Synergy Publications Presents...

A Dollar Outta Fifteen Cent II:
Money Talks...Bullsh*t Walks

An Exclusive by Caroline McGill

Published By:
Synergy Publications
P.O. Box 210-987
Brooklyn, NY 11221-2803

www.SynergyPublications.com

Library of Congress Control Number: 2007930273

ISBN: 978-0-9752980-2-2

Cover Design: Matt Pramschufer for E-Moxie Data Solutions

Book Cover Model: Lady Goines AKA Connie McGill

Written by: Caroline McGill for Synergy Publications

Edited by: Caroline McGill for Synergy Publications

Contact the Author at CarolineMcgill160@msn.com and www.myspace.com/CarolineMcgill

Synergy Publications
718-930-8818

Printed in Canada

For my brother

Khalid (Carnell)

A.K.A.

Casino

You're golden inside and out, baby.

I love you.

You are my heart.

Thanks.

Acknowledgements

Giving honor to God first and foremost. Next, I'd like to thank my readers. This novel, "A Dollar Outta Fifteen Cent II: Money Talks... Bullsh*t Walks", was inspired by you guys. Ya'll asked for it and brought it out of me, so now that it's here I hope ya'll feel me. I'm constantly humbled and awed by the amount of emails, letters, and calls I get from my readers, and I want all of you to know that I appreciate you so much. Thanks for giving me a shot. Without you guys there would be no me. Thank you for the support, and may God bless each and every one of you.

I'd like to thank my mother, Carolyn, my father, Carnell, my sisters, brothers, nieces, nephews, cousins, friends, homies, homegirls, the bookstores (Hi Tru in Hartford), book vendors, book clubs (especially OOSA, Coast 2 Coast, and ARC), libraries, wholesalers, distributors, my fellow authors on the grind, and last but not least, the brothers and sisters in the penitentiary.

Big shout out to my sister on the cover, Lady Goines, AKA Connie (C-Bone). Good lookin' on the classy cover shot. Thanks, mama! Ya'll cop that "Black Girl Lost" CD. It is HOT, trust me! Ordering info is in the back of the book.

A special shout out and special thank you with cherries on top goes out to my partner, Lucky. Here's to us, boo. (smile) Thanks for the ideas and inspiration. I Love you. And love those Budda Belts, baby. Smooches!

Shout outs to Casino, Bless Bigz, Connie, Carleata (Keya) and Ty, Keiecha and Chris, Fanerra, NaQuanda, Jemik, Jaylin, ShaMauri, Zapanga Milan, the whole McGill, the McKoy family, the Norfort family, Kishah B and the crew, Kendell, CJ, Fee-fee, Sparkle, Mo, Tammy, Paulette, Tara, Ice, Maisha, Lisa, Nicole, Tasha, Makeeba, Kadeasha, Kiana,

Tashonda, Boobie, Lisa, Sandra, Terry, Jerry, Mighty, Otis, Sherron, Zayquan, K-Lo, Quick, Dun, Caine, Twan, Un from uptown, Un from the Stuy, Dubo AKA Cappo, Derek Jones, D-Roc, White Bread, Tough Luck, Jehova, Rab, June, Gotti, Honey Comb and Jostle Entertainment, Man Hood Entertainment, The Triangle, Diamond from VA, Ty, and Micah. The crew from Green Haven; Jihad, Boom, Life, Gotti, Lincoln, Hakim A.KA. Deuce, Kenny. My lil' bro Bless Bigz, Trife, Bilal, and the whole crew from Wyoming.

A & B Distributors, African World Books, Hakim from Black and Noble in Philly, K'wan, Meisha, Crystal, Lisa, Kashamba, and everybody else.

Jason and Kione, Christina, Carlene, Mae, Dollar, Tamar, Darlene, Cynthia, Mother Williams, and all the rest of the staff at PPH Taxes on New Lots.

To the east coast, the west coast, the dirty south, and the mid-west, thanks for holding me down. Special shout to North Carolina and Atlanta.

Special thanks to Kevon Thomas. Thanks for the hook-up.

Grandma (Rosa McKoy), I love you. Please get better.

On the day before this novel went to print, my grandfather, Mr. Cary Lee McKoy, passed away. I would like to honor his memory. Rest in peace eternally, Granddaddy.

Rest in peace to all of my loved ones, and to all the fallen soldiers. I would like to honor your memories as well. God bless.

If your name wasn't mentioned above, that don't mean there's any less love. Write me or email me and I'll put you in the reprint. I love everybody. Brooklyn, stand up! Respect to everyone. Thank you and God bless!

Prelude

It was late Christmas night of 2006, around two AM. Portia and Jay were preparing to indulge in some X-rated adult leisure. It had been a wonderful Christmas day. They had celebrated as a family, but now the toys were put away, the kids were asleep, and it was about to be on and popping.

The fireplace was lit, the Christmas tree lights blinked on and off, and the aroma of cinnamon filled the air from the scented candles Portia had lit. She had put on an oldies CD, and one of her favorite songs, "Forever Mine" by the O'Jays, was playing. Jay had gone off to the bar to fix them some drinks.

When Jay returned, Portia was laying under the beautifully decorated, huge nine-foot Christmas tree wearing nothing but a full-length white mink, a pair of sexy Jimmy Choo's, and her wedding ring. The mink coat, which was one of Jay's Christmas gifts, was draped loosely across her naked body, and it was a sexy and inviting sight. The coat's snow white fur really set off Portia's chocolate colored skin and glossy jet black hair, which hung loosely just below her shoulders. Jay stopped to admire her for a second. She looked beautiful. Shit, she looked edible. That was his Kit Kat.

Portia smiled at her husband through lust hooded eyes. She was hot and ready for him. She and Jay had been smooching all day, due to her strategically placing mistletoes all over the house. She had done this just as an excuse to kiss him. Their little girl Jazmin had also loved the mistletoe game. She had showered them with kisses all day.

Portia was grateful to God that she and Jay were still in love. He always made her feel like a woman. She loved Jay to death. He was just the perfect man, and she couldn't get enough of him. Portia felt like she had the best husband in the world, and she was excited like it was their first Christmas together.

Jay still looked good as hell, with his fine, pecan brown self. And he had a fresh haircut, which made him look even more handsome. His goatee was sharp, and his waves were spinning. At the time, he was wearing a wife beater, a pair of navy blue plaid pajama pants, and some comfortable navy blue sheepskin slippers Portia had gotten him for Christmas.

Jay walked over and handed Portia the drink he had fixed for her. He didn't say a word, but his interest in her presence was evident by the sudden rising in the front of his pajama pants. He took a swallow of his drink, and bent down for a kiss.

Portia sat up and kissed him softly. She took the drink from his hand and sipped it. Jay hadn't forgotten the cherries. He really knew her. Portia smiled, and stood up and let her coat fall to the floor.

Jay let out a whistle and nodded appreciatively. He hungrily eyed her up and down, and he reached around and smacked her on the ass. She had on nothing but stilettos, and she looked sexy as hell.

Portia winded her body seductively, and then she turned around and jiggled her booty for him. She bent over and made it clap a few times, and Jay backed up and got a good look. He licked his lips. Damn, Portia had a fat, juicy ass. Jay rubbed it and spanked it a few times, and then he stepped in closer and grinded his hard dick on her ass for a few seconds while he finished his drink.

When Jay was done he sat down his glass. Portia took a maraschino cherry from her glass and handed him her unfinished drink, and he sat her glass down also. Portia seductively licked the cherry, and rubbed it across her lips, and then she placed it in her mouth.

Jay tilted her chin up towards him and gently licked

the cherry juice off her full juicy lips, and Portia slipped
the uneaten cherry from her mouth into his. Jay took the
fruit in his mouth and bit into it, releasing its sweetness
immediately. Portia reached up and kissed him passionately,
hungrily sucking cherry juice off his tongue.

Jay reached down and palmed Portia's ass, and he held her
close. She was so soft. She felt good in his arms. And she
smelled good too.

Portia ran her hands along her husband's back, and along
his broad shoulders. He was so hard and manly. She reached
underneath Jay's wife beater and traced his six-pack slowly
with her fingernails. She wanted him out of those clothes.
She wanted to do things to him. Naughty things.

"Take this off, baby", she whispered softly in his ear.

"Ayight, Ma", Jay replied lowly, breathing heavily. With
Portia's assistance, he came out of his shirt. Next, she tugged
on his pajama pants until he stood in front of her wearing only
his boxers. Those Portia removed slowly with her teeth.

Jay stared down at her. Her face was so close to his
manhood he could feel her warm breath on it. That was
quite a turn-on.

When Portia pulled Jay's boxers down, his erect penis
stood straight out, protruding almost a foot from his body.
Jay's penis, AKA Rocky, was so beautiful, Portia gave it a
long kiss. Rocky was Portia's pet name for Jay's dick because
it was hard and strong, and always knocked her out with
one punch. Afterwards, she reached over and got a candy
cane from the Christmas tree, and hung it on the tip. Portia
gazed at it lovingly, and she looked up at Jay and smiled.
She stroked the length of his shaft with admiration, and he
smiled back.

Jay's big, black, hard dick in Portia's hand was extremely
enticing. She knew it belonged to her, and only her. She
planted soft kisses around the head, and then she slid Rocky
down her throat and made him wet and sloppy, just the way

Jay loved.

Even though he felt his knees weakening, Jay stood tall and ran his fingers through Portia's hair. She knew how to please him. Lately her head game had surpassed his expectations. Boy, his wife had skills. Jay held the back of her head while she deep throated and squeezed on his tip.

"Aaahh, damn Ma. Suck that shit, girl. That's it, just like that."

Portia loved it when he coaxed her to do it. He brushed her hair back out of her face, and she gave it all she had. Before she knew it, Jay was begging her to stop before he came.

Jay pulled Portia to her feet, and he picked her up. She wrapped her legs around his waist, and he hungrily sucked on her right nipple. Portia moaned, and stroked the back of his head. She wanted him so bad her body ached for him.

A few seconds later, Jay laid Portia down on the tan sable fur rug in front of the fireplace. He wrapped his arms around her thighs and spread them, and he kissed their insides and all around her bikini area. After a few seconds of this, he stuck his tongue deep inside her sugar walls.

Portia gasped. Jay slid his tongue in and out, and then he held her vaginal lips open gently with his fingers and sucked on her clit until she squirmed. She moaned and purred as Jay's tongue probed her pussy, until she couldn't take it anymore.

Portia was trembling. She wanted Jay inside of her. Immediately. She begged him softly, "Baby, please put it in. It feels so good. Now, daddy! Please. I need it now!"

Jay didn't have to be told twice. He came up for air, and positioned himself on top of Portia in the missionary position. She loved it that way. Jay slid in slowly, breathing deeply to keep from calling out. Portia had the best pussy he ever had in his life, hands down. She had such a sweet box on her, he felt himself about to bust after only about twenty pumps.

He had to let her know. "Damn, Kit Kat. I'm 'bout to cum."

"Okay baby, but not yet. Don't take it out. It feels so good."

Jay tried to hold it back. He paused, and then he stroked deeper and quicker for a few seconds. Before he was done, Portia let him know that she was about to join him.

"Ooh, Jay! It feels so good! I'm cummin' too, baby! Aahh, yes! Yes, baby! Aaahhh!"

Jay grabbed Portia's ass and made his final three strokes real deep. When he finally ejaculated, it felt like electrical current shot through his body. He groaned into her shoulder, to keep from calling out. Portia's pussy was the bomb.

After their sexcellent lovemaking session was over, Portia and Jay laid intertwined in each other's arms and legs on the fur rug by the fireplace, and they both relished the moment. Christmastime brought back a lot of memories for them. Five years ago that same time of year, some dudes broke into their house to rob Jay, and Portia was violently raped and shot. At the time she had been seven months pregnant, and had gone into premature labor as a result of all the trauma.

Portia and Jay both felt that Christmas was a time for family. What had happened was horrible, but neither of them dwelled on that particular aspect of the holiday. Above all else, God had been very good to them. They couldn't complain about anything. It had been a good year, and life was great.

They had spent Christmas together, but for the first time in their marriage they would bring the New Year in apart. Jay was leaving in a few days. He had some business to tend to, so he was flying south. There was some social function going on that he had obligated himself to attend. Jay said it was for a man who held a lot of weight in the music and film industries, named Benny Chen. He had invited Portia

to come along, but she refused. She told him she'd prefer to
stay home and bring the New Year in with her girls.

Jay didn't have a problem with that. He loved the fact that
Portia always understood when he had to handle business.
She knew he was constantly trying to make power moves,
and she didn't nag him. That was part of the reason their love
had always been strong.

Chapter One

New Year's Eve of 2007 was a few days later, and Portia, Laila, and Fatima all gathered at Club Paradise in celebration. The girlfriends had made a tradition of celebrating life, especially after their best friend Simone had died. All that they had been through together in the past had taught them that life was precious indeed.

In Club Paradise there were lots of flat screen TVs hanging on the walls, and they were all showing the ball about to drop at Time's Square. The ladies stood over by the bar, and held hands and counted down. *"Seven, six, five four, three, two, one. Happy New Year!!!"*

Portia and her girls hugged, and wished each other peace, prosperity, and many New Year blessings for the year to come. In the spirit of festivities, they popped a bottle of Dom Periogn, and shared a toast to friendship and family.

Portia, Laila, and Fatima partied hardy until around one AM, and then they made a trip to the ladies room. Each of them had to tinkle from all the champagne they drank, and it was also time for a mirror check.

After they all used the bathroom, they stood side by side at the adjoining sinks and washed their hands. Then the girls all put on fresh coats of lip gloss in their favorite shade. Equally attractive sisters just hitting their thirties, they had all maintained their figures, and still looked great.

Laila, the pretty, petite, coffee bean colored vixen of the crew, had her long glossy black hair pulled back into a chic chignon. Laila wore her hair up a lot because she couldn't stand it in her face all the time. She was wearing a stylish, cream, silk Prada blouse, and a pair of low rise D-squared jeans, with a pair of bad ass, cream colored, alligator Jimmy Choo boots that came up to the thighs.

Fatima stood next to her, staring at her caramel complexion in the mirror through honey flecked light brown eyes. She wore her coolie hair naturally curly that night, with an aqua, silk Fendi scarf tied around it. She had on a matching aqua, silk Fendi blouse that hung off one shoulder seductively, and a pair of faded, hip hugging Roberto Cavalli jeans. On her feet she wore aqua suede Botegga Venetta stiletto boots.

Fatima was braless, in commemoration of her recent breast lift. It was the third in a series of little procedures she had undergone the past year, to enhance her figure to her liking. She had also had gotten her tummy tucked, and liposuction done on a couple of places. Her new svelte figure had her dressing like she was eighteen again.

Portia was third in the row of homegirls. She had her hair done in a pompadour in the front, with a ponytail in the back. She had put on a few pounds, but it was all in the right places. She could fit into a size ten easily, so she didn't mind that she had gotten a little thick. Luckily, she carried the weight in her butt and hips, as opposed to her waist, which was still small.

Portia was wearing a long-sleeved, black and white pinstriped Gucci bustier, tight black leather cigarette pants by Diane von Furstenberg, and knee-high, black and white pinstriped Giuseppe Zanotti boots. As usual, she and her homegirls' outfits were tight, and their footwear was the truth.

Before they left the bathroom, Portia took out her cell phone and called Jay, who had left to go out of town the day before.

Jay picked up on the first ring. "Oh shit, I was just about to call you. I had the phone in my hand about to dial. Happy New Year, ma! You gon' live a long time."

"Me and you both, together forever. Happy New Year, baby", Portia said gleefully. "How you doin'?"

"I'm good, Kit Kat. I'll be home in like two days,

ayight?"

"That's what's up! I miss you, baby."

Jay laughed. "I miss you too, Ma."

"I miss you more. And I miss my Rocky too."

She got him with that one. Jay blushed into the phone. "He misses you too, Ma. Trust me." He thought about the rendezvous he and Portia had under the Christmas tree the night before he left, and Rocky stiffened.

Jay was in a room full of dudes, so he didn't really want to be standing there with a stiff cock. It just wasn't appropriate. He quickly changed the subject to take his mind elsewhere.

"Ma, you think it's too late to call your moms' crib, to check on the kids?"

Portia said, "Jazmin was dozing off when I talked to Mommy a little while ago, so she might be asleep, but you know Jayquan's behind is still up. Go' head and call."

Portia told Jay to be safe, and he told her not to drink and drive. They agreed to speak again when she got home.

After Portia hung up she saw that Laila and Fatima were both done using their cell phones as well. They all did one last mirror check before they left the john. They were satisfied with their appearances. They all looked great. Now it was time to go get their party on a little more.

After a few more drinks and a lot more dancing, Portia, Laila, and Fatima decided to call it a night. They went and got their furs from the coat check, and they made their way through the crowd to exit the club.

When they got out front, some young asshole walked up behind Laila and slapped her on the ass hard as hell. Another boy, who was obviously his homie, laughed.

Laila knew she looked young, but she was a grown ass woman, and she didn't play that shit. And she wasn't about to have her night ruined by being disrespected by no young, punk ass dude. Fuck that, she was from Bed-Stuy. She spun around angrily, and slapped that mothafucka hard across his face.

The boy, who didn't look a day over twenty, touched his face and looked startled. "Bitch, what the fuck is wrong with you!? Is you crazy!?"

Laila looked at him in shock. Did that nigga just call her a bitch? She rolled her eyes at him, and spat venomously, "Keep your fuckin' hands to yourself. And if you see a bitch, slap a bitch, nigga!"

After Laila dared him to slap her, the boy looked at her like she was stupid. He shook his head, wondering why she had to test him. He couldn't look like a sucker in front of his mans. Now he had no choice. He drew back his arm to slap her for running her mouth, but his hand never got the opportunity to make contact with her face, because Portia quickly came out of her black leather Gucci bag with a stun gun, and zapped him in the ribs.

The sudden and unexpected jolt of electricity put him on his ass. The dude's mouth hung wide open for a minute. He was really stunned.

Laila, Portia, and Fatima stood over him with facial expressions that told him to keep it moving. They all had weapons. Laila had gone in her purse and retrieved her blade, Portia had the blue spark shooting stun gun, and Fatima had a can of pepper spray, ready to blind his ass if he got up and acted stupid. Onlookers watched in amusement, tickled at the sight of the ladies handling the disrespectful young dude.

The boy got up, and took a step back. He shook his head and held up his hands in peace, like he surrendered. He had never run into a set of bitches like them. He looked at Laila and said, "Damn shorty, I was just try'na get wit' you. Ya'll try'na assassinate me and shit. My bad."

He laughed it off. He didn't want to beef with no girls. That wouldn't get him any cool points. "Yo, ya'll must be from Brooklyn, 'cause ya'll like the black Charlie's Angels, and shit. But yo, that shit is kinda' sexy. Word."

Laila said, "Just learn how to keep your hands to yourself. You don't just hit nobody on the ass. That shit ain't cute. I'm a lady, and you should respect that."

Laila was mad tipsy. She placed her hand on her hip, and sassily told him, "And besides, you couldn't even afford this. I got mortgage payments, baby. You probably still live at home with ya' mama, so go 'head with that bullshit. Money talks, nigga. And bullshit walks. That's the rule for '07. It's a new year. You better stay in your league." Laila rolled her eyes at him, and spun around on her heels, and she and her girls bounced.

The dude looked around to see who had witnessed him get dissed that way. He started to respond with some type of disrespectful comeback, but he just let it go. He had known better anyway. He had just been drinking and trying to impress his man Howie, who had just stood there and laughed at him. That was the main reason they went to clubs, to feel on asses. Shorty had a fatty, and he was just being a dude. But he had obviously touched the wrong ass that time.

On their way to the car, Laila, Portia, and Fatima shook the incident off, and joked about how they had handled that dude. Having static as soon as the New Year rolled in was a sure sign that the year to come would be drama filled.

$$$

Meanwhile, down in Atlanta, Jay, Casino, and Wise had just left the after-party of the huge New Year's industry event they had all attended earlier that evening. Wise, Nas, and a few other big names in hip-hop had performed and got the party crunk.

The event was sponsored by Benny Chen, a bigwig in the music and film business. He had thrown the impressive

gala to launch his new distribution company. Street Life
Entertainment had previously done business with Benny,
and wanted to again in the future, so they had showed up
out of respect.

After the after-party, Jay, Casino, and Wise parted ways
with two of their key players. Jay's nephew Dave, AKA "Dave
Brave", was now a super-producer charging two hundred
grand for a track, and Moe, who was Street Life's promotions
guru in the south. Moe had been living down south for a
while, but Dave had recently relocated, and made a home in
ATL. Both Moe and Dave had wives that they were anxious
to get home to.

Wise broke Moe and Dave's balls about acting so square
all of a sudden. "Ya'll some pussy whipped ass niggas. Man,
let's go hit up a tity bar."

Moe and Dave refused, and Jay understood where they
were coming from. He was thinking about his wife too. But
his Portia was miles away, so he figured he might as well hang
out. Jay, Cas, and Wise each gave the whipped husbands,
Dave and Moe, a pound, and they all said goodnight.
Afterwards, they loaded up in their limo and headed for Blue
Flame, a landmark strip club in Atlanta.

Less than thirty minutes later, they were watching exotic
women of all nationalities and sizes gyrate. Jay and Cas were
just there to look and kill time, but as usual Wise was the one
who wanted to pick out a stripper, and go further.

The girl on stage was collecting money from Wise like it
was the first of the month. She was dancing to the song, "I
Wanna Fuck You", by Snoop Dogg and Akon, and he was
throwing dollars at her by the fist full. Wise liked what he
saw, so he mouthed the song lyrics to her.

*"I see you windin' and grindin' up on the floor. I see you
lookin' at me and you already know. I wanna fuck you, fuck
you, you already know. I wanna fuck you, fuck you, you already
know…"*

The stripper bent down in front of Wise and flirted with him. When she was within earshot, he told her, "Yo, I'm puttin' a down payment on you for later on, shorty." Wise ended his statement with a wink, and tossed another handful of bills at her.

The girl looked at Wise like he had lost his mind. In a deep southern drawl, she said, "Ha! Down payment, my ass! You better gon' on 'head with that bullshit, nigga. You must be crazy. You gotta pay more than singles for this here. Money talks, and bullshit walks. You better come high, or stay yo' black ass home."

She stuck her tongue out at Wise playfully, and backed up and palmed her breasts. She ran her hands along her body seductively, and then she went back to working the pole again. At the end of her set, she slid down the pole upside down with her legs wide open, and she winked at Wise.

Wise found that shit sexy. He was feeling her. He wanted some of that country pussy. That Georgia peach looked ripe. He watched her leave the stage, unable to stop the hard-on growing in his pants. He was glad he was sitting down.

When the girl came back on the floor, Wise summoned her over. Now she had on a white corseted mini-dress, thigh high fishnet stockings and garters, and white patent leather stiletto boots. Her whole attire just screamed *"Come fuck the shit outta me"*, and Wise wanted to bad as hell.

The girl was light skinned, with green eyes and pale blonde hair. She told him her name was Heaven. You could tell from her roots that she wasn't a natural blonde, but her hair looked like it was all hers. Wise figured he would find out later on, when he ran his fingers through it while she was on her knees pleasuring him. He knew he could go on and pretty much count his chickens before they hatched, because no matter what her price was, he wanted to hit that. She had a nice, fat, juicy ass.

Wise asked, "Yo, why they call you Heaven, shorty?"

She seductively told him, "Because I take dudes to paradise. You wanna go, boo?"

Wise was definitely interested. "How much?"

Heaven reconigized Wise from his videos, but she wasn't selling herself cheap. Hell, he had it. She didn't bat an eyelash. "Just a thousand."

Wise almost spit out the Henny he was sipping on when she said that. He had expected her to be more expensive than a hundred dollars, but a grand? Shorty was wilding.

Wise wasn't short in the pockets. He had the bread. Money wasn't a thing, but he wasn't paying no bitch a thousand dollars to blow him. He got that shit free all the time. Bitches threw pussy at him. He was a celebrity now, with three solid platinum hits under his belt, so he had access to round the clock pussy by the pound.

Wise decided to counteroffer, only because he really wanted to fuck her. "Ayight, I'll give you a pound. Five hun'ed. Go get dressed. Let's go."

Heaven stared at him for a second. She looked like she was thinking about it. "Ayight, tell you what. Seven fifty. Only 'cause you cute as hell."

"Well then fuck me for free, shit", Wise told her.

Heaven laughed, and drawled, "Don't push it, nigga. I done told you. Money talks, and bullshit walks. Now if you wit' it, big spender, I get off at three." She winked at him, and walked off.

Wise told Jay and Casino about his plans to get in Heaven. They tried to talk him out of it as usual, but it was no use. Wise was a grown ass man, so Jay and Cas went on about their business, and let him do him.

About an hour later, Wise had gotten his shit off but he wasn't really impressed. He politely put Heaven out of his suite, and went over to check his mans in the adjoining suites they were staying in.

Jay and Cas asked him if he felt the pussy was worth all

Caroline McGill   17

the risks, and Wise told them the truth. "Man, that bitch's pussy was garbage. Straight trash. I should've kept my mothafuckin' money."

Jay and Cas just laughed, and shook their heads. That dude Wise would never change. He would fuck a deformed hyena with one leg, but you could count on him for a laugh.

$$$

Back in New York, Portia was on her way home. She and Fatima had ridden together in Fatima's burgundy BMW X5, because they both lived in New Jersey now. Laila still lived in Brooklyn so they had dropped her off at home, bid her farewell, and hit the highway.

Despite Jay's warning about drinking and driving, Portia drove home bent. But she felt like she could handle it. She was definitely in better shape than Fatima, who had fallen asleep as soon as she got in the passenger seat.

When they got on the highway, Portia turned on the radio. Her song, "Be Without You", by Mary J. Blige, was on. She turned it up and sang along.

"Look him right in his eyes and tell him, we've been too strong for too long- and I can't be without you baby. I'll be waitin' up until you get home, 'cause I can't sleep without you baby. Anyone who's ever loved knows just what I mean. To hard to fake it, nothing can replace it. Call the radio if you can't be without your baby. He-ey-ey-eyyyyy-ey-ey-eyhhh. Oh-oh-ohhh-oh-oh... He-ey-ey-eyyyyy-ey-ey-eyhhh. Oh-oh-ohhh-oh-oh..."

That was Portia's damn song. Mary J. really did her thing with that one. That song reminded Portia of her and Jay's marriage. She couldn't be without Jay. He was her soul mate, and he personified the word "love" for her. And they were still strong because she had followed her mother's advice.

When Portia first got married, Patricia had schooled her on certain things that were necessary to be a strong wife.

There were a list of things, but the most important two pieces of advice her mom had given her were, "learn when to fall back, and when to assume the dominant role", and "choose your battles wisely." The latter had been the gem of Portia and Jay's relationship. Portia definitely chose her battles wisely. She and Jay never fought about little shit because they were both pretty sensible people. They went well together because they knew each other well.

Their bond was in stone, partial credit to that incident they never spoke about anymore. It happened five years ago. Against her will, Portia thought about the worse night of her life, when those niggas broke into the house and raped her. Even though she knew that lowdown, dirty bastard Wayne-o was probably rotting in hell, every time she thought about him she was overcome with the urge to spit in disrespect of his memory. Portia instinctively coughed up some phlegm, and rolled down the window, and spit into the night.

Portia would forever be grateful to Jay for coming to her rescue that day. She had been helpless and pregnant at the time. She was shot, and being violently raped by Wayne-o's sick ass when Jay had crept up out of nowhere, and blew that nigga's brains out. Portia could remember it vividly, like it was yesterday. After Jay shot him once in the head, she had jumped up and grabbed the gun from him, and emptied the clip on Wayne-o. To protect her, Jay had taken the wrap for all the bullets.

Portia had gone into premature labor that night, but thank God, her daughter was okay. Jazmin Simone, who had the middle name of Portia's deceased friend, who was like a sister to her, was born weighing only four pounds and two ounces. But by God's grace, she made it through.

Portia whispered a prayer for her, her husband, and their children's safety in the year to come. She was lucky to have Jay. He was her black knight, and he always treated her like a lady. He had given her everything she ever wanted, and even proved that he would kill for her. What more could a girl ask for?

Chapter Two

About four months had passed since the New Year came in, and everything was everything. Good news was bubbling throughout the industry waves about Street Life Entertainment Inc. Their distribution deal with Universal Records was almost up, and rumor had it that there were multimillion dollar offers on the table from other majors. They would be free agents once again, and they had the clout to pretty much go in any direction they pleased. Their record company's numbers had spoken for themselves.

Jay smiled to himself when he thought about it all. The rumors were all true. The other majors had been circling them like sharks in the water, waiting for the opportunity to bite. Those mothafuckas smelled new blood. So far Street Life had been courted by just about all of Universal's competitors. And now those offers had made Universal up the ante, to try and get them to stay there. Jay felt good about this. He was glad Street Life had a big enough name to stay in the game so strong. And it wasn't by chance. They had put their work in.

It was a late Thursday afternoon in early April, and Jay was in Brooklyn, driving down Myrtle Avenue. He was headed for the bridge, en route from his mother's brownstone in historical Fort Greene, to his office in Manhattan.

He had gone by to check on his moms, and also to check out a piece of real estate she'd told him about. Her next door neighbor was selling her home, and she wanted to sell it fast because she didn't believe she had long to live. She told Jay she would sell it to him below market value if he would move fast. She had recently been diagnosed with a chronic illness, and she kept saying that she didn't want to die in Brooklyn. The woman said she had no children to leave her house to, so she wanted to take the money, and see the world before she died.

Jay was thinking about how sad that was. He really wanted to help her. His cell phone rang just then, and interrupted his thoughts. He knew by the ring tone that it was Portia. He'd been expecting a call from her an hour ago. She was supposed to let him know what time her flight was leaving. She had been out of town for three days.

Jay answered the phone, and Portia quickly told him she was about to board her flight in two minutes. He told her that he would see her in a little while, and he prayed that she would have a safe trip.

After they hung up, a hip-hop song Jay liked came on the mix CD he was bumping. He turned the volume up in his Bentley, and rapped along with Cam'ron.

"Ma, I been huggin' the block. That's right, hustlin' rocks. I know I've been puffin' a lot. Babygirl, a nigga wanna know if you gon' suck it or not."

As Jay passed the corner of Vanderbilt Avenue, he slowed down, and had a look at a crew of young boys engaged in a dice game. Jay didn't recognize any of the young heads, but his love for the game caused him to pull over.

Jay double-parked, and reached under his seat and retrieved one of the two handguns he always kept in his possession. He knew those Brooklyn streets well. They were mean, and had no love for a dude. Jay knew that from firsthand experience. Dudes had already tried him. He didn't trust anyone, so carrying two guns, that was like his trademark.

Jay carefully adjusted his .45 in his waist, and hopped out of his midnight blue Bentley Arnage T. He smoothed the wrinkles out of his black Zac Posen shirt, and walked over to the crew of young dudes.

The one holding the dice in his hand looked up at Jay, just before he rolled. "What up, O.G.? I hope you brung some good luck with you. 'Cause if you jinx me, I'ma be highly upset with you for interrupting this game. Word."

Another lil' dude with a blue Yankees fitted cap on said, "Son, that's ayight. We take old ass money too. This old nigga bread ain't stale."

Jay was only thirty four, but they were clowning the shit out of him about his age, like he was on a respirator, with one foot in the grave. But it was okay, he wasn't mad. In fact, he found them to be humorous. He scratched his chin, and laughed. "I got fifties and hundred dollar bills older than all you lil' pocket-sized bastards. Now stop all this cacklin' like little hens, and roll the dice."

A third kid out of the crew of four laughed. "Yo, old-timer, you look like you ain't from around here. You better know what it is, steppin' foot on our corner. Old-school, you gon' fuck around and leave here broke. One way, or the other." With his last words, he shot Jay a menacing look.

Jay could tell that one thought he had the most heart, but he didn't really feel threatened by him. They all looked under twenty one, and he could tell that none of them were killers. Not to say that younger age made a man less dangerous, because Jay knew a lot of little dudes who really put it in. But this crew seemed a little more tamed than some of the wild lion cubs he knew.

Jay figured the young boys were trying to play tough because he had an air about him that they were forced to respect, and they didn't want to look like they were dick-riding.

The fourth kid in the crew, who hadn't been laughing at his comrades' antics, finally spoke up. "Yo, ya'll niggas is stupid!"

He stepped up and gave Jay a pound. "What up, Jay? They call me Humble. Can I speak to you?"

Jay greeted him in exchange, appreciating the revere. He and Humble stepped a few feet over to the side, to speak privately. "What up, lil' man?"

Humble said, "*You* what's up, man. Pardon these dick head ass niggas. These lemons obviously don't know who you are. These dudes just came out the house. Man, I've heard nothin' but great things about you. All due respect. You and ya' mans Cas and Wise bubblin' with Street Life Entertainment. And I know ya'll dudes really put it in to get where ya'll at too. You a legend to niggas like me, try'na come up. My older brother Nate used to run with you and Casino, before he got clapped a couple of years ago." Humble was truly honored to meet Jay in the flesh. Jay was iconic to him. God-like almost.

Jay thought that lil' dude looked familiar. He was the spitting image of Nate. He reminded Jay so much of his deceased homie, he immediately became fond of him. He gave Humble another pound and told him what a real dude his brother was, and how much love he had for him. Jay gave him a business card, and told him to get at him to let him know what he and his family needed. Jay suddenly had a strong urge to keep Humble off the streets.

Humble had a list of things his family could use Jay's help with. Amongst other things, his moms was about to lose their family house in foreclosure, because she got hurt on her job. Their only tenant had stopped paying rent a month later, due their own hardships. But Humble decided to keep that conversation for another day. He didn't want everybody in his personal business like that.

The other three boys looked on, and tried to eavesdrop on Humble and Jay's conversation. They hadn't known who Jay was when he walked up, but he looked familiar to them. They knew he had to be somebody, hopping out of such a bad ass Bentley.

The wanna-be-tough one spoke up again. "If ya'll niggas done reminiscin', we in the middle of a game."

Jay assured Humble they'd finish their conversation later on, and he got in the game and placed a bet. Humble just stayed on the sidelines and watched. By the time Jay rolled the dice three times, he had taken all of their money. Now it was his turn to talk shit to the three who had been hassling him.

Jay raised an eyebrow at them, and feigned confusion. "Damn, you mean I got all ya'll little ones already? Ain't that a bitch. The tables done turned. I don't hear you mini-niggas talkin' no more. Why ya'll so quiet? Why the long faces?"

No one said anything, so Jay answered himself. "I'll tell you why. 'Cause I'm pickin' up money off the ground, and all ya'll pickin' up is ya' faces. Learn the rule, lil' niggas. Money talks, bullshit walks. If your pockets too short to go the distance, fall the fuck back when long money come through."

Jay nodded his head at them, and continued. "That's right, I said *long* money. Not old money. Learn the difference, 'cause I wasn't born rich. But I'm rich as shit now. And furthermore, it's just like my man Jigga said." Jay quoted Jay-Z, *"Thirty's the new twenty, I'm so hot."*

Jay laughed, and counted their money. He put it in his left pocket, and he walked off. When he looked back, they all looked tight, except for Humble. He had a little smile on his face.

Jay grinned at the frustrated looking lil' dudes. They looked so pitiful he felt sorry for them. His intentions weren't to leave them broke. He had a good heart. He'd only wanted to teach them a lesson. He turned around and headed back over to them, and pulled out a roll of money from his right pocket, and he peeled off a nice walk for each of them.

The five hundred dollars Jay handed each of the boys was more than they had actually lost to him, but he told them to go buy themselves some lunch, on him. The lil' dudes appreciated the kind gesture. They all stepped up and gave Jay a pound, and thanked him.

The little "tough" guy said, "O.G. Long Money, you ayight wit' me. Let me push that Bentley around the block."

Jay laughed, and told him next time. He bid the young bros farewell and told them to stay out of trouble. Jay headed for his ride, and looked back over his shoulder. "Yo Humble! Come on, man. Let's roll."

Humble played it cool, but he was thrilled at the prospect of sliding off with Jay and leaving those dudes on the corner. He didn't give a fuck where they were going. He gave his mans a pound, and he had to stop himself from running behind Jay to hop in that Bentley. He was glad he had invited him along, but he couldn't look like he was thirsty.

$$$

Portia was on a flight heading home from L.A. She stared out of the airplane window at the clouds for a while. She smiled at the thought of being so close to heaven. Up there where her father was. And her sister from another mother, Simone.

A flight attendant walked by and handed out trays of hot food. Portia sat hers in front of her, and she reclined her seat and closed her eyes. She didn't want to eat just yet. She was too busy reminiscing. Simone had passed over five years ago, and her birthday was the following week.

Portia, Laila, and Fatima always celebrated Simone's birthday as opposed to the anniversary of her death, because they preferred to rejoice her life, and not dwell on her untimely passing.

Simone's memories made Portia happy, but tears came to her eyes nonetheless. She missed her so much. As soon as she landed, she was going to call Laila and Fatima to schedule their annual brunch dedicated to Simone's memory for the following week. Every year on her birthday they all visited her grave, and updated her on the latest going on in each of their lives. It was an emotional time for all of them. Afterwards, they would go celebrate her life over food and drinks.

Another thing they did each year in commemoration of Simone was AIDS Walk New York, an annual march and fundraiser dedicated to AIDS research and awareness. Portia, Laila, and Fatima, collectively called "Team Simone", solicited donations from others, and went in their own purses as well to raise money. They were down for the cause, and every May they were right there in Central Park, wearing red ribbons, and tee-shirts with Simone's photo on the front, ready to march.

The date was approaching fast. Portia knew she could count on Jay, and all of his friends and business associates to make hefty donations. Fatima and Laila knew a lot of people too. Last year together they had raised more than a hundred thousand dollars. Hopefully they would top that this year.

Portia realized that she hadn't connected with her girl Laila in over a month. It seemed like time was going by so fast. She wondered what was going on with Laila.

Portia had spoken to Fatima the day before. Part of the reason they stayed in touch so much was because of their involvement in business together. Portia and Fatima co-owned a book publishing company called Sinclair-Lane Publishing. And both of them were pretty well off, because of their husbands' success with Street Life Entertainment. Street Life had produced millions in revenue, so they didn't have to work, but the publishing company was their hustle. That company was their baby. They still had a long way to go, but they had independently pushed more than eighty thousand copies of Portia's first two novels, "It's Official", and its sequel, "It's 2 Official". Now Portia had a third, so far untitled urban fiction novel almost completed. That book was scheduled for release in a few months.

Portia also had her hands in film a little now. She had

written and directed a few independent, straight to DVD films. Jay was always supportive of her endeavors. He had paid for her to go to film school, and he financed all of her projects. The film company was theirs together, and they had some big plans for the future.

Portia couldn't wait to get home. She had left California three hours ago, and was en route to New York. She had flown to L.A. to meet her new agent, Penelope, who was trying to line up some foreign distribution channels for her last film, "Do It or Die". Through some of Penelope's connections, Portia had premiered "Do It or Die" at the Worldwide Film Festival a few months ago.

Truthfully, it was sort of a wasted trip because there was nothing in stone yet. They were still negotiating because Portia wasn't really happy with the offer they had on the table. She wanted to take her time and make the right decision. Fortunately, she was blessed, and not pressed for money. God was so good. That being said, she wasn't desperate to give up her film rights for the peanuts they'd offered her.

Portia yawned again. She needed a nap. When she landed in New York she had to go pick up the kids from her mother's house, and it took a lot of energy to run behind her little one, Jazmin. Portia knew Jay wouldn't be home until late, so she would probably chill at her mom's house for a while. That was also where she had parked her car.

She remembered that she had to make two stops in the City on her way home, to pick up about eight hundred dollars due to her for some books she had dropped off at the stands of these book vendors who sold books on the street. There was an African brother down by 34th street she had to stop by, and several of them uptown on 125th street. Portia gave out books on consignment to a few, but only those who had done square business for a while. The street vending brothers and sisters pushed her books, and contributed to her success. For that she was grateful.

Portia's mind drifted to Jay. When she finished her running around, her and the kids were heading home to their lovely, big house in New Jersey. She missed her husband like crazy. They had been apart for three long days.

Chapter Three

Laila sat outside of her house in her Lexus GS and dreaded going inside. That was really ironic because a short time ago in her life, there was no better feeling in the world than to get home after a long day at work. Lately Laila had often contemplated not even going home. She felt like just driving off and disappearing into the night. Her life had done a 360 degree turn over the past year. As God was her witness, were it not for her children, she would've left that day.

She'd gone back to work as an R.N. six months ago, when she and Khalil had been forced to close their store, due to her husband's poor accounting practices. Laila had enjoyed being self-employed. She wished she'd gotten more involved in the financial part of the business. They had to shut the doors and go out of business because Khalil had repeatedly spent all of the proceeds, and didn't pay any of the bills. Not the rent, not the suppliers, and not the utility bills.

Laila had figured she could trust her husband. She had quit her damn job to help him pursue his dream. In their arrangement she had overseen the sales marketing and store management areas, and Khalil had handled the financial part. She believed in him, so she had taken his word that he'd been paying everything on time. It wasn't a cash flow issue, because the store had been making a profit. They were out of the red, so Laila didn't really understand what had happened at the time. But now she did. And she was ready to leave that mothafucka.

Khalil was getting high. There was no point in denying it. He had all of the signs, and Laila found evidence. She wasn't stupid. Her husband was getting high. Laila couldn't for the life of her understand why he would wait until he turned thirty three years old to start smoking crack. He was weak, and Laila's patience was wearing thin. She was sick of being his rock. They had children. He was the man, so he was supposed to be the leader of the family. Laila thought back over the years. She had always been Khalil's crutch.

Her first instinct was to leave him. Just pack up her and her kids' shit and go. She made good money, so they would be alright. She had sacrificed too much in her marriage and life already. Maybe it was just time to throw the towel in.

Laila's daughters, Pebbles and Macy, were now eleven and twelve years old, and both of them were going through adolescence and smelling themselves. And the younger one, Pebbles, was the fastest. Laila knew she had to keep a close eye on that one. She wanted to wear tight clothes and belly revealing tee-shirts all the time.

Both of Laila's girls had long hair like her, and she wouldn't let them wear it out until they got older. But she found out from Macy the other day that Pebbles had started taking out her hair in school, like she was grown. When Laila found that out, she whipped Pebbles' little hot ass. Her daddy should have intervened in the situation, but now Laila realized that he didn't because he was too damn busy getting high. It was like he wasn't even in the house anymore.

Khalil was obviously going through another one of his phases. He was in his second childhood. If he wanted to experiment with drugs he should've done that shit years ago. Laila was no hypocrite. She smoked a little trees, so she tried not to judge people with dependencies. But crack was a hard narcotic, and she couldn't help but have little tolerance for her husband getting addicted to it.

Shit had started disappearing in the house a couple of months ago, but she had overlooked it. Then about six weeks ago the television in the den turned up missing, and Khalil told her that he took it to the repair shop because the picture tube had blown late one night while he was watching the fight. She had believed him, but after she asked him when he was getting the TV back he kept making excuses, which got lamer and lamer.

The final straw was the night before. That's why she was so fed up. Laila caught him going through her pocketbook. She usually only kept petty cash on her because she preferred plastic, and Khalil knew that. The fact that he was trying to steal twenty dollars from her was even more pitiful. A petty thief was the worse kind. There was no level they wouldn't stoop to.

Knowing this now, Laila couldn't trust him. She had gone online at work to check the balance of their joint checking account, and she found more than fifteen extraneous withdrawals from ATM machines that month, for five hundred dollars a piece. And he was unemployed, so he hadn't been contributing anything to their household for a while.

This new information had really, really pissed Laila off. He was throwing away her fucking money! Thousands of it. She was going to the bank the next day to open up a separate account so she could manage her family's household expenses without bouncing checks all over town. That sorry mothafucka had caused them to go out of business, but she'd be damned if that nigga was gonna put her in foreclosure.

That's why Laila had gone back to work. They'd been behind two mortgage payments, and she wouldn't jeopardize the roof over her children's heads. Khalil had once felt that way too, but not since he got hooked on crack.

"Shit, I can do bad by my damn self. Fuck this shit", Laila mumbled to herself.

She knew she could handle her situation in one of two ways. She could just pick up and go, or she could talk to him about getting some help and saving their family. She was a woman, so she knew she had to confront him. Enough was enough. Laila shut off her car and got out, and headed inside her once happy home.

$$$

Fatima laid poolside at the back of her home, basking in the afterglow of good sex. She was soaking up the last of the sun before dusk fell. It was a little chilly out, but it was nice. Fatima smiled to herself. She just felt so sexy. And so naughty. She had just escorted her lover, Ray, out after a long afternoon of illicit sex. She knew she was playing it close. Fatima had taken a chance that day by fooling around at her house. She and Ray usually met at a hotel across town.

Fatima didn't really feel bad about being unfaithful to Wise. Not anymore. He was a good man and a good provider, but he had been cheating on her ever since before they'd celebrated their first wedding anniversary. Barely a year after they'd exchanged wedding vows. The signs were all there, and Fatima was done trying to ignore them. Two could play that game, so she didn't get mad, she got even.

Just then Fatima's cell phone rang. She reached over and picked it up, and she peeked at the caller ID before she answered. It was her mother, who was babysitting her three year old daughter Falynn that weekend as usual. Fatima was lucky because her parents couldn't get enough of their only grandchild. She flipped open her Razr phone. "Hey, lady. What up?"

"What's up, Miss "No Responsibilities"? I wish I had your life", Mrs. Doris Sinclair teased.

"Is there a problem, Ma? You want me to come and get Falynn, or somethin'?" Fatima wasn't in the mood for her mother's sarcasm.

"Don't be silly", Doris told her daughter. "When I'm ready to return my angel, I know where to find you. I'm calling to give you a heads up about next weekend, though. Your father and I have plans. We're going out of town."

"That's nice, Ma. Ya'll *need* to get away. Will you be takin' your granddaughter with you?"

Doris laughed, and burst Fatima's bubble immediately. "Oh no, you spoiled brat, you. This will be the first weekend since God knows when that you won't be able to go traipsing all over town, because you will have your child for a change. So put the brakes on those hot feet. And tell Mr. Wise I said the same thing. Now I'm gettin' ready to watch this Disney movie "Madagascar" with my grandbaby. You have a good evening." She hung up.

Fatima stared at the phone for a second. She was shocked. Where the hell were her parents going? Shit, if they were going some place, they should've chosen Disney Land, or some other child-friendly spot.

When Fatima thought about it, she knew she was being a bit selfish. And she knew she did that a lot. It was true. She was a spoiled brat, and she was guilty of hating to take up time with her child. Fatima never told anyone, but she had never really wanted to be a mother. She'd just wanted to have Wise' baby.

Oh well, Falynn was there now. And Fatima did love her. When Wise came in, she would let him know that they'd be staying in that weekend. She wasn't babysitting alone. It wasn't that she couldn't. She just didn't want to.

The more she thought about it, that seemed like a good idea. They could use some family bonding time. Fatima loved Wise, and she didn't want the two of them to drift apart any further.

When she thought about their baby's little angelic face, she knew she and Wise had to make it work. She had never considered just having a "baby daddy". Wise really loved his daughter, and he asked that Falynn stay home more often on the weekends. It was Fatima who always rushed her to her parents' house to get rid of her all the time.

Fatima decided that she would play a bit fairer when it came to parenting. She knew Wise was a good daddy. That weekend would be good for them. Fatima would cook, and they would have a real family weekend. She called Wise to let him know not to make any plans.

By the time she got off the phone, it was nighttime and getting a lot cooler out there. Fatima gathered her towels and drink, and she headed inside the grand five bedroom, five bathroom house she and Wise shared.

Just as she walked in the house, her cell phone rang again. This time it was Portia, calling to confirm the date for Simone's annual memorial tribute. Fatima and Portia winded up talking for about thirty minutes. Before they hung up, they agreed to meet Laila at the graveyard Simone was buried in that following Saturday morning. Afterwards, they would head to Mr. Chow's for brunch.

Chapter Four

Jay had flown out of town on business for a few days. He had been busy running around getting ready for the release of Wise' new album, so he was dog-tired. He was in his hotel suite dozing off in a comfortable recliner, finally taking a much needed nap when his cell phone rang.

Jay ignored the phone the first two times, but whoever it was kept calling him back. The ringer told him that it was a private number. Jay liked to screen his calls, so he hated those. Annoyed that the phone had interrupted his good sleep, he answered.

As soon as Jay put the phone to his ear, he was greeted by the sound of a screaming woman.

"Yo Jay, this nigga got knocked again! You gotta get him outta there! I went down to the precinct, but they won't tell me nothin'. He need a lawyer. I'm scared this time, Jay. What me and my baby gon' do without Hop?"

Now Jay knew who it was. It was Nisha, the baby mother of his so-called artist, Hop. Hip-Hop was the latest act they had signed to their label, and that dude was living up to his no-good reputation. They hadn't known he was that much of a fuck up. Every time he got locked up, people in the streets joked that he went "home", because he spent more time in jail than out on the streets.

Jay told Nisha not to worry, and he assured her that Hop would be fine. After he hung up, he called Sollie Steiner, his attorney.

Sollie specialized in entertainment law, but he had the best connections and contacts in the industry and the system that a person could hope for. When Jay explained the situation to Sollie, Sollie voiced his distaste for Hop's reoccurring criminal activities. Nonetheless, he assured Jay that he was on the case. He told Jay he'd see him when he got back to New York the following afternoon.

Jay hung up, and he pondered the "Hop" situation for a minute. That dude was something else. He was just too much of a hard head. No matter how many times Jay had preached to him about the benefits of longevity, he still took stupid chances that he didn't have to take.

Jay knew Hop was younger than him, but if he didn't change his way of thinking he wouldn't live to see thirty. It would've behooved Hop to listen to Jay because he knew all about it. He had been through it all. But he had the formula for success now, so a dude couldn't tell him shit.

Life was good. Damn good. He and his mans had really gone hard at the music thing, and it had paid off. Fuck houses, niggas had estates. And they had wills too. In the unfortunate event of anyone's demise, God forbid, their children would be set for life. With bread that was legitimate.

$$$

A uniformed police officer yelled into the pen, "Stevens! Russell Stevens! Let's go!"

Hip-Hop heard his government name, and came forward, and the officer opened up the cell. Hop was a handsome, lanky built, brown skinned dude around 5'11", with a light Caesar, and a cut right above his eyebrow. He kept a stone expression on his face until he walked out of there pass all those dudes he had been locked up with, and then he broke into a huge grin. Boy, them niggas Jay and Casino were on time. That was the fastest he had ever gotten out of jail. He knew them crackers didn't have anything on him.

Hop had been charged with armed robbery in the first degree. The cops claimed he was identified by the victim, but Hop had kept his mouth shut when they interrogated him. He was guilty, but he planned to lean on the witness and persuade him not to show up for court. That's why he wasn't really worried about the charge. Taking money was what he did.

Hip-Hop's real name was Russell Stevens, but everybody in the 'hood called him Hip-Hop because he had been shot in the hip a few years ago, and had to undergo hip replacement surgery, which had left him with a slight limp. But right after his hip surgery his limp was more like a hop, so dudes had christened him with the nick name "Hip-Hop". Later on it turned into "Hop" for short. The streets were cold, but the name stuck.

Hop's name was well-known, and feared as well. Niggas knew how he got down. His name rang bells. He was notorious for taking money. He was a rap artist himself, but he had several well-known, supposed to be tough rappers paying him protection money every month.

Hop was a grimy dude from Brownsville, Brooklyn. He didn't give a fuck about anything, or anybody. He was a cutthroat type of nigga. He didn't have any friends, or any remorse.

$$$

Later on the following evening, Jay and Cas sat at the crib they had recently rented for Hip-Hop, and listened on as he emotionally thanked them for springing him from the pen again.

Hop had been drinking heavily, and at the moment he felt indebted to be home. He looked around his newly furnished uptown apartment proudly, and then he downed another double shot of Petron tequila, and slammed his glass down.

He slurred, "Yo, ya'll know somethin'? I really love you dudes, man. Ya'll the only ones that ever gave a fuck about me. I ain't never had nobody. My moms and pops both

O-D'ed on dope when I was a little kid, and I ain't have no grandparents on neither side. The mo'fuckin' streets raised me, man. Literally. I ran away from this orphanage when I was eight, and I was homeless and living in the streets 'til I was twelve. And then I got sent to a group home. Them crackers got me for stealin' cars. Grand theft, auto. That was my thing back then. Stealin' cars. I hooked up wit' this Puerto Rican cat named Tito, who taught me the game when I was a lil' nigga."

Hop paused, and shook his head. He looked nostalgic for a second. He leaned back in his chair and slurred on. "Now Tito, *that* was a real nigga. But he got killed in a car accident, when he was runnin' from the po-lice. That nigga could drive like he was in NASCAR, but them crab ass pigs did some foul shit to make him crash. God bless the dead. But yo, I ain't mean to get off the subject. I was just thinkin' 'bout my past and shit."

Hop sat up abruptly, and banged on the table loudly two times with the palm of his hand. He loudly exclaimed, "I got mad mothafuckin' love for ya'll dudes! Ya'll know that? Ya'll gave a low life, good for nothin' dude like me a chance! I never thought I would be shit! I used to think about takin' myself out all the time. Felt like I was a waste of life, and shit."

Hop nodded his head slowly, reflecting on his last words. He looked like he was winding down again. Then all of a sudden, he reached under his shirt and took his burner out his waist, and cocked it. He placed it on his temple, and remained silent for a minute. It seemed like he was really contemplating doing it.

Jay and Cas glanced at each other nervously. What the fuck was wrong with Hop? He was on a series of highs and lows, like he was bipolar or something. That dude was a mental case. He needed to get checked out.

Hop looked at them and noticed how uneasy they were.

He laughed, and put the gun down. "Nah, yo. Nah! I ain't gon' kill myself. Relax, man. I got somethin' to live for now, thanks to ya'll."

He grinned at Jay and Cas like he was real proud. Hop poured himself another double shot, and raised his glass in a toast. "To ya'll. My niggas." He threw back the tequila, and belched loudly before he continued.

"And I promise ya'll, I'ma stop all this bullshit. I know ya'll runnin' out of patience wit' a nigga. Fuck that goin' back to jail shit. I'm ready to eat. Some real bread, man. And I'm ready for my Street Life medallion. I'ma wear that shit proud!"

Cas said, "Well, you gotta earn that. If you can stay out here on the streets long enough to follow through, we got some plans for you. But you gotta get in the studio, son. You just been bullshittin', and not doing anything productive."

"Word", Jay said.

Hip-Hop nodded his head in agreement. He couldn't front, they were right. He had to listen. Money talked, and those dudes knew how to get some bread.

$$$

The following Saturday morning, Portia and Fatima drove to the graveyard where Simone was buried. When they reached there they parked in the parking lot, and glimpsed around for Laila. She wasn't there yet. Portia and Fatima got out of the car, looking equally fabulous in low waist designer jeans and pink ski jackets. They hadn't planned to color coordinate, it was just a coincidence. Portia had on a hot pink Marc Jacobs jacket, with blue jeans and pink Louis Vuitton sneakers, and Fatima wore a cotton candy pink Just Cavalli jacket, blue jeans, and a pair of pink Pradas.

Portia complimented Fatima on her newly svelte figure. Girlfriend had lost almost thirty pounds, so she deserved it.

It was no secret how Fatima had struggled with her weight after she had her daughter. Portia knew she'd had a little work done, but it didn't matter. She still looked good. She had teased Fatima, and called her "Nip & Tuck", but she was right there with her during her surgeries, to make sure everything went okay.

Fatima and Portia waited a few minutes, and Laila finally pulled up. She grinned at her girlfriends, and waved. She shut off her gold Lexus GS, and hopped out looking real cute in a light blue, pink, and yellow, fitted Juicy Couture velour suit, and beige Gucci sneakers with the pink and yellow web down the side.

It had rained hard the night before, so all three homegirls had on comfortable footwear, so their heels wouldn't sink down in the graveyard dirt. Laila reached in her car and retrieved a pink scarf, and tied it around her neck because she had a little cold. She took the flowers she had picked up along the way from the backseat, and locked her car doors.

They all headed over to Simone's gravesite together. Simone's baby, Imani, was buried right next to her. After they dusted the fallen leaves off their graves, the ladies placed a beautiful bouquet of pink tea roses on baby Imani's grave, and a lovely sprawling arrangement of white roses on Simone's. All of the friends greeted Simone loud and jovially, and they commenced to celebrate.

Portia, Laila, and Fatima shouted *"N.I.B. forever"* and threw up their N.I.B. signs. N.I.B. stood for "New Improved Bitches", which was the name of their clique back in their teenage days. They were the most hated, flyest set of bitches the 'hood ever knew.

After the girls reminisced for a little while, they all stood around in a circle and held hands while Portia led them in prayer.

"Heavenly Father, we stand here holding hands in unity, humbled by your greatness. Lord, as you know, today is the

birthday of our dear friend and sister, Simone. And while we
are still hurting from our loss, we ask that you watch over us and
give us the strength we need to cope."

Portia got a little teary eyed, but she continued. "*...Our*
hearts are heavy today, God. We truly miss her presence amongst
us. Lord, we pray her soul will rest in peace. And Imani's too."

The friends all said "Amen", and then they sat on Simone's
grave, talking and giggling like schoolgirls.

About two hours later, Portia, Laila, and Fatima left the
graveyard. Now they were ready to grub. They changed their
minds about Mister Chow's, and decided on BBQ's because
there was one located right in Brooklyn.

When they got to the restaurant, the hostess asked them if
they needed a table for three. Portia told her that it was four
of them, but they only needed three chairs. The girl smiled,
and asked if one of them was expecting a baby.

Portia laughed, and shook her head no. She didn't bother
trying to explain that Simone's spirit was with them. The girl
just looked at Portia kind of strange, and told them to follow
her to their table.

Shortly after, they sat at a table sharing a full basket of
sticky wings, and sipping on Texas sized strawberry coladas
and Long Island ice tea.

Laila was fairly quiet for the first few minutes of their
conversation. She was thinking about her situation. She was
tired of playing it off. She knew she needed to confide in her
girlfriends. She needed some type of support system to get
through what she was going through at home.

After Laila ordered her second drink, she decided to spill
her guts. "Yo, I got somethin' to tell ya'll. Guess what?"

Portia and Fatima looked at Laila asked in unison, "You
pregnant?"

Laila laughed, and said, "Hell no! My husband is on
crack."

Portia said, "You so stupid." She knew Laila was joking.

Laila said, "Yo, P, I'm not kiddin'. Khalil is smokin' fuckin' crack. That stupid ass, weak son of a bitch!"

Laila felt relieved. It was good to get it off her chest. There was something therapeutic about telling her homegirls. They were the only ones she could talk to.

Portia and Fatima were quiet for a minute. Fatima asked Laila, "How do you know, girl? You got any proof?"

Fatima had dealt with a loser named Larry, who'd starting smoking in the nineties, so she felt she was a pro at knowing the signs.

Laila said, "That nigga done started stealin' my fuckin' money. Thousands of it. I had to close all my accounts and shit he had access to."

Portia and Fatima looked equally shocked. "Get the fuck outta here, Lay", said Portia. "You gotta be kiddin'. I don't believe this shit."

Fatima shook her head. "Child, that crack shit is a mothafucka. Can't nobody but God save him from that monster. Has he become violent?"

"Yeah. He got real stupid the other day, when he found out he didn't have access to my money no more. I told you I closed all our joint accounts."

Portia was just quiet. It was hard to picture Khalil as a crackhead. Poor Laila. Portia couldn't even imagine how she would feel if Jay started smoking.

Laila held her head down and tried to regulate the tears that were starting to well up in her eyes. She hated when that happened. Crying didn't solve anything. Even though she had a lot to cry about. Her fucking family was falling apart.

Laila dabbed her eyes with a napkin, and got it together. She told her best friends about everything, including the drastic change she saw in Pebbles' behavior since Khalil had been fucking up.

Portia and Fatima were surprised at all of the things going on in Laila's life. Both of their hearts went out to her. They each offered her a place for her and her children to stay, until she figured out what to do.

Portia felt like it was up to Laila to make her decision, but Fatima urged her to pack her shit and leave Khalil's ass. They both agreed that it wasn't healthy for her kids to be around him if he was getting high.

Laila appreciated their concern, but she didn't feel she could leave him yet. In the back of her mind, she still wanted to save him. He was her children's father.

Portia and Fatima didn't pressure her. They knew she was smart enough to make the right decision. They moved on to a lighter conversation topic, to take her mind off things.

Portia let them know that she was planning an intimate celebration for Jay's upcoming birthday. Her baby was an Aries, and the party was scheduled for the following weekend. She told them that it was a gentleman-oriented gala but it would be real classy. She knew Laila wasn't in much of a party mood, so she told her she wouldn't be upset with her if she chose to sit that one out.

Chapter Five

Barely two weeks had passed since Jay and Casino bailed Hop out of jail, and he was up to his usual antics already. He sat outside of a club called Ocean's Twelve, and scoped. He was on the lookout for somebody he could gank. Hop didn't feel bad about it either. He needed the bread. Jay and Cas had recently given him another advance, but he'd lost the bulk of the money gambling. The last thousand, he had tricked on this bitch named Nicole, who could swallow his whole dick.

Just then, Hop spotted a vic he'd had his eye on. He knew he would see that nigga again. He was a dapper dude, with a royal blue suit on. Hop couldn't front. Homeboy was dressed to the nines, on some real player shit. The dude wasn't actually a celebrity. He was more of a baller. He was amongst the C-list "who's who", simply because he had the bread. He was rumored to be from Detroit, and he was shining to an impressive extent. Hop wanted nothing more than to relieve him of his many jewels.

He got his opportunity shortly after, when the dude stepped off from his mans for a minute, to take a piss. Hop hopped out, and crept up on his left, and he caught him with his dick still in his hand. He waited politely until the nigga finished pissing before he stuck him up.

When Hop saw the stream of urine hitting the ground turn into a drip, he yelled, "Yo, run ya' shit, nigga! Now mothafucka!" He startled the dude so much, the last few drops of piss landed on his royal blue gators.

Duke struggled to put his dick away, but Hop demanded that he put his hands up immediately. He wanted to rob him quickly and quietly, so him having his johnson out was a real plus. That would give Hop a few seconds to get away.

He didn't think that nigga would run after him with his shit out like that.

Hop stuck him for about eighty thousand dollars worth of jewels, and about ten thousand in cash. He smiled at his take, and slipped away into the darkness just as quickly as he had come.

Hop looked back, and saw the dude trotting after him with his dick still out. His penis was just flapping against the side of his royal blue suit pants. Hop turned around and fired two shots at his feet. The dude stopped in his tracks, and cursed. *"Mothafucka!"* He pumped his fist in the air in anger. He was vexed, but he knew he had no wins.

Hop laughed, and hurried to his car. That was a nice come-up. Another day, another dollar. Jay and Casino didn't have to know. What they didn't know wouldn't hurt them.

$$\$\$\$$$

True to Portia's word, she gave Jay a small, but intimate birthday celebration that was out of this world. There were only about twenty guests, and it was a classy affair. Portia had chosen a circus-like theme, with a grown and sexy urban twist.

She had worked closely with a circus ringmaster, a brother from the African American owned UniverSoul Circus, to achieve the effects for the theme she chose. It had cost her a grip, but everything turned out awesome.

Each guest had their own small, candlelit table, and there were four sexily dressed women serving drinks from the fully stocked bar. Everything, including lap dances, was on the house. Instead of regular strippers, Portia had hired exotic dancers that were specially trained in burlesque. They were sexy sisters in classy costumes, with finger waves, pin curls, and big feathers in their hair. Some of the dancers hung from the ceiling on ropes and swings, and twirled about seductively, and the others worked the floor and stage for the gentlemen's entertainment.

Portia had individually interviewed each of the fifteen girls she'd hired, to make sure they were down to earth. She hadn't wanted any prissy, pompous broads, because they wouldn't know how to handle Jay's friends, who Portia knew could get a little rowdy at times. The girls had all been well paid in advance, and instructed to make sure the men had a great time.

The fellows that attended the party, including Jay's mans, Cas and Wise, all acted like they appreciated Portia's efforts. Those girls were a lot different from the strippers they were used to. Jay's party was definitely a celebration fit for grown ass men.

At the end of the night, Jay was so engrossed in the grand finale the dancers performed for him, he didn't even notice Portia had disappeared. After the girls' show, there was a drum roll, and a spotlight shone to the left of the room. A pair of fancy burgundy velvet curtains parted, and revealed Portia being slowly lowered down. She was sitting on a chiffon draped swing. She smiled seductively, and crossed her legs sexily.

Portia had completely transformed. She was always pretty, but now she looked like a runway model in a Victoria's Secret Angels fashion show. She looked way sexy, in a light blue and silver corseted Cosabella one piece, and silver open toe Versace stilettos. She wore a pair of silver trimmed, light blue wings on her back, and a silver halo atop a mass of bouncy curls in her hair.

To say that Portia looked beautiful would have been an understatement. The word "breathtaking" would have been a more appropriate adjective to describe her. She looked like a real goddess.

Jay just stared at her. He was mesmerized, and so were the others. Portia stood up, and danced to Ciara's

"Promise", moving her hourglass shaped body seductively. Her performance was classy and tasteful. She had practiced for two whole weeks, so she moved with the grace of a ballerina.

Portia finished her perfectly choreographed routine sitting on Jay's lap sideways with one leg up in the air. When she was done, everybody clapped. Portia stood up and took a bow, and she took Jay's hand, and led him over to a silver gift wrapped door, with a huge light blue bow on it. Jay watched Portia's big heart shaped booty bouncing in front of him, and shook his head. That girl was the truth. Together, they disappeared into a private room in the back. Jay was all smiles.

The room was dimly lit, and sweetly scented by the aromatic candles that were burning. There was a special chair waiting for Jay. It was actually a real throne Portia had rented, especially for the purpose of giving her king a royal birthday lap dance.

Portia sat Jay down, and stood in front of him. She eyeballed him sexily, and teased him by slowly undressing and winding her hips to the beat of the music. Minutes later, she wore only wings and stilettos.

Portia moved closer and grinded her crotch on Jay's lap. That night he learned what it was like to be touched by an angel. He palmed Portia's ass, and massaged it in circular motions. She was so soft. He still loved her just as much as he did the day he married her. And the few extra pounds she had put on were right where they should've been. Jay had no complaints.

He leaned back in his chair, and watched Portia clap her booty for him. Boy, what a beautiful sight. Jay bit his lip in anticipation. He was ready to slide up in that pussy immediately. He wanted to hit it with those sexy wings on.

Jay told Portia to bend over. She obeyed, and he slid deep in her valley, and hit it from the back. The wings rustled, and

Portia moaned.

Jay leaned down and kissed the tattoo of his name on her ass, and he continued to stroke. It wasn't long before he was ready to cum. It felt like it was traveling from his toes on up. Jay grinded his teeth to try to hold it in, but he was forced to let it out. "Ma, I'm 'bout to cum! Aaahh!"

Damn, Portia had some good ass pussy. He leaned forward and kissed her on the back of her neck. That was his baby. She had made sure his birthday night was on fire. He had a good wife. Portia was always on her job.

$$$

Jayquan looked out the window and saw his father's black Maserati pull up. The passenger door opened, and Humble stepped out. Jayquan was glad to see that Humble was in the car with his father. He grabbed his basketball, and ran outside.

Jayquan yelled, "Yo, Humble! Catch", and he tossed him the basketball.

Humble turned around, and was forced to think fast. He caught the ball in time, and laughed, and he gave Lil' Jay a pound. "What up, lil' man? What's shakin'?"

Jayquan just shrugged. "Ain't nothin'. Same toilet, different day."

Humble laughed. He was pretty sure that "toilet" wasn't the terminology Jayquan would've used had he been around his friends at school. Lil' Jay was a funny little dude. Humble really got a kick out of him.

Humble threw Jayquan the ball. "Man up, son. Come on, let's take it to the court."

Jayquan grinned, and dribbled a few times, and he threw the ball back. "Come on, coward. Let's play ball."

Jayquan was just kidding with Humble. He took after his father a lot. He loved to talk slick. Lil' Jay looked at Humble

like an older brother. His little sister Jazmin and his little
cousin Jahseim loved him too.

Jayquan and Humble jogged over to the court to play a
little one on one. Jay had a full-sized basketball court on the
side his house. Jayquan loved to play, and he tried to get a
game going every time Humble came over. Either that, or he
wanted to play video games on his Playstation III.

After Jay and Humble pulled up, Jay stayed in the car talking
on his cell phone for a minute. He was on an important call.
When he was done, he got out and grinned at Humble and
Jayquan running towards the court. As usual, Lil' Jay hadn't
wasted anytime.

Humble was like an addition to the family now, because
Jay had sort of adopted him as his honorary little brother.
Jay had become quite fond of that dude. It was probably
because Humble reminded him of himself at that age. When
he was twenty years old he had been a go-getter too.

By conversing with Humble, Jay discovered that he had
a lot of potential. And that made Jay take him on as an
understudy of sorts. He wanted to teach Humble how to
make profitable power moves without getting caught up in
the white man's system.

In effort to keep him off the streets, Jay had taken care
of all his problems, starting with paying up his mother's
mortgage, and saving her house from foreclosure. He also
copped Humble a nice whip, and unofficially put him on
the payroll.

Jay and his mans kept a close-knit circle. Humble was
around them so much that Cas, Wise, and the rest of the crew
at Street Life considered him part of the team. Especially
since he was Nate's little brother. Nate was real a stand-up
dude. And Humble was just a likable person. Even Portia
adored him.

When Jayquan and Humble came in from playing ball,
Jay was in the kitchen with Portia. Lil' Jay and Humble were

both panting and sweating, so Portia offered them a cold drink.

"Hey fellas. What up, ya'll want some lemonade, or iced water?"

Jayquan nodded. "Gimme lemonade. Thanks."

"Me too. Thanks, Lady P", Humble said. He smiled and tipped his fitted cap at Portia like a gentleman. "How you feelin' today?"

Portia smiled. "I'm blessed, thank you. And how 'bout you, Humble Bee? You ayight, baby?"

"I'm good, Lady P. Now that I've been blessed with your presence." Humble took Portia's hand, and kissed it.

Portia blushed, and waved her hand at him. That boy was crazy. She knew Humble was just kidding. He'd been flirting with her ever since he had seen her in that sexy costume at Jay's birthday party. She headed over to the refrigerator in her state-of-the-art stainless steel kitchen.

Portia retrieved two glasses, and placed them in the ice dispenser on the front of the double door, stainless steel fridge. She half-filled their glasses with crushed ice, and then filled them to the rim with lemonade. Portia stuck a lemon slice on the side of each glass, and she handed the cold drinks to the boys.

Jay sat at the table drinking a cold bottle of formula 50 flavored Vitamin Water that Portia had handed him from the fridge when he came in. He watched Humble flirting with his wife, but he didn't pay it any mind because he knew it was innocent. Humble was always telling him how bad Portia was, and how he wished she had a sister his age, so Jay knew he had a little crush on her.

Humble took a sip of his lemonade, and he nodded his head in approval. "Umm, this is perfect. It's so sweet, you must've stuck your finger in it, Lady P."

Portia laughed. She liked Humble. He always made her laugh. He was a good kid, and always so well-mannered.

And she loved the nickname he had given her, "Lady P". Humble was a gentleman, and Portia also loved the way he treated the kids. His demeanor was really humble. Portia had started calling him "Humble Bee".

Humble grinned at Jay, and told him he was just fooling around. Jay playfully told him to fall back. Humble just laughed. He really enjoyed being around Jay and his family. That man had made his life a lot easier, and he was extremely grateful. Jay had really looked out for him. He had even purchased him a brand new car. All he told him to do in exchange was stay out of the streets, and do something with his life.

Humble looked up to Jay and respected him, so he listened. He didn't frequent the 'hood much anymore. He was only seen coming and going. No more hanging around. He had bagged this shorty named Ysatis, and he had been on some laid back stuff lately.

But around Humble's way, dudes were starting to hate a lot. They didn't like seeing him coming through the 'hood pushing the new Lexus ES 350 Jay had set him out in. It was like he had come up overnight, and dudes were anxious to pull him back down.

$$$

A few days later, Jay, Casino, Wise, and Hop were having drinks at an upscale gentleman's club in the City called "Bada Bing". The club belonged to their man Wings. Wings had recently obtained a cabaret license, so he now featured topless dancers in what used to be just a sports bar.

Wings had been their acquaintance for a while. They went back about twelve years. Wings and Jay had shared the misfortune of losing their loved ones at the same time. Jay's baby mother, Stacy, and Wings' shorty, Maisha, were killed in a car accident on their way home from a club a few years ago.

Unfortunately, Stacy had been drinking that night. Jay hadn't had a particularly magnificent relationship with her before she passed, but she was Jayquan's mother. For that reason he would always love her. He hoped she was resting in peace.

Jay was blessed that Portia had stepped up, and helped out in raising his son. That really meant a lot to him. She loved Jayquan like he was her own.

Jay snapped back to reality, and looked around at his homie's establishment. It was classy, and decorated tastefully. Jay was happy for Wings. He had come a long way.

Jay and the crew had gone out for a nightcap because they'd had a long day of promoting Wise' upcoming album. A few hours later, they piled up in Casino's Maybach, and headed for a diner to get some breakfast.

Hop had drunk too much. When they got to the restaurant, he got overly emotional as usual. Cas was on the phone with his wife, so he started on Jay.

"Yo Jay, man. I just want you to know how much I appreciate what ya'll did for me. I owe you, man. So just so you know, any dude that disrespects you, Cas, or Wise is finished. The nigga son is a bastard, straight up. No questions, big homie."

Jay appreciated his little homie reaching out to him like that, but he never trusted anyone to do his dirty work for him. And Hop was too anxious to prove that he would bust his gun.

A lot of young dudes in the streets knew of Jay and Killer Cas' legend, and some of them tried hard to prove to them that they were killers as well. Nowadays, that image sort of bothered Jay and Cas both. They were well respected, legitimate, self-made millionaires now. They didn't want their legacy to be a few dead bodies left in the 'hood.

Hop had obviously misinterpreted what he and Cas had

meant when they told him he had to earn his stripes. Jay tried to tell Hop that wasn't the way. Dudes weren't living like that anymore. They couldn't risk blowing everything they had accomplished over some petty bullshit.

Wise listened to Hop tell Jay about all the so-called killing he would do for them, and he just couldn't stand it anymore. For some reason, that dude really got under his skin sometimes. He hated a wanna-be.

Wise was so impatient with Hop, he butted in him and Jay's conversation. "Nigga, shut the fuck up with all that bullshit. Always frontin' like you such a killer. Yo' ass won't bust a fuckin' grape."

Hop got tight when Wise said that. "Nigga, don't test my aim", he stated. He was sick of Wise always breaking his balls.

Wise said, "What? Man, you ain't gon' do *shit*." He stared Hop down, to see what his response would be. Hop just shook his head, and walked away for a minute. You could tell he was tight.

Jay and Cas never really thought anything about the rivalry between Wise and Hop. They took it to be sort of sibling-like. Wise thought lightly of it too. He usually laughed it off. He knew Hop wanted to take a shot at him, and he always welcomed the challenge.

Before the night was over, Hop cornered Jay again and asked him when he was going to get his Street Life medallion. He was the only one in the crew without one. Jay patiently explained to Hop that once he calmed down, and stopped trying to terrorize the industry, he would get an iced out Street Life Entertainment medallion immediately.

Hop got arrested all the time, and they just didn't need the bad press. They were respected businessmen, and didn't want the likes of Hop's grimy antics to be associated with them. Not for the robbery thing. He couldn't be wearing a Street Life medallion, and running around yapping niggas.

They didn't need the beef. They were just try'na get bread.

Hop didn't know yet, but Jay, Cas, and Wise had discussed dropping him from the label. Wise especially thought it was a good idea to get rid of him. He couldn't really stand Hop. He was just too extra, with his "I'm a thug, I bust my gun" shit. And he was in jail more than he was in the studio. The amount of bail money they had spent on getting him out of jail was ridiculous.

Hop didn't know that they were starting to think of him as a liability, not an asset. He had an ignorant type of street mentality, so he didn't understand Jay's reasoning about the bad press he was bringing to the company. He always took it personal. He felt like they wouldn't give him a chain because they were trying to play him.

Wise overheard Jay and Hop's conversation again, and he couldn't resist butting in one more time. "Yo Hop, shut the fuck up, man. You stay cryin' about a chain. Soundin' like a lil' hoe and shit." Wise laughed, and kept teasing him.

"Here, Hop. You want a chain? You can wear mine." Wise jokingly sang that Nas song to him, *"Shorty, you can hold my ice."*

Hop didn't find Wise funny at all. What did he look like holding his chain? He wasn't his bitch. Hop was tired of niggas clowning him. If he didn't get his Street Life medallion soon, he was gonna have the last laugh.

Chapter Six

It was the beginning of May, and the weather was getting nice. Portia was ready to start planning her family's summer vacation. She, Jay, and the kids usually went away for a few weeks every summer.

Portia wanted to go to Europe that year so she could shop in Paris and Milan. The kids had passports too, so it wouldn't be a problem. They could all go. She made a mental note to ask Jay. He had been so busy lately. Portia looked forward to having him all to herself for a few weeks.

She didn't want to seem insecure, but she had started to feel a little neglected lately. It seemed like ever since Jay's birthday had passed, their sex life had declined a little. They hadn't made love in almost two weeks. That might've been normal for some married couples, but Jay and Portia usually did it at least four times a week, even when he went out of town. Jay's sexual drive was usually pretty high, so she was beginning to wonder if he had been fooling around on her recently. He had to be getting it from somewhere.

Portia thought about that phone call a few days ago. She had walked in the kitchen on Jay when he was on his cell phone. He had told whoever the person was that he would call them back, and hung up the phone. Portia hadn't commented, because it wasn't that serious. Not at the time anyway. But if something was going on, she wanted to find out as soon as possible, so she could nip it in the bud. She'd be damned if she was sharing her husband with some other bitch. Over her dead body.

Portia wanted to be totally sure before she accused Jay of anything. When he came home that night, she just played it cool. She asked him if they could take their family vacation in Europe that year. To her delight, Jay told her to schedule the trip for early August. Portia decided to invite Fatima and her family too. And it would be nice if Laila and her kids could come too. Portia knew Jay wouldn't mind.

Before they went to bed that night, Jay announced that he had to go out of town to Miami the following day on business. Portia knew they were promoting Wise' album, so Jay was running a lot, but why hadn't he mentioned it before? Portia's suspicions were further aroused. Now she really suspected something was up. Jay was a good man, but she wasn't naïve, damn it. He was still a man. She wanted to talk about it, but he was so tired he fell fast asleep.

The next day, Jay told Portia he would be gone for two or three days. As usual, he let her know exactly where he would be staying. He always disclosed his itinerary to her, whenever he traveled. Portia didn't trip. That evening, she kissed him goodbye before he left, and wished him a safe journey.

That night she tossed and turned in bed until dawn. She spoke to Jay after he got there, so she knew he was okay. She just had a funny feeling in her stomach. A part of her felt ashamed and silly for not trusting him, but she wanted to know what the hell was going on.

The next day, Portia took the kids over her mother in-law's house, and she went for a manicure and pedicure. While she was getting her feet done, she called and booked herself a first-class flight to Miami for that evening. Portia wanted to creep up on Jay at nighttime. She just wanted to see if he was fucking around on her or not. She trusted Jay for the most part, but she needed to ease her suspicions.

Portia landed in Miami at about two AM. It was the perfect time of night to bust a man cheating. Jay definitely wouldn't be expecting her. And she was dressed incognito in a short, black, satin Yves Saint Laurent trench coat, and black YSL shades. She had packed light, stuffing everything into a large, black, leather Gucci hobo bag.

Portia knew Jay would've had a limo waiting for her if he'd

known she was coming but she had to surprise him this time. She flagged a taxi and headed for The Savoy, where he said he was staying. She had a big knot in her stomach during the entire ride. Twenty minutes later, she arrived at the hotel.

As she crossed the enormous lobby Portia looked up at the lovely cathedral ceiling, and it dawned on her that she forgot the room number. She stopped at the front desk and told them that she was there to meet her husband, Mr. Jay Mitchell, and she needed to know what suite he was in. After she obtained the information she needed she headed for the elevator.

The elevator concierge, who was a handsome elderly blue eyed gentleman in a burgundy and gold uniform, asked her if she needed any assistance. Portia told him what penthouse suite Jay was in, and he told her he'd have her there in a second.

When they reached the top floor he gave Portia directions. She kindly thanked him, and the gentleman gave her a warm smile. She smiled back and bid him a goodnight. Just before the elevator doors closed he tipped his hat and bowed, and then he winked at her.

Portia smiled at him again through the closing doors, and then she shifted her thoughts back to Jay. "That nigga better not be up here with no bitch", she said aloud to herself. Portia didn't know what she would do if she caught him with somebody.

All she knew was that she wasn't going out like no damn white woman. She was gonna wild the fuck out. Portia mentally pumped herself up, preparing for the worse. Though heaven knows she was certainly hoping for the best.

When Portia located Jay's penthouse door she stood outside and tried to listen for activity inside. It was like time stood still for a few minutes. Her heart was beating triple times. She didn't hear anything, so she knocked on the door.

Just then, Portia heard voices. There were some people getting off the elevator. They were guys, and one of those voices sounded like it belonged to Jay! Damn, she should've had a room key. She should've tried to get one from the front desk. She quickly scuttled behind a big plant in the hallway corner and hid.

Portia peeped through the leaves and saw Jay, Wise, and three scantily clad girls coming around the hallway corner. She got so tight her nostrils flared. Fire almost shot out of them like she was a dragon. She had caught that mothafucka dead in his tracks. She couldn't believe his nerve. Portia wanted to jump out on them and spazz out but she fought the desire. She waited because she wanted to see which of those scallywag bitches was with Jay. Or did they have some type of orgy planned?

Portia was fuming. She wouldn't have been surprised if they could see the smoke that was coming out of her ears. She tried to breathe steady but it felt like someone had cut off her oxygen supply. Jay was about to fuck one of those hoes. How could he? No, the question was "how would he?" Because that shit was only going down over her dead body that night. That fucking bastard!

Portia's bit her lip in anger as she watched Wise and Jay walk to different suites. The tallest of the girls, this awful long weave having brown skinned bitch, seductively stroked Jay's arm and whispered something in his ear. Portia stood as still as death. If Jay went for it she was going to jail that night because she was gonna kill him.

What Portia saw her husband do turned her frown into a grin. She was glad she didn't react because Jay politely shook that bitch off and told her he wasn't with it. He said goodnight and went inside his suite and closed the door in her face. The girl looked real disappointed.

Portia had to restrain herself from shouting, *"That's right, bitch! Get off my husband dick!"* Instead she shouted for joy within. O glorious day! Jay obviously hadn't been lying to her. That bitch was half naked and he hadn't looked the least bit interested.

The groupie just stood there outside his door for a second, clearly unpleased at Jay's brush-off. She knocked on his door but he didn't answer. The girl looked defeated, but she still stood there for a minute. Portia guessed she was determined to wrap her lips around Jay's dick.

Well Jay never came to the door, so the bitch finally walked across the hall to Wise' suite. When she knocked on that door, it opened and she went on inside.

Portia couldn't believe Wise. What the hell was he going to do with all those groupies? She knew he wasn't about to mess with all those bitches at the same time. She was telling Fatima on his ass.

Portia usually minded her business but she had to look out for her girl's safety. Wise was always promising Fatima that he was going to be faithful to her. That lying bastard. Portia decided she would pull Tima's coat as soon as she got back home. As a matter of fact, it couldn't wait. She was going to call her that night. How could she not let her know immediately? If Fatima found out some information like that and sat on it, Portia would be pissed off.

But at the current time she was more concerned with her own husband, with his sexy, faithful, fine ass. Jay always insisted that he didn't fuck around with the groupies that threw themselves at them, and now Portia really believed him. She waited about two minutes, and then she came out of hiding and knocked on his door.

Jay heard the knock and he started to ignore it again but something told him to go look out the peephole. When he saw that it was Portia, he held back his grin and opened the door. That girl was crazy. "Ma, what up? What the hell you doin' down here?"

Portia smiled brightly and said, "Just checking on you to

make sure you're behaving yourself."

Jay laughed, and pulled her inside and shut the door. Portia dropped her bag and slipped into his awaiting arms. They hugged and shared a long kiss. It was late, but they could both tell it was going to be a long night.

"I thought you were cheatin' on me", Portia whispered in his ear.

Jay raised her chin and forced her to look in his eyes. "Why you actin' so insecure all of a sudden? Have I given you any reason to believe I fucked around on you?"

Portia put him dead on the spot. "How come we haven't done it lately?"

"Come on. It's only been a few days. I just been tired, Ma. I've been rippin' and runnin' on three and four hours of sleep a day."

Portia said, "I know, boo." Her poor baby wasn't lying about that. She paused for a second. "So what about that phone call that day?"

Jay made a face. "What phone call?"

Portia said, "That phone call last Tuesday. I walked in the kitchen and you said *'I'ma call you back'*, and hung up your cell phone."

Jay sighed impatiently. "Ma, come on. That was Hop's baby mother, Nisha. She was gettin' on my nerves that day. And if you had a problem with that, why didn't you address it then?"

"Because I wanted to trust you. I ain't wanna feed into it."

Jay looked at Portia and shook his head. "This is what you call trust? You be wildin', P."

Portia just shrugged her shoulders and pouted. She wasn't going to admit that she was wrong, but that time she was sure glad she was.

Jay couldn't resist saying it. "You smoke too much of that shit. That weed got you paranoid."

Portia punched him in the arm. "Shut up, Jay! I ain't paranoid."

"You're right, you *crazy*. But I love your stinkin' ass. You lucky."

Portia laughed. "No, *you* lucky!"

Jay grabbed her around the waist and they kissed again.

Afterwards, Jay helped her out of her coat like a gentleman. After Portia took off her trench she went to the bathroom to freshen up. She took her cell phone with her so she could call Fatima while she was in there.

While Portia took forever in the bathroom, Jay mused over her. He was happy that she came, but that girl was crazy. His wife wasn't playing with a full deck but he couldn't front, he loved that gangsta' way she handled shit. She had really suspected something was up so she just popped up on him.

After about fifteen minutes, Jay grew impatient and opened the bathroom door to rush her. He was turned on, and ready to hit that.

When Jay busted in the bathroom, Portia just laughed. He was so impatient. She could tell what was on his mind from the look on his face. Her baby was horny. Portia played it off and told him she was tired from her flight, and not in the mood.

Jay just looked at her like he wasn't trying to hear that. He wasn't taking "no" for an answer. Without a word, he walked over to Portia and took the liberty of undressing her. She tried to play hard to get like she didn't really want it, but Jay knew better. Her protests weren't real. She kept on saying no but she was smiling.

They played these little games every now and then. Sometimes Portia liked for him to take it. Jay picked her up and threw her over his shoulder like he was a caveman. Portia shrieked and squirmed like she was trying to get away, so he spanked her on the ass and told her to behave. He carried her out of the bathroom and sat her down on the table, and then he pulled up a chair in front of her. Portia looked as scrumptious as a mighty feast, and he was about to chow down.

Now that his face was between her legs, all of a sudden she wanted to participate. Jay reached under her skirt and pulled off her thong, and she eagerly spread her legs and scooted her pussy closer to his face. Portia was funny. Jay had to laugh. He knew she loved when he did that to her. And he loved doing it too, but since she was so anxious he took his time. He started out by placing tiny butterfly kisses along her inner thighs.

Portia squirmed with the anticipation of feeling Jay's warm mouth down there. Her little joy button was throbbing like there was no tomorrow. She placed her hands on the back of his head and softly persuaded him to go for it.

"Go 'head and kiss it. Please, daddy? Kiss it, baby", she moaned.

Jay liked the sound of that. He decided it was time to give her what she wanted. He wrapped his arms around her thighs and dug his face in like he was searching for buried treasure. He skillfully used his tongue and lips to whip Portia's body into a frenzy and ate her out like there was gold at the bottom of her pussy.

Portia trembled in pleasure. It felt so good she couldn't even speak. Damn, Jay was the man.

After he was sure she came, Jay came up for air. He stood up and placed his hard dick on Portia's throbbing clit. She stared down at it like it was a fine piece of art. Portia reached down and massaged it, and she guided him into her wet, steamy valley.

Jay slid into her cocoon and caught his breath. It was hot and tight, just the way he loved it. He gave it to her missionary style for a minute, loving the way she kept saying how good it felt over and over.

Jay paused. He wasn't ready to cum yet. He pulled out and flipped Portia over. He wanted to hit it from the back now. She looked sexy as hell on the table down on all fours. She sexily wiggled her fat ass in the air. Jay palmed it and rubbed it, appreciating its abundance. He looked down proudly at the tattoo of his name. There it was. The proof that she was his. That ass belonged to him.

The thought of that was arousing. Jay smiled mischievously. It had been a minute since Portia let him put it back there. He leaned down on her back and whispered in her ear, "Let me slide up in here, Ma." He traced the length of her crack lightly with his finger.

Portia smiled back at him seductively. She and Jay had been married for six years, and they had entertained anal sex a few times. Portia referred to it as "H.B.L.", short for "Hot Butt Love". It was only like a once or twice a year thing for them. After the first horrible time, Portia had honestly started to enjoy it a little. She was feeling freaky so she said fuck it and gave Jay the green light. "Alright, boo."

Jay kissed her on the neck and reached under and massaged her clit with his fingers. She was soaking wet. He coated his penis with her moisture and slid in her bottom gently, stopping each time she protested. Jay took his time and was sincere in his efforts not to hurt her.

Before long, Portia found herself throwing it back. Jay was packing, so just a little. She just relaxed and let him take control. She couldn't believe how good it felt this time. She felt like she was about to cum again.

Jay felt Portia's body start twitching and he got real excited. Damn, she was cumming. She started bucking and moaning louder and louder. The fact that she came, and the sweet suctioning of her juicy ass overwhelmed him so much he couldn't hold it back any longer. Jay called out Portia's name and climaxed right after her. Just before his volcano erupted, he pulled out and shot a load of hot cream all over her milk chocolate ass.

Afterwards, they both breathed heavily. Jay shook his head. What an episode. That shit was unbelievable. He smacked Portia on the ass, and she looked back at him and smiled lazily. Damn, he was glad she had shown up.

Lovemaking between the two of them was always great. Portia knew how to please him, and to Jay that was priceless. She always knew what he needed, and when he needed it. As a matter of fact, Mother's Day was coming up. Jay was glad too. That gave him an excuse to get her something nice. He saw a new set of car keys in Portia's near future.

$$$

When Fatima got the phone call from Portia about Wise and those groupies she was hurt but not really shocked. In her gut she'd had a feeling he was still cheating. A woman's intuition never lied. Fatima knew she had to make a decision about their marriage before Wise' high-risk lifestyle caught up with her.

And lately she had been hearing a lot about something called HPV. It was one of the latest scares for women. HPV was the acronym for human papillomavirus. From what Fatima understood, it could lead to a lot of serious things, including cervical cancer. She had done some research online and printed out some information. She learned that HPV wasn't new. It had been around for a long time, and it could even be spread with a condom. After she found that out, Fatima knew that being with Wise had too high of a cost.

She was fed the fuck up. She wanted to go down there to Miami and kill his ass but it was three in the morning, and there were no more flights out until six thirty a.m. At the time there was nothing she could do to that bastard. But wait until he got home the next day. Just fucking wait.

Fatima was enraged. She sat up all night crying and

smoking weed to calm her down. It was the same old love song. Wise would never change. Fatima contemplated taking all of his shit outside and setting it on fire like Angela Bassett did her husband in the movie "Waiting To Exhale". Fatima smiled at the thought but she didn't go through with it because she realized that her life was not a movie, and she could get in trouble. Or worse, the wind could blow the fire towards her house and she could burn down her own crib. She wasn't crazy or emotional enough to do that. That was her home. Even if her and Wise were to split up, she knew she was getting the house.

Fatima suddenly had an idea. It was so crazy she laughed out loud. The more she thought about it, the harder she laughed. There was this website called "Craig's List". It was where she'd posted a profile under the "casual encounters" section and met her lover. She remembered also seeing a "men seeking men" link.

Fatima decided to log in and post an ad for Wise requesting a one night stand with an old fat white man. She would include Wise' cell phone number so the responders could contact him directly.

Fatima hurried and turned on her PC, and she logged on to the internet. When she got on Craig's List she posted an ad under "men seeking men" with the headline, *"Hot Young Black Stud Seeking No Strings Attached Romp With Overweight White Grandfather"*.

Fatima could just imagine how many old homos and perverts were online that time of morning wishing they had a nice hot piece of young black ass. She knew Wise would kill her if he found out, but she typed the following ad:

I'm bored, and ooh me so horny. Anybody out there with a nice big stiff one wanting to poke me in my ass?

You are… Old (at least 55 years old), Caucasian, hairy (gray beard also preferred), overweight, and well hung.

I am… 28 years old, Black, fit and handsome, with

huge cock.

    *I've always had this fantasy to get fucked by Uncle Sam.
I will supply red, white, and blue suit and hat.*

    *If you want to play, call me ASAP at (347) 699-0121.
I'm in NYC, and I can host. I'll be all lubed up and waiting...*

Fatima clicked her mouse and sent the post through, and she couldn't stop laughing. She placed her hand across her chest and tried to catch her breath. There was no turning back now. She grinned wickedly and imagined how lewd some of the responses to that ad would be.

    That was good for Wise. Let's see how well he could perform in an orgy with three bitches when his cell phone was ringing off the hook with old freaks and homos wanting to fulfill his sick requests with old white wrinkled cock. That would serve his no-good ass right for trying to play her.

    Fatima's actions had given her a little bit of relief. It was after three in the morning so she finished off her blunt and decided to go to bed.

    Fatima tossed and turned until she finally fell asleep. It wasn't easy because she had unwanted visions of her husband's adulterous, unsafe sexual behavior floating through her head.

$$$

    Meanwhile, down in Miami Wise was laying on a king-sized bed enjoying a dual blowjob from two women. A third chick stood on the bed in front of him dancing provocatively.

    Wise coaxed the two girls with their mouths on him. "That's it, right there. Suck my balls too. Yeah, that's it. Do that shit, bitches. Hell yeah."

    Just then, Wise' cell phone rang. He hoped that wasn't Fatima. The phone was over on the nightstand next to the bed, so he reached for it and looked at the caller ID. It was a New York number he didn't recognize.

Wise flipped the phone open and answered it. "Yo, what up?"

There was heavy breathing on the other end, and then a man's voice Wise didn't recognize said, *"Hey there, you young black stud. I'm as old, fat, white and hairy as they come, and I'd love to dress up like Uncle Sam and fuck the shit outta you with my big hard cock."*

That was some fuckin' faggot on the phone! Wise was immediately enraged. "Yo, who da' fuck is this!? Nigga, you call my phone wit' some shit like this again, and I'll smoke yo' ass. You hear me, mothafucka?!"

Wise angrily slammed his phone shut and took a deep breath. After he heard that old foulmouthed ass perverted cracker on the phone, his hard-on shrunk. Wise shooed the girls off of him. He wasn't in the mood anymore. It was time for them to go. That shit had turned his stomach. Duke had him ready to spazz.

Was that some kind of sick ass joke? Wise made up his mind to smack fire out of whoever was behind it. But that really sounded like some old ass white man. He would kill that freak mothafucka.

After Wise got rid of his company, who were all very disappointed that they had to leave, he fired up a blunt and tried to relax. After he took a few pulls, his cell phone rang again. Wise walked over and picked it up, and he saw another New York number he didn't recognize. He answered, and it was yet again another man.

This caller sounded like an extremely Gay dude. He said, *"Well hello there, hot and bothered. I've always been attracted to young, black studs. I'd love to dress up like Uncle Sam and suck you off, and then swallow when you shoot your load."*

Wise cut him off right there. He almost threw up! "Yo nigga, if you call my phone again, I'ma cut ya' fuckin' throat. I'm tellin' you! I ain't no fuckin' faggot! You sick ass mothafucka! I'll cut ya' fuckin' heart out!"

Wise slammed the phone closed once more. What the fuck was going on? How'd all those homos get his phone number? Before he could put the phone down, it rang again.

It was another man. This one said, *"Hey buddy, this is Uncle Sam. I'll be seventy-two years old come August. Is that old enough for you? I'd like to put some of my steamy milk in your hot cocoa. Do you like to suck cock too?"*

When Wise heard that, steam shot out of his ears. *"What!?* I'ma make you suck on this big .45, nigga! I'll blow ya' mo'fuckin' brains out if you call my phone again wit' this gay shit!"

Wise hung up and threw the phone against the wall. If another faggot called his phone he was gonna fuck somebody up. Where were those freaks getting his cell phone number from?

About ten minutes later, Wise received another call. He barked on the homo and threatened to kill him if he called him again.

That one had a smart assed mouth. He told Wise off. *"Well just calm down there, closet-queen! You shouldn't post your phone number on dirty websites if you don't want people to call you. Now you go straight to hell!"* He slammed the phone down.

Wise stood there holding the phone with his mouth open in shock. A dirty website? What the fuck? When he heard that, he knew for sure that he was changing his phone number first thing that morning. He was obviously the butt of some stupid asshole's practical joke, and he didn't appreciate it one bit. His night was ruined. He shut off his phone so no one else could disturb him, and he went to bed alone.

Chapter Seven

Late the following Sunday evening, Laila sat soaking her tired limbs and muscles in a hot herbal bath. Her legs were sore from marching all those miles at AIDS Walk New York the day before. She, Portia, and Fatima had finished the walk, and Laila was feeling it now.

It was Mother's Day Sunday, and her kids had cooked her dinner earlier and cleaned up the house. They had even baked her a chocolate cake. Laila smiled at the thought. Her little girls were the saving grace in her life. When she thought about her sorry excuse for a husband, her smile faded into a frown.

Laila leaned her head back and closed her eyes, wishing Calgon could really take her away. She just had so much on her plate. She was still in limbo about her marital situation. Everything had taken a turn for the worse over the past few weeks, and she felt partially responsible. Khalil really needed help. Things had gotten out of hand. She was tired of sleeping with one eye open.

After Laila got out of the tub, she peeked in on her daughters to make sure they were okay. When she stuck her head in her oldest girl, Macy's bedroom, she saw that she was still up.

When Macy saw Laila, she said, "Hey Mommy. Can you come here for a minute? I wanna talk to you."

Laila went inside and closed the door behind her. She smiled at her baby. Macy was the spitting image of her daddy, with the exception of Laila's slanted Cleopatra-like eyes. Laila sat down on the edge of her bed and smoothed her long hair back. "Hey, baby girl. What's up?"

Macy sat up and began twirling her hair. She stared down at the carpet. "Ma, I just want you to know that I know about daddy." She looked up at Laila to see her reaction.

Laila played it cool. "You know what about daddy?"

Macy looked her dead in her eyes. "I'm not stupid, Ma. I know he's messin' with that stuff. And Pebbles knows it too. That might be why she been actin' so fast lately." Macy gave Laila a look that reinforced her last words about her sister.

Macy saw that Laila looked real saddened by her news. "We know it's not your fault, Ma. You don't have to look so sorry. It ain't you. Daddy's the sorry one."

Laila regained her composure and checked her. "Look, Macy. That's still your father, and you will show respect for him at all times." Laila was stern with her but she was also flabbergasted that she was having such an adult conversation with her twelve year old. That child was wise beyond her years. She knew entirely too much.

Macy had initiated it so now Laila was forced to talk about it with her. "Macy, your daddy is just a little weak right now. He'll get it together. He just needs some time."

Macy said, "You know what, Ma? Remember the other night, when you and Daddy had that big fight? I heard you keep tellin' him that you didn't have any money, so I gave him twenty dollars so he would go and leave you alone. And I know what he wanted the money for."

Laila couldn't believe Macy had just told her she gave her father money to get high. And all to protect her. Oh, hell no. She had to straighten that shit out. Khalil was messing her fucking kids up.

"Macy, you're a twelve year old child. You don't have to give nobody money to leave me alone. And you do *not* have to feel responsible for me. I'm *your* mother. Don't you do that again, you hear me?"

Macy nodded her head. She stared at Laila for a second. "Ma, are you and Daddy gettin' a divorce?"

"I never said that", Laila told her. "But baby, some changes have to be made. Your daddy has to get his act together."

"I know that's right", Macy said.

Laila laughed. Macy sounded just like her when she said that. She leaned over and kissed her baby on her forehead. "You better take your butt to sleep. You have school in the morning."

Macy's smile faded and she put on a serious face. "Well, speaking of school... Ma, all the kids at school be sayin' Pebbles is a hoe. And she been actin' like one too. You need to get on her. I tried to talk to her but she don't wanna listen."

Laila looked at Macy like she was crazy. "Don't talk that way about your sister! What the hell are you talkin' about, Macy?" Laila didn't like the terminology "hoe" being applied to her eleven year old.

Laila had to admit it. She had seen a change in her baby daughter lately. Pebbles was trying to wear clothing that was inappropriate for her age and letting her hair down in school so she could look older.

Macy said, "Ma, the other day I heard she let some boys feel on her. And when I asked her about it, she told me to mind my business. And then I heard..." She paused and let out a long sigh. "She might be having sex, Ma."

Laila's jaw dropped. It took her a moment to respond to that one. She didn't want to seem like a naïve type of mother but Pebbles was just a baby. Laila couldn't fathom the idea of her being sexually active. Not at eleven. Laila didn't know what to say.

"Macy, I pray to God that isn't true. About Pebbles, *or* you. 'Cause both of ya'll ain't nothin' but babies."

Macy rolled her eyes. "I ain't *thinkin'* 'bout no boys, Ma. I'm try'na do me. Your daughter has big plans." She mocked Jay-Z. "I'm focused, man."

Laila laughed. "You better be because you are a young black woman. That means you're gon' have to try twice..."

Macy cut her off. "Ma, please stop. I already know that

speech by heart. We gotta try twice as hard to succeed. You have been tellin' us that since we were babies."

"Well, I'm glad it stuck."

"It did. I'm just tellin' you to keep your eyes on your youngest child. Now, Mommy I love you, but if you'll excuse me, I have a test in the morning in Biology, which is my first period class. I gotta get some rest."

Laila couldn't believe how mature Macy was acting. She stared at her for a second. Macy sat up and hugged her, and kissed her on the cheek. She whispered in Laila's ear, "Ma, me and you are the only sane ones in this family. I got your back, don't worry."

Laila hugged Macy tight. At that moment she almost cried on her shoulder. Her daughter had the strength that she needed. It felt good to know she had an ally. Her child didn't know what she had done for her. Laila kissed her on the forehead. "Say your prayers, lil' ma-ma. And look out for your sister. Okay, princess?"

Macy smiled at her mother. "I will."

"Good night, baby." Laila got up and left the room. She loved her daughters more than anything in the world. She was glad Macy had pulled her coat about Pebbles. Now she had some serious investigating to do.

Both of her girls were still in middle school. Pebbles was in the seventh grade going to the eighth, and Macy was in the eighth grade, soon to be a freshman in high school when school started back that Fall.

Laila remembered back when she was in junior high school. There were some loose girls in her class, so it wasn't impossible for Pebbles to act up at such a young age. Laila didn't want to believe the things Macy told her she heard, but she wasn't going to ignore them either. She had to start spying on Pebbles. She needed to know exactly what that child was up to.

Before Laila went to bed that night, she called Portia to

give her the rundown on her discussion with her very mature daughter. She was still shocked so she had to tell somebody.

Portia told Laila that she'd better be glad Macy told her about Pebbles' behavior. And once again she told her she was there for her if her and the girls needed a place to get away for a little while. They chitchatted for a few more minutes before they told each other Happy Mother's Day again, and goodnight.

Laila got in bed and dozed off that night seriously considering Portia's offer. She just needed to talk to Khalil first to see where his head was at. If he agreed to get some help, she wouldn't leave his side. But if he resisted the help he needed, Laila decided she would take her kids and go away for a little while to teach him a lesson. School would be getting out soon, and she could commute to work from New Jersey if she had to.

No sooner than Laila had fallen asleep did Khalil come in the house acting stupid again. He told her some cockamamie story about him getting his car towed and needing a hundred and fifty dollars to get it out of some twenty-four hour pound.

Laila didn't believe him but she didn't feel like fighting. She was too tired and she just wasn't in the mood. She couldn't believe that bastard was harassing her like that on Mother's Day. And he hadn't even wished her a happy one. How selfish. She gave him the money but she decided it was time to tell him the truth.

She took a deep breath. "Khalil, you have to get some help. If you don't, I'm leaving you. And that's my word."

Khalil turned around and looked at her like she was crazy. "What? Laila, let me tell you somethin'. Ain't nobody goin' nowhere. And get some help for *what*?" He raised his voice. "I don't need no help for *shit*."

Laila should've just left it alone, but she was a strong willed black woman. Her home was in shambles and she wasn't about to back down from the issue at hand. It needed to be addressed too urgently.

Her husband needed a reality check, so she gave him a hand. "Stop fooling yourself, Khalil. We both know you have a fuckin' problem. Enough of the bullshit. You have to get some help. Think about your children. *They* even suspect something is up. Nobody's stupid, you know."

Khalil was too anxious to get high to talk about that shit with Laila right now. Shit, he was the man of the family. He'd be damned if he was about to roll over and be the bitch. To hell with her demands.

Just to prove to Laila that he was in charge, he hissed, "You must be stupid, talkin' to me like that. Don't make me fuck you up in this mothafucka', Laila. Get the fuck out my face, and stop talkin' stupid."

Khalil started to walk out but he stopped short. "Oh yeah. Gimme your car keys."

"Hell no! You got a car. *Wherever* the fuck it is!"

Khalil tried to look sincere. "Yo, I told you my truck got towed. Stop playin' with me. I'll bring your car right back. Where's the keys?"

"You heard what I said", Laila countered.

Khalil's patience wore off. "Yo, gimme the fuckin' keys!"

Laila didn't budge. Khalil was starting to fiend so he got enraged. He shoved Laila to the side and grabbed one of her Louis Vuittons, and a yellow Marc Jacobs bag from the closet. Khalil saw that she had her wallet and lip gloss in the Louis, so he dumped its contents on the bed.

Amongst about twenty other things, Laila's Lexus key fell out. Satisfied, Khalil stuck the key in his pocket and ignored her protests. He shoved Laila out of his way again and just broke out.

Khalil shoved her really hard that time. He knocked Laila down on the floor and it felt like she pulled something in her back. She ignored the jolt of pain she experienced in her back and got up and ran to the window just in time to see him pulling off in her car. That son of a bitch better not let anything happen to her Lexus. She couldn't stand that piece of shit.

She flirted with the idea of calling the police on his ass, but she decided against it. A diehard Brooklyn chick at heart, Laila was from a time and place where people didn't involve the law in their affairs. That was against the code of the streets. Khalil was one lucky nigga that night. Laila hoped his stupid ass would be back in time for her to go to work.

The next morning Laila woke up and discovered that Khalil hadn't come home that night. She was so pissed she called out of work that day. She could've taken a cab but she was so hurt that he would do that she couldn't leave the house. She spent the entire day crying, up until the kids came home from school.

Khalil didn't come back until late that Monday night. And when he came in he didn't even say anything to her. He just dropped her car key on the dresser and laid across the bed and fell asleep.

Laila figured he must've been pretty rundown from the mission he had obviously just come off of. She was so through with Khalil after that incident, she made up her mind to take her kids and go when they got out of school. Luckily, there was only about a month left until their summer vacation started.

$$$

The night before, Wise dropped his family off at home and he headed back out for a while. He had to make a run to the studio to lay down a track. He had been asked to get on this R. Kelley remix with his mans Beef & Broccoli. Beef and Broc were his homies. Those two were some cool dudes. He had been up north with Broc.

That night Wise was driving his big boy Mercedes because he didn't like to take his daughter out in cars that were too fast. The Benz was the family car. He, Fatima, and his little angel Falynn had just come from Chez Bono's, an upscale family oriented restaurant. It had turned out to be a nice evening. Wise was glad because he and Fatima had a terrible fight a couple of weeks ago when he came back from Miami. Fatima had been mad at him ever since. He wanted to get out of the doghouse. That was also why he had given her a twelve carat diamond bracelet for Mother's Day.

Wise thought about his wife and baby, and he smiled. His family brought him great joy. All of the success he had wouldn't mean a thing without his family to share it with. He knew Fatima only wanted him to be faithful, and that was the only thing in this world he couldn't give her. He didn't know what the fuck was wrong with him. He just couldn't help cheating on her.

For the first time ever, Wise considered getting some therapy for his infidelity. He didn't want to blow a good woman, and it seemed like Fatima was at the end of her rope. He knew she wasn't playing this time.

Honestly, Wise hadn't even given her a full year of not cheating on her since they'd gotten married. His dick just seemed to lead him to fuck around all the time. He really had to change. That was the bottom line.

Inside the house, Fatima put her daughter down for a nap. She was tired herself from all that walking she did the day before when she, Portia, and Laila marched in AIDS Walk New York. Fatima was tipsy as well from the wine she drunk at the restaurant so she sat on the couch to take a load off.

Wise had recently bought a little Pit-bull puppy for Falynn. At first Fatima had been concerned about the type of dog it was because she knew Pit-bulls could be vicious. It was only a few weeks old and it was cute but she knew it would grow fast and be bigger than the baby in no time.

Wise promised to get rid of the puppy when it got too big for Falynn and buy her a Teacup Yorkie. Fatima dozed off thinking about it.

Falynn woke back up while Fatima was still asleep. And she was fully charged and ready to play. When Fatima noticed she was up she told her to be a good girl, and she dozed back off.

A little while later, Falynn woke her up again. Fatima groggily opened one eye and saw that her daughter was trying to feed her some bubblegum or something. Fatima was tired as hell but she patiently opened her mouth and let Falynn shove it on in.

"Here Mommy, eat your food. Eat your food, Mommy. Atta girl. That's a good little girl", Falynn said.

Fatima smiled sleepily. Falynn was mimicking the way she talked to her when she wanted her to eat her food. She was such a smart little girl. Fatima sniffed the air a few times. There was a really unpleasant odor. Something smelled just like shit. Had Falynn messed on her self? She got up to see what was going on.

Damn! Her child had dog shit in her hand. The puppy had apparently shitted, and her daughter had picked it up. Realization dawned on Fatima, and she gasped. Oh my God! That's what Falynn had put in her mouth. Falynn had stuffed dog shit in her mouth! She had eaten fucking dog shit! And on Mother's Day!

Fatima screamed at the top of her lungs and ran to the bathroom to wash out her mouth. She quickly gargled and brushed her teeth over and over again, trying hard not to throw up. That was the most disgusting thing that had ever happened to her in her whole life.

If Falynn wasn't her child she probably would've killed her. Fatima hurried back to get her so she could clean her up. She picked her little shitty daughter up and carried her to the bathroom at arms length.

After Falynn and everything she had touched was sanitized, Fatima brushed and gargled about forty six more times. She felt like she could still taste it. That was how foul the taste of shit was.

Fatima popped Falynn on the hand three times and warned her not to touch dog doo doo ever again. Falynn started crying when she hit her. That made Fatima feel bad. She was just a child. She didn't know any better.

And where the fuck was Wise? He told her he would be back in about two hours. Fatima picked up the phone and called him. She cursed his ass out for buying that stupid assed puppy, and then again for not being there to help watch his daughter. She then proceeded to give him the gross horrific details of her ordeal.

After she told Wise what happened, he laughed so hard she wanted to jump through the phone and strangle him. Fatima told him what an asshole she thought he was.

Wise tried to sound sincere. "My bad. I'm sorry, Ma. I guess you don't find that *shit* funny, huh. No pun intended." He started cracking up again.

"Go to hell, you bastard", Fatima scoffed.

"And look, you *still* talkin' *shit*." Wise laughed again. He was on a roll. He knew Fatima was tight but he couldn't help it. He couldn't stop laughing. Tears even came out of his eyes.

It took Wise about two whole minutes to get it together, and then he promised Fatima he would be home as soon as he could. In the spirit of good humor, before Fatima hung up she told him she didn't appreciate him laughing at her "shituation".

Wise got home pretty late. It was almost five o'clock in the morning but he woke up Fatima. Falynn was asleep in the bed beside her so he quietly shook her awake. He was tired but he didn't want to go to bed yet. He wanted to be put to sleep.

Fatima was groggy but she got up to keep Wise company. After she brushed her teeth, they went downstairs so they wouldn't wake up the baby. It wasn't the first time Wise had awakened her in the wee hours of the morning when he came in, and it wouldn't be the last.

Wise picked up a blunt Fatima had left on the coffee table next to an ashtray and a lighter. He knew she had left it for him so he sparked it up. She usually had a blunt rolled for him when he came in. When she wasn't mad at him. And she never put it out until the baby was asleep for the night because Falynn was in that stage where she messed with everything.

Wise took a few tokes and passed the el to Fatima. She hit it good and passed it back. He stared at the outline of her breasts through her nightgown and became aroused. She was braless and her nipples protruded at him. And if he knew Fatima well, she was panty-less too. She never slept with panties on. At the thought of that his penis hardened. Wise was horny and in the mood for some action so he was upfront with her. "Ma, get up and take off your clothes."

Fatima smiled. Her husband was such a freak. After she hit the blunt again, she stood up and slipped out of the ivory silk Oscar de la Renta chemise she was wearing.

Just as he thought, she wasn't wearing any panties. Wise liked that. "Damn, girl. Look at them big ass tities. Come here and let me suck on them shits."

Fatima shook her head and backed away from him playfully. "No. You come over here and get 'em, baby. And bring that big ass dick over here with you." She palmed her breasts and massaged them slowly, and licked her lips at him tantalizingly.

"Suck on your tity for me, Ma", Wise ordered. He loved to see her suck her own tities. She'd had that reduction but her breasts were still very ample, and that shit turned him on.

Fatima lifted her right breast and bent down and licked the nipple. Wise looked really interested. He got up and walked over and passed her the blunt again. She stood there naked and got her smoke on while he explored her body with his mouth and hands like it was new territory to him. He kissed allover her neck, and then he hungrily sucked on her nipples. He squeezed her tities together so he could suck both at the same time.

Fatima moaned and held the back of Wise' head. "Ooh boo, that feels so good. Yeah baby, you know how I like it. That's what's up."

"You so fuckin' sexy, girl. Turn around and let me see that ass."

Fatima smashed the blunt out in the ashtray and she turned around and shook her ass for him.

Wise screwed up his face and shook his head. "Damn, look at all that peanut butter colored ass. Shake it, girl! Shake that fat ass. That's what I'm talkin' 'bout."

He was so smitten he bent Fatima over and ran his tongue along her ass crack. He licked up and down a few times and asked, "You like that, Ma?"

She moaned and told him she did. She placed her hands on the floor for support and spread her legs as far as she could. Wise spread her ass cheeks open and licked her ass for a few more seconds, and then he ate her pussy out from the back. He put his face all up in it and went for the gold. He didn't give a fuck because Fatima was wifey. Anything went with her. That treatment was definitely not used on the groupies and birds he sometimes bedded.

A few minutes later, Fatima laid facedown on the floor trembling from the star treatment Wise had given her. She came two times and had begged him to stop.

Wise was satisfied that she had gotten hers, so now it was time for him to get his. He got up and sat on the couch in his boxers. His dick was so hard it was sticking straight up.

He winked his eye at Fatima to give her the message. "Get your sexy, pretty ass over here. Get on your knees and crawl to me, Ma. Come on, crawl to daddy."

Fatima laughed but she got on her knees and crawled over to him seductively. She was wearing nothing but a long ponytail weave she was experimenting with that week. She stopped in front of Wise and laid her head in his lap and rubbed her cheek against his rock hard dick. It was lovely. She placed a soft kiss on its tip through his boxers.

Wise urged her to go on. Fatima knew he loved getting head, so she freed his penis from his underwear. She took him in her mouth and stepped to her business, swallowing him until the tip hit the back of her throat. Wise moaned and wrapped her ponytail around his fist. Damn, it felt good. He didn't want to cum yet so he stopped her. He wanted to feel those sugar walls.

Fatima knew her man. She knew what he wanted. She got up off the floor and straddled him on the couch. She placed the tip at the opening of her vagina and slowly lowered herself down on his pole. It took her a few seconds to get comfortable and find her rhythm because he was so large.

Wise coached Fatima and squeezed her ass, and before he knew it she was riding him and bucking wildly like she was on a real horse. She whipped him across the face and chest with her ponytail.

Wise found that to be a real turn-on. She spun around and rode him from the back. He kneaded her ass like it was dough and gritted his teeth. Fatima bent down and placed her hands on the floor and kept riding. That shit felt so good he almost came again. He had to stop her fast so he told her to get up. When she stood up a lot of air came out of her and made a long suctioning sound. Wise knew that meant she was soaking wet. He had that pussy farting.

He looked down at his dick and saw all the cum she had left on him. He said, "Ma, look at your cream allover my dick. Come put your mouth on this thang again."

Fatima gave him the sexy eyes and started to wipe it off before she sucked it again but Wise stopped her. "Nah, don't wipe it off. Stop cheatin', girl."

He was so nasty. Fatima couldn't front, she loved it though. She liked it when he took control. She slid him in her mouth without wiping her juices off. It did come from her pussy. She figured that if she couldn't trust it, neither should he.

She pleasured him intensely for a few more minutes, giving the head job all she had. Wise couldn't take it anymore. He got up and bent Fatima over the couch and stood behind her. He slid back in her pussy and didn't stop beating until he shot off so far up inside of her he probably glazed her ribs.

When they were done, the sun peaked through the wood blinds. After Wise caught his breath, he went upstairs and checked on his daughter to make sure she was sleeping okay, and then he got in the bed. Fatima went to the bathroom to freshen up, and then she snuggled up under him and laid her head on his chest. Their bed was king-sized, so they didn't disturb their little sleeping angel on the other side. The two of them fell asleep just like that.

Chapter Eight

The following week, Kira drove along the highway in her cotton candy pink Porsche listening to a few songs from her upcoming CD. Her shit was banging so she had the volume on ten. Kira was open. She had been in the lab all weekend, and she was proud of the outcome of her efforts.

But now it was Monday afternoon and she needed to unwind. She had a break from the studio and a break from her five year old son for a few hours so she was on her way shoe shopping. She had a few shows coming up and she had to represent. She was usually the only female emcee on the roster with a bunch of dicks, and she liked to make a statement.

Kira didn't employ a stylist fulltime. There was a girl named Ginger she used to find her gowns for awards and stuff sometimes, and Portia and Fatima found things for her sometimes too. But she usually liked to pick out her own stuff. Kira used to play ball and she still had a little tomboy in her. She liked to be sexy with a boyish twist, and she threw it down in the outfits she put together. She was definitely a fly ass bitch.

Kira was long legged, lean, and chocolate. She had been voted one of King Magazine's top five sexiest female emcees. As a matter of fact, she was scheduled to be on the cover of an upcoming issue wearing a tiny two-piece Dior swimsuit. Cas and Jay hadn't approved of the cover shots. They thought the photos were too revealing but Kira was stubborn and she liked to do her. She and her manager, Nicki, thought the pictures were fine.

A few minutes later, Kira parked in the parking lot in front of Neiman Marcus. She hopped out of her Porsche in a pair of metallic gold Chloe stilettos with the matching gold Chloe Paddington bag. She wanted to make it quick so she hurried to the shoe department. She shopped so much it didn't really excite her anymore. When she first got on she used to like to make a day of it, but not anymore.

Within minutes, Kira selected four pairs of the hottest new season Gucci shoes in a size nine, two pairs of Manolo Blahnik's that were absolutely to die for, and some Jimmy Choo's and Donald J. Pliner's she couldn't take her eyes off of.

At the register Kira handed the cashier her Black card and didn't bat an eye at the eighty six hundred dollar total. After she paid for her merchandise she picked up her shopping bags and left the shoe department. On her way out, a sales girl that was just coming off her break recognized her.

The girl pointed at Kira and shrieked, "Oh my God, You're Kira! Oh my God! Oh shit! Can I please get your autograph?"

"Sure", Kira said and smiled. The level of the girl's excitement was flattering. She was clearly a fan. It felt good to be noticed. But contrary to what Jay and Cas said about her, the fame hadn't gone to her head. She was still down to earth. The money had just changed her a little.

The girl was still smiling. She handed Kira a pen and a piece of paper. Kira put her bags down and asked for the correct spelling of her name, and she gave her an autograph. Afterwards, she agreed to pose for a photo on her camera phone.

The girl thanked Kira over and over and kept saying that she couldn't believe she met her in real life. She told her how much she loved her first two CDs, and she said she would be the first person to cop the new one.

Kira smiled brightly at her. "Thank you much for your support, sweetie. Stay gold, babygirl."

Kira picked up her shopping bags and headed on, and her cell phone starting ringing. She knew from the ring tone that it was Vee, this popular rapper from ATL that she had been sort of kicking it with on the low. Kira was dying to answer the phone but her hands were full so she let it go to her voicemail. She would call him back when she got in the car. Just then, a middle aged white male employee walked up and offered to assist her with her bags.

When they got out to her car, Kira thanked him and tipped him a twenty. She started up the engine and leaned her seat back and called Vee.

He picked up on the third ring. "Yo, what it is, shawty?"

Kira smiled, like she did each time she heard his southern drawl. That shit was so sexy it drove her wild. She played it cool. "Ain't shit. What's good, Pa?"

"Ain't nuntin', shawty. I just called to holla' at you, guhrl. To see what you was up to."

Kira smiled again. "Well that was nice, boo. That's what's up. I was kinda' busy when you called me. My hands were full. But it's good to hear from you. What you doin'?"

Kira flirted with Vee lightheartedly for a few minutes, and then they agreed to speak the following day. Before they hung up, she told Vee that she looked forward to seeing him again.

Kira had met Vee down in Atlanta last month when she had flown down to record three singles for her upcoming album with her nephew, Dave Brave, who was a well-known producer in the industry now. Dave did a lot of her production, and his beats were fire.

That particular weekend Dave just happened to be working on some tracks for Vee as well. Vee and his entourage had come to the studio to check out the beats he was purchasing, and he and Kira locked eyes. The magnetism had been completely mutual. Before he left, he had slipped her his number and winked at her.

Kira had given him a call when she got back to New York,

and they'd been talking on the phone ever since. It was still innocent but she wanted more.

Kira was married to Cas and they had a fine son, but she was missing something. Cas gave her everything a woman could ask for but he was lacking in the excitement department.

Kira loved drama, and that was the bottom line. Her marriage had gotten dull because Cas was all business all the time. And the fact that Kira was also an artist on his record label didn't help either. All she saw was the business side of him all the time. And Cas was especially hard on her, whether they were in the studio, or at their six bedroom home. He was always demanding that she grow up and act more mature. Kira hated the way he still treated her like she was a little kid. She loved him, but that dude was just too serious sometimes. At times she deliberately ticked him off just to spark some type of emotion.

Now Young Vee was different. He was loud and jovial, and he joked around all the time. Kira's thing with him was still kind of high school but it was fun. She knew she shouldn't be pursuing an affair with him but the attraction between the two of them was real strong. They hadn't been intimate yet, but she wanted to.

Vee hadn't pressed her for any ass so far. He had basically left the ball in her court. Little did he know, she was itching to give him some. Vee had respectively fallen back when she told him she was married. He didn't exactly know Cas but he knew of him, and his manager knew him pretty well.

Kira knew Cas would probably stomp a mud hole in her ass if he found out about her and Vee. Shit, it would be nice to get some type of reaction out of him. She was sick of Cas' fucking nonchalance all the time. Every now and then she flirted with dudes in front of him just to make him notice her.

Kira noticed a few raindrops hit her windshield so she snapped out of her daydream. All of a sudden it was real

dark and the sky looked like it was about to fall in. That
was weird because it had been a bright and sunny day so far.
Damn, she didn't even have an umbrella in the car. Kira put
on her seatbelt and threw her car in drive, and she headed on
home in attempt to beat the storm.

$$$

Portia hurried around to the driver's side of her brand new
midnight blue four door Mercedes CLS coupe and hopped
in just in time. It was about to storm. As soon as she shut
the car door and started her up, huge raindrops began hitting
her windshield harder than bird droppings. The new car was
her Mother's Day present from Jay. The sounds of R. Kelly's
"Flirt" came blaring through the speakers and startled her so
she turned the volume down a little. A second later it started
pouring down outside.

Portia thanked God they didn't get wet. She looked back
at Jazmin, whom she'd just strapped in her child safety seat
in the back, to make sure she was okay. She was bobbing her
head to the music. Portia laughed. Jazz loved that song. Her
baby had soul.

Portia's four year old replica grinned at her. "Hurry
Mommy, drive the car. I wanna see my Daddy! Let's go!"

Portia couldn't help but laugh again. Jazmin loved Jay
to death. He had been out of town for a few days and was
due back that afternoon. Portia and the kids missed him like
crazy. Jazmin was about to turn five years old, and Jayquan
was eleven. He looked more and more like Jay every day.

Portia was used to Jay's absences. Wise' album was scheduled
to drop soon, and that was the way it was every time they put
out a new record. Portia drove towards Jayquan's school.
She was going to pick him up because she had to take him to
football practice. He played in a peewee league. Then again,
practice was outdoors so it might be cancelled now that it

was raining.

When Portia pulled up in front of Lil' Jay's school, her cell phone rang. She knew it was Jay because she had a special ring tone for him, "The Chosen One", by Jaheim. She grinned and flipped open her mint green Chocolate phone. "What up, boo?"

Jay said, "What up, Ma? Where ya'll at?" He had just gotten home, and he missed her and the kids.

Portia said, "I'm picking up Jayquan. You home?"

"Yeah, I'm home. I'm 'bout to take a shower. I'll see you when you get here. Ya'll be safe, Kit Kat. It's raining hard out there. Be careful." Jay hung up.

Portia closed the phone and she looked back at Jazz and grinned. "Hey, doll baby. Your daddy's home."

Jazmin's face broke into a huge grin. "Yeah! Hip hip hooray! My daddy's home!" She looked out the window and started singing. *"It's raining - it's pouring - The old man is snoring, and he bumped his head and he went to bed..."*

Just then, Jayquan came out of his school. He was dressed cute as usual, just like a big boy. When he spotted them, he ran over and jumped in the car.

Portia smiled and greeted her stepson affectionately. "Hey, stinky. How was your day?" She leaned over and wiped the raindrops from his forehead.

"What's up, Portia?" Jayquan looked serious. "My day was average. I'm glad school is over. I really hate it sometimes. Is Pop home yet?"

Portia nodded, and he looked pleased. Jayquan looked back at his little sister and grinned. He was protective of her, and Portia loved that. Jazmin gave him a million dollar smile in return, and he leaned in the back and pinched her cheek lovingly. They were both great kids.

Portia loved Jayquan like he was her real son. She had helped Jay raise him ever since his mother, Stacy, was killed in a car accident six years ago. Just as Portia thought, he told her his coach had cancelled practice because of the weather.

Portia headed on home, driving at a safe speed in the thunderstorm. She couldn't wait to see her husband, and she couldn't wait to get back to her novel as well. That was her baby too. She hated to leave it unattended too long. She was preparing to release it soon so she was in the process of editing and polishing it up.

$$\$\$\$$$

Fatima was about to go to the supermarket but she changed her mind because it had started to rain. She decided to stay in and do some laundry instead. She turned the stereo on and popped in Fantasia's CD, and took a few pulls of a blunt she had rolled.

A few moments later, Fatima whistled along with her favorite song on the album, "When I See You", while she separated her family's dirty clothes. She sung her favorite part. *"Baby, when I see you, see you... Something has taken o-ver me..."*

Amidst putting a load of white clothes in a laundry basket, she came across a pair of Wise' boxers and did a double take because she thought she saw something. Fatima held the underwear up and examined them closer. When she realized what it was, her heart fell in her ass. It was a red blood stain!

Luckily for her, Wise was at home. He had just come back from out of town a few hours ago. He told her he was tired, and had fallen asleep. Fatima had something for him. That was the final straw. That nasty mothafucka!

Fatima quietly walked into their bedroom and into the huge walk-in closet. Wise kept a gun in there, and she was on the verge of using it on him. After she retrieved the heavy black fully loaded automatic weapon from the closet, Fatima stood over Wise with tears in her eyes. She couldn't believe

he had done something like that. He was nothing but a
lowdown, lying, cheating, no-good piece of shit. He had no
respect for her, or the fact that she was his wife.

Wise had kicked the cover off in the bed, and he was
wearing plaid boxers and a wife beater. Fatima glanced
down at his dick, which laid to the left of his thigh. He was
packing so its print was well visible even while it was soft.
Fatima looked away because the sight of his penis weakened
her desire to hurt him.

She didn't want to kill him. She just had to figure out a
way to put an end to his cheating. She had to put the fear of
God in Wise. Fatima was tired of letting him walk all over
her. She pumped herself up mentally. When she got up her
nerve she reached down and slapped Wise across the face as
hard as she could.

Wise quickly sat up and opened his eyes. He looked
shocked to see Fatima pointing a gun in his face. He rubbed
his eyes and tried to focus because he thought he was bugging.
He knew Fatima knew better than that.

Fatima slapped him upside his head again and thrust
the boxers in his face. "I found these bloody boxers in the
hamper. You runnin' up in bitches with they period on now?
You nasty, disgustin' piece of shit! You just out there try'na
deliberately contact AIDS and give it to me, huh? You try'na
kill me, huh Wise?"

Wise looked at Fatima like she was crazy. What the fuck
was she talking about? She was wilding. He was tired. He
didn't feel like going through this shit.

Fatima kept on. "Oh, you ain't got shit to say now, huh?
You try'na catch somethin' and kill me, nigga? Well, how
'bout I kill *you*, mothafucka? How does it feel to stare death
in the face? That's how I feel every time we fuck! I don't
know *what* you might give me. Fuckin' express AIDS, or
some shit! *A bitch with her period?* Why, Wise? Why? You
disgust me!" Fatima started crying.

Wise didn't really believe she would kill him on purpose. He was more worried that the gun might go off by accident. He had enough. "Yo, get that gun out my face. What the fuck is you talkin' 'bout? I ain't run up in nobody with their period. What are you talkin' about?"

Fatima kept the gun on him. "I see the blood, Wise. Right there on the front!"

"That ain't no blood, stupid." Unafraid, he got up and walked towards her. "Put that gun down and stop fuckin' playing, Tima. Give it here!"

Fatima backed up a few steps. "No! That *is* blood, nigga! I should kill you for this shit! I ain't puttin' up with this shit no more. Nigga, if you cheat on me again, I'll cut ya' fuckin' dick off and stick it down your throat and then shove it up yo' ass! Don't fuckin' play with me!"

"Stop yellin' and listen to me. That's *ketchup*, Tima. Gimme that gun before you fuck around and make a mistake!" Wise' patience wore thin with her. He stepped up and took the hammer from her.

Fatima gave up the gun without much of a struggle. She hadn't really wanted to shoot him. She loved him but she was fed up. "I know you didn't say ketchup, nigga. *Ketchup?* Please, I look that *stupid* to you?!"

Wise said, "You heard what the fuck I said. Ketchup!" He grabbed Fatima by her throat and shook her hard a few times. "Point another fuckin' gun at me and see what the fuck I do to you. That's my mothafuckin' word! You hear me?"

Wise grabbed the boxers from the floor and showed her the red stain. "I was watchin' the game in my boxers, and eating a burger. Some of the ketchup spilled on the front of my boxers. Look."

Fatima took the drawers and held them up in the light. At closer inspection, she realized that Wise was right. The red stain was too bright to be old blood. Being a woman, she'd messed up enough panties in her lifetime to know that a blood stain darkened when left on underwear. She'd been wrong that time.

Wise said, "Now look at you, lookin' stupid. Yo, you crazy, man. You gotta stop buggin', Tima. Real talk."

"Okay, I was wrong *one* time, but that's *your* fault. I can't fuckin' trust you, Wise. I'm insecure, paranoid, and always expecting you to fuck up. This relationship is not healthy for me. I can't keep doing this to myself. I want a divorce."

Wise acted like he didn't hear her last sentence. She was talking crazy. Nobody was getting a divorce. He sighed. "Fatima, I know I've been fuckin' up a lot lately but I promise I'ma stop, okay?"

"You said that before, I don't know how many times. I don't believe you no more, Wise. I don't believe nothin' you say. And I'm tired of waking up scared. I bet you don't wake up scared after we fuck. Do you?"

Wise shook his head.

"Well, I do. Every fuckin' time! That's pathetic, Wise. I'm your wife." Fatima broke down and couldn't stop crying.

Wise felt terrible. He put the gun down and held her in his arms. Fatima just buried her face in his shoulder and cried. He felt fucked up. He knew she loved him more than any other girl he had ever been with. And he loved her too, that's why he didn't know why he did her like that.

Wise used to feel like he was a good husband and took care of her, just because he paid the bills and gave her nice things. Now he was starting to realize that taking care of a woman required more than that. She needed more. He hadn't meant to make her insecure. Fatima was so confident when he'd first met her. He'd loved that about her.

"Don't cry, Ma. I'm sorry", Wise whispered in her ear. He rubbed her back and smoothed her hair. "I'ma change, Tima. I promise. I'ma change, Ma. That's why I changed my number. So we can make a new start."

Despite the fact that she was upset, Fatima laughed to
herself because she knew the real reason why Wise had
changed his cell phone number. Fatima had heard all that
bullshit Wise was saying before but she wanted to believe
him. She truly did.

"You promise?"

Wise nodded. He looked sincere.

"Okay, baby", she said. She knew it probably wasn't true
but she savored the moment nonetheless. Sometimes it felt
good to be lied to. Especially when you had nothing else.

$$$

The following Wednesday, Laila got a call from Pebbles'
guidance counselor, Ms. Richards. She called to inform Laila
that Pebbles had missed too many days from school that past
week, and her grades were slipping. In fact, Pebbles wasn't in
school that day either.

Laila told that woman the truth, which was that Pebbles
left her house every morning for school, so she had to be
playing hooky. Laila thanked Ms. Richards and assured her
that she'd get to the bottom of things immediately, and they
hung up.

Laila was pissed off when she got off the phone. Pebbles
had been lying to her! And obviously pretending to do her
homework too. She was gonna get her ass tore up when she
got home.

The girls wouldn't be home from school for a few hours.
To kill time, Laila sat down and puffed on an el while she
checked her email and paid a few bills online. The more she
thought about it, a plan came into play in her mind. Laila
decided to play it cool. She was going to follow Pebbles
in the morning to find out where she was going everyday
instead of school.

When the girls came home from school Laila didn't say

anything about the phone call she'd received from Pebbles' guidance counselor. That night she served dinner as usual. Lately her daughters had developed the bad habit of eating in their bedrooms, instead of at the dining room table where they were supposed to. Laila figured that could've had something to do with Khalil not being around like he used to.

The next morning Laila took the day off work, but she left the house at eight AM as usual. Macy and Pebbles went to school right around the corner, and they usually left the house about twenty minutes after her so they would be there by 8:45. Even though Laila had told them to walk to school together a million times, they rarely did. Both of them had their own little crews. That's how Laila knew it was possible for Macy to be unaware of Pebbles' absences from school. They also had different lunch periods.

Laila drove around the corner by their school and parked inconspicuously, and she waited for Pebbles to turn the corner. First Laila saw Macy and two of her friends. They were laughing and jiving around, but they all went inside the schoolhouse.

"One down, and one to go", Laila said to herself aloud.

Finally, at five to nine, Pebbles turned the corner straggling all by her lonesome. Laila noticed that her hair and blouse were different from a little while earlier. Pebbles looked older with her hair styled the way she had it, and Laila looked closer and realized that Pebbles' grown ass had on her blouse. And one of her cleavage revealing blouses at that. Laila wanted to jump out and beat her ass, but she just held her breath and prayed Pebbles went inside that school.

To Laila's horror, she witnessed something that she was extremely unprepared for. Instead of going to school, Pebbles walked over to a strange car. It was a black BMW 525 with rims, and it was parked just feet away from the junior high school. Pebbles appeared to be well acquainted with the driver. She said something to him and grinned, and she hurried around to the passenger side and hopped in.

Laila panicked and opened her car door. She started to jump out and run over there to save her little fast assed ignorant daughter but the BMW pulled off. She quickly started up her car and followed them. She dialed 911 on her cell phone and started to call the police, but then she hesitated. She wanted to see where this grown ass, German car-driving mothafucka was taking her dumb ass, naïve child.

It took everything in Laila to keep cool and not let her presence be known. She couldn't wild out yet because she was determined to find out where they were going. She imagined herself killing the man in that BMW ahead of her for harming her child. Laila was prepared to go to jail that day before she let him hurt Pebbles. She tailed him closely, not allowing space for any cars between them. She didn't think he would recognize her car. And she was willing to bet that Pebbles' dimwitted ass was so busy grinning in his face that she wasn't paying attention.

Laila was worried to death and pissed off at the same time. She was in no way prepared to let Pebbles do as she pleased at eleven damn years old. She would be twelve in July, but that didn't mean anything either. She was just a baby, and Laila knew that perverted mothafucka driving that Beamer knew that. Come on, he picked her up at a junior high school. Pebbles had a pretty well developed shape for an eleven year old because she inherited Laila's big butt, but her face was still that of a baby's.

The BMW made a couple of turns, and Laila followed the car to Saratoga Avenue. The driver parked and got out, and Pebbles followed him. She was trying hard to act grown up but she looked like she was out of place.

Laila parked a few cars down and got out. She paused, and stood about eight feet away and watched three extremely scantily clad young women approach the guy Pebbles was with. He was a tall, slim, light skinned dude with waves in his hair. He looked about twenty two years old, and he had two icy earrings in his ears and a mouth full of gold and diamonds. He was wearing a white tee shirt, baggy blue Evisu jeans, and a pair of beige Timbs.

Pebbles stood by his side looking stupid while he conversed with the girls, who all looked like they were in their late teens. The guy seemed real familiar with the girls, and Laila saw each of them pass him some money. After they were done talking, he smacked each one of them on the ass and shooed them off. You could tell he was a cocky dude.

Laila had already seen enough to know what type of scumbag she was dealing with. He was some wannabe-pimp mothafucka. He didn't strike Laila to be a thug because he didn't look tough. He was more of a pretty mothafucka. Not that it really mattered, because Laila was ready for a showdown regardless. He could act like he was stupid if he wanted to, but there was no way her daughter was going with him in that building they were heading for.

The dude turned around and told Pebbles to come on, and she followed him like a damn lost puppy. Laila quickly intervened and shut him down. She was so angry she used Pebbles' real name. "Khalia Janae Atkins! What the hell are you doin' with this grown man?! Girl, if you don't get yo' ass over here!"

Pebbles' eyes widened like she saw a ghost. "Ma! What are you *doin'* here?"

"Get over here right now!"

Pebbles hesitated and looked at the guy like she needed his approval.

That shit pissed Laila off beyond words. She couldn't believe her. Laila said, "I'm only gonna tell you one more fuckin' time. Pebbles, get your behind over here before I snatch a knot in your ass!"

When Pebbles heard that, she quickly walked over to where her mother was standing. She didn't want to get embarrassed out there. Laila just looked at her for a second, thanking God that she was okay, but at the same time wondering how long she had been involved with that grown man.

The dude obviously didn't understand that Laila had come for her child because he called Pebbles like she was his property. "Yo Pebbles!"

Pebbles looked frightened. She started to go to him, but she looked at Laila and knew better.

Who did that nigga think he was? Laila grabbed Pebbles by the arm and marched over to him. She was about to tell him off. He was really trying her patience. She hoped she didn't have to kill that bastard.

She said, "Excuse me, what is your name?"

The dude crossed his arms in front of him and stared at her coolly. "They call me Ice."

Laila nodded, and she was direct. "Look, *Ice*. I'm only gonna tell you this once. This little pissy tailed eleven year old girl here belongs to me. So, unless you have a death wish, don't let me find you within a million feet of her, ever again. Stay away from my child, or I will personally make sure that you're sorry. Trust me, bro. You don't know who you fuckin' wit'. Do we have an understanding?"

That bastard looked at Laila and smirked, which really irritated her. He said, "Hell no, we ain't got no understandin'. And I didn't know that Pebbles was only eleven, 'cause she sure don't act like it. Miss, I don't know what to tell you. Your daughter belongs to me now. Ain't that right, Pebbles?"

Laila took a deep breath and tried hard to keep from losing it. "Oh, is that so?"

Pebbles was shook and afraid to speak. She just looked down at the ground and didn't respond.

Ice said, "You heard what I said. And you lookin' good too, mama. I got room for one more in my stable." He rudely stared Laila up and down.

Laila almost spit in his face, but she refrained. She was trying to avoid a physical confrontation if possible. Her only objective was to take her child home with her, but that asshole was sure asking for it.

She pointed her finger at him. "Yo, just as I thought when I first saw you, you ain't nothin' but a cowardly young punk who preys on little girls. Don't fuck with my child again."

She looked at Pebbles and asked her, "Has this man ever hurt you?"

Pebbles shook her head. "No, Ma."

Even though Pebbles said no, Laila still let that nigga know how she felt. "If I find out that you hurt my child in any shape, form, or fashion, you gon' see me again. And I won't be alone next time. You've been warned, mothafucka!"

Laila grabbed Pebbles' arm and hurried her to the car. She didn't say a word to her until they got home. It wasn't that Laila didn't have anything to say. She was just angry, and frightened beyond her imagination. She didn't know what had occurred before that day. Pebbles could have been involved in some very adult stuff. All kinds of things ran through Laila's mind. Was her daughter still a virgin? Was she some kind of child prostitute? Had she had sex with that guy? Those were questions with answers Laila was afraid to hear. Nonetheless, she had to find out everything that had gone on.

When they got home, Laila took out one of Khalil's thick leather belts and tore Pebbles' ass up. She tried to set her ass on fire with that belt. She had to catch herself to keep from killing that child. When she was done whipping her she had welts all over her behind. That's what she got for being so damned stupid.

Laila didn't think she would have had to for a few more years but that day she called and scheduled Pebbles' first gynecological exam. Pebbles said she hadn't done anything, but Laila wasn't taking her word. That damned man she was with was a pimp. There was no telling what Pebbles had been exposed to.

Chapter Nine

A few blocks across town, a young girl named Ysatis had just dozed off into a light sleep when she heard keys turning in the front door. The pace of her heart quickened. She knew it was her older brother, Neal. Ysatis lay there still, frozen with fear, listening to see what state of mind he was in.

Over the years, she had learned to listen for signs of her brother's upcoming abuse. If he was loud when he came in, he was either drunk or high off angel dust, and she would more than likely be raped by him that night. But if he came in quietly and went straight to his room then Ysatis would be spared. That hardly ever happened, but it meant that Neal was either sober, or had female company.

Ysatis heard the familiar uneven pattern of disoriented footsteps coming down the hall, and they stopped at her room door. Damn, Neal was coming to fuck with her. And she had a test in the morning. It was her last year in high school, and time for finals. She tried hard to maintain her average so she could get into a good college. Ysatis knew that getting an education was the only way she could escape the hell she was living in, getting raped and molested by her own flesh and blood.

She mentally prepared herself for the horror that was to come. She wasn't going to put up a fight this time. It was three o'clock in the morning, and she was tired. Ysatis had learned a while back to just lay there and get it over with. The few times she'd fought back, Neal had beat her up pretty bad. There was no point in her going to school that morning with a black eye she couldn't see out of. She couldn't take her final exam like that.

Her bedroom doorknob turned, and Neal stepped in the

room. Ysatis played possum and prayed he would just leave. He closed the door behind him and walked over and stood over her bed. Neal pulled her blanket back and leered at her body like a panting dog in heat. He quickly stepped out of his Timbs, and then his pants and boxers. He was hard already. His gross penis stood up in the air.

"Ysatis!" Neal shook her a few times but she ignored him and acted like she was asleep. He wouldn't let up. "Yo, wake up and take this fuckin' gown off!"

She didn't respond so he said, "Oh, you wanna play it like that, huh? Okay, I see. You want me to take it."

Neal climbed in the bed on top of his little sister and ripped her nightgown open and exposed her breasts. He groped them roughly, and took one in his mouth and sucked on it sloppily. Ysatis bit her lip and laid there like a log. One thing she had learned over the years was that rejection turned her brother on.

As usual, she flirted with the notion of killing that mothafucka. If it weren't for her sick mother, she would have done it a long time ago. A murder in their household would make the authorities come snooping around. Then Ysatis would wind up in jail or some group home, and they would put her mama in some rehab or old folks home where she would be neglected and eventually shrivel up and die, just like her grandmother did. Her grandmother's health had failed rapidly after she was put into one of those old folks homes.

Ysatis endured Neal's sexual abuse but she took care of her mother well. She spoon-fed her and bathed her everyday, and also turned her from side to side several times a day so she wouldn't get bedsores. Before her grandmother died she had developed bedsores so bad they were big enough to fit baseballs in. And the smell of the infection and pus was unbearable.

Neal pried his sister's legs open and stuck his finger inside of her. She wasn't wet yet so he bent down and licked her pussy a few times, not really to pleasure her but to lubricate it with his spit. Ysatis thought about any and everything she could to keep her mind off of what was happening to her. She hated him.

Neal got back on top of her and placed her legs over his shoulders, and he entered her with force. Ysatis cried out in what he took to be was pleasure, but was really pain and despair. Neal humped her and whispered in her ear how good her pussy was. He told her that it was his, and if she gave it to any other nigga, he'd kill him.

Ysatis had once begged Neal's sick ass to use a condom, but he refused and told her not to be stupid. He told her that she was the only girl he ran up in raw, and he wouldn't risk giving her anything because she was his sister. Then he'd backhanded her across the mouth and raped her.

Ysatis prayed every single day that he wouldn't give her any type of disease. She often went to Planned Parenthood and got tested for STDs, and so far she had been lucky. And she took her birth control pills faithfully so she wouldn't get pregnant and have a mutant baby with three heads.

Neal grabbed Ysatis' ass and plunged deep as he could inside of her. His heart rate increased, and all the blood in his body seemed to rush to his dick. "Aahhh! Aargh, oh shit! I'm 'bout to cum!" He grabbed his sister's hips and shot off deep inside her.

Ysatis' stomach turned as usual but she swallowed the vomit that rose in her throat. She used all of her strength to push her drunk and disgusting slobbering brother off of her, and then she jumped up and ran to the bathroom to clean herself of her sick sibling's semen.

Neal watched his sister run from the room and he looked at her fat ass with pride. He was responsible for pumping that ass up like that. To his understanding, sex made a girl develop into a woman real fast.

When Ysatis finished in the bathroom, she peeked in on her mother to make sure she was okay. Satisfied that she was breathing well, Ysatis went back to her room. She saw that Neal was gone and she was relieved. Just like every other time it happened, she got back in bed and cried herself to sleep.

$$$

Laila sat in Portia's living room on the sofa weeping her heart out. She was engrossed in a heavy therapy session with her two best friends. Portia and Fatima consoled Laila and rubbed her back. Girlfriend had a lot to cry about.

When Laila had taken Pebbles to the gynecologist, she discovered two things. One, her daughter had an STD, and two, she was pregnant. The STD Pebbles had contracted was curable, thank God, but the combination of that one-two punch had Laila in shambles. If Pebbles had the baby she would be a thirty-two year old grandmother.

Laila told Portia and Fatima that after they left the doctor's office and got in the car she had lost it and beat the shit out of Pebbles with a brush like Claudine did her daughter in that old seventies movie "Claudine". But instead of a hairbrush she had used the snow removal brush in her trunk.

Portia and Fatima felt her pain. They were hurt too because Pebbles was just a baby. The two of them listened as Laila spilled her guts and gave them the rundown on how she'd found out that her daughter was running around with a pimp, who had also given her gonorrhea.

Laila couldn't stop crying. She took another tissue from the box of Kleenex Portia held in front of her and blew her nose, and she tried once again to speak. Laila stammered, "I -I-I just can't believe this shit, ya'll. My eleven year old b-b-baby is pregnant, and has g-gonorrhea. What k-kind of mother have I been? I thought I was doin' a good job. I don't know w-where I went wrong." She put her head down and started bawling harder.

Portia and Fatima hugged her. It was unlike Laila to get hysterical so they knew she was at the end of her rope.

Laila shook her head. "And Khalil stupid ass ain't a bit of help. He don't know what's goin' on with his kids. And the state of mind he's in, I don't even know if I should tell him. What do ya'll think I should do?" Laila looked at her friends through teary eyes.

"Don't tell him", Portia and Tima said in unison.

Portia said, "I think there are just some things a man doesn't need to know. I mean, tell him for what? She's not keeping the baby, right?"

The friends were all quiet for a minute, each deep in thought. Portia's million dollar question lingered in the air. They all agreed that Pebbles was way too young to be a mother, but Portia knew that Laila and Fatima were both pro-life. She was pro-choice but she knew she was outnumbered so she attempted to reword her question.

"Pardon me, Lay. I should've asked you what you were gon' do first. But I know that child ain't ready to have no baby. Mentally or physically. Pebbles' little body is not ready to carry no baby."

Fatima said, "But an abortion could mess her up too, God forbid. She's just a little girl."

Portia didn't bother to dispute what Fatima said. It was true. Abortion was a serious procedure, especially in the case of such a young girl. She didn't know what to say. It was all Laila's decision.

Portia thought about it for a second and said, "Pebbles will be twelve in a few weeks. She's barely a pre-teen. What is she gon' do with a baby? She's a baby herself. Laila, *you're* gonna wind up raising it. And if you want to, that's cool. 'Cause I'll be right there by your side helping you change the pampers. All I'm sayin' is, just think things through and know what to expect."

Laila sighed and shook her head. "I don't know what to do, ya'll. I don't mean to sound cruel, but a part of me just wants to beat that baby out of her. I'm so fuckin' mad at that girl!"

Laila felt bad after she said that but it was the truth. She looked up at the ceiling. "Lord, please forgive me. I'm sorry."

She took a fresh Kleenex from the box and dabbed her eyes again. She knew she had to pull it together. Crying damn sure wasn't going to solve the problem. Laila took a deep breath. She had made her decision.

She made her announcement. "Even though it's against everything I stand for, I think I'ma have to take her to the clinic ya'll. That child can't have no baby."

After that, Laila excused herself to the bathroom. She needed to splash some cold water on her face.

While Laila was in the bathroom, Jay and Casino pulled up outside and came in. They had gone to the City earlier that morning, and were just getting back. They only lived about a mile apart so they rode together sometimes.

When Jay and Cas came in they saw Portia and Fatima sitting in the living room. Jay said what up to Fatima, and bent down and kissed Portia on the cheek. Even after all the years they had been together he still greeted her with a kiss every day.

Cas greeted Portia and Fatima. "What up, ladies? How ya'll feelin'?

They both smiled and spoke in unison. "Hey, Cas. We ayight. How 'bout you?"

Cas laughed. "That sounded rehearsed. Everything is everything. Portia, I gotta use the bathroom."

Portia just nodded at him, and she and Tima smiled at each other. They were both thinking about Casino and Laila's past affair. Seeing Cas would be a nice surprise for Laila so neither of them told him that she was in the bathroom.

Cas saw that little secret smile they shared but he didn't know what it was about. All he knew was he drank a bottle of Vitamin Water on the way, and he had to go bad. He hurried off to take a leak.

Jay handed Portia some receipts to file away. She still handled some of the bookkeeping for Street Life. Just light stuff because the company had grown so much they had hired an accounting firm. They wanted to stay straight with the IRS.

When Laila came out of the bathroom she bumped dead into Casino. She was so surprised she couldn't even talk for a second. Damn, why hadn't she applied a fresh coat of lip gloss?

Cas was just as surprised. All he could do was simply say her name. "Laila."

Laila was so nervous she just waved and mumbled hello, and she tried to walk on pass him.

Cas blocked her path for a second. He just wanted to look at her a little longer. He hadn't seen her in a long time. To keep her in his company for a few moments Cas made small talk. That was something he never did. Laila always did have the power to make him do things he didn't. "So what up, miss? How you been?"

Laila knew here eyes were swollen from crying because she had just looked in the bathroom mirror. Shit! Why did she have to run into him when she looked so tore up? She took a second to breathe deep and relax before she spoke. "I'm alive, thank God. How 'bout yourself?"

"I'm good, thanks." Cas looked at her closer. It looked like she'd been crying. He voiced genuine concern. "Yo, you ayight, Laila?"

Cas wondered what was wrong with her. Was she getting a divorce or something? For some reason his hopes rose when he thought about that. He knew he was married, but the attraction he felt to Laila at that instant made him wonder if she was the one.

For some reason Laila almost broke down when Cas asked her if she was okay. Instead she nervously cleared her throat and nodded her head. "Yeah, I'm good." Cas couldn't be her shoulder to cry on. Not about the shit she was going through.

Damn, he was still fine. She hadn't seen him in almost three years. They had become real close at one point but Laila had broken it off with him, so keeping in touch just hadn't seemed proper.

Laila had the feeling she had really fucked up by letting Cas slip through her fingers. As vulnerable as she was feeling, she almost had to stop herself from jumping into his arms. Instead, she played it cool and told him it was nice seeing him.

As she headed back to the living room where Portia and Tima were, Laila wanted to kick herself. How could she have blown it with Casino? He was perfect. She was an idiot.

Cas watched Laila walk away and couldn't take his eyes off of her. Her ass was so fat and juicy it looked like a ripe peach. That was what you called bountiful booty. Cas started to say something but then he remembered how she had dissed him. Her crab ass husband had beaten the shit out of her and almost killed her, and Cas had rescued her and took her to the hospital. And after all that, she ran right back to that lame.

Cas had told her he understood because she and the dude were married and had kids together, but he had actually considered it a slap in the face that she'd turned him down. He could've given her anything she wanted and she turned him down. *"Man, fuck Laila"*, Cas thought, and headed in the bathroom.

In spite of the facts, Casino thought about Laila while he took a leak and washed his hands. He couldn't front, when he saw her he felt something. He loved his wife Kira but deep inside he felt he and Laila had unfinished business. He felt like they had really started something before. Damn, why had she showed up? He and Kira were a family now. Their son was almost six years old.

Cas was family oriented but he and Kira were on a rocky road. They had a lot of differences, and that usually overpowered what they had in common. Kira was messy and liked to sleep late. Cas wanted a woman who was neat and got up early and cooked breakfast for him sometimes. Kira was hard-headed and her mouth was too slick. Cas preferred a woman who knew how to listen and kept her mouth shut sometimes. Kira liked to do shit to rile him up on purpose, and Cas didn't like getting upset.

Cas could've gone on about the things he disliked about Kira for days. Instead, he tried to think of a way to get Laila by herself again. He wanted a contact number so he could holler at her, but he didn't want everyone in their business. Cas dried his hands and went back out there with the others.

Jay had gone upstairs for a minute. Just as Laila had, Cas received these little knowing smiles from Fatima and Portia. Cas kept his poker face on and had a seat across from the ladies. He wasn't about to act nervous. He was a grown ass man. He glanced over at Laila. She was trying to look serious too. They were playing the same game.

Portia and Fatima tried to clear up some of the tension in the room by talking to Cas about the video schedule for Wise' new single called, "Fall Back". Cas answered their questions and conversed with them for a few minutes.

Laila was quiet the whole time. She didn't know what to say. Cas probably didn't want to be bothered with her anyway after the way she had broke it off with him. But she was beginning to feel an overwhelming attraction to him. Laila realized she wanted him back. She felt like she had to have him. She wished she could get his phone number somehow before she left.

A minute later, Jay called Portia upstairs to help him locate whatever it was he was searching for. Laila finally got up the nerve to say something to Cas but before she could open her mouth a car horn beeped outside.

Cas stood up and looked out the window. He saw that it was Kira so he excused himself and went outside. Cas was cool about it but he went out there so quickly to keep Kira from coming in and seeing Laila.

Laila stood up and peeked out the window. She saw that Kira had pulled up in a pink Porsche. Laila figured Cas must've really loved her the way he had hurried outside to meet her. She stared on enviously from the front window and watched as he bent down for what looked like a kiss, and then opened the back door for his son. When the little boy got out he hugged Cas and smiled. He looked just like him. They looked like a real happy family.

Laila's heart sank. Boy, she had been a fool. That should've been her pushing that whip. She'd chosen her sorry ass husband and children's father, and her life had taken a turn for the worst ever since. Well to be fair, she and Khalil did have almost two good years after they renewed their wedding vows. But that was it. Since then everything had gone from sugar to shit.

Fatima watched Laila staring out the window at Cas. She knew what was going on in her head. She interrupted Laila's thoughts and startled her. "You still like him, Lay", she stated.

Laila sat down and tried to look nonchalant. "No I don't, Tima."

Fatima gave her a look like she knew she was lying. "Yeah, whatever. Who do you think you talkin' to? You better make a move, sis. Ain't nothin' wrong with having a friend." Tima winked at Laila.

Laila smiled for the first time that day. For a brief second she felt like a teenager in love. She was a step away from singing *"Laila and Casino kissing in a tree. K-I-S-S-I-N-G...
"*

Portia and Jay came back downstairs, and Laila snapped back to reality and remembered that life wasn't a fairytale. Her smile faded. Cas was outside with his family. And she had a crackhead for a husband, and her eleven year old daughter was burning and pregnant. Her situation was looking type grim. She could certainly use some sunshine in her life.

$$$

Wise sat in Street Life's main office going over some paperwork he had to pass on to his lawyer. This new hip-hop clothing line called Budda wanted him to model some of their personalized handcrafted belts. The Budda belts were hot, and they were paying him so he had agreed.

After he finished reading the contract, Wise reflected on his past weeks activities. He was feeling real bad about the heartache and pain he had caused Fatima. She had indirectly caught him cheating again. She found the phone number of this jump-off and called her, and the dumb bitch leaked too much information. She was a video hoe, and needless to say, she was fired after that.

Fatima was mad so Wise decided to go home early and do something nice for her. The more he thought about it the guiltier he felt. He loved his wife. All those groupies and bitches he fucked around with didn't mean shit to him. Before Wise left headquarters he got the receptionist, Nelly, to contact a florist and have a hundred red roses sent to Fatima. He was going to spend the whole day pampering her. And she deserved an expensive gift. Whatever she wanted.

Wise decided he'd take her on a shopping spree, and then dinner and maybe a movie. Then later, he would run her a hot bubble bath and let her relax, and then give her a sensual massage. That was something he hadn't done in a while. He even used to rub her feet when she was pregnant. Determined to treat his wife like the queen she was that day, Wise put a little more lead on the accelerator. He was pushing one of his favorite toys that day, a yellow Lamborghini Gallardo, so he was lucky to make it home without getting a speeding ticket.

When Wise got home he saw a strange car parked in one of their garages. It was a dark green X-Type Jaguar. He wondered who that was. It could have been one of Fatima's homegirls but he didn't recall any of them driving a Jag. Wise headed inside the house.

He didn't see Tima in the front room, or in the kitchen. He went further inside and looked in the parlor. She wasn't in there so he headed upstairs to the bedrooms. She wasn't up there either. Wise was anxious to surprise her but the house was so damn big he couldn't find her.

Then it occurred to him that she and her company might be out by the pool. He slid open the terrace doors in the master bedroom and stepped out there and looked down at the pool.

Fatima and her company were out there all right. Wise' jaw dropped in shock. "What the fuck!?"

Fatima was sitting on the low side of the pool with one foot in the water and one up on the side. Her head was thrown back and she was writhing and moaning in pleasure from getting her pussy eaten by some mothafucka standing in the pool between her legs. Fatima's eyes were closed, and she was panting and holding their head like she couldn't get enough.

That cheating bitch! Wise couldn't believe her. He grabbed his hammer from the closet and ran downstairs and outside to the pool to let her know she was busted. He felt like an asshole. He had come home early to surprise her like he was some sucker. He was gonna fuck that bitch up.

Fatima was engrossed in an orgasm so she didn't even see him walk up. He watched her making the sexy faces that should've been reserved for him. The faces she made when she was about to cum. Wise cringed in anguish. That was his pussy. That shit almost made him cry. But fuck that. He was no bitch.

He had seen enough. "Yo, Tima! What the fuck is this?! You try'na *play* me, bitch?"

Fatima opened her eyes and thought she saw a ghost. Oh shit, it was her husband! Her jaw dropped in surprise, and she pried Ray's face off. Fatima jumped up and started copping a plea.

"Wise! Baby, it's not what you think! Listen to me..." Fatima realized that there was nothing she could say. Her bikini bottom was on the ground next to her, and Wise had caught her dead in the act. She had no wins. She unconsciously placed her hands in front of herself and tried to cover up. She had never been so ashamed.

Wise was fuming. "Nah, fuck that! Don't try to front and cover up your pussy now, bitch! You just had your ass spread wide open *outside* gettin' ate out! This how you get down, Tima? Huh, bitch? I should kill ya'll mothafuckas."

Ray scrambled out of the water and grabbed her towel from the side of the pool, and she made a beeline for the house as fast as she could.

Wise pulled his gun from his waist and went after her. "Don't run now, bitch! Here, take this wit' you!"

Fatima saw the gun and screamed, "NO! No, Wise! Oh my God, please!"

Wise wasn't listening to her. He was enraged, and there was no telling what he would do. Fatima ran after him. She grabbed Wise' arm and tried to stop him. She managed to subdue him for a few seconds but he was stronger than her. He got fed up and pushed her aside.

"Run, Raven! Run! Hurry", Fatima yelled after her lover, praying that she made it out of there in time. She knew what Wise was capable of doing, and she didn't want him to kill her.

Wise heard tires screech out front. Damn, that bitch got up outta there fast. She was lucky as hell. He turned his anger back on Fatima. He grabbed her by her throat and hissed, "You fuckin' dyke!"

Fatima cried out in pain but Wise didn't listen. He was infuriated. He picked her up by the neck and slammed her on the ground. Wise stood over Fatima and grabbed a handful of her hair, and he slapped her three hard times.

"You a fuckin' carpet muncher, Fatima? You ate her pussy too? Huh, you fuckin' *bitch*? Answer me!" He choked her again and shook her violently, and her head rolled around like she was a bobble head doll. Wise didn't care. He wanted to break her fucking neck.

Fatima was crying like a baby. "No! I didn't eat her pussy, I *swear*! Let go of my neck, Wise! Please, I can't breath. For real, please." She was petrified. She tried to pry his hands from her throat. Wise was really wilding out.

"Bitch, I'll kill you out this mothafucka! I ain't got no use for no dyke ass, pussy suckin' bitch. You supposed to be my wife!" Wise got angrier and choked her harder. He saw Fatima's eyes bulging out of her head so he loosened his grip a little. He didn't really want to kill her but he was gonna put the fear of God in her ass.

Wise placed his gun to her temple and stared at her coldly. "Fatima, you wanna fuckin' die?"

"*No*", Fatima cried. She knew Wise had really lost it now. He had never beat her up, or pulled out a gun on her. She was scared to death. She pleaded with him through sobs. "Wise, I am so sorry. Please don't do this, baby. I love you. Please, you know I'll do anything for you. We got a daughter, baby, please! Think about Falynn."

When she spoke about his daughter she struck a cord in him. Wise calmed down and put his gun down. He brushed the hair out of Fatima's face and leaned down and kissed her on the forehead. "Shhh. It's okay. Stop crying."

Wise' whole demeanor had changed. He gingerly stroked the side of her face and said softly, "If you ever cheat on me again, with a nigga *or* a bitch, I'ma fuckin' kill you, Tima. You hear me?"

Fatima knew he wasn't kidding. Her lips quivered and her voice shook when she answered him. "Yes, I h-h-hear you. I'm s-sorry."

Wise stood up and tucked the gun in his waist. He reached down and extended his arm to help her get up. "Now go wash your ass and put on some fuckin' clothes."

Fatima nodded her head, and she ran in the house wearing just her bikini top. When she got inside she locked herself in the bathroom for a while and thought about her thwarting reality. Her husband had caught her engaged in lesbian sex. Fatima was glad Wise hadn't killed her. The oral sex was good but now she doubted that shit was even worth it. Fatima thought back to the day she first met Raven.

Around Valentine's Day weekend of the past year, she had received an e-vite to a "girls only" adult toy party. Anxious to find something to spice up her and Wise' sex life, she accepted the invitation and attended the affair.

When Fatima had arrived she was absolutely delighted. She wanted to purchase something that would blow Wise' mind, and there was a whole lot to choose from. There was every type of sexual toy a person could dream of on display. There were dildos, vibrators, anal plugs and anal beads, clit massagers, vibrating vaginal balls, strap-ons, whips, and even synthetic pussies and blow-up dolls for the women who wanted to safely invite another woman into bed with her and her man.

Raven was the hostess of the party, which was also held

in her uptown apartment. She had a great sales pitch so she'd auctioned off toys by the dozen. The women attending carried on like they were at a Tupperware party. They bought up everything. Fatima had bought three toys herself.

After most of the guests had made their purchases and gone home, Raven and Fatima had winded up engaged in a "how-to" conversation about the clit massager Fatima had purchased. When Fatima thanked her and was about to leave, Raven invited her to stay for a glass of red wine.

Fatima had agreed, and after they'd almost finished the whole bottle, Raven volunteered to show her how her new toys worked. Fatima had been tipsy and said what the hell. At Raven's request, she took off her pants for the demonstration.

A few minutes later, Raven had her crawling up the walls. Before it was over, she replaced the clit massager with her warm hungry mouth. Fatima was so caught up in tongue rapture from Raven's oral assault on her pussy she didn't even protest. Instead she grabbed the back of her head and fucked her pretty face until she came. Twice.

The orgasmic wave Raven had taken Fatima on was breathtaking. She was panting like she had just run a two minute mile. Girlfriend had given her the best head she'd ever had in her life. And to top it off, Raven made it clear that she didn't expect anything in return. She said she just loved pussy so she got off on doing her.

That was cool with Fatima. She could certainly get with the thought of having another orgasm like that just a phone call away. They had both agreed to keep in touch.

Fatima had enjoyed their little affair while it lasted. She had really loved getting tongue fucked ever so often but it was over now. Wise had caught them in the act, and it was all due to her carelessness. She had gotten too bold. She never should've started letting Raven come to her house.

Raven was Fatima's dirty little secret. She hadn't even

told her friends about her yet. And now she wouldn't. There was no point. Besides, she didn't want to be judged. Even though Fatima had participated in oral sex with Raven, she was still an old fashioned girl at heart just like her homegirls, Portia and Laila. She wasn't exactly proud of her semi-lesbian activities. What could she say? The flesh was weak.

Chapter Ten

That weekend Humble got a call on his cell phone from his new shorty, Ysatis. She said she wanted to see him. He went through to pick her up because he wanted to see her too. Humble had bagged Ysatis around his way, and he was kind of feeling her. In fact, he had picked up a surprise for her the day before. He would give it to her that night.

As usual, he picked Ysatis up on the corner of her block, down the street from her house. Humble knew she was a little younger than he was so he never questioned her about that. He figured her moms must've been strict or something.

A few minutes later, Ysatis watched Humble pull up. She hurried over to his car and jumped in the passenger side. "Hurry up, drive!"

Humble pulled off quickly and he looked over at her. "Ysatis, why you actin' like the Feds is chasin' us and shit?"

Ysatis just looked down and shook her head. Humble didn't know the half. Her older brother Neal suspected that she was messing around. It was all too complicated to explain so she didn't bother to go into details about the incest, rape, and sexual abuse that went on in her household. Besides, she didn't want to turn Humble off. He would surely think she was some kind of freak for not blowing the whistle on Neal.

Humble noticed how troubled Ysatis looked and he wondered what was wrong. "What's the matter, Ma?"

Determined to have a great time that evening, Ysatis shook it off and forced a smile at him. "I'm good, boo. Let's go to the movies."

"That sound like a plan. Whatever you want." Humble reached over and stroked her hair affectionately.

Ysatis beamed. That uncommon display of positive affection from a man made her feel special and loved. And it

seemed genuine. She was really starting to fall for Humble.
Ysatis just wanted to get away from the madness, and it felt
like he offered her an escape.

About four hours later, Humble dropped Ysatis off down
the street from her house. It was still early but he wanted to
make sure she got in at a decent time. He didn't want her
to get in trouble. They'd had a good time at the movies, and
then they'd gone for a bite to eat afterwards.

Humble wished the night didn't have to end so soon but
he knew she was young so he didn't beef about it. He really
dug shorty. He had given her the surprise he had at the
restaurant. It was a pair of gold bamboo earrings with her
name on them. And he had sprung for the biggest ones too.
He had ordered them the week before and picked them up
yesterday.

Ysatis thanked Humble again for the earrings and kissed
him goodnight, and she floated down the street. She was
ecstatic. Humble was just so sweet. There was no doubt
about it, she was in love. Wow, she had her first boyfriend.
Ysatis grinned from ear to ear.

When she got inside her house she realized that her brother
was at home. She made a beeline straight for her bedroom,
but Neal heard her come in. He quickly came down the
hall and pushed her door open and began questioning her
immediately.

"Yo, where 'da fuck your little hot ass comin' from this
time of night?"

Ysatis sucked her teeth impatiently. "It ain't even eleven
o'clock yet."

Neal noticed the new earrings she had on. "Where 'da fuck
you get them big ass earrings from? What dead nigga bought
those for you? And what the fuck you did for them?"

Ysatis wouldn't answer him. Neal popped her upside
her head real hard to generate a response. She just kept a

stone face and wouldn't say anything but she had to restrain herself. He hit her in her head hard, and it really hurt. She almost hit his ass back that time.

Neal wouldn't back off. He grabbed her by the shoulders and shook her hard. "You hear me fuckin' talkin' to you!"

"I bought them *myself*', Ysatis said with an attitude.

He looked at her like he didn't believe her. "Yeah right. Get the fuck outta here. I know who probably bought 'em. That lil' nigga Humble. I heard you been sneakin' around ridin' in that nigga car."

Neal poked Ysatis in the forehead with his index finger and pushed her head back. He forced her to look at him. He wanted her to know how serious he was when he said what he was about to say. "Yo, let me tell you somethin'. If you give my pussy away, I'ma *smoke* that nigga. *And* you. You hear me, bitch?"

He grabbed Ysatis by the neck with his left hand and snatched the earrings from her ears with the right. He threw them down on the floor and stomped them in rage. "You heard me?"

Ysatis was forced to say yes but her bottom liptrembled in rage. He didn't have to destroy her earrings like that. Her brother was just evil. Against her will, a lone tear ran down her face. It wasn't because she feared him. She felt nothing but pure hatred towards Neal. She was sick of the sick way he controlled her life.

Neal noticed Ysatis' resilience but he wouldn't let up. Determined to find out whether or not she had been out screwing, he demanded that she take off her clothes so he could inspect her vagina.

Ysatis refused, and Neal hit her across the face. She clawed his eyes and tried to put up a fight but he gave her a pimp smack that sent her flying to the floor. Ysatis was so full of hate her body was cold and numb. She couldn't even cry.

Neal forced her out of her clothes, and he sniffed her

panties and checked their crotch for cum stains or discharge. He inspected Ysatis' body for hickeys, and then made her lie down on the bed spread-eagled while he examined her with his fingers like he was a gynecologist. Afterwards, he stuck his dick in just to make sure it was the same fit.

Satisfied that it didn't feel tampered with, Neal continued to stroke. He figured he might as well go on and bust a nut while he was in there.

Ysatis just laid there crying, thinking of a hundred ways to kill that bastard. She just couldn't take it anymore. She wanted him dead.

$$$

A few days later, Humble was cruising through the 'hood when he saw his man Dee on the corner of Myrtle and Clinton. Another dude named Chewy was out there too, whom Humble had a minor dispute with last year over a package. Ysatis' older brother, whose street name was Nasty Neal, and this dude named Tone were also on the corner.

Humble had a feeling he should've kept going but he couldn't let those niggas think he was a sucker. He pulled over to holler at his man Dee. Jay had given him an iced out Street Life Entertainment medallion and chain the day before, so this gave him an opportunity to show it off a little. And he just happened to be bumping Fabolous and Young Jeezy's new joint "Diamonds in My Damn Chain" in his Lexus. What a coincidence. Nah, he had been running that song since he got that chain. Humble knew he was fronting a little bit but it was almost summertime and he just wanted to shine for a second. Fuck it, he was still young. This was the time of his life he was supposed to floss. He was in his prime. He left the music playing and hopped out and gave dudes a pound.

Just as Humble figured, Chewy came out of his face with

some slick shit and tested him. He was just in straight hate mode. First he said Humble was pussy and his diamonds were just glass. Then he said he would take his Street Life chain and run him off the streets. He was really trying to impress the other dudes on the corner so Humble had to answer. Chewy kept on disrespecting him so he slapped fool out that nigga.

After that, Chewy was humiliated and tight as hell. Humble tucked his chain in his tee shirt and told him to throw up his dick beaters so they could shoot a fair one. But Chewy didn't want to fight fair. He wanted to pop Humble but he didn't have a burner on him at the time. He promised Humble he'd be back.

Humble had a hammer on him, and something told him to end that beef right then and there before Chewy became a reoccurring problem. But Humble had never killed before and he had compassion for life, so he hesitated.

The following day, Humble let Jay and Cas know about the altercation he'd gotten into with Chewy. He kept it real and told them he'd thought about offing that dude.

Jay told Humble to chill and let it ride because niggas weren't worth it. Humble agreed, and Jay gave him strict orders to stay out of the 'hood until things cooled down.

Being partners for so long, Jay and Cas had developed the habit of never disagreeing in front of other people because it showed weakness. They had the mutual understanding to remain a united front at all times, so Cas held his tongue until they were out of Humble's earshot.

When Humble went to the john, Cas calmly voiced his opinion to Jay. He felt that Jay should just mind his business and let Humble handle that. After a man to man debate in which neither party raised their voice, Cas agreed with Jay's reasoning. The two of them had done their share of dirty work, and he didn't want to influence a young brother to do something that could possibly get him put away for the rest of

his life. Them crackers weren't playing with those sentences
they were giving out now. There were new gun laws and
mandatory sentences for violent felonies, so nowadays some
street shit could fuck around and put you away for natural
life.

$$$

A few weeks later, Chewy came back. And he had an
accomplice. Nasty Neal had put a battery in Chewy's back.
He'd been amping him up to shoot Humble ever since he
smacked him on the corner.

Earlier that day, Nasty Neal and Chewy were riding
around in a hooptie getting fucked up off angel dust, and
Neal convinced Chewy that it was time for him to save face
because the whole 'hood was laughing at him. A few minutes
later, they just happened to see Humble's car.

They tailed Humble and rolled up on him when he was
going up the stairs of his mother's house, and they opened
fire without warning.

Humble's back was turned so he didn't even see it coming.
He had a gun on him but he never even had a chance to
reach. He was murdered in cold blood, right on his mother's
doorstep.

When they dropped him, Neal told Chewy to run up
and get his chain. Chewy quickly scurried up the steps like
the little rat he was and snatched the dying man's Street Life
medallion and chain from his neck. He remorselessly looked
into the eyes of his fellow young black brother and spat, "I
told you I was gon' take this shit, nigga!"

Chewy dug in and removed the stack of money from
Humble's left pocket and hurried back down the stairs and
jumped in the hooty with Neal, and the two of them sped
off.

Humble's mother, a widow named Mrs. Landry, was in

her kitchen washing dishes when she heard the shots. The gunfire sounded close and that gave her a bad feeling. She ran outside praying it wasn't anybody she knew. Much to her dismay, she found her son at her front door bleeding to death. She knew he was going because blood was coming out of his mouth.

The distraught woman fell to her knees and cradled her dying son's head in her lap. "Just hold on baby", she told him. She prayed and she prayed.

But it was too late. First her oldest son Nate was murdered, and now her baby Humble. There was no one there to comfort Mrs. Landry as she lost another son. Someone took away the only child she had left. And there was no one around to blame. His killers were already gone when she got outside. She cried and asked God to take her boy's soul so he could rest in peace.

$$$

That night Jay was driving on his way home when he got the call about Humble's murder. He was deeply saddened by the news, but more than anything he blamed himself. Damn, he should've handled that beef for Humble before it escalated like that. It had led to him getting killed over some bullshit. Jay had called that one wrong, and he would regret it for the rest of his life.

When Jay got in the house, Portia was sitting in her office in front of her computer. When she heard Jay come in, she spun around in her mahogany leather executive chair. She had her hair wrapped with a scarf tied around it, and she was wearing a black sports bra and a pair of sweatpants.

Portia smiled at Jay, and she got up and walked over to where he was. "Hey boo, what up?" She stretched up on her tiptoes and kissed him on his cheek.

"Ain't shit. What's shakin', Ma? Where're the kids?"

Portia knew Jay, and could tell something was bothering him. "They're sleeping. Baby, what's wrong?"

Jay could barely bring himself to say it. He sighed heavily. "My lil' man just got killed."

Portia looked shocked and worried. "Oh my God, baby! Who?"

Jay looked real sad. "Humble", he said unhappily.

Portia couldn't believe it. She placed her hand across her heart. "Oh my God! Oh no, not my Humble Bee. That is so fucked up. Baby, I am so sorry."

Portia couldn't help but cry. That news hurt so bad. She really loved that boy. The senseless violence just had to stop. It didn't make any sense. She hugged Jay, and then she stepped back and cradled his face in her hands. "Baby, are you okay?"

Jay's eyes watered up a little so he looked away. He couldn't let Portia see him cry. He knew she cared. She loved Humble too. He nodded his head. "Yeah, I'm good."

Portia knew that wasn't the case but she would allow him his privacy to grieve alone if he needed to. She hugged Jay again and caressed his back, and she told him she was there for him.

Jay said he just wanted to take a shower so Portia got out a clean pair of boxers, socks, and a tee shirt from his dresser, and she turned on the shower in the master bathroom for him. She got his slippers and robe ready for when he was done.

Jay thanked her and took of his clothes, and he headed for the shower in his boxers. He needed a minute to think. To say that his heart was heavy would be understating his pain. Jay was crushed. Someone had to pay.

While Jay was in the bathroom, Portia cried her heart out. She couldn't believe Humble was dead. She saw so much in him. That boy was destined to be something. Lord, how would she tell the children? They loved him.

After Jay got out of the shower, Portia asked him if he was hungry. He told her he didn't really have an appetite but he accepted her offer to fix him a drink. He told her to make it stiff.

When Portia was done, Jay threw back the double shot of straight Hennessy she handed him in seconds. Afterwards, he just sat there quietly deep in thought. Just then, Jay-Z's "Lost One" video came on the big flat screen LCD television on the bedroom wall. That record was one of Jay's favorites, and it really triggered some emotions in him that time. He really needed to vent.

Humble's death had really fucked him up. He voiced his feelings to Portia about the whole ordeal, speaking as calmly as he could but blatantly hinting about his plans for retaliation.

"Yo, P, the nigga responsible for this is done. You hear me? His moms gotta feel what Hum's moms is feelin'. She gotta experience that same pain", Jay said.

Portia could tell from the look on Jay's face that he wasn't playing. She knew he was upset but she didn't want him to get into any trouble. She tried to be the voice of reason.

"But Jay, what's that gonna solve? That'll just result in another black mother in tears, another sister that lost a brother, or another child that lost their father. No, baby. That's not the answer."

Deep down inside Jay knew Portia was right. Retaliating wouldn't really solve anything. But having the head of the mothafucka who did it would ease his guilty conscience. Street justice was the only way to handle shit like that. An eye for an eye and a tooth for a tooth. That was the only way he would get some closure.

Before Portia and Jay went to bed that night, she convinced him not to get involved. Or so she thought. Jay just didn't want to worry her. He already knew what had to be done.

Late that night, Jay got phone calls from Casino, Wise,

and Hop, all expressing their sympathy, concern, and grief
for Humble. There was one thing all of the men agreed on.
Humble's killer and everyone involved had to go.

The following morning when Jay woke up, he laid in bed a
little longer than usual and pondered the situation. He really
felt like he needed some get-back. That thing was eating at
him too bad. He had to do something. If he didn't, dudes
would start thinking he'd gone soft. There wasn't anything
ice cream about him.

Jay was especially upset because he felt that his bad
judgment was the cause of Nate's little brother's life being
taken. He had really let Nate down by failing to protect
Humble, and he felt low. He wanted the person responsible
for his little homie's death dead. It was that simple. Someone
had to go.

That afternoon, Jay and Cas went over and sat with
Humble's mother for a while. Before they left they gave her a
huge check so she could handle all of the funeral arrangements
and do something nice for herself. They told her that Portia
and Fatima were stopping by later to help out with things.

When the partners talked the situation over, they decided
to put a fifty thousand dollar cash bounty on the killer's head.
They figured the bastard should be easy to find because he
had stolen Humble's chain. When the missing Street Life
medallion popped up they would have their man. Jay wanted
him brought to them alive because he wanted to be the one
to murder the scumbag. He and Cas used a blow-up cell
phone number as the contact hotline for info on the reward,
and they sent a few little soldiers to put word on the streets.

Even though Jay knew Cas had advised him to let Humble
handle that beef he had before it escalated, Cas never once
said "I told you so" because he was a real friend. He knew Jay
had mad love for their little man Humble. He didn't mean
for that shit to happen.

Wise was ready and willing to assist Jay and Casino in the

head hunt. None of them had really had to pop off lately, and the fact that it was time was sort of exhilarating. They had been busy baking bread but now they needed to send a message to the streets. That was just the way it was. Anyone who violated them got it. Those mothafuckas who killed Humble were finished.

$$$

Across town, two armed and dangerous men sat at a roundtable deep in discussion. The men were debating who their next vics would be. The two of them were Philadelphia natives who had made a special trip to New York to scope out potential victims and plan their next jux. Armed robbery was their profession, and they were diligent in their craft. They made a living off the blood and sweat of others, particularly young, black entrepreneurs coming up in the music industry.

The streets had christened the grimy pair "The Scumbag Brothas". They were infamous for yapping some of the most popular rappers in the game for their chains, iced out medallions, cars, and money. The men were blood brothers named Melvin and Michael, and they had both spent their whole lives in and out of prison. They went by the street names Powerful and Mike Machete, due to the strong-arm techniques they used to take what they wanted from others. There were only two of them but when they got at niggas, they swore there was an army after them.

The Scumbag Brothas had recently been plotting and scheming on the fellows who owned Street Life Entertainment. Upon observation, they had discovered that those niggas Jay, Casino, and Wise were really getting it. They had come up a lot over the past few years, and Mike Machete and Powerful had their eyes on them. The Scumbag Brothas wanted nothing more than to get into their pockets. If they did shit right that lick would set them straight for a while.

Mike Machete and Powerful worked on formulating a concrete plan. The two of them never rushed on a job. They would sit back in the cut and wait until the time was right. They were experienced enough to know when to strike. They had been watching those Street Life mothafuckas for quite a while, and those guys were careful. They didn't move about sloppily, so The Scumbag Brothas weren't dumb enough to think they were just sitting ducks waiting to be got.

But Powerful and Mike Machete were fearless. When the time was right they would hit them, and they would hit hard. Niggas better be ducking when The Scumbag Brothas came through.

Chapter Eleven

Friday night, Jay, Cas, and Wise were up in the studio when the blow-up cell phone rang. This was the second call they got that day, and they hoped that this caller would have more information than the last.

This time the caller was a female. She told them she used to mess with Humble and that she loved him, and that she could hand his murderer to them on a silver platter within hours. She said them capturing him couldn't get any sweeter because she had a key to his house. Jay told the girl to meet them at a discreet location in forty-five minutes so they could talk in person. He told her he was sending a car for her.

The girl turned out to be a slim brown skinned little cutie with braids. She said her name was Ysatis with a silent "y", pronounced Sah-tees, and she had a pretty smile. Jay and Cas could see why Humble had been involved with her.

In person, she assured them again that she held the key to them getting their man. The only catch was that she said she needed seventy five thousand dollars instead of the fifty they were offering. Jay and Cas told her that if she was telling the truth that wouldn't be a problem.

"So when I'ma get my money?", she asked.

Cas looked at her like she was crazy. "Hold up. Shorty, calm down. When we're sure that the information you've provided us with is accurate, then you'll getcha' money. How do we even know you got the right address?" Cas asked her.

The girl laughed bitterly. "I know the address is correct because I live there too. That foul ass scumbag piece of gutter shit that pulled the trigger is my brother. And I know part of the reason he killed Humble was just to make my life miserable."

Jay and Cas looked at one another in disbelief. This chick

was turning the situation into some soap opera shit. They both grew impatient and irritated with her.

Cas said, "Yo, what kind of games is you playin', man?"

Ysatis looked both of them square in the eye and said, "I ain't playin' no games. Trust me. Nobody wants that nigga dead more than me! I hate that mothafucka!"

Jay said, "Damn, shorty, that sounds personal. But if that's your brother, then why do you want him dead?"

Ysatis said, "Yeah, he's *some* kind of big brother. That nigga been gettin' dusted and rapin' me ever since I was twelve years old. And my mama can't walk or talk, 'cause she done had three strokes, so she couldn't do nothin' to help me."

Cas and Jay sympathized with the girl. That was fucked up. Cas asked, "Yo, how old are you?"

Ysatis replied, "I'm almost eighteen now. And if you wanna know how come I didn't break out, it's because my brother kept a roof over me and my mother's heads, and food on the table. My moms had her first stroke when I was twelve. I didn't wanna go in no foster home so I was grateful when my brother promised to hold the family down so we could all stay together. But about a month later he came in my room dusted out his mind and told me that if I didn't take off my clothes and do what he told me, he was gonna put my mother in a home, and put me in the system. So I went along with it that time, and it just turned into years of abuse. But I swear to God I only took that shit off Neal so I could be close to my mother, and take care of her."

There wasn't much Jay or Cas could say after that.

Ysatis' eyes watered up a little, but she continued. "Ya'll don't know, my brother is really sick. He used to always tell me that he would kill any nigga I fucked with. And he knew I cared about Humble. We'd been messin' around for a few months. Everybody in the 'hood knew we was talkin'."

After that she told them about the night she went home after Humble gave her those nameplate earrings and Neal stepped on them, beat her up, and raped her.

Ysatis paused and wiped a tear from the corner of her eye, and she sighed. "Yo, I hate my brother. He even had the nerve to come home with Humble's chain the night it happened. He was like, "I told you so. Look what you did to that nigga. His blood is on your hands", and then he held up the chain and laughed."

She started crying again. "That nigga Neal is really sick. I would probably kill him myself if it wasn't for my moms. I gotta look after her. I just want Neal out of our lives once and for all. Then we can start over. That's why I need the extra twenty five thousand dollars. Now that I'm like grown, I can buy a house in my own name. Down in North Carolina I can buy a big ass doublewide manufactured home with four bedrooms and two baths for forty thousand dollars cash, if I get a used one. And I know I can find a piece of land for a few thousand. So basically, around fifty thousand will put us in a nice crib with central air conditioning and heat. I need the other twenty five grand to pay bills while we get situated, buy me a little piece of car to get around, and enroll myself in college. I really wanna go to school. I found out I can get my mother a nurse to sit with her during the day."

If that girl was telling the truth, she'd had a hell of a life. Jay and Cas both really wanted to kill that dude. That mothafucka was sick! They both played it cool though. There was always the chance that she could be lying.

Jay said, "So it looks like you already got your new life all planned out, huh?"

"Pardon me ya'll, but my brother's dead body will be just the welcome mat I need to get started. Me and my moms will be livin' good when we get down south, God willin'. With Humble gone, I don't even want to stay up here. Plus I don't want to be around to answer nobody questions about Neal."

After that, Jay, Cas, and Ysatis set everything up. Ysatis'

only request was that they not kill her brother in the house where her mother was. She said she would make sure they caught him "with his pants down" so it wouldn't be a problem taking him out of there. Then they could kill him as they pleased.

Just because they were meticulous, Jay and Casino checked out Ysatis' story to see if she was really Neal's sister, and really had a history with Humble. Humble's mother confirmed the fact that Humble was dating some girl named Ysatis before he passed away, so Jay and Casino decided to trust her.

When the time came, Ysatis set her brother up like she was professional. He should've known something was wrong because she initiated sex with him for the first time ever. Neal was so ignorant he thought that she was finally coming to realize that she liked it too.

Through lust hooded eyes, Neal leered at his sister's naked body. He quickly got undressed and stepped out of his boxers, and he held his hard dick in his hand. He told Ysatis to give him a little head but she refused. He didn't sweat it because he figured in due time she would learn to love that too. For the time being, he would give her what she wanted.

As soon as Neal got on top of her, the door opened and four dudes dressed in all black came in and stood over him. Neal looked surprised as hell. Who the fuck were they? And how had they gotten into the house so quietly?

Neal glanced over at Ysatis. She had pulled a sheet over herself but she didn't look scared. He started to break out but he heard the sound of four guns cocking, so he thought the better of it.

Jay, Cas, Wise, and Hop allowed Ysatis a moment before they made a move. Ysatis didn't try to hide anything. She wanted that bastard to know she was involved. She grinned at her brother coldly. She wanted him to know that this was her get-back for him taking away her childhood and making her life so miserable all those years. And for taking Humble away from her.

Ysatis greeted the four armed men jovially like they were old friends. "Hey fellas, what up? Hot damn, ya'll right on time. Take this piece of shit up outta here, please."

Casino said, "With pleasure, lil' ma. With pleasure." Cas looked at Neal and nodded like his number was up. "You bitch ass nigga, get the fuck up!" He snatched Neal out of the bed by his neck.

Jay stuck his hammer on Neal's forehead and bit his lip in anger. He wanted to kill that nigga so bad he could taste it.

Neal was butt naked and that really disgusted them. Wise sneered, "Nigga, put ya' fuckin' drawers back on before I shoot that shit the fuck off." The sight of Neal's penis was grossly offending him.

Hop added, "This nigga need his shit shot off anyway, molestin' his little sister!" He shoved his gun in Neal's mouth. "Bitch ass niggas like you should get it in the throat", he growled.

They made Neal put his clothes back on before they continued. After he was dressed, Jay told him, "Yo, you shouldn't have killed Humble, man."

Contrary to the sea of emotions Jay was feeling, his voice was pretty calm. "He was like a little brother to me, and I take the lost of his life extremely personal. We're supposed to look out for our little brothers and sisters, you know. I got a little sister too, and the way you've been abusing yours sickens me to my stomach."

Jay paused for a second and shook his head. "Scum like you doesn't deserve to live. And by the way, catching you about to pipe your sister just put another nail in your coffin. But I'm having a little dilemma about the way you should die. A part of me just wants to pop you in the head and kill you quick. But another part of me wants your death to be slow and miserable so I can watch you suffer. But maybe we'll just let your sister decide."

Jay looked over at Ysatis. "Ysatis, sweetie. How do you want this prick to go, fast or slow?"

Ysatis was sitting up on the bed with the cover over her because she still didn't have any clothes on. She wrapped the sheet around her middle toga-style and covered her intimate parts, and then she stood up. "I have an idea. Let *me* kill him."

"Ayight shorty. Here you go." Jay handed Ysatis his gun, and he pulled out another one from the back of his pants waist.

Ysatis took the gun and pointed it at her brother with hatred. Neal pleaded with her through his eyes. He knew he was wrong for having sex with her all those times but she was his sister. He didn't believe she was going to kill him.

Ysatis raised the gun and aimed at his head. He looked so pitiful she couldn't do it. She looked at Jay and shook her head, and she directed her next words at Neal. "Neal, I hate you. I hate your fuckin' guts, you son of a bitch. But for some reason, I just can't kill you."

Ysatis stepped up and kneed him hard in the dick. Neal hollered out in pain but her last words had given him a little hope.

Ysatis said, "I should cut that little nasty shit off and shove it up your ass! But like I said, nigga. *I* can't kill you. But my friends here can. They're not scared little girls that you can just take advantage of, you bastard. But not no more. I really loved Humble. Did you know that? And he loved me too. But you just couldn't let me be happy, could you? Neal, I hope you rot in fuckin' hell." She spit in his face.

When Neal heard that he knew it was a wrap. He looked around at the faces of the four gun toting men. He could tell that none of them was playing with him. They meant business, and he detected that they had the hearts of killers. It was in their eyes. He tried to think of a way to buy himself more time.

Ysatis gave the hammer back to Jay. "Please don't kill him here. Just out of respect for my mother, because he is her child too. And please make his body disappear, so me and my mama don't have to waste no money burying him. He ain't worth it."

She looked at Neal and said the last words she would ever say to him. "Good riddance, Neal. You were a waste of breath. I hope maggots eat out of your eyes *and* your ass."

There was no more to be said after that. Neal was quickly forced into his boots and marched out of his home on a journey that he was certain would end in his death. He decided he wasn't going out without putting up a fight. He tried to get away and make a run for his bedroom where his hammer was but he was stopped in his tracks by Cas' big black Mac.

Cas didn't say a word. He just smiled at Neal coldly and nodded his head like he wished he would. Neal got the picture. He held up his hands and surrendered peacefully. He knew he didn't have any wins. Boy, his little sister had really done him in.

Before they left, Jay handed Ysatis an envelope that he knew was going to change her life forever. She didn't know it yet but there was a bonus in there. He and Cas thanked her, and they exited the house just as quietly as they had come.

Outside, they instructed Neal to get in the back of the black Range Rover with dark tinted windows that was parked in front of his crib. Wise drove and Casino rode shotgun. Hop sat in the backseat on Neal's left, and Jay sat on Neal's right. They sandwiched him in the middle and kept their ratchets on him the entire ride.

Neal turned out to be a big rat. They hadn't known anyone else was involved but he started snitching as soon as he got in the car. He gave up Chewy's whereabouts without any persuasion at all. And it wasn't even that he believed that snitching on Chewy would save him. He was just selfish, and didn't want to go down alone. It was Neal's idea but Chewy still played a big part in everything. And it was him who had robbed Humble.

After Neal told them about Chewy, Jay insisted that he call him and lure him out to the car. Neal was a snake anyway so he didn't have a problem with that.

Jay handed him the blow up cell phone, and he called Chewy and asked him to ride with him to these bad ass Puerto Rican bitches' crib in Sunset Park. Chewy said okay, and told him to come pick him up from his house.

As Chewy waited for Neal, he brushed his teeth and then sprayed on Cool Water cologne just in case he got some pussy from one of those bitches later. A few minutes later, Neal called and told him to come on outside.

When they parked outside of Chewy's house, Hop got out and stepped to the side and lit a Newport. When Chewy came out, his face looked like he was wondering whose Range Rover that was. Wise rolled the back window down so he could see Neal's face.

Neal was one grimy dude. He called out to his man, "Yo, Chewy! Come on, son. These my peoples. Get in."

Chewy hesitated so Hop figured he needed a little more persuasion. He stepped over and stuck his gun in his ribs, and he directed him to climb in the backseat quietly.

Chewy tried to get away but Hop smacked him with the gun. "Get in the car, nigga!"

Chewy was taken by surprise. The only thing he could do was make a scene so someone would hear him. "Yo, they kidnappin' me! Somebody help! Yo, Ma! Ma, I'm gettin' kidnapped!" Chewy looked up at his mother's window, praying that she'd heard him.

Hop forced him into the truck and quickly glanced around to see if anyone had seen him, and then he got in and shut the door.

Wise pulled off immediately, coasting along at a speed

that wouldn't seem suspicious. He drove to a warehouse in Queens that belonged to Jay and Cas' former connect, Colombian Manuel. Jay and Cas had quit doing business with Manuel as friends, and sometimes they still did favors for one another.

Jay had made a call along the way and asked Manuel if they could use his facility to handle some business, and he agreed. Manuel referred to his warehouse as "The Meat House" because he said that's where he dealt with the snakes, rats, and cockroaches that made the mistake of crossing him.

When Manuel got the call from Jay he didn't hesitate to offer his assistance. He had done a lot of good business with Jay and Casino, and he knew they were both standup dudes. Anything he could do to make their lives easier, he would do. It was all a part of the code of honor. They were good men.

Manuel wasn't upset with them when they had informed him a few years back that they were set, so they were getting out of the game. They had parted on good terms, not owing each other anything. The two young brothers had even thrown Manuel a lovely parting gift of twenty grand just out of appreciation.

Manuel had helped them out in the beginning by trusting them enough to front them the weight they needed to bubble. Jay and Cas had been grateful for that, and they hadn't messed up and blown the opportunity like a lot of young boys their age would've. Manuel really respected that. Those two had their heads on straight.

He was actually impressed that Jay and Cas had vacated the narcotics game for the music industry. Now that the Reggaeton boom was in effect, Manuel himself had an independent record label with artists of his own. Jay and Casino had showed him the ropes, and he'd had the money to back his own project. The music thing was really paying off too.

Manuel had a lot of love for Jay and Cas. They were smart young men, and he thought of them as his sons in a sense. He had watched their progress from when they first came to him and copped their first big eighth of coke, up until they handled kilos of cocaine and heroin like the pharmaceutical business was their second nature.

Manuel knew he was partially responsible for their success. He had helped them grow. He smiled at the memory like a proud dad, and then he took out his cell phone and called Loco to give the order to assist his young friends. If they needed his help, they had it.

When Jay and them finally arrived at the warehouse, Wise drove up to the gate. Just as Manuel promised, he had one of his sidekicks waiting there to let them in. The guy must've seen them on camera when they came up because the gate opened just in time. Wise drove in and parked, and they got out and marched to the door with their hostages at gunpoint.

Manuel's sidekick, whose name was Loco, didn't speak a word of English but he had been briefed by Manuel already. He understood the part he was to play in the murders that were going to take place. He was the cleanup man. It was his job to get rid of all the mess for Manuel.

Loco greeted them with a simple nod of his head, and he took them on a tour of the butcher shop just as Manuel had instructed. The fellas couldn't believe how much it really looked like something straight out of a mobster movie, complete with meat hooks and the whole nine. The kind of meat hooks you hung a nigga on and left them to die.

Neal and Chewy were the only ones who weren't fascinated by the butcher shop. They were both too busy shitting bricks because they knew they were about to die.

As Hop looked around he got more and more open. He'd always wanted to do some mafia shit like this to a nigga. He was anxious to get on with the torture. He turned to the two would-be victims and told them what they were in store for.

Hop said, "You niggas are meatloaf. Ya'll know that, right? By the time it's over, you mothafuckas gon' be prayin' to die! Oh yes." He rubbed his hands together. "It's time for the good part now."

Hop expected Jay, Cas, and Wise to co-sign with him and scare the dudes up real bad before they killed them but that wasn't any of their styles. None of them talked about the shit they were gonna do because talk was cheap.

Jay looked at Hop running his mouth and shook his head. Without a word, he stepped up and put two bullets in the back of Neal's cranium. Hop flinched. Neal's body had barely hit the floor when Cas followed suit and put a hot slug in Chewy's temple.

Hop stared down at the two bodies' with now disfigured heads in disbelief. It had happed so fast. He looked over at the faces of his accomplices, and they were all expressionless. Loco's face was blank too. It was like they saw shit like this everyday. Hop could tell that he was surrounded by real killers.

Jay motioned for Loco to show them where to put the bodies. Loco shook his head and waved his hands to let Jay know he would take care of everything. The bodies would be disposed of in-house. They were going in a meat grinder, and then they'd be cremated. And then their ashes would be disposed of as well. They'd be poured into the cement at one of Manuel's contracting company's jobs. Both Chewy and Neal's final resting places would be in concrete in someone's driveway or sidewalk somewhere.

Loco showed them to the door and said "adios". He didn't mind cleaning up. That was what he did. And Manuel made sure he was well compensated for it too.

When they got back outside to the truck, Hop was quiet. He had the feeling dudes had words for him. Just as he thought, Wise started in on him first.

"Yo, check this out, son. You talk too fuckin' much, man. Niggas ain't wit' all that talk. You gotta learn how to stop runnin' your mouth all the time." Wise shook his head, clearly irritated with Hop.

Jay or Cas didn't say anything to Hop but they had each already decided that would be the first and last time they ever took him along to do any dirty work. He was just a bunch of talk. They had seen that for themselves. He was shook when he saw them murder those dudes. Hop's gangsta' was definitely questionable.

Chapter Twelve

The next morning, Portia woke up feeling scared for some reason. She just had a bad feeling about something, and her gut told her it was Jay. He had been acting sort of quiet and reserved the night before. Portia knew Jay like a book. That meant he had been up to something.

Portia knew what it probably was too. He had probably gone and retaliated on the dudes that killed Humble. She had asked him to let it go. Portia knew the type of dude Jay was and how he got down, but they had a family now. At one point in their relationship that street part of him had excited her but sometimes it frightened her now. He couldn't be getting himself involved in things that could lead to trouble. And why would he risk being taken away from her and the kids? Portia decided to have a word with him. She had to. She had too many concerns.

When Jay got in later that night, Portia cornered him in their bedroom and asked him what he was up to. At first he tried to act like he didn't know what she was talking about. Portia was worried about him so she didn't back down.

"Don't think I'm stupid, Jay. I know what's going on. Are you tryin' to fuckin' destroy yourself or something? Look around at all the things you've accomplished. Why are you risking it all by gettin' involved in this street shit again?"

Jay still wouldn't respond but Portia knew he knew what she was talking about. He could play that distant shit on somebody else. Portia knew he knew better, so she kept on trying to get through to him.

"Jay, you keep pushin' it. Don't you know that God only allows us a certain amount of fouls before He says, *"Enough is enough. I know you know better, so now I'm gonna punish you."* Jay, you have to keep your soul slate clean. Every negative thing you do puts another mark on your soul."

Portia took his hand. "Baby, you know God knows everything. And when judgment day comes He's gon' count the marks, and that's how He's gonna judge us. Jay, God knows you've killed before, for whatever reasons, and He forgave you. He gave you another chance. Don't you remember your trial? They were try'na give your ass life! But God gave you another chance. And if you keep on, He's gonna show you that He's *not* playin' with you. And you have children, Jay. What about them? Baby, stop try'na play God. You gotta learn to let go and let Him handle it! Please! I'm scared, Jay. I don't wanna lose you. And baby, don't you wanna go to heaven?"

Jay kept his poker face on but he was deeply touched by Portia's words. She almost broke him a couple of times during her speech. He knew she was right. He couldn't front, he was still angry and in need of somebody to take it out on. He needed the talk she gave him. He kept his thoughts to himself and nodded in agreement. "You right, Kit Kat. You right." He could barely look at her.

Jay kissed Portia on the forehead and told her not to worry. He knew a change was in order. He was a man. He knew what he had to do.

$$\$\$\$$$

After Laila took Pebbles to the clinic to terminate her pregnancy, she decided to move out for a while. Laila did this for two reasons. Number one, she wanted Pebbles out of the City and away from that damn pimp. And number two, she needed some space between she and Khalil. He was so far gone she never even discussed Pebbles' situation with him.

Laila wanted Pebbles to understand why she had taken her to get an abortion so she talked to her about the whole ordeal.

She allowed Pebbles to speak freely about her feelings, and the poor child just broke down in tears. She hugged Laila tight and told her how sorry she was for getting tangled up with Ice, having sex, and getting pregnant. She even apologized for catching gonorrhea. Laila told her it was okay but she advised her to play smart from then on. Then she reminded her that even though she tested negative she would still have to get tested for HIV every six months, just to make sure she was okay.

Laila took a couple of days off work to nurse Pebbles. She wanted to monitor her closely. Everything from her body temperature, to the amount of blood she was passing on her pads. Laila knew her daughter had gone through a very serious procedure for an eleven year old child, and she needed a few days to rest and heal.

Ironically, Macy and Pebbles' birthday was the following week. Macy would be thirteen, and Pebbles would be twelve. She had become a woman way before her time, and it saddened Laila's heart deeply.

The day after she took Pebbles to the GYN for a follow-up to make sure she was okay, Laila packed about a weeks worth of clothing, and loaded her girls up in the Lexus and headed for the Holland tunnel, en route to New Jersey. She needed a break for a few days. Hopefully she would get a little peace of mind.

Along the way, she and her daughters talked about their family situation. They seemed to understand that Laila's hands were tied. They knew their father needed help. But Pebbles still cried about leaving her daddy. That proved she was still just a baby, no matter how grown she had been acting lately. Laila consoled her and told her that everything would be okay. She told her that nothing was permanent, and she should really look at it as a vacation for a few days.

Laila had called Portia ahead of time and let her know that they were coming, so Portia was at home busy preparing

their rooms for them.   She and Jay had an eight bedroom
house, and they only had Jayquan and Jazmin.   Their whole
family only used three of their bedrooms so there was plenty
space.   Portia looked forward to Laila and the kids coming.
She had already talked it over with Jay, and he didn't have
a problem with it.   He said they could stay as long as they
needed to.   Portia had told him about Khalil's getting high,
and he felt that Laila deserved better than that.

Laila called Fatima from her car and let her know that
she and the girls would be spending the week at Portia's.
Fatima wasn't offended that Laila hadn't chosen her place
as a retreat because she knew that Portia and Jay had three
more bedrooms than she and Wise had at their crib.   Five
bedrooms were more than enough for Fatima because she
had no plans of having anymore children.   Plus, she knew
that Portia's stepson Jayquan had all the cool stuff teenagers
liked so there was more recreation for Laila's daughters over
there.   Fatima told Laila to go on to Portia's and get situated,
and she would be over there later on.

Knowing that her girlfriends were waiting for her with
open arms caused Laila to accelerate and try to cross that state
line a little quicker.   She asked her girls if they were okay, and
they said they were fine.   Hearing that, Laila turned up the
volume on the car stereo and sang along with one of her
favorite oldies, Earth, Wind, and Fire's "The Reasons".

The kids laughed when Laila tried to hit the high note at
the end, and they begged her to stop.   But they were both
happy to see their mother in high spirits again.   It had sure
been a while since they saw her laughing.

When Laila drove into New Jersey's posh Marquis County
where Portia and Fatima lived, Macy and Pebbles looked
around at all the huge mansion-like houses and couldn't
believe it.

Pebbles said, "Dang, Ma!   Are Auntie Portia and Auntie
Fatima filthy rich now?"

Macy answered her sister. "Shoot, they *must* be if they live in *this* neighborhood. Right, Ma?"

Laila saw how impressed they were, and she just laughed. "I *told* ya'll to think of this as a vacation."

A few minutes later, they turned down Portia's long winding driveway. The house sat up on a hill. Laila had to admit it did look like a castle. Especially in the dusk with the lights twinkling through the windows. Portia was living good, and she was happy for her girl.

Laila pulled up out front and beeped the horn. Portia had been watching out for them for the last twenty minutes so she ran out front to greet them. Jazmin followed close on her heels. Laila hopped out, and she and Portia hugged like they hadn't seen each other in years.

Macy and Pebbles got out, and Portia hugged each of them tight too. She couldn't believe how much they had grown. She had just seen them a few months ago when she was in New York. Portia looked closely at Pebbles to make sure she was okay. Poor baby. She didn't stare long because she didn't want to make her feel uncomfortable. And that would also let her know that Laila had told her business. Portia's heart went out to that little girl because she knew what she had been through. She had been there once herself.

Laila picked Jazmin up and kissed her and tickled her. Jazz just grinned and enjoyed it. She loved her Auntie Laila. Macy and Pebbles took her away from Laila and pinched her cheeks. They kept saying how cute she looked with the two puff-puff ponytails Portia had styled her hair in.

Portia popped Laila's trunk, and she called Jayquan out to help her get their things inside. He came outside to lend them a hand. Jayquan was a well-mannered kid so he welcomed Laila by hugging her and kissing her on the cheek. But he was too cool to hug Pebbles and Macy. He just said "what up" to them. But Portia could've sworn she saw his shoulders straighten up and his walk change after he saw them. She laughed to herself. She couldn't believe Jayquan. Wait until she told Jay that he was starting to like girls.

Portia told everyone to come on inside the house. When they got inside, she showed everyone to their rooms. The girls were delighted that they'd have their own rooms with televisions in them. Portia and Laila left them to get settled in, and they headed for Laila's room. When Laila saw that Portia had set her up in a master suite she broke into a grin. She had her own bathroom and a huge walk-in closet.

She thanked Portia for the umpteenth time. "Girl, I feel better already. I really needed to get away. Thanks, P. You true-blue, Ma-ma."

Portia smiled. "Oh, stop it, honey cabbage. You know how we do. If the shoe was on the other foot, you'd do the same for me."

Laila nodded. She certainly would. She and Portia went back downstairs, and they saw that Macy and Pebbles had already made themselves at home. They had taken off their shoes, and were in the den with Jayquan and Jazz watching videos. Pebbles was showing them how to do that dance, "The Chicken Noodle Soup". She was getting down too. Laila and Portia laughed when they saw her.

A warm, good feeling overcame Laila. Tears came to her eyes. She was happy to see her daughter acting like a normal kid again. She could already tell that week would be good for all of them.

A little while later, Jay came home. When he saw Laila and the kids, he hugged them all and welcomed them. He told them that they were not guests because his house was their house. Macy and Pebbles liked the sound of that.

Macy asked Jay, "Uncle Jay, are you rich?"

Jay just laughed. "Nah. I'm just an old bum. I live in a cardboard box."

Macy looked around and loudly exclaimed, "This sure as hell ain't no doggone cardboard box!"

Laila's mouth dropped in shock but she laughed along with everyone else. That girl was something else.

Jay had a long day so he said goodnight to everyone and headed upstairs. He was tired but he also had a lot on his mind. No sooner than he had gone upstairs then Jazmin came running up there behind him. She peeked in the bedroom where he was. Jay knew she was going to jump out and try to scare him, but he saw her first. He hurried over and scooped her up.

"Ah ha, I saw you! You can't scare me, girl. You can't scare your daddy." Jay planted kisses all over her face, and then he picked her up high in the air. Jazmin laughed and screamed at the top of her lungs. Jay laughed and threw her down on the bed, and she started jumping up and down.

Jazmin was smart for her age. She knew not to jump on the bed around Portia but she took advantage and did it every time she was alone with Jay. She knew her daddy would let her. He always spoiled her rotten.

Jay sat down on the edge of the bed and unlaced his Timbs. Jazmin got down and helped him pull them off. Jay laughed and asked her if she was ready to go to bed. Jazmin quickly said no, and she gave him a goodnight kiss and went back downstairs with Portia.

Jay watched his daughter walk away and he counted his blessings. He had a beautiful family, and he found peace at home around them. He had a good woman who had his back, a wonderful son who his good woman loved and cared for as if he was her own, and a little chocolate princess for a daughter. That was the whole package. A man couldn't ask for anything more.

Jay was wealthy but money wasn't shit without happiness. He knew some dudes with major bread that were extremely unhappy and in need of hugs. Thinking about his family made Jay think about the dirt he had recently done.

He couldn't front. Doing away with those dudes that

killed Humble hadn't really made him feel any better. He was still feeling his little man's loss. And furthermore, he had a family. Why was he out there doing shit like that? And then he dragged Cas and Wise into it too.

The music business had been lucrative to them. Their money had grown pretty long over the past few years. They were respected businessmen, and they had to display proper decorum now. And they all had wives and children so it wasn't even about them anymore. It was about their seeds.

Dudes were in their thirties now so they had to act accordingly. There was no time for them to be going through phases. They had too much coming up on their roster. Wise' new album was about to drop, Kira was back in the studio, and they had to figure out what to do with Hop.

Jay laid down and stretched out across the bed for a minute. He looked over at the silver framed photos of him, Portia, and the children sitting on the nightstand. Jay smiled at the images. The new duvet Portia had just put on their king-sized bed was so comfortable, he closed his eyes and snoozed.

$$$

A few days later, it was the night of Wise' album release party. It was held at Club Billions, and the turnout exceeded their expectations. Luckily everything went smooth. All of Wise' peoples came out to show their support. There were some pretty big names in the hip-hop there too, including Jay-Z, Nas, Busta, Jermaine Dupri, Three-Six Mafia, T.I., Irv and Chris Gotti, Beef & Broccoli, and more. There were some R & B dons and divas up in there too, like Mary J. Blige, Usher, Jahiem, Neyo, and Lady Goines.

Wise had danced with Christina Milian earlier that night but shorty was fronting. She told him she loved his music, and she kept flirting with him, so he knew he could score.

He wanted to hit that but he couldn't really press her because every time he turned around Fatima was right by his side.

Fatima was his wife, and Wise did the honorable thing by courting her on his arm and posing for photos all night. And he didn't mind because Fatima was largely responsible for his success. Her prior experience working at a record company had really helped them when she came on board at Street Life when they first started out.

At the end of the night Wise was tipsy and found himself feeling extremely frisky. He loved his wife but he was in the mood for something a little different. Wise knew if he wanted to get something popping that night it would have to be with a straight jump-off, because Tima was on him. But where there was a will, there was a way. After he'd caught Fatima getting eaten out by that lesbian out by the pool, he felt a lot less compelled to be faithful to her. He still got tight at her every time he thought about that shit.

Wise had a little too much to drink, but it was thinking about Fatima with that bitch that really powered his next move. He got bold and decided that he was going to get some head from one of the broads at his party. He drank straight from a bottle of Cristal and scanned the room for some easy action.

As if on cue, a jump-off from Wise' past came right into his radar. Portia's cousin Melanie was standing on a table to his right, dancing and seductively winding her hips. She had on an extremely short and tight denim dress with hot pink colored leggings on underneath, and a pair of hot pink stiletto ankle boots. Wise' interest level peaked.

For a second, he reminisced about the way he used to face fuck Melanie. He remembered how much her throat felt like a pussy, and his dick got hard. She was a "yes girl". She used to agree to every single dirty thing he suggested. Wise had even foot fucked her once.

He decided to go on and make that happen. His only

problem was that Fatima was there. A few minutes later, Fatima, Portia, and Laila went to the ladies room. As soon as they walked off, Wise sent his little homie Reg to tell Melanie he wanted to get with her later.

When Fatima came back from the ladies room Wise told her he was leaving because he was tired. He asked her if she was ready to go. To his dismay, Fatima said yes. Wise' hopes fell, but they rose once again when she told him she was riding with her girls because they were stopping at a diner to get some breakfast.

He knew he had a window of opportunity now. He could go get right and still beat Fatima home. Hell, as drunk as he was he only needed a minute. He wasn't about to romance Melanie or anything. Shit, she probably wouldn't get anything out of what he was in the mood for.

Wise chuckled to himself because he knew that wasn't true. Melanie would be getting something out of it. Her pleasure would come from the opportunity to pleasure him. He was a million dollar mothafucka. He could have any bitch he wanted.

When Melanie got the proposition from Wise' messenger, she told him she was with it and gave him her cell phone number to give Wise. Melanie smirked to herself because she couldn't wait to see the look on Wise' face when she told him there was a price to spend time with her now. That nigga had to cough up before she gave it up. It was a new day, and Melanie had stepped her game up. She earned her bread the horizontal way now. A dude had to look out. Especially Wise, because he had dissed her and cut her off after he married Fatima. Melanie had accepted it and moved on but she was still a little scorned. She knew Wise would be back, and she had vowed to tax him when he returned.

Wise located Casino and Jay. The two of them were wrapping up a conversation with two bigwigs from Columbia Records. Street Life Entertainment's contract with Universal had just ended and so far they'd opted not to renew. Word traveled fast, and all of the majors were courting them again. The offers were getting sweeter and sweeter.

Wise gave his mans a pound and told them he was about to be out. Jay saw the Cristal bottle in his hand and expressed his opinion. He didn't think he should drive when he'd been drinking so much.

Casino agreed, and he took the bottle from Wise and told him he'd had enough. He told Wise to go home with his wife. Wise just laughed and told them he was going to get his dick sucked first.

Jay and Cas didn't really approve of his plans but they didn't care where he went, as long as he didn't attempt to drive himself there. He was their man, as well as an artist on their label so it was their duty to protect him.

Wise ignored the looks Cas and Jay gave him. He knew they were looking at him like that because he had told them a thousand times how he had to stop cheating on Fatima before he lost her. But Wise couldn't tell them that he was only about to cheat because he caught Fatima cheating with another woman. Jay and Cas were his mans but he had been too ashamed to tell them about that one. Wise gave both of them a pound and said goodnight.

Before Wise knew it, Casino threw him in a headlock and held him while Jay went through his pockets and got his car keys. After Cas saw that Jay had the keys, he gave Wise a noogie on the forehead and let him go. He and Jay laughed.

Cas said, "Friends don't let friends drink and drive. Try to leave without these keys. I dare you, nigga."

Jay laughed again and co-signed. "Word, son. You don't need to drive like that. You're bent, so just take a limo."

Wise started to tell his boys that they couldn't stop him. He had a code to unlock his car doors and start the keyless ignition, but he agreed to have a limo take him home. That would be perfect. He could get some brains right in the back.

When Wise got outside to his designated limousine, he called Melanie on her cell phone and told her to meet him down the street. She agreed, and about five minutes later she came walking up to the limo. Wise quickly let her in and told the driver to pull off.

In the back of the limousine, Wise began fondling Melanie immediately. He figured she knew what it was already so they could go on and get straight to the shit. Wise saw that she wasn't wearing a bra, so he attempted to free her left breast from the denim halter dress she had on. Her tities were just spilling out at him.

He was being a little rough and Melanie was beginning to feel like a piece of meat so she grabbed his hand and stopped him. "*Hello*. Hi Wise. Yes I'm fine, and how are you?"

Wise laughed. She was right. Damn, he could've at least spoken to her. "Yo, my bad. What up, Mel? What's shakin'? I ain't seen you in a minute."

Melanie sucked her teeth. "Oh, nigga please. I've been around. You just been ignorin' a bitch. And now you try'na get some ass. Damn, Wise. You must really think I'm stupid." She rolled her eyes at him and crossed her arms.

Wise didn't usually hold his tongue but he had to stop himself from saying, "*I wasn't try'na get some ass, I just wanted some head. And I do think you're stupid. That's the only reason I called you out here.*"

Instead he just said, "Come on, Mel. You know how we do." That was all she was getting. He wasn't about to beg no scallywag to suck him off. Fuck that. Wise knew Melanie wasn't very intelligent. He could talk her out of some ass in less than twenty seconds.

Melanie stuck to her guns. "Yeah, I know how we *used* to do, but things changed a little. I'ma need to be compensated now, if you want me to play mistress. You understand,

Wise?"

At first Wise looked at her like she was crazy. He started to say, *"Bitch, I'll pay you no mothafuckin' mind!"* But instead he opted to tell her what she wanted to hear. "Ayight. So what's your price?"

Mel looked thoughtful for a second. She didn't want to sell herself cheap. Wise was getting it. An expensive gift wouldn't hurt him. Without blinking an eye she looked at him and stated, "I want a mink. Full-length."

Wise almost laughed in her face. What type of wife-like, main-bitch demands was Melanie making? Was she on drugs? Who was she kidding? She was nothing but a skeeze. The lie Wise told her rolled off his tongue so naturally it almost seemed true. "Ayight, Mel. I got you."

At first Melanie looked at him like she didn't believe him. "You promise?"

Wise acted like he was offended. "Yo, I said I got you! A mink ain't shit to me. That's light, Ma. I got you." Wise sealed it with a sincere look.

After that, Melanie believed him. Her face lit up. She hadn't known it would be that easy.

Wise could tell she bought it so he continued gaming her. "Mel, my money is long. Just like this big, black snake I want you to see." Wise unzipped his pants and pulled out his penis.

He placed Melanie's hand on his dick. "Look, he won't bite you. Go 'head, give him a lil' kiss."

Satisfied that she was getting her fur coat, Melanie was prepared to work for it now. She leaned forward and slowly swallowed the whole length of Wise' dick and squeezed her throat on the tip.

Wise leaned his head back and enjoyed the moment. Damn, that was just what he needed. He wrapped Melanie's hair around his fist and guided her head up and down. She was working on his joint like a pro. Wise raised his hips and started humping her face. He wanted to slide his dick all the way down in her chest. Melanie gagged and choked but she didn't complain.

A few minutes of this was more than Wise could stand. He was about to bust. Oh shit! He gritted his teeth and groaned, and he squirted hot jizm right into Melanie's digestive system. When she realized he was cumming she tried to get up but Wise wouldn't release her head until she swallowed every drop.

As Wise' penis shrunk, he laughed to himself. He had promised Melanie a mink for that blowjob but somebody should've told her dumb ass to get her money up front. It wasn't that he didn't have the bread for the coat. He just wasn't into trickin' on chickens. He could've bought her ten furs if he wanted to but Wise didn't regard Melanie classy enough to muscle a gift that nice out of him. Besides, he had already got what he wanted from her so the only way Melanie would get a mink coat from him now would be if she stole it.

Wise went in his pocket and pulled out a brick. He peeled off five c-notes and handed them to Melanie for cab fare and pocket money. She could squeeze a hairdo, lunch, and a couple pairs of $54.11 Reeboks out of that. That was the best he would do for her. He was sleepy now, and he just wanted her out. Wise assured her that he would call her the following evening, and he dropped her off at the next corner. After that, he instructed the driver to take him home to Jersey.

Melanie stood on the curb in Manhattan where Wise had dropped her off, trying to flag a taxi. She couldn't help but gloat because she had earned herself a mink that night. It wasn't in her possession yet but Wise had promised. And the five hundred dollars he had just given her showed good faith on his part.

Melanie smiled. She used to really like Wise. Maybe they

could establish something this time around. She thought about it, and she realized that she hadn't even gotten his cell phone number. He'd better call her like he said he would. Mel peeped at the five crisp c-notes in her purse and felt assured that he would.

Chapter Thirteen

Late the following morning, Cas woke up in bed beside Kira but there was nothing but Laila on his mind. To be honest, he had fallen asleep thinking of her as well. At Wise' album release party the night before, Cas had got a chance to corner her briefly and get her cell number.

He had learned from a casual conversation with Jay a few days ago that Laila and her kids had been staying at him and Portia's crib for a little while. When Casino found that out he played it cool but truth be told, there had been nights he'd wanted to creep over there and scoop her up.

But now that he had Laila's number safely stored in his cell phone under a business contact's name, he felt positive that their time would come. The night before, he had been a little tipsy so he had almost been candid and told her he wanted her back in his life. He had just wanted to lean forward and kiss her lips so badly.

But Cas knew if he'd done that all eyes would have been on them. Even though Kira was busy grinning in that little rapper dude from Atlanta, Young Vee's face like some unmarried slut all night. Cas hadn't even spoke on it because he didn't really care.

He was preoccupied with wanting Laila. He wasn't the type to not get what he wanted. The more he thought about it, he knew he had to have her. It was like she had something over him. Something mystical. Perhaps he was charmed. He closed his eyes and imagined her pretty face with its smooth coffee bean colored skin, full succulent lips, exotic slanted eyes, and long silky black hair.

Cas longed to run his fingers through her tresses and make love to her. That was the part that really got him. He didn't want to just fuck Laila. He wanted to make love to her.

With passion. He was attracted to her soul.

To Cas, the fact that she had that effect on him was strange. The urge to touch her overcame him so much his penis hardened. He laughed at himself when he realized that he was laying in bed with a woody from thinking about some chick, like he was a teenaged boy. He was a millionaire, and could have any woman he wanted.

But at the time there was no woman he wanted more than he wanted Laila. Cas made up his mind. Laila was going to be his. That was all there was too it. He was willing to put money on it.

$$$

Meanwhile, Laila was at Portia and Jay's house laying in her bed thinking about Cas too. He was so attractive she found it hard to think about much else. She could still smell his cologne from the night before when they'd conversed briefly. Casino was just such a real man. He was the kind Laila needed in her life. A genuinely good brother, inside and out. Cas just possessed so many of the qualities she loved in a man.

Laila reminisced about the few precious times they had been intimate years ago. Cas was packing, and he had some good ass dick too. Laila wished she could've awakened in his arms. She had given him her cell phone number so she really hoped that would happen sometime in the near future.

She knew Casino was married to Jay's sister, Kira, but Laila guessed that their marriage was on the rocks because last night she had seen Kira acting real friendly with that dirty south rapper, Young Vee. Seeing that had helped influence Laila's decision to slide Cas her digits. Boy, Kira was a dumb bitch. If Laila had Cas now, she wouldn't have fucked that up for the world. Homegirl obviously didn't know what she had.

Laila wouldn't have admitted it to anybody, not even Portia or Fatima, but she wanted to be the woman in Cas' life. She wanted to be his wifey. The attraction between the two of them was just so strong. But Laila was smart enough to know that everything was far too complicated to be that simple. Hell, she had more baggage than Cas did. But regardless of the facts, Laila secretly had high hopes for her and Cas' future.

Laila snapped back to reality and got out of bed a few minutes later. It was time to get her day started. She had to go to Brooklyn to get some more clothes for her and the girls, and she needed to check on her house.

Laila got in the shower with Casino still on her mind. The thought of him aroused her. When she was done washing her body she turned the shower massage on full blast and aimed between her legs. She targeted her joy button, which was literally thumping with the anticipation of Cas. Laila sprayed a jet stream of water on her clit until she couldn't stand it anymore. She moaned, and when she came she came hard. The water left Laila breathing hard and trembling like she had just gotten her pussy eaten by America's finest. What an orgasm! She leaned onto the shower wall for support.

After Laila regrouped, she rinsed her sticky pleasure juices away and got out the shower and got dressed. She put on a cute but casual green safari styled Proenza Schouler pants suit. After she got ready, she woke up her daughters to see if they wanted to go with her.

To Laila's surprise, neither Macy nor Pebbles wanted to ride. Their lazy behinds had stayed up all night playing video games with Jayquan. When Laila and Portia came in from Wise' party the night before, all of the kids had been awake. Even little five year old Jazmin and her cousin Jahseim. Jayquan and Pebbles were talking about they were all "breakin' day".

Laila let Pebbles and Macy go back to sleep because she

knew they were okay. They were comfortable, and Portia was their auntie. She would look after them. Laila went down the hall and saw that Portia's bedroom door was closed. She figured she was still asleep too, so she left a note that said she would be back in a few hours. Laila went outside and hopped in her Lexus, and she headed for the City.

For some reason, her stomach tightened more and more as she got closer to her house. There was no telling what she was in store for. She kind of hoped Khalil wasn't at home so she wouldn't have to face him.

The more Laila thought about Khalil, the more concerned she became. She had been thinking about Cas so much that Khalil had received very little attention in her mind the past few days. New Jersey just seemed like a whole new world. A better one.

But as Laila neared her exit on the New Jersey Turnpike, she wondered if Khalil was okay. Was he eating well? She hadn't left him any money because she knew he would've misused the funds anyway. She made up her mind to stop at the supermarket and pick up a few things.

Laila took out her cell phone and dialed *67 to block her number, and then she dialed her house phone to see if he picked up. Nobody answered so she figured he wasn't at home. She was relieved. It was sad to say, but she was avoiding him. The weakness he had displayed by getting hooked on drugs had really turned her off.

When she got in Brooklyn, Laila stopped at Pathmark for the groceries, and she arrived at her house about thirty minutes later. When she got inside, she froze in the doorway.

Laila dropped her bags in shock, and her mouth just hung open. What the fuck?! She looked around and couldn't believe it. The front room of her house looked like it had been burglarized. All of the electronics, including the widescreen LCD television that was mounted on the wall and the state of the art surround sound stereo, were missing. The framed art on the walls was all gone, and so was her beautiful eight thousand dollar sheepskin rug. The room looked so bare Laila broke down and cried.

It took her a second to get herself together. She picked up the grocery bags and carried them in the kitchen and sat them down on the counter. The kitchen looked okay. At least he didn't sell the refrigerator. Laila headed upstairs to inspect the rest of the house, holding her breath along the way.

As she walked upstairs, she thought about the time when Khalil had found out she cheated on him and beat her up, and Cas had winded up coming inside her house to rescue her. He had even taken her to the hospital to see about her broken ribs. Laila wished Cas would show up and rescue her from her nightmare this time. The abuse wasn't physical, but seeing that Khalil had sold all of the stuff in her living room was quite a gut shot.

Laila checked the kids' bedrooms and everything seemed intact, but when she got to her bedroom she started crying again. It looked like a scene from a documentary called "A Junkie's Monologue". All of Laila's pocketbooks were strewn about like he had been checking them for money, and he had dumped all the clothes in the drawers out onto the floor. The bedroom TV was missing as well, but the icing on the cake was the hundreds of little colorful crack vials all over the floor.

Laila sat down on the foot of the bed. She felt weak. It took her a minute to digest that one. It was evident that Khalil had been on a serious mission. Laila felt like she was at her breaking point. This was all she could take. Khalil was behaving like he was trying to kill himself. It seemed like he had been smoking enough damn crack to bust his heart. He was traveling high-speed on a path of self-destruction, and she didn't think she could save him.

Laila decided to wait around to see if he came home

anytime soon. She wanted to look in his face and ask him why he was doing that to himself, and to their family. She had to make him see that he was destroying everything they had built together. He had to tell her something that day because if he had no intentions on bettering himself, then she was giving up on him.

While Laila waited, she packed all of the valuables left in the house that she could fit in her car. When she looked in the closet, she noticed that the chinchilla coat Khalil bought her was missing too. She didn't know if she was more angry, or more hurt. She calculated more than fifty thousand dollars worth of stuff to be missing from her home. And what had he gotten for it? Probably just a few bullshit dollars, or a little bit of crack. That was another reason Laila wanted to see him. She wanted to know where her damn stuff was.

She knew if he'd sold it to strangers or hustlers she had slim chances of ever seeing it again, but if he'd taken it to a pawn shop she could get it back. She hoped and prayed he'd pawned it.

After Laila made her last trip to the car she looked down the block and saw Khalil walking up. Or rather, it was a shadow of Khalil because this man looked wild and unkempt. His clothes were dirty, he needed a haircut and a shave bad as hell, and his face looked sunken in. Damn, homeboy had lost a lot of weight. Way too much.

Laila was overcome with the urge to get in her car and flee. The sight of him brought tears to her eyes. Maybe she was too emotional to face him right then. Laila could tell from the look on Khalil's face that he'd noticed her. At first he looked happy, and then he looked shamed.

When Khalil saw Laila, he unconsciously looked down at his attire. What was she doing there? Were the kids home too? Oh shit, had they seen the way he'd left the house? He hadn't cleaned up after himself after a little party he'd had, during which he'd stayed awake smoking for fifty seven hours straight. Khalil remembered the fact that he had sold a couple of things in the house for some extra cash.   He wondered if they'd noticed anything missing.

Khalil knew he had to do something. If Laila wasn't serious about leaving him permanently before, she would be after she saw the house. He tried to play it cool.

He walked up to her and tried to put his arm around her. "Laila! Welcome home, baby. I sure missed my wife. You hear me, girl? I missed you. Where's my kids?"

Laila froze in disgust when Khalil tried to hug her. She took a step back. Was he crazy? She tried to find the right words for him. She just couldn't believe how bad he looked.

Laila took a deep breath before she spoke, hoping her voice wouldn't crack. "The kids are not with me, thank God. They sure don't need to see you like *this*. What are you doin' to yourself, Khalil?"

Khalil tried to make light of the seriousness of the matter, but he could see in Laila's face that she wasn't playing with him. He brushed the question off and changed the subject. "You know what, Laila? I've been thinkin'. I think we should have another baby. You promised you were gonna give me a son. Remember? Let's go 'head and try for that boy." Khalil winked at her and licked his chapped white lips.

Laila just stared at him like he was stupid. Did he actually think she would let him touch her looking like that?   And especially after he sold all her shit. Speaking of which, she proceeded to question him about her belongings.

"Fool, ain't nobody 'bout to have no damn baby. Where are my televisions, my framed art collection, my rug, my chinchilla, and all the rest of the stuff that's missing from my house?"

Khalil didn't answer her at first. After a moment he just said, "Here and there."

Laila tried to be patient with him. "Okay. And where is here and there?"

Khalil replied nonchalantly, "Oh, a little here, and a little there. I just needed a few dollars to pay a couple of bills. I'm gon' replace everything that's missing, so don't worry."

Laila sighed. "So where is it? Is there anyway I can get it back?"

Khalil could hear the hopefulness in her voice, and that made him feel terrible. There was no point in leading her on because he knew the chances of him getting back that stuff were probably nonexistent.

"Look, Laila. I *said* I'ma replace everything. It was time to remodel anyway. I just wanted to make some changes before you and the kids came home, but you caught me off guard."

Laila listened to his sorry ass excuses and she knew it was a wrap. She could kiss her things goodbye. What really pissed her off was the fact that he couldn't look her in her eyes and admit that he needed some help. Why couldn't he just man up? That nigga was living in a fog of denial.

Laila loved him dearly because he was her children's father but she had to leave him. She couldn't sacrifice anymore for him than she had. There was nothing left to do but put him in the hands of the Lord.

Laila didn't really want to leave their house in his care, but there wasn't much else in there he could sale. She still had a soft spot in her heart for Khalil so she didn't insist that he leave the house. She simply asked him not to sale anything else for the sake of their children, and she said goodbye.

Laila climbed in her Lexus and headed back to New Jersey, but she left a huge piece of herself with him. A great big chunk of her heart.

$$$

Back in Jersey, Jay woke up pretty late in the afternoon. He stretched and looked over at Portia in the bathroom with the door open. Their master bathroom was huge. It had two toilets, a urinal, two sinks, a huge hot tub, and two huge walk-in showers.

Portia had just got out of the shower, and she was still was naked. Jay was immediately aroused. He was laying under the cover on his back with his arms crossed behind his head. He looked down and watched the cover rise as his penis hardened.

Portia bent down to rub lotion on her calves and Jay stared at her fat ass up in the air. From the angle he was watching he could see all up in it. He got up and headed for the bathroom to take a piss, deliberately brushing against Portia's butt on his way to the urinal. She smiled at him and watched as he took a leak. Jay farted after he peed, and Portia wrinkled her nose and laughed.

"And good morning to you too, sunshine", she teased. She didn't care about Jay passing gas. They had been together for a long time, and they were comfortable around each other. They didn't tiptoe around one another.

Portia rubbed peach scented Platinum Secret deodorant under her arms and got ready to step into her thong. Jay stopped her and told her to wait until he brushed his teeth. Portia grinned. She knew what that meant. She was about to get some action.

She waited patiently for Jay to wash his face and brush his teeth. When he was done, Portia crawled in front of him seductively and kneeled down at his feet. She gently removed his hard penis from his boxers and stroked it gingerly. She lovingly placed it against her cheek.

Jay looked down at her in front of him on the bathroom floor and was down for whatever she had in mind. He urged her to go on with his eyes.

Portia could take a hint. She held Rocky with both hands and licked the tip like it was a big lollipop of her favorite flavor. Then she slid the length deep down her warm throat.

Jay breathed deeply in effort to hold back his moans. Portia's head game was lethal. He had taught her well. She continued pleasing him until his knees felt like they were going to buckle.

Jay didn't want to cum yet so he stopped her and pulled her to her feet. Portia rose, and she tiptoed and placed a light kiss on his lips. Jay picked her up and sat her on the sink, and he kneeled down and stuck his tongue in her pussy and twirled it in and out. Portia breathed heavily and humped his face. He guessed she liked that. Jay stuck his tongue in as deep as he could. That was his pussy so he didn't mind diving in. He knew she kept it super clean.

Portia came all over Jay's face, and then she begged him to make love to her. Her body ached with desire for him. Jay got up and grabbed her ass and slid his dick in right there on the sink. Portia held her legs up in the air while he deep stroked inside of her. She purred that she loved him over and over again.

Jay was amazing. She held on to his shoulders and wrapped her legs around his waist while he pounded her with intensity. The sex was so good both of them were approaching their peak. Seconds later, their bodies trembled with orgasmic waves and they breathed heavily in each other's arms.

Jay kissed Portia on her shoulder. He loved her sexy brown skin. She was so soft. After he caught his breath a little, he turned on the shower and hopped in. Portia joined him for a second to wash away their juices between her legs.

A few minutes later, Jay got dressed and thought about his partner, Casino. Jay knew something about Cas that he hadn't let on. He had seen him talking to Laila the previous night at the party. Jay didn't talk about Laila to Cas but he knew he still dug her. Jay couldn't really blame him either because Laila was a fine woman. And not even just in the looks department. She was a classy broad who carried herself well.

Jay couldn't front, it had crossed his mind that the possibility of Laila being so close would be too much temptation for Cas to handle. Cas was married to his little sister but he was his friend first. Jay didn't put him and Kira together, and he wasn't about to play super sleuth trying to hold them together. Jay was a realist, and he had time and time again witnessed what patience Cas had for Kira's childish ways. She was spoiled and sometimes she could be real immature.

Like that shit she had pulled at the party last night. Kira had played that little rapper dude from down south, Young Vee, way too close all night. She had been disrespectful, and Jay himself had wanted to check her about that. So he could just imagine how Cas had felt. But Cas was a cool levelheaded dude, so he had just let Kira play herself.

That being said, Jay wasn't about to clock Cas' every move because Kira was no angel. If Cas chose to rekindle whatever flame he and Laila had then that was his business. Jay knew he was a good dude, and his sister and nephew would be well taken care of regardless.

Chapter Fourteen

Melanie had gone for her weekly ten dollar wash and set that Monday, and she sat under the dryer and watched Francesca, her Dominican hair stylist, removing rollers from the long healthy hair of a popular neighborhood transvestite named Jacinta. Jacinta was a regular at the salon like Melanie, and many women envied his glossy, bouncy, always perfectly coiffed mane.

Melanie's dryer stopped, and she listened to Jacinta give Francesca an account of his prior weekend with some very wealthy, married man. He-she was carrying on about how he had the man in his pocket, and if he didn't get everything he wanted he was going to expose him.

Jacinta said, "That's right, I'll let every mothafuckin' body know. His wife, his mother, his pastor, his neighbors, and his kids." He-she snapped his fingers up in the air ethnically.

"I am a fly ass, vindictive bitch. I play by the rules but if a mothafucka tries to shit me, I'll destroy his ass. Umm hmm, honey. That's right. You can't play with these mothafuckas. They gots to pay up."

Francesca finished styling him so Jacinta looked in the mirror and shook his hair and tossed it over his shoulder like a certified diva. "Oh yeah, that's nice. I look simply amazing." He-she got up and headed for the register to pay.

"Melanie", Francesca called out in her thick Dominican accent. "Come mommy."

Melanie got up from her dryer and went and sat in Francesca's styling chair. Francesca smiled at Melanie in the mirror and started taking her rollers out. On his way out, Jacinta stopped and stuck Francesca's tip in the side pocket of her jeans.

"Thank you, mommy", said Francesca.

"No, sweetie. *Thank you!*" Jacinta flipped his hair to the side and winked at her. He-she waved at Melanie and the rest of the ladies in there, and put on his Chanel shades like he was Jackie Onassis and made his grand exit. He had on a pair of tight Versace jeans and stilettos, and he had a supermodel walk that was ready for the runway.

None of the women could front. That mothafucka was one fly ass bitch. He-she stayed designer down from head to toe, and had a pair of breasts and a high firm ass women envied. He-she dressed classy, and rocked a variety of furs in the wintertime. Mink, chinchilla, coyote, beaver, raccoon, sable, fox, lynx, you name it.

Wise hadn't bought Melanie's mink coat yet. In fact, it had been a month and he hadn't even called her. Melanie was beginning to believe that she had been played. She felt slighted, and that day she decided to do something about it. Jacinta didn't know it but he had given Melanie an idea. He-she was right, you had to be vindictive with niggas. Melanie put her plan together while Francesca blew out her roots with a comb and a blow-dryer.

When Mel left the salon she felt pumped. She was going to make Wise come up off that coat, so he might as well get ready to ante up. She needed to get in touch with him but she didn't have his number. Melanie called Portia and tried to get it from her.

Portia was braiding Jazmin's hair when her phone rang. She saw Mel's number on her caller ID. She answered quickly so she wouldn't wake up Jazz. She only had two more braids left. Her little girl was very active, and it was hell trying to braid her hair while she was awake. "What up, Melly Mel?", Portia asked softly.

Mel said, "Hey, Porsh. What up, Ma? What you doin'?"

"Braidin' Jazz hair. What up, girl?"

"Nothin'. Everything is everything. Since you busy, I ain't gon' keep you long. Listen, I need a favor. I need Wise' phone number, P."

Portia got quiet. Why was Mel asking her to get caught up in her shit? "Mel, I thought you stopped messin' with Wise. Why do you want his number?"

"I did stop messin' wit' him, but we hooked up after his album release party. I really need to speak to him, P."

Mel sounded serious but Portia couldn't give her that number. Wise was married to one of her best friends. "Mel, don't take this the wrong way, but if he wanted you to have his number he would've given it to you. I told you to think smart and stop lettin' Wise play you. He is married, Mel. You were the jump-off. Now you gotta live with that. I don't understand you. You *had* a good man, and you let him go. Montrell treated you like a lady, but you prefer the drama and shit."

Melanie was sick of Portia throwing that in her face all the time. "Trell was a good dude, but I'm a free spirit. And plus, he didn't have enough money. I want me a rich nigga like you got, P. You can't fault me for that."

Portia just sighed. "Girl, you don't know what you want. Just be careful, Mel. You can't trust these dudes. And I hope you're protecting yourself. Don't fuck around and catch something. You're getting out there too much again, Mel."

Melanie cut Portia off before she went further into another one of her long lectures. She didn't want to hear that shit. She saw that she had to lie to make Portia give her that number. She acted like she was beginning to cry. "Portia, please. Not now. I *really* need this dude's number. I'm pregnant, P."

Portia couldn't believe her cousin. "What!? By *Wise?*"

"Yes! That's why I need his number. I gotta tell him."

Portia asked, "You sure it's his, Mel?"

"Yeah! Come on, I don't get down like *that*", Mel said defensively.

Who was she kidding? Portia didn't want anything to do with this one. If Fatima found out all hell was gonna break

loose. But if Mel was really pregnant, she had the right to
speak to Wise. She was a slut but she was still Portia's family.
If Wise hit that raw he needed to man up. "Mel, you try'na
keep it?"

Melanie sighed. "I don't know yet. I wanna see what he
talkin' about first."

Portia understood that part. "Mel, you better not tell him
I gave you this number. You hear me?"

"I won't, Porsh. Thanks."

Portia gave her the number, and then she asked her if she
was okay.

"Yeah, I'm okay. I'll let you know what this dude says,
ayight? Later, Porsh. Good lookin', boo." Melanie hung
up.

She called Wise seconds later. He picked up on the fourth
ring.

"Yo", Wise answered.

"Hello? Wise?"

When Wise heard that it was Melanie on the phone, he
asked her where she got his number from. She told him
she got it from the phone company but he knew that was
bullshit.

Melanie asked Wise why she hadn't heard from him lately,
and he told her he had been real busy. She asked him if he'd
forgotten about his promise to buy her a mink, and he said
he hadn't. Then he told her he would call her back and hung
up the phone.

After Wise hung up, he was tight at first. That bitch had a
lot of nerve calling him and pressing him about some fucking
coat. But then Wise thought about Mel's full soft lips on his
cock, and that changed his whole outlook. He decided that
he would call her back a little later. He wasn't buying her
stupid ass no mink, but he could sure use some head.

After Wise hung up on Mel, she knew she was going
through with her plan. He had sounded annoyed and

dismissed her like she was nothing on the phone. She felt cheap. She vowed to get him the next opportunity she had. No matter how long it took.

Melanie got her opportunity a lot quicker than she had anticipated. Wise called her back about two hours later. Mel's first thought was that he was calling to tell her he was coming to pick her up to go fur shopping. Now she felt bad that she had been scheming on him. Maybe he really did care about her.

When Wise got Mel on the phone, he told her to take a cab to a discreet but classy hotel where he'd reserved a suite. He didn't tell her but he got the suite solely for the purpose of getting off in her mouth.

When Wise didn't say anything on the phone about going shopping, Melanie realized that he was just trying to use her for sex again. She decided to pull everything she had up her sleeve out on his ass. She told Wise it was good that he called her because she was in the mood for something real freaky. She asked him if he had another friend they could ménage with.

Wise wasn't with the threesome thing unless it was with two bitches, but he lied and told her he could accommodate her request. He told Mel to take a cab, and to hurry. He only had a two hour window before he had to go pick up his daughter from her grandparents' house.

Mel told him she was on her way, and to be ready to pay for her cab. Wise didn't bother trying to find another dude like Mel asked him too. He wasn't about to dick wrestle with no nigga. He just wanted some head.

Twenty minutes later, Mel arrived. After Wise went down and paid for her cab, the two of them headed upstairs. In the elevator, he took Melanie's hand and placed it on his crotch to show her he was already hard.

Mel smiled at him seductively and licked her lips, and she massaged him over the pants. The look on his face said that he approved. Her plan was to get Wise so hot and bothered that he agreed to do anything she said to get the pussy. She was going to tease him.

When they got inside the suite, Mel saw that they were alone. "Where's your friend?", she asked.

"Dudes are busy. It was too last minute. I got you next time, though."

Mel laughed. "That's what's up." She shook her shoulder length hair and flipped it to the side like Jacinta had done. "I just came from the salon. You like my hair, baby?"

Wise raised an eyebrow and checked it out. "Hmm, from the front it's nice. Now let me see the top. Come here. Get down on your knees and let me get a bird's eye view." He lewdly grabbed himself and winked his eye at her, and he unzipped his pants and freed himself.

Melanie knew what it was. She normally wouldn't have had a problem wrapping her jaws around his dick because she knew there was nothing Wise enjoyed more than a blowjob. But she had a slightly different agenda this time. To put it simple, she was out for blood.

Melanie told Wise that she'd wanted to be gang banged, but she would settle for him roughing her up. At first Wise refused to honor her requests but she kept begging him to rough her up, insisting that she couldn't suck his dick until he hurt her. She said she was in the mood for pain and torture.

Wise noticed how much time had gotten away from them already so he got impatient and slapped the shit out of Mel like she kept begging him to. After he slapped her, she fell to the floor and begged for more. Wise looked down at her like she was crazy but he couldn't help but get a little turned on. He slapped her a few more times. Then that crazy bitch started begging him to piss on her.

She said, "I'm serious, Wise. Please take your dick and piss on me. And then hit me again. More please, baby!

Hurt me, daddy! Spank me, punch me, kick me, and choke me nigga! Show me how much you want me! Please, I'm begging you! I need it! Please! Do it, you fuckin' *bitch*!"

Had she just called him a bitch? She must've been losing her mind. *"Fuck it"*, Wise thought. He reached down and pimp slapped her about five more times, harder and harder.

Mel took those blows like a champ. She looked up at him and said, "Is that all you got, you stupid bitch ass nigga? I said fuckin' *harder.*"

Melanie got up and slapped fire out of Wise. Her strategy worked too. After she hit him, he fucked her up pretty bad. He even made her nose bleed.

After Wise finished beating the shit out of Mel he just looked at her and shook his head. "Yo, you's a *crazy* ass bitch."

Melanie crawled over to him and quickly took his dick in her mouth. That ass whipping must've really turned her on because now she seemed anxious to suck him off. She sucked and licked his cock for a second, and then she looked up into Wise' eyes with it in her hand. "Pee on me, Wise. Come on, I always wanted to try that shit."

Wise looked unsure. Was she serious? That was kind of sick so he avoided the request. "Come on, stop playin'. Go 'head, suck it."

Melanie said, "I'm *serious*. Gimme a golden shower, boo. Come on, so I can suck this big dick."

Wise didn't really have to piss but that being said, he concentrated for a minute and shot hot urine on Melanie's chest. He had been taking some new system cleansing herbal pills that Cas had given him, and for some reason the first pee that came out after taking a pill was always real yellow. So Melanie definitely got a golden shower. And it splashed all over her face.

After her golden shower, Mel took Wise in her mouth and sucked his dick better than she had ever before. She literally made his knees buckle. When Mel sensed Wise was about to bust she pulled back so that his semen landed all over her face and chest. Wise was a little disappointed that she didn't swallow, but he couldn't complain.

Afterwards, Melanie didn't bother to clean herself up. She just wiped her mouth with the back of her hand, and she grinned at Wise and told him she'd had a great time. Mel told him she'd be seeing him soon, and left the hotel room.

In the hallway, she stopped short when she realized that she hadn't gotten cab money from him. She went back and asked, and Wise gave her three hundred dollars. She went downstairs to flag a cab.

Wise wiped his dick off with a soapy washcloth, and he sat down for a minute to catch his breath. A few minutes later he checked out of the hotel and got his Lamborghini from the parking lot, and he innocently headed to pick up his daughter so they could go home. Wise had done this hundreds of times, cheated and gone home like nothing had happened. But little did he know, today would be different.

Melanie asked the cabdriver where the nearest precinct was. She told him she had to file a report, and she began to cry. When the driver pulled over at the precinct, Melanie paid him for her trip and got out. He told her he hoped she would be okay. She thanked him, and then she limped into the precinct with crocodile tears in her eyes.

Melanie was an aspiring actress. She had done a few cameos in Portia's films, a bunch of videos for rappers, and even a couple of low budget porno movies she hadn't told anyone about. But nothing had pushed her to stardom yet. Nonetheless, her performance in that precinct was nothing short of Oscar winning.

When the female officer at the front desk asked how she could help her, Mel stammered through tears and told her how Wise had violated her.

When Officer Sicarro learned that Melanie had been

raped and assaulted by a famous wealthy rapper, she moved quickly to assist her. Within seconds, she found an officer to take the report.

When the male officer questioned Melanie, she broke down in tears again. She told him that she had been forced to perform oral sex on Wise, and when she refused, she was beaten and pissed on until she agreed.

The officer told her it was good that she came forward because she definitely couldn't let him get away with that. Wise had beaten her up and raped her, and he had to pay.

Mel was a lot smarter than Wise gave her credit for. She did the Monica Lewinsky on his ass. Her shirt was soiled with his cum and piss, and she had his semen on her face and in her mouth too. She figured that, along with her police report, was all the evidence she needed.

Melanie went on record saying that Wise raped her and assaulted her repeatedly, and that was the foundation she cleverly laid for the lawsuit she set him up for. That was how she planned to come up. Mel hadn't gotten her big break yet so she needed this opportunity bad as hell.

Even though she only set Wise up because he wouldn't buy her fur coat, Mel didn't feel any remorse. She wasn't trying to kill him. She just wanted to hurt him in the pockets a little. Her acting career wasn't taking off like she thought it would've, and she needed a nice chunk of bread to get herself a crib and a car. Wise just happened to play her at the right time. Melanie wanted to live a certain lifestyle, and it was comforting to know that now Wise was going to finance it. In the end, that nigga would wish he'd have bought her ten damn furs.

$$$

About four hours later, Wise was just ending a family night with his wife and daughter. They were on their way out of Clowny's, a kid's palace that Falynn loved to go play at. Clowny's was similar to Chuck E. Cheese's, but it was a little more upscale.

As they left the building, Wise was approached by two white men in cheap dark suits. Even Fatima could tell they were detectives. She looked more surprised than him. These cops, Detective Sutland and Detective Sneider, had a passion for taking down what they referred to as "rich black hip-hop niggers". The two of them had picked up another rich asshole, Henry "Hen-Rock" Jacobs, for similar charges a while ago. It was their pleasure to bring in another one of those lucky black bastards.

They informed the couple that they had a warrant for the arrest of Mr. William Page, which was Wise' government name, for the rape and assault of Melanie Lane. They intentionally revealed this information in front of Wise' wife just to shame him and put him in deeper shit. They asked Wise to come with them, and one of them produced a pair of handcuffs and smiled at him sarcastically.

When Fatima heard them say he was being accused by Portia's slut cousin Melanie, she wanted to go upside his head for being so fucking stupid. And at the same time she wanted to find that bitch Melanie and fuck her up for lying on her man.

Before the cops took Wise away, he gave Fatima the car keys and told her to call Jay and Cas, and his lawyer. Fatima couldn't help but shed a tear but she had to be strong for her baby. When Falynn saw those cops handcuff her daddy and take him away she had a fit.

Fatima got on the phone and called Cas and Jay immediately, and she gave them the facts as she knew. They both told her they would handle it so she should go take the baby home and not worry. They assured her that they would have Wise out as soon as possible. Fatima thanked both of them, and after she hung up she felt a little better.

Instead of taking Falynn home, she took her over her parents' house for the night. Fatima told her parents that she had an emergency because Wise had been arrested. They were concerned, and asked her what he was being charged with. She just lied and told them she wasn't sure yet. She thanked her parents for helping her out, and she went on home.

About an hour later, she got a call from Cas. He told her that Wise would be out as soon as he could see a judge and get a bail, and he assured her that he and Jay had already secured the best of legal representation for him. He asked Fatima if she was alright, and she told him she was good. Cas told her that Wise would more than likely be in jail overnight so she should try and get some rest and get ready to go to court for him in the morning.

After Fatima hung up, she rolled herself a blunt and got ready for bed. She half-watched TV and puffed on her trees, and she thought about her situation. How was a nasty slut like Melanie accusing her husband of rape? Fatima figured Wise probably fucked that bitch again but she didn't believe he raped her. Fatima was smart and levelheaded, and she knew this shit was probably leading up to some type of lawsuit. Melanie's cum thirsty ass was more than likely seeking some type of monetary settlement.

Fatima wondered how that dumb mothafucka could put himself in that position. It might be good that this shit happened to Wise. He was always fucking around with bitches who didn't have shit. He could've at least stayed on her level. It was a slap in the face that he would even mess with such a bird when his wife was so classy.

Melanie was Portia's cousin and they shared the same last name, but that was where their similarities ended. Fatima loved Wise, and she tried to give him the benefit of a doubt but she had a feeling he'd set himself up for that one.

A few minutes later, Portia called her to make sure she

was okay. Fatima could hear Laila in the background yelling for her to "be strong and don't let that shit break her". They asked Fatima if she wanted them to come over. She only lived five minutes away, so it wouldn't have been a problem.

Fatima assured her best friends that she was fine, and they didn't need to trouble themselves that late at night. She told them she was going to bed soon anyway. For some reason she was exhausted.

After they got off the phone, Fatima ate Ben & Jerry's Chunky Monkey ice cream from the carton and watched TV. She had a lot of thoughts running through her mind, and she was unsure about a lot of things. The only thing she was certain of was the fact that she was standing by her man. He didn't leave her when he caught her getting her pussy eaten by Raven out by the pool, and come what may, she wasn't leaving him either.

Thinking about that incident made Fatima realize that it was the only secret she had ever kept from Laila and Portia. She was too embarrassed to tell them about that one. Maybe one day. A few minutes later, Fatima dozed off into a light, troubled sleep.

Chapter Fifteen

The next morning, Portia gave Mel a call to find out what was going on between her and Wise. She had called her the previous evening as well, but kept on getting her voicemail. This time Melanie picked up.

Melanie told Portia she hadn't answered the phone last night because she was at the hospital getting treated for the bruises Wise had given her before he raped her. She told Portia how badly he'd hurt her and even busted her nose, and then she said he needed to learn how to treat a woman. Then Melanie hinted that Wise should try making her a peace offering that would sooth her pain. She told Portia to advise him to make it sweet.

Portia asked Mel if money was all she wanted. Mel said it was nothing personal. She was sticking to her guns so the ball was in Wise' court.

Portia got off the phone and went downstairs to give Jay the rundown. He and Cas were on the west wing of the house, in the recreation section shooting pool. The entire second floor of their three-story Victorian-style home was reserved for entertainment.

The second floor consisted of the theater and the rec section. The theater had a real movie-sized screen and thirty comfortable reclining movie chairs. The rec section was really a huge game room with two pool tables, a ping pong table, and every game you could imagine, including Portia's old school arcade sized Ms. Pac-man and Jayquan's X-Box, Playstation 3, and Nintendo Wii, which were all hooked up to seperate 32 inch flat screen TVs.

When Portia came down and told Jay and Casino what Melanie had said, they ended their game of pool. Both of them wanted to know what Wise had to say about Melanie's accusations.

They had bailed Wise out of jail earlier that morning, and dropped him off at home to get cleaned up. Jay and Cas hadn't really gotten a chance to grill him about what happened. They both doubted that Melanie was telling the truth about him beating her up and raping her, but they wanted to know what led up to all of that. They had to have a talk with Wise. They didn't want to call and disturb him yet because they knew he had a lot of explaining to do to Fatima first.

About an hour later, Wise pulled up outside. When he came in the first thing he did was assure Portia that he did not rape her cousin. And he knew Jay and Cas were going to bust his balls more than the detectives did at the precinct, so instead of waiting for them to ask, he began to voluntarily explain how Melanie had set him up.

Although Melanie was her cousin, Portia was impartial to the situation. She wasn't taking any sides. Wise had gotten himself tangled up in that mess. He had no business cheating on Tima anyhow, with his loose dick self. If he had to pay up, he just had to pay.

Just as Portia predicted he would've, Wise asked her to try and talk some sense into her cousin. Portia told him she had already called Mel and spoke to her about it, and she told him what she said about him making her an offer sweet enough to give her amnesia.

Wise got tight when he heard that. He frowned and mumbled under his breath, "I ain't givin' that dirty bitch shit."

Portia, Jay, and Cas all looked at him like they knew better. His ass was in deep shit.

Portia asked him the million dollar question. "Wise, why does Mel keep insisting that you hurt her? She said you beat the shit out of her and busted her nose, and then raped her. If that's not true, then why would she make that up?"

Wise' expression said he couldn't believe what Melanie
had said. "What?! Get the fuck outta here, that freak bitch
wanted me to beat her up! She begged me! Talkin' 'bout
pain and torture turned her on. And she begged me to piss
on her and shit. She said she wanted a golden shower."

Portia twisted her mouth to the side like "yeah right,
nigga". That shit sounded a little unbelievable but she didn't
say anything. Jay and Cas didn't say anything either. They
just wanted to know the truth.

Wise saw that they were all scrutinizing his story. He
knew he was telling the truth. They had to believe him.

"Yo, that's word on my daughter and everything I love,
Melanie begged me to beat her up. Pardon me Portia, but
she said she wouldn't suck my jump-off if I didn't do what
she said. She kept yelling for me to slap her and pee on her
and shit."

They all wanted to know, but Casino asked the question
first. "So, did you?"

Everyone looked at Wise for an answer.

Wise shrugged his shoulders. "Yeah. What the fuck I'ma
lie for? But she *asked* me to. She kept saying how much it
turned her on. Ya'll ain't gotta believe me if ya'll don't want
to, but I'm *tellin'* you that bitch set me up."

Portia said, "Well with all due respect, Wise, you fell for
the bait."

Jay said, "Man, how could you have been so naïve and
dumb? You might as well have just given her the combination
to your safe." Jay shook his head in disbelief.

Cas found it irresistible to cosign. "And then you had
to R. Kelley the girl, pissin' on her and shit. Oh well, son.
There's a sucker born every minute." He patted Wise on the
back in mock pity.

Cas continued. "But what the fuck did you do to piss that
chick off so bad? If you *been* hittin' that with no problem,
why is she cryin' rape all of a sudden?"

Wise said, "Man, stop sayin' *rape*. I didn't rape that bitch! I didn't even fuck her. All she did was give me some brains. That slut bitch just got mad 'cause I ain't cop the mink she kept askin' me for."

When he said that, Jay, Cas, and Portia all looked at one another like a light bulb came on in their heads.

Portia said, "Oh, *now* I get it. All this is over a mink, huh?"

"Yeah, I guess so", Wise admitted. "Shit, I can't think of no other reason. Me and Mel ain't never had no misunderstanding. I ain't see her like that, but we was cool. She was just wildin' lately, with this mink shit."

Portia was sold. She believed Wise. It sounded to her that Mel had finally gotten tired of getting played. She said, "Look, Wise. I believe you, and I'm sure everyone else in this room does too."

Jay and Cas nodded in agreement with her, and she continued. "But as much as we all believe you, they are charging you with rape, nigga, so you better come up outta this fog of denial you seem to be in. Those are some serious charges against you, Wise. I told you Mel said she wants some bread. You know how it is. Money talks, and bullshit walks. You better come up off somethin'. Because all the sluts and bitches she may be, she got you by the balls, bro. And I don't need to remind you that your album just dropped, so this is a terrible time for a rape charge." Portia shook her head. "Damn, I ain't even know Mel was that smart."

"Me neither", Wise agreed. As much as he hated to admit it, he knew Portia was right. Jay and Casino didn't even bother getting on him anymore because Portia had given him the full business, straight with no chaser.

Wise wished he could've turned back time. He hadn't expected Melanie to be anything different from the passive jump-off she'd always been. He couldn't front, she had stepped her game up. She got him real good with that shit.

Fuckin' bitch.

Wise thought about it for a second, and he asked Portia to call her. He was ready to make her an offer he knew was skimpy but he figured he'd start out low. He just hoped she took the money and ran. He told Portia to tell Melanie he would give her twenty grand to drop the charges.

Portia called Melanie right in front of them. Although she tried to make the offer sound great, Mel scoffed at it like it was peanuts. She told Portia to tell Wise not to waste her time insulting her like that again.

Portia told her she should really reconsider but Mel wasn't trying to hear that. She told her to ask Wise if prison looked more appealing than a measly dent in his bank account. Then Melanie told Portia she loved her like a sister, and she was holding out because she knew that's what she would've done. Portia couldn't front, that part was true.

After Portia hung up, Wise saw that she had tried but she hadn't gotten through to her. That bitch Melanie was really starting to get under his skin. He copped an attitude but it was himself he was angry at for letting a bitch get the upper hand that way.

Wise told Portia to call Mel back and offer her fifty thousand, and a full-length mink coat. He was sure she'd go for that.

When Portia called Mel back, she turned down that offer too. That wasn't enough money for her to get right. Mel told Portia to tell Wise to stick that mink coat up his ass. She said he should've bought it as a gift from the heart, but now she would buy her own. This was like a one shot deal for Melanie. She wasn't letting Wise off that easy.

Portia hung up again and told Wise that Mel said come higher, and stick that coat up his ass. She couldn't help but laugh. Jay and Cas did too.

Wise wasn't laughing. He was visibly vexed. If he was light skinned his face would've been beet red. His teeth were clenched in anger. A fucking whore had the nerve to try and strong-arm him. He couldn't believe that shit.

After they waited a half-hour to see if Melanie called back and took the bait, Wise told Portia his final offer was eighty thousand dollars, and she could take it or leave it.

Melanie haughtily turned that offer down too. She knew she could get more, and she planned to show Wise that she wasn't playing with his ass. It wasn't like he didn't have it.

Wise was getting frustrated. He finally told Portia to just ask her what she wanted. Melanie said to tell him that she would get back to him another day. Now it was his turn to wait on her call like a broad with high hopes.

Portia looked over at Wise and shook her head. She had to break his balls a little. He shouldn't have lied to Mel about that coat. "Wise, Wise, Wise. You poor thing. What a tangled web we weave when we conspire to deceive, bro."

Wise just made a face. He didn't want to hear that shit. He knew Portia was right though.

About twenty minutes later, Jay, Wise, and Cas were leaving the house about to head to the City when Laila pulled up in the driveway. She was just getting home from work. She smiled and said what's up to all of them, and she made her way inside the house.

Cas waited a few seconds, and then he announced that he had to take a piss before they hit the road. He went inside the house acting all nonchalant and shit. Jay peeped his best homie's transparent attempt to go holler at Laila, but he didn't comment.

Wise was the one who blew it up. He said, "Son, look at Cas. Laila pulls up and shakes that fat ass rump pass him, and now all of a sudden he gotta go take a piss. That nigga full of shit."

Jay couldn't help but laugh. Wise had hit the nail on the head.

Laila played it cool but her heart had literally fluttered

when she saw Casino. When she got inside, she paused at the door for a moment to catch her breath. The next thing she knew, Cas came in behind her. He scared Laila, so she jumped and placed her hand over her heart.

The two of them just looked at each other for a second, both unsure of what to say. Cas stared at her from head to toe. He imagined her naked, wearing only the olive green peep toe Bottega Veneta high heels she had on. Laila always kept a pair of bad ass heels on. Her shoe game had been on point ever since Cas first met her. He was careful to keep his expression cool but he very much appreciated the sight of her. His eyes traveled from her hips to her eyes.

Laila saw the once-over Cas had given her plain as day but she was busy scanning him too. He was damn sure one good looking brother, with his sexy ass frame. Cas made her feel weak. She couldn't help it. She gave him the sexy eyes and sent him a signal that let him know what she had on her mind. Laila couldn't believe she had been so bold, but she was tired of playing footsie with him. Now the ball was in his court.

Cas caught it. He just stared at her for a minute. "I'ma call you later."

Laila just nodded in response. She didn't say anything but she really hoped he meant that.

Portia had gone upstairs to check on the kids, and on her way back down she saw Laila talking to Cas. Portia paused at the top of the stairs so she wouldn't interrupt their conversation. She couldn't help but smile, hoping whatever they were discussing would lead up to something. Laila needed a happy place in her life. She was going through a lot. Portia knew Cas was with Kira, and things were a little more complicated now, but there was something between him and Laila. Anybody could see that.

Portia didn't know what Cas said to her, but after he left Laila spun around smiling like hell. She looked dead in

Portia's face, and when she realized she was caught grinning like a school girl she burst out laughing.

Portia laughed too, and gave her the "thumbs up" sign to let her know she was on her side. Laila just waved her hand at her and kept laughing.

$$$

That evening around eight o'clock, Laila got her wish. Cas called her cell phone and asked her to meet him at a nice restaurant in the next town over. She agreed because she didn't think it was a good idea for him to come pick her up either. She didn't want her kids to know she was going out with another man. After Laila hung up, she grinned at Portia and did a little old school happy dance consisting of The Cabbage Patch and The Running Man.

Portia knew what that meant so she didn't even have to say anything. Homegirl was stepping out that night. The two of them quickly went in Laila's room and shut the door. Within minutes, they went through the walk-in closet and picked out what they agreed to be the most appropriate outfit for the evening. It was casual and sexy but not too revealing. Laila didn't want to look too thirsty. She didn't dress like a hoochie anyway. She never had. Ever since they were younger, she had always been the more conservative one of the bunch.

Portia volunteered to take the kids to the movies so they wouldn't miss her. Jay wasn't home yet, but she'd just call and let him know where they were going. Portia went off to tell Jayquan, Macy, and Pebbles to get ready, and she located Jazmin so she could change her clothes. She had on shorts, and Portia knew it would be chilly in the movie theater.

When Laila's daughters asked her if she was coming with them and Auntie Portia to the movies, she told them she was tired and wouldn't be joining them. They both kissed her and told her to get some rest, and they left without hesitation. After they went downstairs, Laila hopped in the shower and got dressed. By the time she left the house everyone was already gone.

Laila set the security code on the door like Portia had taught her, and she hopped in her freshly detailed Lexus and headed out to meet Cas. She was glad she had gone to the carwash earlier that day. Her baby was shining.

When Laila pulled up in front of the restaurant, she realized that there was valet parking. She thought that was a nice beginning to the evening. She got out of her car and was escorted to the front of the restaurant by a uniformed gentleman, and another one parked her car.

Inside, the maitre d' saw that Laila fit the description of the young lady one of his most prominent guests was expecting. The tuxedo wearing gentleman smiled at her and bowed, and then he snapped his fingers and summoned a waiter to escort her over to Cas' table.

When Cas saw Laila walk up he fought back a smile. For some reason he had been a little doubtful about her showing up. He stood up and greeted her as the waiter pulled out her chair. Laila reached over and gave him a quick hug, and they sat down. Cas told the waiter to give them a minute.

Laila smiled brightly. "What's up, Cas? How are you?" She reached across the table and touched his hand.

That smile and her touch automatically disarmed all that cool shit Cas had planned. He smiled back at her. "I'm good, Ma. How are you?"

"I'm livin', thank God."

"Well you certainly look well", Cas complimented.

Laila blushed. "Thanks. And so do you."

The waiter returned and asked if they were ready to order drinks or appetizers. Laila chose white wine, and Cas ordered Courvoisier. Shortly after, they sipped their beverages and conversed.

By round two of their drinks, Laila was smiling from ear to ear. She and Casino had warmed to each other, and now they chatted like old friends. Laila let her guards down and told him everything that was going on in her life, about her husband getting high and all. She told him she was staying with Portia and Jay until she figured out what to do, but she was leaning toward putting her house on the market and getting a new start somewhere other than Brooklyn.

Cas sympathized with her, and he had this urge to try and fix all of her problems. He almost blurted out, *"Fuck that weak ass, crackhead nigga. I'll put you and your kids in a house somewhere safe"*, but he kept his mouth shut. He just asked her where she thought about moving to. Cas and Laila ordered their entrées, and then continued their conversation over lobster.

After they ate and it was time to go, they each shared the same thoughts. Neither of them was ready to leave the others company but nobody wanted to come on too strong. When they got outside the restaurant it was Cas who broke the ice. He just came right out and asked her what she wanted to do next.

Laila wished she could have been honest and told him that she really needed to get laid but she didn't want to seem desperate. Besides, she was a lady. Cas sensed her hesitation so he told her to relax, and suggested she park her car and ride with him.

Laila agreed and hopped in the silver Aston Martin with Casino, and he drove to the shore. When they got there Cas parked the car, and they got out and walked on the pier. The late evening breeze was warm and inviting. Laila slipped her hand into Cas' hand and squeezed. She felt safe with him.

Laila stared out at the water and her spirit was calmed by its peacefulness. She really needed that. She was so moved by the beauty of the ocean under the moonlight she leaned over and whispered in Cas' ear. "Come on, let's go somewhere."

Cas understood what that meant. But did she? He looked at her closely. "You sure?"

Laila nodded her head. She boldly took Cas by the arm and pulled him towards the car. He followed without a word.

Cas started up his ride and headed for a discreet getaway along the Jersey shore. He checked them into a suite within minutes. As soon as they got to the door of their suite, Cas' cell phone rang. He answered it and excused himself to the bathroom.

Laila could hear water running through the closed door. She couldn't make out any of Cas' muffled conversation but she was willing to bet he was on the phone with Kira. Laila actually got jealous for a minute. She really had to check herself. That was what happened when you crept around with a married man.

Laila knew deep in her heart that she had given Cas to Kira on a silver platter. He had been into her first but she had tried to make her marriage work. There was no way she could fault that brother for moving on. Hell, he was an excellent catch. Bitches were lined up for miles to snag a good man like Cas.

Casino came out the bathroom drying his hands. "I had to get in there before you. You know how long you chicks take in the bathroom", he joked.

Laila rolled her eyes at him playfully. Cas was right but she wasn't going to take long that night. She had just taken a shower before she left home. She headed in the bathroom while Cas flipped through the channels on the television.

While Laila was in the bathroom, he went downstairs and bought some condoms. Luckily they had the Trojan Magnum joints. He wasn't prepared because he hadn't known things would go that far.

When Laila came out, he was on the bed watching "The Conan O'Brien Show". She took a deep breath and walked over and stood in front of him.

Cas tried to play it cool and be patient but she started to undress. This grabbed his attention so much that he sat up on the bed and watched her.

Laila slowly and seductively removed her blouse, and then she unfastened her belt and pants button. She paused and looked at Cas. His eyes told her to go on.

Laila looked so sexy in that lace turquoise bra and thong peeking out at him, Casino felt compelled to stand up and help her out of her pants. After he pulled them down he palmed her ass and squeezed it. Damn, it was soft. Next, he caressed her breasts. She had on the kind of bra that fastened in the front. Cas unhooked it and bent down and took her right nipple in his mouth and sucked on it gently.

Laila let out a low moan and palmed Cas' face in her hands. She stroked his waves lovingly, and ran her hands along his sexy broad shoulders.

"Take your shirt off, baby", she said softly. She wanted to feel his brown skin against her brown skin just like that India Arie song.

Cas took off his shirt, and Laila's knees literally weakened. He was so fucking sexy. You could tell he worked out regularly by the muscle cuts that adorned his tight frame. Laila needed the comfort of a man bad as hell. She walked into Cas' arms, just wanting to be held. She was a lot shorter than him, especially now that she had taken off her heels. Her head barely reached his chest.

Cas hugged Laila tight. She felt good in his arms so he squeezed more. He could tell by her reaction that she needed that so he held her for a while. Laila was short so bending down so long put a strain on his back. Cas picked her up and held her in his arms.

Laila wrapped her arms and legs around him, and she buried her face in his shoulder and inhaled. Umm, he smelled so good.

Casino sniffed Laila's silky hair and thought the same thing about her. She smelled wonderful. Just like apricots. Laila leaned back and placed a light kiss on Cas' lips. He kissed her back, and they winded up smooching like lovebirds.

Laila was putty in Cas' hands. He was a great kisser. The way he flicked his tongue in and out of her mouth sent tiny jolts of electricity through her body. She was on the verge of creaming. Cas sensed her urgency so he carried her over to the bed and laid her down. He handled Laila delicately, like she was a doll made of fine silk.

Laila laid spread-eagled awaiting more of him. Cas stood over her for a second and admired her beauty. Laila blushed. He was staring at her all sexy. Not the corny kind of sexy, but the irresistible thuggish kind. Laila wanted him inside of her so bad. She reached over and ran her fingers along the waistline of his boxers. She could see that he was hard.

Cas unbuckled his belt and let his jeans fall to the floor. He stepped out of his clothes and joined Laila on the bed. When he crawled between those warm welcoming brown thighs, he was forced to take a slow deep breath. He was too excited. He didn't want to blow his first time making love to Laila in five years by cumming too fast. Cas laid there for a second trying to will his penis to calm down.

Laila took Cas' laying there as a sign that he wanted her to take control. She got up and straddled him like a horse, and she traced her name along his chest with her fingertips. L-A-I-L-A. Laila replaced her fingertips with her lips and kissed his chest delicately. She ran her tongue along Casino's ear and kissed him on the neck.

The way Laila was kissing on Cas had him on fire. He squeezed her ass and ran his hands along her back, caressing her soft skin in a way that drove her mad. Cas rolled Laila over so that he was on top, and he kissed from her forehead all the way down to her belly.

Laila squirmed and panted as Cas slipped off her thong

and kissed her inner thighs. He was making her feel so good. They had never entertained oral sex during their previous affair but it looked like Cas was going for it. Laila held her breath and crossed her fingers.

Cas hadn't done that to Laila before but he really dug her and he wanted to make sure that she didn't get away from him this time around. He knew she was a clean woman. He wrapped his arms around Laila's thighs and spread her pussy lips open, and he put his face deep in the place. She was soaking wet and her juices were tasty.

Cas whirlwind-tongued Laila's pussy and literally made her scream for joy. Afterwards, Laila smiled at him appreciatively through lust hooded eyes and sat up and kissed him in the mouth. She could taste her essence. She reached down and took Cas' well endowed tool in her hand and stroked it affectionately. She wanted to kiss it but it was too soon. Cas took off his boxers and his immense soldier stood proud and tall. Laila gasped at its beauty. Her body ached for it.

Cas felt the same way. He reached over and got a condom from the nightstand and tore it open. After he rolled it on, he positioned himself atop Laila missionary style. When he slid inside her love canal they both sighed in unison, as if the relief was reciprocal.

Laila's body trembled and she met Cas' strokes until they created a rhythm more melodic than an African drum symphony. Their bodies were perfectly in sync. That was what you called lovemaking. It just felt so right. Cas got all up inside of Laila, in places she hadn't even known existed.

The combination of the unbelievable sex and Cas' manliness overwhelmed Laila and racked her body until she lost control. She didn't think their lovemaking could get any better but Cas deep stroked her until she exploded so hard tears ran down her face.

When Laila came, Cas came too. Afterwards he collapsed on top on her, breathing heavily. Boy, boy, boy. Laila's pussy was out of this world. He could've sworn he heard trumpets and shit.

After Cas laid there for a second he got up and saw that Laila was crying. He wiped away her tears and gently kissed her eyelids. He wanted her to know that she didn't have anything to cry about. Not when she was with him.

$$$

The following day, Portia was washing dishes when what sounded like a grown man called her cell phone and asked to speak to Pebbles. He sounded so much older than Pebbles was, Portia got nosey and asked who he was. He said his name was Ice, and that Pebbles had called him from that number a few times the night before.

Portia remembered that at the movies the past night Pebbles kept asking if she could use her cell phone, and then going to the bathroom. Portia had just assumed that the obviously personal conversations were with a little boy she liked.

Now Portia thought about what Laila had told her about that pimp dude, and she suspected that was him. Oh shit, the dude's name was Ice. That was him! Portia asked him how old he was, and he told her he was twenty two. Portia told him Pebbles was just a little twelve year old girl, and if he called her phone again for her he would be in big trouble. Before she hung up on him she told him to stay the fuck away from her niece before he got dealt with.

Jay overheard Portia on her cell playing phone gangsta', so he asked her what the problem was. Portia didn't want to tell Laila's business but she told Jay about how that pimp dude had tried to turn Pebbles out, and how Laila had caught her cutting school and sneaking off with him.

Portia told Jay how Pebbles had kept on borrowing her cell phone at the movies and calling that nigga, after Laila forbade her to see him. Jay agreed that Portia should get involved and tell her mother because Pebbles was just a little girl. Jay had a daughter, and he hated the idea of some old dude trying to take advantage of her. He would leave that nigga where the fuck he stood. He knew Pebbles' father was out there getting high so he told Portia to let Laila know that if she needed a man to intervene, he would be more than willing too.

Chapter Sixteen

A few days later, Melanie made her move. She called the office of a well-known female attorney named Liza Satchers, who was infamous for going after wealthy celebrity athletes and entertainers. Liza loved to pursue paternity, child support, and other anti-male lawsuits. And she was good at what she did. That's why she got paid the big bucks.

Liza advised Melanie briefly during a ten-minute consultation, and Melanie retained her. Two days later, they filed a civil suit against Wise for 3.5 million dollars.

When Wise found out about the lawsuit, needless to say he was very upset. It even crossed his mind to have Melanie killed. That was the way he would have preferred to handle it, but he knew that bitch wasn't worth it. She was playing hardball so his hands were tied.

Wise talked it over with Jay and Cas, and they scheduled a meeting with his attorney. Wise' lawyer, Dennis Cohenberg, said that if Melanie was willing to drop the charges it would be in his best interest to settle. He told Wise that the system was designed to protect women, and in cases like his there was a slim chance for a man. Especially when she had so much evidence against him. She had a shirt with his DNA on it. And to top it off, they were threatening to go public, and the media portraying him as a rapist during a time his album was climbing on the charts could really hurt his record sales. Wise had a lot of female fans, and women hated a rapist. Cohenberg advised Wise against gambling when the stakes were so high.

Wise didn't really have a choice, so he agreed. His lawyer got on the phone with Melanie's lawyer and they agreed to settle, if the offer was feasible. They made an appointment to meet the following day so they could talk turkey.

That night Wise tried calling Melanie but as instructed by her attorney, she wouldn't take any of his calls. Wise asked Portia to call her to try and see what kind of numbers she was looking for. He had bread but it would still sting him to part with a chunk. Especially over some bullshit like that.

Portia got Mel on the phone but Mel just kept on saying she was under a gag order. She said she couldn't discuss the case with her because her attorney had instructed her not to talk about it. Then Mel told Portia that when she got paid she was going to take her out to a fancy restaurant and treat her to a day at the spa, just for being a great cousin. Portia couldn't help but laugh. That damn girl was already spending that money.

Portia hung up and she let Wise know she had no luck with Mel. She could tell that he was worried, but she told him to relax and quit stressing over the situation. She told him to be easy because whatever he had to kick out would be a lot less than he was being sued for.

Wise figured Portia had to be right. But he still worried all night. He went in the house early and smoked two blunts with Fatima, and he laid in bed and tossed and turned all night.

Fatima couldn't help but feel sorry for him. She had been giving him a hard time about getting caught up in that mess with Melanie but that night she hugged and kissed him, and assured him that she was in his corner. She told him not to worry because that was a small thing, and he was a giant. She said whatever Melanie cost him would be replenished in no time.

Fatima's support about the situation was invaluable to Wise. He was touched. She was a real woman. He didn't deserve her. Wise knew he had to get his shit together because he couldn't lose Fatima. She was his woman, and he needed her by his side.

The following day, Wise and Melanie settled their differences for three quarters of a million dollars. Melanie's attorney got a third, and she was left with half a million bucks.

The first thing Melanie did was buy herself a brand new fifty thousand dollar Mercedes off the lot for thirty five thousand dollars in cash, and then she purchased a lovely two bedroom condo in North Jersey for one hundred seventy thousand. She spent another twenty grand on expensive Italian furniture.

Mel spent almost half of her money the first week but she had the deed to a piece of real estate that she knew would appreciate, and the title to a car she knew she could sell and get her money back out of if she needed to. Next, she wanted to go on a shopping spree. It would be the first time she'd be able to shop without looking at the price tags, and she was anxious.

Mel also decided to treat herself to that full-length mink coat she never got from Wise. She laughed to herself about it because Wise was buying it for her after all.

When Melanie was done splurging on a mink, a blonde chinchilla, and a new wardrobe full of high-priced designer clothes and shoes, she kept her word and set up an appointment for her and Portia at Crème de la Crème, an upscale spa in the City.

The following day, she and Portia spent the afternoon getting pampered, and then they went to Mr. Chow's for dinner.

While the Lane cousins dined, Portia advised Melanie to do something smart with her money before she found herself broke again. Portia knew she couldn't have had much left after all of her extravagant purchases. She was glad Mel had bought herself a crib but she told her to keep on working to pay her bills because living off her stash would only make her penniless in the long run.

Mel told Portia she was right, and she thanked her for the advice. The following day she sat with a financial planner, and she split her remaining two hundred thousand dollars up and put part in savings, part in a mutual fund, and the rest in an interest bearing money market account.

Mel had spent a lot of money the last few days so she knew how fast it could go. She was grateful for her new lifestyle. She didn't ever want to be broke again.

$$$

Jay and Casino headed for the old opera house in Middleton. They were going to attend an "invitation only" benefit art auction that was to be held that evening. Wise was still tight from having to pay Melanie all that money so he didn't want to come along.

Jay and Cas were both dapper in fine tailor-made Salvatore Ferragamo and John Galliano suits, and expensive hard bottom shoes. They were going to mix and mingle with old money, and they both looked the part.

About an hour later, they settled into their seats at the auction and waited patiently to see what item had enough appeal to make them bid. Jay and Cas were both financially stable, and therefore not the least bit intimidated by the number of million dollar figures being casually tossed about the room.

After they were there for about a half hour, Jay saw something that struck his interest. It was a rare painting. An eighteenth century piece done by Stratinsky. Jay knew fine art, and it was a classic. He decided he wanted it so he raised his hand and confidently outbid an elderly Caucasian gentleman to his left. They went back and forth a couple of times, and the old dude backed off.

A lady sitting in the row behind them was now interested. She raised her hand and outbid Jay by ten thousand dollars. Jay refused to let anyone outbid him. Especially a woman. In the spirit of friendly competition, he upped his bid another twenty grand.

The woman didn't stop there. She topped Jay's bid by another thirty. He put up fifty more, and she raised her bid another hundred grand. Jay bid another hundred twenty five gees, and she raised her bid two hundred thousand more. It was obvious that girlfriend's money was real long. And she really wanted that painting. Jay couldn't help but look back at her. She was a middle-aged redhead. She had a pretty face, and wore her hair in an upsweep.

Cas elbowed Jay in the ribs. He wanted to stop him before he winded up paying more than that Olivier Stratinsky was worth. Jay knew Cas was right. He let it go and let the lady have it. She looked over at him, and Jay could've sworn he saw her stick her tongue out at him.

Before they left the auction, Jay and Casino had both purchased masterpieces of substantial worth. Together they had spent way over a million, but they didn't regret it. They were both cultured gentlemen, and had done their homework. They knew they had purchased fine art that would only appreciate.

$$\$\$\$$$

A few days later, Portia was mopping up some apple juice Jazmin had spilled on the kitchen floor when her mother called and said she was coming over to visit that weekend. Portia had been begging Patricia to come and stay with her for some time now so she was thrilled. She and Pat talked for about five more minutes, and Portia told her she would see her the following morning.

Even though they hired a cleaning lady to come in once a week, Portia decided to stay up late cleaning. She knew what a watchful eye Patty Cake had, and she was eager to get her mother's approval.

When Portia told Jazmin, she was excited too. She just

loved Patricia. She kept running around singing *"My mam-ma's coming over, my mam-ma's coming over!"* Jazmin had been calling Patricia "mam-ma" instead of "grandma" ever since she started talking. Pat loved it, and everyone else seemed to think it was cute too.

Patricia arrived early Saturday afternoon, and she and Portia spent the day catching up. They spoke on the telephone at least three times a week but there was still a lot to be said. Portia loved her mother so much. Everyone loved Pat. She had a good spirit about her and it always showed.

She had brought gifts for all the kids, Jazmin, Jayquan, Pebbles, Macy, and Fatima's little girl, Falynn. The kids loved their presents, and they stuck up under Patricia. But Jazz was possessive of her. She climbed up in Pat's lap and wouldn't get down.

Patricia loved all of them like they were her grandkids. She'd always been a great mother, and she treated Portia's friends like they were her daughters. Laila, Fatima, and Simone, may she rest in peace.

Fatima came over a little later. Her daughter was with her this time. Falynn was so sweet and adorable. She hugged everybody, tore open her gift from Patricia, and ran off to play with Jazmin and their new dolls.

Fatima, Portia, Pat, and Laila stayed up late talking and eating munchies. Patricia had wisdom beyond their years and ever since they were little girls, they cherished her advice. She was fair, down to earth, she told it like it was, and she pulled no punches.

Patricia knew Portia and her friends smoked a little weed and got their drink on so she didn't mind that the girls passed a blunt back and forth while they all sipped on "Tima-tinis" and frozen "Laila-ritas". Those were Laila and Fatima's ghetto versions of the classic martini and margarita.

Patricia knew that Portia and her girlfriends were all successful young women who had accomplished things so she certainly didn't knock them for what they did in their leisure time. She was proud of the women they had become. They were all grown with their own children now. Pat was just glad they made sure the kids didn't see what they were doing. The children were all upstairs in the rec section playing games.

Patricia was amused by the girls and she had advice for each of them. She told Fatima to be strong and stick by Wise, but only if she thought he was worth it. She commended Laila on her strength and told her not to give up helping Khalil, but not to let him drain her and let her spirit die with his. She told Portia that her thing seemed together but always be strong and keep a level head because no marriage was beyond tests.

Then Pat went on to tell them similar things she had been through with Portia's father when he was alive. Portia hadn't even known some of the stuff she told them went on. But Pat said she stuck by her husband through the good and the bad, and that was what the marriage vow "for better or for worse" meant.

After a long night of Pat analyzing all of their relationships like she was Dr. Phil followed by them grooving to their favorite oldies and getting down, the ladies decided to call it a night. Or morning rather, because it was already after five AM.

The following Sunday afternoon, Patricia asked Portia to join her in the kitchen for a cup of green tea. She said she had to talk to her about something. Portia got a little nervous because Pat looked like it was serious. She had a feeling she wasn't going to welcome this news her mother had.

During their conversation, Patricia announced that she had uterine cancer. She said she was scheduled to start chemotherapy to try to combat it. When Portia heard that her hand shook so bad she almost dropped hot tea all over herself. Oh God, that was serious. Cancer was nothing to play with. People died from it everyday.

It felt like Portia's heart stopped. How could her mother have cancer? That couldn't be true. She looked great. Portia was so scared she grabbed her mother and hugged her tight, and broke down in tears.

Patricia hugged her daughter and rubbed her back, and she told her to quit crying over something that was God's will. She said she was going to beat it so Portia shouldn't worry. Portia nodded her head in agreement but she couldn't stop crying.

Patricia cupped Portia's chin and raised her face so that she looked in her eyes. "Hush, child. Stop that crying. Where is your faith?"

Portia was awed by her mother's strength. It shone through her eyes. She was a Godly woman. She knew Pat was right. She had to have faith that she would be okay. Enough faith could move a mountain.

Portia regained her composure and told Patricia that she was right. She was going to be fine. She was too good of a person for God to take away. And there were too many people depending on her. Portia was grateful that she could feed off her mama's strength.

Portia begged her mother to stay at her house so she could look after her but Patricia insisted that she was okay. She said she wasn't sick, she just had a little condition. She assured Portia she was fine. She left to go home that Sunday night.

$$$

After her mother left, Portia stayed up late talking to Laila. She told her about her mother having cancer and then she cried in her arms like a baby.

Portia knew Laila had to get up early the next morning for work. She didn't mean to keep her up. She was just grateful to have her there. It was really nice having a friend who was like a real sister staying with her.

Laila told Portia to just pray because prayer changed things. That was the best advice she could give her. Laila had lost both of her parents years ago and Portia had lost her father, so both of them knew firsthand how it felt to lose a parent. It was like no other pain in the world.

While they were alone, Portia figured it was a good time to tell Laila about that pimp calling her cell phone and saying that he was returning Pebbles' call. When Laila heard that she was so pissed off that her first instinct was to go upstairs and tear Pebbles' ass up with a thick leather belt.

Portia told her to wait and analyze the situation. Apparently this dude had gotten into her daughter's head and convinced her that they had some type of relationship. This was a little more serious than an ass whipping could cure. This problem had to be addressed from both sides.

Laila and Portia agreed that if this dude wouldn't fade away he'd just have to be dealt with. Portia told Laila what Jay said about letting him know if she needed some man power.

At first, Laila was a little upset that Portia had told Jay her business but Portia explained to her that she was in the room with Jay when that asshole called, and he overheard her cussing him out. Laila told her she was sorry but she was just embarrassed that it looked like she couldn't control her twelve year old. But she knew it took a village to raise a child, and being that Pebbles' own father was strung out she really appreciated Jay's concern.

Laila knew that the best thing she could've done was get her child out of New York City. One thing she knew for sure was that Pebbles could sneak around and call that mothafucka all she wanted, but she couldn't get to that bastard. Not from New Jersey. Or so Laila thought.

Needless to say, Laila still knew she had to put the fear of God in Pebbles. She had defied her. She was still running behind that old ass man. Laila wasn't some white mother who was gonna just put Pebbles on timeout. Her ass was going to pay for not listening.

That night Laila waited until Pebbles got out of the shower and surprised her in the bathroom. Pebbles quickly covered herself with a towel, and Laila scolded her and let her know that she knew she was still communicating with Ice.

"Khalia, didn't I tell your hot ass to stay away from that damn man? Why is he calling Portia's phone for you? You takin' me for a damn joke?"

Pebbles knew Laila was serious because she had used her real name. She just sighed and rolled her eyes like she was tired of being accused. "No, Ma. Ain't nobody takin' you for no joke. I ain't been talkin' to no Ice."

"Oh, so Portia's lying then, huh?" Laila gave Pebbles an opportunity to respond but she was getting angrier by the second. She couldn't believe she had the nerve to lie to her face.

Pebbles just shrugged and blew her off. That was it for Laila. She ran in the room and got an extension cord. She was back in the bathroom in seconds, and she tore Pebbles' behind up butt naked, the old-fashioned way.

As Laila whipped her daughter's ass she yelled, *"Your ass gon' learn how to listen! You only twelve years old, what the hell is wrong with you? Your stupid ass wanna get pregnant again? Huh, Khalia? You want that mothafucka to give you AIDS? Stop being so damn stupid, try'na live like you grown! What the fuck are you rushing for? You can't make your own decisions! You my child! You hear me? My fuckin' child! Stay the fuck away from that mothafucka!"*

Sweat was rolling down Laila's forehead like she was working out. She was so mad she had to stop herself from killing that child.

Pebbles just laid on the floor with her body balled up. She was stubborn and tried to act tough at first, like she

wasn't going to cry. She tried hard not to but Laila broke her
behind down. She put fire to her ass. Before it was over she
was screaming and hollering like somebody was killing her.

Everyone else in the house overheard the commotion
but no one dared to interfere with Laila's discipline. Portia
didn't get involved because she knew that the ass whippings
she received when she was a child had saved her from a lot
of stuff in life.

$$\$\$\$$$

Even though Pebbles had just gotten her ass beat, two
nights later she sneaked on the phone in Portia's office and
called Ice. In a matter of minutes, he convinced her to sneak
out of the house and take a cab to Brooklyn to be with him.

Pebbles still had welts on her body from that extension
cord her mother beat her with, and she knew Laila would
take the skin off her ass next time if she found out but that
didn't stop her from getting ready to go meet Ice.

She was only bold enough to sneak out because her mother
and Portia weren't at home. They had gone out, and they
instructed Macy to keep an eye on all of them because she
was the oldest. Macy had cramps so she was taking a nap.
Jazmin had fallen asleep beside her. The only one awake was
Jayquan.

Pebbles wasn't worried about getting pass him. She just
had to figure out a way to make him keep his mouth shut
and cover for her when Laila and Portia called to check on
them every hour.

Pebbles changed into a grownup outfit and she went to the
rec section where Jayquan was playing NBA Live. Pebbles
walked over in front of the TV and stood in front of him
with her hand on her hip.

Annoyed, Jayquan kicked her out of the way. "Move out
the way, dummy!"

Pebbles sucked her teeth. "Pause your stupid game for a minute! I need a favor."

Jayquan reluctantly paused his game and asked her, "What you want?"

Pebbles said, "I'm gettin' ready to go somewhere, and I need for you to cover for me when my mother and Aunt Portia call."

Jayquan looked at her suspiciously. "I'm not lyin' for you! Besides, you gon' get in trouble. You better stop being so grown. And take that stupid lookin' stuff off your lips! Ugghh!"

Jayquan was referring to the lip gloss she had on, that she had taken from Laila's dresser. Pebbles said, "Stop hatin', boy." She imitated Lil' Mama and sung, *My lip gloss is cool. My lip gloss be poppin'. All the boys be watchin'. They chase me after school.* She started dancing in front of Jayquan. *"What you know 'bout me? What you, what you know 'bout me?"*

Jayquan made a face and said, "Your lip gloss ain't poppin'. It looks stupid."

Pebbles said, "Mind your business, dummy. You gon' cover for me, or not?"

Jayquan didn't say anything, but he looked like he wasn't buying it. Pebbles knew she had to persuade him. Since he was a boy, she used what she knew boys liked. She lifted her shirt and bra, and showed him her tities.

Jayquan's mouth hung open in surprise and his eyes almost jumped out of his head. They were the first real pair he had seen on a girl his age. He had seen his mother's, his grandmother's, his Aunt Kira's, and Portia's all by mistake at some point or other but they were all old so it didn't count. Jayquan would be forever grateful to Pebbles for what she let him do next.

Pebbles said, "I'll let you feel 'em, if you promise to hold me down. All you gotta do is say I'm sleeping when my mother calls."

Jayquan's curiosity got the best of him. "Ayight, come here." He stood up to get a good feel.

"You promise, Jayquan?"

"I said *yeah*", he replied.

Pebbles headed over to him with her shirt still up, and he placed a hand on each of her breasts and squeezed them like they were Playdough. She noticed Jayquan got this real dumb look on his face. She had seen that same stupid look on this boy in her school named Rahleek's face when she let him squeeze her butt. That was why she liked older guys. Young boys were just so stupid.

Now Jayquan was overdoing it. He didn't want to let go. Pebbles got tired of him groping her. "That's enough, boy!"

She pushed his hands away and fixed her clothes. "Boy, you better not forget! Just tell my mother I'm sleep. If you do this right I'll let you touch 'em again. Okay?"

Jayquan just nodded, and Pebbles jogged down the stairs and out of the house. She yelled behind her, "Come lock the door, Lil' Jay! Bye!"

Jayquan ran downstairs and locked the front door, and then he went in the kitchen to get something to drink. For some reason touching Pebbles had made his throat real dry. Jayquan poured himself a glass of lemonade and sat down on a stool at the island counter.

He was still sitting there a few minutes later when his father came in. Jay had intentionally come in early because Portia had called him and told him the kids were home by themselves. He saw his son in the kitchen sitting still for a change so he knew something was up.

Jay said "what up", and he noticed that Lil'Jay was looking all dreamy eyed and weird in the face. Jay couldn't help but ask, "What's wrong with you?"

Jayquan just grinned and shook his head. "Pop, mine eyes have seen the glory."

Jay just looked at him. What the hell was he talking

about? Had Jayquan gotten himself some? Jay knew he was only eleven so he didn't jump the gun. "What glory have your eyes seen, man?"

Jayquan stuck his little chest out and boasted, "I just felt me a nice pair of tities, Pop. A real nice pair." He grinned proudly.

Jay raised an eyebrow at him. "Word? And whose tities did you feel?"

Lil' Jay smiled like he was intoxicated. "Pebbles'."

Jay held back a laugh. Jayquan was too fresh at eleven, just like he was. He was definitely a chip off the old block. Laila probably wouldn't have found his son feeling her daughter up funny, but Jay was amused. Those kids were something else.

Jay played it cool. "Pebbles is like a cousin to you, man. And where is she now? And where is your little sister? Matter of fact, where is *everybody*?" The house was quiet for a change, and that was strange.

"Jazz is upstairs sleep with Macy, and Pebbles just left."

Jay's ears perked up when he heard that. "Pebbles left with *who*?"

Jayquan said, "She left by herself. That's why she let me feel her tities. So I would cover for her when Laila called and say she was sleep."

Jay was worried. What was that little girl doing leaving the house? He had a feeling she was probably trying to go meet that pimp dude Portia had told him about. He asked Jayquan, "How long ago did she leave?"

Lil' Jay thought about it for a second before answered his father. "Not that long. Maybe about fifteen minutes before you came in."

"Go upstairs and check on your sister", Jay told Jayquan. He grabbed his cell phone and hurried back out to his car. He was going to drive up and down the road to see if he saw Pebbles anywhere.

Jay rode up and down the highway several miles each way, but to no avail. She was no where in sight. The matter was so serious Jay knew he had to call and end Portia and Laila's evening early. He dialed Portia and told her that Pebbles had sneaked out of the house and he couldn't find her. Portia relayed the message to Laila, who was standing right beside her.

When Portia told Laila what Jay said, she snatched the phone from her. She had to hear this for herself. "Jay, Pebbles did *what*?!"

Jay calmly and quickly told her what Jayquan had told him about Pebbles asking him to cover for her and say she was asleep. He left out the part about Pebbles bribing Jayquan with her breasts because he felt that was unnecessary information.

Laila asked Jay if Macy was in place, and she thanked him for pulling her coat about Pebbles. After they hung up, she and Portia rushed home.

On their way home Laila got a call from Casino, who was just calling to check up on her. They had been talking on the phone everyday now.

Laila sounded so wired up when she answered the phone, Cas could tell something was wrong. Laila gave him the rundown about her runaway kid and told him she was worried sick. Cas told her he would see her soon, and he hung up.

As soon as Casino hung up, he checked on his sleeping son, and told Kira he had business to take care of, and would be back later. Then he went out to his eight car garage and hopped in his Range, and headed over to Jay's crib.

When Cas rang the bell, Jay knew it was probably no coincidence. Cas was obviously in contact with Laila and knew what happened. Jay didn't have any beef with that. He knew Cas loved kids as much as he did. He also knew that Cas, like him, was probably ready to go roll up on that dude

Pebbles went to see and teach him a lesson about messing with little girls.

Although he and Cas had just seen each other an hour before, they gave each other a pound like always. "What up, son? What it is?", Cas asked.

Jay sighed and shook his head. "Man, it's like a circus around this piece. Fuckin' kids sneaking out the house and shit." He gave Casino Lil' Jay's account of how Pebbles had flashed him and bribed him to cover for her.

Cas had to laugh at that one. Lil' Jay did look like he was standing a little taller now that he had gotten to second base. Cas gave him a noogie and congratulated him, and then he and Jay got back to the seriousness of the matter. They hoped that little girl was okay. She was only twelve years old.

Just as Jay thought, Cas was ready to go lean on that dude Ice. They were just waiting for Laila to come with some information on his whereabouts. Neither Cas nor Jay liked to play the telephones so they preferred to get the address from her in person.

A few minutes later, Portia and Laila finally arrived. After they all discussed the matter at hand they decided that Portia would stay home with the kids, and Jay and Cas would escort Laila to Brooklyn to find her daughter.

Minutes later, the three of them loaded up in Jay's black Hummer and headed for New York City. Luckily Laila, who was sitting in the backseat, had some idea of where that dude lived because she had followed him that day she'd seen him pick Pebbles up from school.

When they got in Brooklyn, Laila directed Cas and Jay to the area where that building was. Minutes later, Jay turned on Saratoga Avenue and parked. God was on Laila's side already. Ice was standing right outside. Laila pointed him out to Casino and Jay, and they hopped out on him. Both of them were packing, and ready to put some heat in Ice's ass if need be.

Ice didn't know the two dudes who stepped out of the black Hummer on twenty-sixes, but he recognized the broad. Damn, that was that little bitch Pebbles' moms. He started to casually step off and go inside his building but he didn't want to look like he was scared. That old bitch had told him she wouldn't be alone if she came back. Ice was a little nervous but he stuck his chest out and played it cool.

Jay and Cas saw the young dude on the corner trying to look hard, and neither of them were threatened by him. They knew that young boys were the ones that would shoot you the fastest but both men had faith in their ability to be the quickest draw. Besides, that little dude didn't look like a killer. He was a pretty mothafucka. The type Jay and Cas would both enjoy smacking up if he acted stupid.

Casino and Jay approached Ice on either side, and Laila stood in front of him. The first thing they all noticed about him was his iced-out grill. The low carat diamonds shone underneath the streetlight.

Ice tried to be tough. He looked the party of three in the eyes one by one and asked, "Yo, what up? Can I help ya'll?"

Cas didn't play with them young boys so he let him know off the back. "I'ma tell you how you can help yourself. You can make this easy by cooperating. You already know who we came for. And we've been told that you'd already been warned to stay away from her."

Just then, a young girl pulled up in a cab. She paid the driver and hopped out, and she adjusted her too short miniskirt and made a beeline straight for Ice. She only looked about sixteen years old but she was obviously one of Ice's prostitutes because the first thing she did was put a small stack of money in his hand. Then she started copping a plea about how she couldn't make any real bread that night, and had been forced to come in early because "those bitches" made the track so hot.

Ice looked down at the money she had given him like it

had a disease. It was evident that he disapproved extremely. He cut his eye at the girl sternly, like a father would a child. In a very low but firm tone, he ordered, "Bitch, go have a seat on the stoop. I'll deal with you in a minute."

The girl looked like she was real scared after he said that, like she knew what was in store for her. She quickly obeyed and scurried to the side to wait for Ice to reprimand her.

Cas and Jay looked at each other in disbelief. That little nigga was really trying to pimp. After the girl walked off, Cas continued where he left off. "As I was saying. This is your second, and final warning."

"That's right, Ice", Jay added. "Three strikes, and you're out. And it would be a pleasure too, man. Seein' as how you like to take advantage of little girls. I got a daughter, man. I would really love to kill a dirt bag like you. So make the wrong decision, and your hoes are pimp-less." Jay gave him a look that cemented his last words.

Ice couldn't deny his affiliations with Pebbles because her mother was right there, and they had already been informally introduced. He just said, "Ay, look here. I can't help it if that chick is on me. She wanna live the life, man. She wanna be with a pimp. *She* chose *me*. What ya'll want *me* to do?"

Laila held her tongue. She wanted to scream, *"You dirty dick mothafucka! You gave my baby V.D. and got her pregnant! I should kill your bitch ass!"*, but she didn't want Cas and Jay to know that particular tidbit of her personal information. She didn't want them looking at Pebbles like some diseased little hood rat, even if she was carrying on like one lately.

Laila said, "Nigga, *she* is only twelve years old. Don't destroy yourself over somebody's baby. Go get my fuckin' daughter! *Now*, so I can take her home."

Cas said, "Yo, you heard the lady. Move, nigga!"

Ice looked at them like he was confused. "I don't know where her daughter at. I ain't gon' front, she called me and told me she was taking a cab over here but that was like three hours ago, and she ain't made it yet. And I ain't heard from her since. For real, yo. That's my good word as a pimp."

Laila , Cas, and Jay all looked at him like they didn't believe him.

Casino said, "Ayight, I see. You wanna make this hard." He glanced around to make sure he didn't see any police and he lifted his shirt and reached for his hammer.

Jay reached for his gun at the same time. It looked rehearsed but it wasn't. They were both just short of patience with that nigga.

Ice got the picture. He kept his voice down so the two young prostitutes sitting on the stoop nearby wouldn't overhear him. "Look, I don't beef over bitches. I said I don't know where she is."

Ice looked at Laila. "With all due respect, Ma. If your daughter's only twelve, you should have more control over her. To be honest, she's becomin' a real headache for me now, wit' her moms comin' over here and shit. Next, you'd be ready to get the police involved. I'm a business, man. I don't need no heat over here. Trust me."

Laila wasn't buying it. She crossed her arms impatiently. Pebbles had to be with him.

Ice could see that she didn't believe him, so he addressed the men. "Look, I ain't got nothin' to hide, and no reason to lie. I'll even let ya'll in my crib to have a look around if ya'll want. You'll find plenty bitches up there, but not Pebbles. Trust me, if she was here I would've given her up by now. I don't fuck with bitches with problems. I got plenty chicks, so one ain't nothin'. Cop and lock, or cop and blow, I celebrate when I lose a hoe. I'm a pimp of honor, man. I'm about gettin' bread, so I don't need the bullshit. That's the golden rule. Money talks, and bullshit walks."

Jay and Cas decided to go upstairs and take a walk through Ice's apartment. When they got up there, they saw that he had meant what he said. There were a lot of girls up there.

At least eight or nine, but Pebbles wasn't one of them.

When they got back outside, Ice said, "I know some of my bitches look a little young, but most of their mothers know they're here. They mostly drug head bitches who know I take better care of they kids than they do."

Ice took the telephone numbers Jay and Cas gave him, and he assured them that he would call if he heard from Pebbles that night.

As Ice watched them leave, he wondered why Pebbles was always running behind him. She was the one calling him all the time. Why was she trying to live that life? He could tell that she was from a good home, and he could see that she had people in her life that cared about her. Back to business as usual, he headed over to chastise Britney, the hoe who had pulled up in the cab with the too short skirt and the too short money.

Laila, Jay, and Cas had no choice but to believe Ice. Pebbles really wasn't over there. All they could do was get in the truck and bounce. Cas and Jay asked Laila if there was anywhere else Pebbles might be hanging out at, but she couldn't think of anywhere.

On the way home, Laila was even more worried than she was on the way there. Lord, where was her child? She hoped she was safe. She was starting to fear that Pebbles had been abducted or something. Laila prayed silently. She needed God to watch over her baby.

$$$

A few hours earlier, Pebbles had left the house believing that she would just flag a cab down like in the City. She had walked down the street and tried to put some distance between her and the house. A good way's down she stuck out her hand at the passing cars on the highway, but she had no luck. She realized that catching a cab wasn't going to be as easy as she thought. And it was getting chilly out there.

As soon as Pebbles was about to give up and make her way back to the house, a car slowed down and backed up. The driver pulled over on the side of the road. It was a middle-aged white man. He was wearing glasses and a necktie. He asked Pebbles where she was headed, and she told him she was going to Brooklyn to see her boyfriend.

The man, who introduced himself as "John", told her he just so happened to be on his way there too. He offered Pebbles a ride to the City. He looked harmless enough, so Pebbles accepted without hesitation. She assured him that her boyfriend would pay him when they got there.

John told Pebbles not to worry about it, and to hop on in. She smiled appreciatively and naively, thinking that him giving her a ride was such a great favor. But what poor Pebbles really did was seal her doom.

John happened to be a former sex offender. He was an ex-con trying to get his life back on track. Needless to say, seeing a little girl out there on the highway was just too tempting for him. He couldn't resist the carnal urge to have his way with her. She just seemed so innocent, and that was what he couldn't resist.

John drove a few miles and then he turned off the highway and headed for a discreet place he knew in South Jersey. He knew he would have the privacy to do as he pleased to the little girl there because the nearest person would be too far away to hear her screams.

Pebbles was so busy daydreaming about Ice she didn't notice John changing his route. She wouldn't have known the difference anyway. Laila had taught her children to pay attention to their surroundings but Pebbles' head was usually in the clouds when she rode somewhere. And that night was no exception. She just assumed they would be in Brooklyn shortly.

Only when she noticed John slow the car down and turn

into the parking lot of some big deserted looking warehouse did Pebbles become alarmed. Where was he taking her?

John could tell by the way Pebbles sat up in her seat that she sensed something was wrong. He placed his hand on her knee and told her to relax. He said they were just making a little pit stop before they got to the City, so she could pay him for the ride.

Pebbles adamantly insisted that he leave from that dark place because her boyfriend would pay him when they got there. She said a mental prayer, wondering what she had gotten herself into. All she could hear in her mind was her mother's mouth. She knew better than to accept a ride from a stranger. Especially a strange man.

John's whole demeanor changed. The nice, friendly looking guy Pebbles had trusted transformed into the sick creep he really was. John was rotten to the core. He had even molested his own daughter, and he didn't have any regrets about it either. His ex-wife had caught him in the act and reported him to the authorities, and the eight-year sentence he had received for that crime had ended earlier that year. He had done six years, and was released on parole. He was required to attend weekly classes with a bunch of other pedophiles, and some of them were even sicker than he was.

Pebbles was a kid from Brooklyn so she had heart. She tried to break bad and demand that John take her to her destination. She told him she wasn't playing with him.

But Pebbles' gangsta' girl routine did little to deter John from his plans. His mind was already made up. He shut off the ignition, and turned around and told Pebbles to shut up. She would be the first African American child he would experience, so he didn't want her to ruin it for him by blabbing off at the mouth.

Pebbles just wouldn't be quiet but John knew how to shut her up. He had one of those anti-car theft devices called The

Club in the back seat. He quickly retrieved it, and without a word he swung and clocked Pebbles upside her head.

John successfully knocked her out with one blow. She fell silent, and her head rolled to the side. John got out and walked around to the passenger side and opened the car door, and he picked Pebbles up and threw her over his shoulder like she was a rag doll that weighed nothing. He shut the car door and headed for an opening on the side of the abandoned warehouse.

John had jimmied open some window bars on the side of the building just three days ago, and he'd created what he liked to think of as a shrine inside. The shrine was really a supply closet with a makeshift homemade alter in it, an old busted beanbag, and a bunch of half burned candles in glass jars. As his final touch of décor, John had carefully scribbled the names and ages of the children he had become "friends" with on the walls in goat blood. The place would probably give an outsider the creeps, but to John it was a place of solace.

In John's mind, he wasn't a monster. He considered what he did with the children to be recreational. He'd never meant to hurt any of them. He had only clubbed Pebbles in the head to shut her up. There were no people around the deserted area they were in but her yelling had agitated him. John had a list of things that pushed him over the top, and yelling was just one of them. He had what he referred to as just a little condition, but was really a serious mental disorder.

John carefully and gingerly laid Pebbles down on the beanbag, and he lit a few candles. The candlelight created what he perceived to be a warm and inviting environment. That would surely let her know that he was a friend. If she wasn't afraid then she wouldn't yell. Satisfied that enough candles were burning, John undressed Pebbles completely and then he nudged her awake.

When Pebbles came to, she looked around in bewilderment. Her first reaction was surprise when she looked at all the candles, and then she was frightened beyond her imagination. She looked down at herself and realized that she was naked, and she started to panic.

When John saw Pebbles wake up, he smiled at her fondly. She looked innocent now. Much unlike the loudmouthed, wannabe tough girl in the car a minute ago. And she had the ever enchanting look of fear in her eyes. John thrived off of other people's fear. Particularly children's.

Pebbles tried to stand up but John shoved her back down. He just wanted her to lay there for a while so he could admire her beauty. Her small, still developing breasts jutted forward proudly like unripe fruit. John reached down and traced his fingers along her torso. He was turned on by the softness of her. The candlelight cast a soft glow over her bronze skin. She was a beauty. John traced her full lips with his thumb.

Pebbles backed up as far away from him as she could and she began to cry like the frightened child she was. She knew she was in sick company. That was evident by the blood writing on the walls of the tiny room they were in, all the candles, and the fact that John had stripped her naked. But poor Pebbles was about to find out the depth of John's sickness.

What he did to Pebbles next could only be described as cruel, inhumane, ghastly, and atrocious. John decided that he wanted to make her into a live wax doll to preserve her beauty. By then most of the candles had melted down. He picked up a glass jar of hot melted wax and poured it over her face. Pebbles screamed at the top of her lungs, and the hot wax clung to her face like a second skin and hardened.

Pebbles knew her face had to be severely burned after that. This man was really crazy. She was afraid he was going to kill her. She had to try and fight her way out. She leaned back and kicked John in his privates and tried to make a run for it, but the fact that her eyelids were scorched shut with wax slowed down her progress a great deal. Pebbles could barely see but she fumbled her way to the door and turned the knob. Unfortunately, she didn't get out in time. John recovered, and he quickly ran over and grabbed her by the back of her neck.

John picked Pebbles up in the air by her neck, and her arms and legs flailed wildly about. He threw her up against the wall and twisted her arm behind her back. He could see that she liked it rough so that was the way he'd give it to her.

He wrapped his fist in her hair a few times, and he banged her head into the wall repeatedly until her forehead split open and she lost consciousness. After Pebbles was out again, he laid her back down on the beanbag. Blood trickled down into her eyes from the huge gash on her forehead. Now John felt that the blood had destroyed her innocence and beauty.

He placed an old pillow over Pebbles' face and held it down tightly, until he saw her chest stop going up and down. Satisfied that she was no longer breathing, John unzipped his pants and freed himself. He spread Pebbles' legs and thrust himself inside of her. She felt so young, just the way he loved. He sickly humped until relief overcame him, and then he removed the pillow from her face. He admired her and affectionately stroked her jaw. In death she was innocent again.

When John was done, he put Pebbles in an old burlap sack he had in the corner, and he blew out all of his candles and headed back to the car with the sack draped over his shoulder like he was Santa Clause. He placed Pebbles body in the trunk, and he drove a few blocks south to get rid of her.

Chapter Seventeen

Days had passed, and Laila still hadn't heard from Pebbles. She had contacted the police the night she discovered she wasn't with Ice, and they had issued an Amber Alert in ten states. But the fact that no one knew anything about who could have possibly abducted her hindered progress substantially.

The upcoming days were hard for everyone, but Laila was a nervous wreck. She was in denial, and still believed that Ice had Pebbles. On various occasions at different times of the day, she hid in Ice's area and watched him come and go, hoping to spot her daughter with him. He interacted with a lot of females, young and old, but to Laila's great disappointment Pebbles wasn't one of them.

Laila was at the end of her rope. She had hit the bottom. She was at a point where she would have been relieved to find her daughter living with a pimp rather than fathom the idea that something terrible had happened to her. She was in such a state of despair she couldn't even go to work.

Two days later, the authorities contacted Laila and told her that the body of a young girl who matched Pebbles' description was found in an abandoned lot in South Jersey. The detective said they had a feeling it was her daughter but they wanted her to come down to the station and identify the body. Laila agreed to come down there, and then she hung up the phone and stood still as death.

Portia was right by her side when she got the call. She placed a hand on her friend's shoulder. Portia was afraid to ask. Laila just looked at her and mumbled softly, "They think they found her body." After that, her eyes flooded with tears and she just collapsed.

Portia sank down to the floor with her friend and held

her. Laila folded in her arms and wept like a baby. Portia had tears streaming down her face as well but she tried to be as strong as she could for Laila. She rubbed her dear friend's back and rocked her in her arms.

A little while later, Laila got it together as much as she could, and they loaded up in Portia's car. Portia made a quick stop to pick up Fatima, and then she drove the three of them to the morgue to see if the poor child's body that was discovered was Pebbles.

When they got there, the girls were led down to a cold room in the basement. The officer opened one of many drawers and pulled out a long table. On the table was a young girl's body with a white sheet spread over it. The gentleman asked the ladies if they were ready, and he pulled the sheet back.

To their dismay it was Pebbles. She had a big cut on her forehead with congealed blood around it, and there was some hard white stuff on her face that looked like wax. Even though Laila had a feeling in her gut, it was different to witness it in real life. That was her baby laying there naked and dead in front of her. Some deranged sicko had raped her and killed her, and then he tossed her in some abandoned lot to rot. And Laila couldn't even murder the bastard because she didn't know who he was yet.

She handled the identifying of her child's body rather well, considering the circumstances. At least now she could give Pebbles a nice home going ceremony and a proper burial. Then her little angel could rest in peace.

Portia and Fatima stood by Laila's side. Both of them were crying quietly. They had all been through a lot but the sight of that little girl dead and bruised in front of them on that cold metal table was indeed the saddest thing any one of them had ever witnessed.

$$$

A few days later, Laila sat on the floor in the corner of her room rocking back and forth with her arms folded around her knees. She was praying, and praying hard. She really needed God to hold her. She needed His strength because she was in shambles. It was hard for her to digest the fact that she had buried her baby earlier that day. She would never get used to the fact that she had lost a child. It had been her duty to protect Pebbles, and she had failed to do so.

"God, why? Why? I don't understand why you let this happen to my baby", Laila sobbed. She just felt like she needed answers. In the blink of an eye she had become a bereaved mother in tears. Tears for her twelve year old. She wasn't supposed to outlive her children. She would've traded her life for Pebbles' in a heartbeat.

Fortunately Laila had been financially situated enough to deal with the untimely tragedy. And financially was the only way she had been prepared to deal with it too. Not mentally, not physically, nor spiritually. She had a hefty life insurance policy on her family, including herself and Khalil.

Laila remembered her grandmother struggling to bury her mother without insurance when she was a child. After that, her grandmother had instilled in her the importance of keeping your loved ones insured. She told her that nobody planned on losing a loved one but a person should be prepared. Because of her grandmother's teachings, Laila had enough insurance on Pebbles to put her away really nice.

Even though Laila had everything covered, Casino and Jay insisted that they pay for everything. They told her to keep her money and do something nice for herself. They had gone all out, and Laila was thankful to them.

Bits and pieces of the ceremony floated through her head. Laila was torn. She wanted to remember it because it was the last time she would ever see her baby in the flesh, but Laila also wanted to forget about it because it hurt so badly.

Pebbles had gone home like a real princess. Laila had

dressed her in all white like an angel, with a halo of curls in her hair. And her custom-made casket was beautiful. It was white and lined in pink satin. Beside it stood a life-sized picture of her, and there had been so many flowers, balloons, and stuffed animals to celebrate her life it was amazing.

Instead of in a hearse, she had Pebbles' body carried on a lovely pink and white carriage pulled by two white horses, and at the end of the ceremony they released one hundred doves into the sky. The doves were symbolic of her soul going to heaven.

Pebbles had a large turnout at her funeral. A lot of her teachers, classmates and childhood friends showed up. Laila didn't have much family because she was an only child, and her mother had been also, but the few family members she'd invited on her father's side showed up.

Macy had recited a poem she had written for her sister. It was titled, "The Birth of an Angel". Laila couldn't remember the exact words but it was about Pebbles' earthly life ending and her heavenly life beginning because she had work to do for God. Macy had struggled through some of the words because she couldn't help crying, but she had done an excellent job.

Laila had cried through the whole poem. Her best friends, Portia and Fatima, and also Portia's mother, were right there by her side throughout the whole ceremony. Casino, Jay, and Wise were there as well, all suited up in nice designer suits, tailored perfectly to their fit.

Even Khalil made an appearance. Laila saw him go up to view Pebbles' body, and she could tell he was crying. But he must've stepped in and out because she couldn't find him anywhere after the service. She imagined the news hadn't been easy for him either because Pebbles was his child too, and sort of his favorite. Laila was just glad he had shown his face. His mother stood by Laila's side on his behalf and offered apologies for her weak son.

Pebbles was a well loved child. Laila smiled and thought
of just a few weeks ago, when Pebbles tried to teach her how
to do the latest dances. That girl knew she could dance her
ass off. Pebbles had laughed so hard when Laila tried to do
the Chicken Noodle Soup tears came out of her eyes.

Pebbles, Pebbles, Pebbles. Boy, she really missed her little
girl. She thought back to when Pebbles was a baby. It was
Portia who had given her the nickname "Pebbles" because
Laila used to always put her hair up in a ponytail on top of
her head like Pebbles from "The Flinstones" cartoon. Laila
couldn't really braid that well, and she had two little ones so
a ponytail had just been easier to do.

A knock at the door snapped Laila back to reality. She
smiled again at the fond memories of her angel and wiped
the tears from her eyes.

That was Macy at the door, coming to check on Laila to
make sure she was okay. She came in and hugged her, and
kissed her on the forehead. Laila was glad to see her. She
was her only living child now, and she was all she had. She
hugged Macy tightly, afraid that she too would slip through
her grasp and wind up getting hurt. She couldn't allow that
to happen again. There was no way.

$$$

Even though he didn't need an excuse because he was
welcome anytime, Cas thought of a reason to go over Jay's
house early the following morning. The truth was he hadn't
slept well because all night he was busy thinking about the
fact that poor Laila was probably awake all night crying. He
had seen how torn she was at the funeral and it had killed
him to not be able to hold her and comfort her. Kira had
attended the service, and he had seen Laila's husband there
too. Cas just wanted to be there for her and make sure she
was okay.

When he got over Jay's house and asked Laila how she was doing, she put up a front at first. She just smiled a little and nodded her head. Cas comfortingly placed his hands on her shoulders and smoothed her hair out of her face. His genuine concern and sincerity made Laila be honest with him. She told him she wasn't okay at all, but he could already tell that by looking at her.

Laila admitted to him that she was enraged because no one had been convicted yet for her child's brutal rape and murder, and she wanted somebody to pay. She told him she was even thinking about going back to the 'hood and smoking Ice because if it wasn't for Pebbles trying to get to him, she would have never been out there in the middle of the night trying to hitch a ride to the City.

Laila was so serious she startled Cas a little. She looked angry enough to kill somebody for real too. Cas didn't want her to get herself in any trouble but he understood how she felt. He didn't say anything but he decided that he would take care of it for her.

Cas hugged Laila and told her he was there for her if she needed him for anything, and he meant anything. He just wanted to protect her. He wished there was so much more he could do.

$$$

Two nights later, Cas and Jay were leaving an upscale gambling joint called Mickey's that was located uptown. They had both been kissed by Lady Luck so they each had a pocket full of money. After they reached the parking lot and got in Casino's Maserati, Jay reclined his seat and bragged about the lucky streak he'd had during the last few days. His gambling winnings had totaled over two hundred grand.

Cas had won some pretty decent bread too but Jay noticed that he wasn't jiving and boasting along with him like he usually did when he won. He looked so deep in thought Jay asked him what was on his mind.

Cas didn't answer him at first because he wasn't sure how Jay would take it if he told him was contemplating taking care of that problem for Laila. He just wanted to ease her mind. He didn't want to be upfront with Jay about the depth of his feelings for her so he didn't respond.

Jay saw that Cas wouldn't answer him. He and Casino could talk about anything so Jay knew he could get an answer out of him. He didn't sense that Cas was in a bad enough mood for him to back off, so Jay asked him again. "Son, what's the deal?"

Cas just shrugged his shoulders. "Ain't shit, man." But the more he thought about it, he knew he had to let Jay know what he planned to do. That was his main man. He sighed, and gave Jay the rundown on his plan.

When Jay heard Cas' intentions, he totally understood. The situation angered him too. He wanted to get involved so he decided to roll with his bro. Truthfully, Jay would've rolled with him no matter what the cause was because Cas always had his back whether he agreed with him or not. Cas and he were like brothers, and they were certainly each other's keepers. They had been for years.

Luckily, they were both dressed in dark colored tee-shirts and fitted baseball caps so they were sort of incognito. Plus the vehicle they were traveling in was black. Jay rode shotgun while Cas drove them to Brooklyn. Along the way, Jay called Manuel and asked him if they could use his facility again. Manuel told him to go right ahead, and said he would have Loco meet them there in about an hour.

When Cas got to Brownsville he pulled up on Saratoga Avenue and parked a few houses down from Ice's building. One of the street lights was out so it was pretty dark where they were sitting. He shut off the car, and he and Jay sat there and late-waited Ice quietly.

Almost two hours later, Ice pulled up and parked his BMW a few cars down and sauntered in his building. Jay and Cas were glad he was alone. That would make things a lot simpler.

They both put on gloves, and quickly hopped out and followed him. When they got in the lobby of his building they glanced around to make sure the coast was clear, and they approached him.

When Ice turned around and saw them, he looked a little surprised. Casino smiled at him, and he took that to be a friendly gesture. He hadn't heard the rumors about Killah' Cas' homicidal grin, so he relaxed. If dudes were smiling they must've come in peace. He hoped so because he sure wasn't prepared. He didn't have a gun on him. Ice noticed that the other dude wasn't smiling. Then he remembered that he had seen the news last week and knew Pebbles had been killed. Damn, this wasn't a friendly visit.

Jay said, "Get over here, cocksucka'. Now!" He grabbed Ice and held him while Cas patted him down to make sure he didn't have any weapons.

Ice was clean. The only thing Cas found in his pocket was a roll of money and a cell phone. He confiscated them both because he knew Ice wouldn't be needing them anymore.

Casino smiled coldly at Ice and clocked him with the butt of his gun. That blow to the head let Ice know how serious they were. He stumbled, and then he tried to make a run for it.

Jay threw a big black .44 in his face and stopped him in his tracks. For trying to escape, Cas double pimp smacked Ice so hard spit flew out of his mouth. After that he got the message and surrendered peacefully.

Jay and Cas weren't new jacks. They knew better than to kill him in the lobby. They walked him out to the car and made him get in the back seat. Jay got in beside him and shut the back door, and Cas drove off. Jay kept the hammer on Ice until Cas pulled up at The Meat House.

It was Ice's first time riding in such an expensive luxury automobile. Cas' black four door Maserati shitted on his Beamer. Ice read a lot of exotic car magazines because he had high aspirations, so he knew that this was the Quattroporte Duoselect model. She was fully equipped too. This was the car of Ice's dreams and he figured he'd be riding in one soon. But this wasn't the joy ride he had anticipated. This was a one-way ticket to hell.

When they arrived, they forced Ice out of the car. Cas and Jay wanted to get it over quick. Ice was scared to death. The fear showed in his eyes. He pleaded with them to let him go. He swore he hadn't laid a finger on Pebbles, and said he was sorry she was dead.

Cas quietly told him that he wasn't sorry yet, but he would be. Jay didn't bother saying anything. He knew Ice was probably telling the truth but his fate was already sealed. There was really nothing he could say.

Loco, the cleanup guy, let them inside The Meat House. Ice wouldn't stop copping a plea. That nigga was on the verge of tears. He was a pimp so he was really good with words but his persuasive game had no effects on Cas and Jay.

Neither of the partners liked to waste time lollygagging. They both had cold hearts when appropriate, and preferred to get to the point. All both of them could think about was that sweet little girl Pebbles, and all of the heartache Laila had been caused on Ice's behalf. The decision to end his life was personal for both of them, especially for Cas. That nigga was a scumbag. Without a word, Casino did cool Ice the honor of putting a hot slug in his cranium.

After Ice's body dropped from the headshot Cas had given him, Cas told Loco he wanted one thing before he disposed of the corpse. Cas already had on gloves so he stuck his hand in Ice's mouth and unsnapped the gold fronts from his top and bottom teeth effortlessly. Luckily, Ice's jewel encrusted grill wasn't permanently bonded onto his teeth. Cas stuck the gold and diamond grill in his pocket and told Loco that was it.

He and Jay thanked him, and they each gave him a pound. Loco didn't speak English but he was Manuel's people so they weren't worried. They knew he would take care of it so they bounced without a second thought.

The following day, Cas called Laila and told her he was coming over because he had something for her. He wanted to see her, and he also had Ice's grill in a little white box in his pocket.

When Cas saw Laila, the first thing he did was hand the box to her because he wanted her to know that it was taken care of. That box contained all that was left of Ice.

When Laila opened the box and saw what was in it she did a double take. Could that really be what she thought it was? She questioned Cas with her eyes, and he gave her a look that confirmed it. The grill belonged to that no-good mothafucka Ice.

To Laila, that was the equivalent of Cas bringing Ice's head to her on a platter. He had taken care of the man she felt was responsible for her daughter's death, be it directly or indirectly. Laila felt a sense of relief now that her wish had been fulfilled. It was good that creep was off the streets. He had messed up enough young girls' lives. Laila wished she could spit on his fucking grave.

Now don't get it twisted. Laila was a woman of God. She knew it was wrong to take the law into your own hands but she was so angry about her baby being taken away from her, she needed some closure. And now she had some, thanks to Cas.

Laila didn't know what to say. She got all teary-eyed. "Thanks, Cas. You don't know what this means to me."

Cas just shrugged like it was no big deal. He just hoped she would sleep a little better at night now. If Laila didn't know before, she knew now. He would do anything for her.

Cas wished they had a little more privacy. He would've offered her a nice massage or something to help her relax, but he knew they couldn't do that. Not while she was staying with Jay and Portia. Something really had to give about that.

Cas briefly toyed with the idea of buying Laila a crib. The more he thought about it, the more he figured it was the right thing to do. His mother was a real estate agent so he could pretty much find her something nice without having to spend a lot of time doing it.

$$$

The next day Laila got a call from Detective Prescott, the cop that was handling the investigation of Pebbles' murder. He let her know that they had a suspect. They had gotten back the autopsy report, and DNA was found on Pebbles from a convicted pedophile named Harvey York.

Harvey York was a recent parolee who was under a strict court order to stay away from children. The detective assured Laila that when they caught that bastard they were going to put him away for good. Laila couldn't wait for them to find that sick mothafucka.

After a massive manhunt, the suspect was in custody within twenty four hours. Harvey York cooperated with the police, and they got a signed confession out of him within two hours. He even took them to the so-called shrine where he had taken Pebbles, and told them what he had done to her. Then he told them exactly where he had dumped her body. That bastard made front page on newspapers across the country the next day and got his fifteen minutes of fame because the media jumped on that story like white on rice.

The following evening, Portia asked Laila if she felt bad about what happened to Ice now that the real killer had been apprehended.

Laila didn't respond. She just had this stoic look on her face. After a minute, she gave Portia an honest answer. "No, I *don't* feel bad, P. Not at all. Hell, I probably saved a few mothers from future tears. So *good riddance*. I hope that bastard rots in hell."

Portia just nodded. She understood. She knew her girl was hurting.

Chapter Eighteen

About a week later, Portia headed to the City to check on her mother. She had made it a point to visit Patricia at least three times a week since she found out about her being diagnosed with cancer. Today was the day for Pat's weekly doctor visit, and Portia didn't want to be late. Morning traffic on the highway was congested so she kept glancing at the time.

That was actually the week their family summer trip to Europe was scheduled but Portia had called it off. There was just too much going on. She wasn't in the mood, and she didn't want to be away from her mother that long.

Her mother's appointment was at ten o'clock so Portia had forty five minutes to get there. She was close to the Holland Tunnel but traffic was just creeping along. She had her radio tuned to the morning show on Hot 97. She turned the volume up to hear Miss Jones badmouthing one of her guests on the show, some wanna-be songstress that she felt couldn't really sing.

Just then, Portia's cell phone rang. It was Patricia calling to see where she was. Portia told her she was coming through the tunnel and would be there as fast as she could.

When Portia finally got to her mother's house, she called her and told her to come on downstairs. Pat walked out looking healthy as ever. Her shoulder length silky black hair shone in the sun. It blew in the wind, and her cocoa skin glowed. She was dressed in flare leg jeans and a cute lavender sweater, with a stylish pastel colored Dooney & Burke bag hanging on her shoulder.

Portia smiled at the sight of her. Her mother looked good. She looked too young, and was too pretty and healthy for Portia to believe she had cancer. Every time she thought about it a wave of fear swept over her and made her stomach flip. She couldn't stand the thought of losing her mother.

Portia shook it off and brightened up. She unlocked the car door, and Pat got in on the passenger side. Portia smiled, and leaned over and kissed her on the cheek. "Hey, Mommy. How you feelin'?"

Pat nodded her head and said, "I feel pretty good. How 'bout you, baby?"

Portia told her she was okay. After Patricia fastened her seatbelt, Portia pulled off and headed towards the Brooklyn Queens Expressway. Along the way, Pat revealed to her that her doctor had suggested that she have a full hysterectomy to try and remove the cancer. She said he told her that if that didn't work she should undergo radiation treatments. Then Patricia told Portia about all the side effects and possible repercussions the treatments could have.

Portia admitted to Pat that she was scared, but would stand by her side on whatever decision she made. Next, they discussed the possibilities of holistic healing. Pat said that even though there was no medical evidence that it worked, she wanted to give it a shot. That along with prayer could certainly change things if they had enough faith.

After Patricia saw her doctor, he confirmed what he had told her the previous week. He said he felt she needed to have a full hysterectomy as soon as possible because the tests he'd run showed that the cancer was spreading.

Pat thanked him and told him she would make a decision soon, and she left his office. Portia was right by her side.

Portia and Pat were both quiet on the way home. Pat was thinking about the fact that she might have to part with her uterus. She wasn't thinking of having anymore children but that was part of what made her a woman. She didn't know if she was quite prepared to part with it. She would have preferred to leave here just as she came if she could help it. Pat voiced her feelings to her daughter.

Portia understood how her mother felt about parting with her uterus but she felt like if that was what could save her, than it had to go. She told Pat that losing a uterus could never take away from all the strength, beauty, and glory she possessed as a woman.

When Pat heard that her eyes got a little teary. Portia was right, she was strong. She had been raised by a strong woman, and she'd raised her daughter to be that way as well. She knew Portia was afraid, and truthfully she was scared too. She definitely wasn't ready to leave yet. Pat rubbed Portia's hand and assured her that she would do whatever she had to so she could be there for her and Jazmin.

Patricia didn't tell Portia that the doctor told her she had to do something immediately because the cancer was spreading so fast. She kept that tidbit of information to herself. She had a lot of thinking to do that night.

$$\$\$\$$$

Back in New Jersey, Wise and Fatima were involved in another heated shouting match about Wise' infidelity. Well, Fatima was really the one shouting. Wise was just standing there looking stupid. He had been served with some papers that morning, and it turned out that he was hit with another lawsuit. But this one was the ultimate. It was a paternity suit. A woman named Angela Thomas had a two year old son, and she charged Wise with being the daddy. She was demanding child support and legal recognition of her son by the famous wealthy rapper, William "Wise" Page.

Fatima was glad her daughter was at her mother's house because she was at the point of snapping. She wondered if she should just grab a butcher knife and stab Wise in the heart. He had broken her heart so many times it only seemed fair that she mess up his. Shit, her heart was permanently damaged. The worse part was that he never allowed it time to heal before he broke it again.

Fatima was taking the news about that baby real hard. She thought about leaving that mothafucka. But that was her damn house. So what if he bought it. She wasn't going anywhere! His ass was leaving. As a matter of fact, kicking him out was the right thing to do. His getting a bitch pregnant was the final slap in the face.

Fatima couldn't take it anymore. "Wise, get the fuck outta my house. Get your shit and get out, Wise!" Fatima was so angry she was pulling her own hair.

Wise remained cool, and was patient with her. "Tima, this shit is bogus. That ain't my baby, you crazy? Whoever this bitch is, she's lyin'!"

"Nigga, she ain't lyin'! Your dumb ass be out there having unprotected sex with all these hoes and shit. You stupid mothafucka! Get the fuck out before I hurt you, Wise. I'm telling you. For real."

Fatima ran upstairs and started dumping shit out of his drawers on the floor. She was crying, and she kept screaming on "Get out! Get the fuck out!"

Wise could see that Tima was serious. She was straight wilding. He didn't even recognize the name of the bitch who was trying to set him up. And he knew he hadn't piped any bitches raw. Maybe in the mouth, but not in no pussy. There was no way that could be his baby but Fatima wouldn't listen to reason.

Wise couldn't front, this paternity shit was serious. And for a paternity suit to come so soon after Melanie accused him of rape, now that was crazy. It was like those bitches were in cahoots.

Wise didn't know what to do. Maybe he should really move out for a little while. Just to give Fatima some space. From the way she was tossing his shit in those suitcases, it didn't look like he had a choice.

Wise decided to check into a hotel that night. And not

to mess around either. He really just wanted to be alone for a change. He was having a bad luck streak with broads, and he was beginning to wonder if it was in fact payback for all the times he was unfaithful to Fatima. But what did he do to deserve this one?

Fatima locked the front door after Wise left, and she sank to the floor and held her head in her hands. She just cried her heart out. She was so tired. Wise had drained her. She didn't have anything else left for him to suck out of her soul. That was it.

Fatima sat there for what seemed like hours, and then she got up and took a long, hot shower. The hot water made her feel a lot better. She put on an oversized comfortable tee-shirt and flopped down on the couch.

As always when she got upset, Fatima craved ice cream but she thought the better of it. She had kept her weight off so far, and she didn't want to backslide. A perfect size eight, she was thinner than she had been in years. And it felt good. But being with Wise seemed to take away the joy from her accomplishments. It was definitely time for a change.

$$$

Around three AM, Hop was sitting in the cut in his black BMW 750. He was parked down the street from Club Duvet. He had just left the club a few minutes ago because he was trying to get a head start on this rapper dude he'd been scoping out. The dude's name was Trey-Black, and he was in town from St. Louis.

Hop had watched that nigga flossing all night, throwing money around and ordering champagne for the house. Hop had his eye on that big quarter million dollar diamond chain he had on. He had every intention of relieving Trey-Black of it, and all the money in his pockets too.

While Hop was waiting, his cell phone rang. It was

Mikey, his man from Lefrak City, calling to let him know about a golden opportunity someone had pulled his coat to. Mikey said that it would be easy for Hop to pull off, because for him it was an inside job.

Hop listened as Mikey told him about some out-of-town dudes called The Scumbag Brothas, who had their eye on those Street Life cats he rolled with, Jay, Cas, and Wise. Mikey said The Scumbag Brothas were willing to split the proceeds with Hop sixty-forty if he set things up, and he told Hop he only wanted five percent of whatever he cleared as a finder's fee.

Hop told Mikey he would let him know later, and they hung up. He pondered the idea of setting Jay and them up. Those dudes had been good to him. But on the other hand, they hadn't yet presented him a Street Life medallion. That was an indirect insult. And Hop hated the way Jay and Cas always took Wise' side when they had a disagreement. They hadn't shown him the love he felt he deserved. He had been a team player but dudes still ain't show him no love.

The more Hop thought about it, he decided to do it. If Jay and them would just give it up then nobody would get hurt. Niggas got robbed everyday. That was how the shady lowlife in Hop justified the foul act he was ready to commit. He was a grimy dude anyway, so nothing was beneath him.

Hop called Mikey back and got contact numbers for The Scumbags, or whatever the fuck they called themselves. Mikey was glad he had decided to take the bait. He and Hop agreed to stay in contact. Before they hung up Hop told Mikey that if he ever needed another gunman to pull some shit off, he would be the first one he called. Mikey just laughed because Hop knew he didn't get his hands dirty. He always got other dudes to rob dudes. That way they could take the fall if something went wrong.

Hop closed his cell phone and snapped back to his current project. He zoomed back in just in time to see Trey and his little entourage coming out of the club. There were three of them. Hop was outnumbered, but not enough to back down from his goal. He wanted that chain, and he had to strike before they got to their vehicles. He knew they probably had guns in their cars but he was pretty sure they didn't have any in the club.

Hop pulled his hat down over his eyes, and he cocked his gun and tucked it in his waist under his hoodie. He got out and followed them. The time had come to set it off.

Trey and his homies had seen Hop in the club so they didn't really feel alarmed when they saw him limping behind them. But when Hop got close up on them he made sure that shit changed. He swiftly pulled out and pointed his ratchet in their faces. "Yo, you niggas put ya' hands up. Now!"

Hop's tone and expression told them shit was for real. He kept his eyes on all three of them and demanded their shine. Trey's two homies had on some nice pieces too, although theirs were miniscule in comparison to Trey's. But Hop didn't give a fuck, he wanted those too.

He kept his gun on Trey's head. "C'mon, ya'll know what it is. Give it the fuck up. C'mon, let's go!"

From the looks on the dudes' faces, they were all tight that they had gotten caught out there like that. Trey bit his lip in anger and reluctantly took off his chain, and one of his homies made a move. Hop stopped him in his tracks by aiming at his head. The dude grimaced at Hop but they all gave it up with no problem after that.

In a deep southern drawl, Trey said, "Gon' and take it. I don't give a fuck! It ain't nuthin', man. I got ten mo' of these mo'fuckas at the crib, partna'. This here a small thang to a giant, nah mean."

When Trey referred to himself as a giant, Hop laughed. That niggas was only like 5'4". "You lil' leprechaun ass nigga, you ain't no mo'fuckin' giant. Nigga, my *dick* is bigger than you."

Trey defiantly said, "Nigga, fuck you!"

Hop laughed and let that one ride. After he patted their pockets down and took their car keys and cell phones, he said, "Ya'll niggas lucky I let ya'll keep ya'll grills. Now get the fuck up outta here before I start blastin'!"

The trio took Hop's advice and headed in the other direction. Trey looked back and nodded at him to let him know he would see him again. He never forgot a face.

Chapter Nineteen

Casino was sitting in his office at Street Life Entertainment's headquarters in Mid-town. He was engaged in a telephone conversation with his mother. She had just informed him that she closed the deal for him on a "lovely four bedroom, two bathroom ranch style house with a three-car garage, a huge backyard, and an outdoor swimming pool". Cas thanked his moms for her time and effort. She reminded him about her hefty commission from the 1.2 million dollar purchase and told him that was thanks enough. Cas laughed and told her she had a point. After a few minutes, he told her he loved her and they both hung up.

Before Cas left the office he had Trina, an office assistant, send his mother some flowers for him. That lady had been advising him on good real estate investments for some time now. He owned a number of houses in New York he could have put Laila up in but he wanted her close. And this house he hadn't purchased as an investment. It was solely a gift, and he hoped she accepted it as such.

Cas knew Laila was a real independent sister who held her own so he hoped she wouldn't trip over him taking charge like that. How did he know that she wanted him to decide where she and her daughter lived? Was he being too controlling?

Casino mulled it over a great deal, and about a week later he finally decided to proposition Laila on his offer. They met for dinner at their favorite spot, and he laid it on her right before their drinks arrived.

Cas cleared his throat. Damn, he was nervous. "Laila, there's something I wanna tell you."

Laila prayed it wasn't bad news. She looked at Cas expectantly but she played it cool. "Well, yes?"

Cas sat back in his chair and looked directly at her as

he spoke. He wanted to see her initial reaction. "I got you a house. It's a four bedroom joint. It's nice, and it's only minutes away. It doesn't have to be permanent but I figured you could use your own space."

Laila looked surprised as hell. Did he just say he bought her a house? Laila knew Cas had bread but that was quite an extravagant gift. Wow, a house. She looked at him and asked, "But why?"

"What you mean why? I just thought you could use your own space, that's all. I don't have any angles, or ulterior motives. And the deed will be in your name", he assured her.

Laila was glad he thought so highly of her but the truth was she didn't want a house from him that he wasn't living in with her. She had really fallen off the deep end for Casino. She was head over heels. Laila had grown so attached to Cas it was ridiculous. She felt like she needed him. And it wasn't just the sex. She looked forward to being with him because of the safeness his personality radiated. But she knew he was married, and so was she. Her living in a house he bought would only complicate things further. Laila just shook her head. She couldn't take it.

Casino was a little confused. He had spent a lot of money on a nice crib for her and here she was, acting like she wasn't interested. Was Laila serious? The only woman he had ever spent that much bread on before was his mother. Not wanting to play guessing games, he came right out and asked her. "Yo, what's wrong wit' you?"

"What's *wrong* wit' me?" Laila took a deep breath, and she chose her next words wisely.

"Cas, what am I supposed to do? Accept this house and just comfortably assume the role of your mistress, or your *whore*? I'm s'posed to just be your jump-off when you wanna creep, but meanwhile you still playin' one big happy family with Kira?"

Cas hadn't even really thought about leaving Kira because they had a son together. "Damn, it sounds bad when you put it like that. That's not what I meant, Laila."

"Well, it is what it is. Why sugarcoat it, Cas?"

"Listen, Laila. You won't have to worry about nothin'. You hear me? You can have anything in this world you want. Trust me."

"If I could have everything I wanted, then I wouldn't have to creep around and be your mistress. Right?"

Cas didn't respond.

Laila said, "Umm hmm. Exactly. Well, I can't deal with those terms. Sorry, but I'm not your fuckin' whore."

Cas didn't have a comeback for that one. What the fuck did she want him to do? Shit, when he wanted her to leave her husband, she wouldn't. He just had to be honest with her.

"Look, Laila. I understood when *you* were married, and you said you weren't leaving your husband because I had no choice. But now when it's *your* turn to be so *understanding*, you got a problem with that. What's that about, Ma?"

His words stung. Laila had to get away from him fast because she was on the verge of tears. She knew he was right but she stuck to her guns. "Look, Cas, thanks for the house. I really appreciate it but I don't need your pity. And I'm not your whore. So no thanks, boo. Now you have a nice life."

Laila got up and walked away with her head held high, leaving Cas sitting there alone. When she got her car back from valet parking, she drove down the road and pulled over. She couldn't have kept driving if she'd wanted to because her vision was blurry from crying.

Cas sat at the table for a few minutes. He still couldn't believe Laila walked out on him like that. It deeply disturbed him. He felt as if he'd hurt her but there was nothing he could do. Laila was just too unpredictable. What if he left Kira, and she fucked around and went back to her husband? He didn't want to gamble on her. Not yet. He just couldn't.

Casino also wanted to raise his son, Jahseim, in a two parent household. Having an old man around was something he never had the opportunity to experience so he wanted to be there for his boy. That was really the only thing keeping Cas with Kira because most of the time he couldn't stand her. Lately it seemed like she was turning into some superficial Hollywood bitch. And he wasn't stupid. He knew she was probably fucking around. But he wasn't on her like that.

Kira was the type of chick that thrived in drama. She loved to do shit to make him angry. But in all actuality Cas wasn't even mad at Kira. He knew deep down that was partially due to him having another love interest. But what could he do? That was just what it was.

$$$

Laila, Portia, and Fatima sat around chilling in Portia's office later that night puffing on a blunt. Portia sat in her leather executive chair with her feet up on her desk, and Fatima and Laila were sprawled on the oversized leather loveseat in the corner. Portia had been running scenes from her novel by them to make sure they seemed realistic. She didn't want to come off sounding too over the top so she was happy her girls liked what she had. Laila and Fatima had both given her positive feedback, and were egging her on to tell them more. Portia laughed and told them to wait and buy the damn book.

Laila had kept the house Cas had purchased for her a secret so far. She figured that now was as good a time as any to spring it on her girls and get their advice. Laila passed the blunt to Fatima and cleared her throat. "Yo, I gotta tell ya'll somethin'. Check it out. Cas bought me a house."

Portia and Fatima looked at each other with open mouths. They said in unison, "A *house*? *Word*?"

Laila nodded her head slowly. "Yup. A house. But I ain't take it though."

Portia and Fatima looked at her like she was crazy. They spoke in unison again. "You *crazy*? Why not?"

Laila just shrugged. "I don't know. I just said "no thank you", and walked out the restaurant."

Fatima said, "Wow. You ungrateful fuckin' bitch. You should've dropped and gave that nigga some head."

Laila laughed. She knew Fatima was kidding. She said, "No, it's not that. I am grateful. I really appreciate his thoughtfulness, but I *like* him ya'll. A *lot*. So I can't just be layin' up in some shit he bought and being his fuckin' *mistress*. Lettin' him just stop by and fuck me every now and then, whenever he feels like it."

"Wait, that doesn't seem like such a bad idea", Portia joked.

Laila sighed. "That is true. That nigga got some good ass dick. And it *is* time for me to get up outta you and Jay's house. I've been staying with ya'll long enough."

Portia made a face at her. "Girl, please. That's nonsense. You can stay as long as you want. My house is your house. And you know that, Lay. Right?"

Laila smiled and nodded. She knew Portia was sincere. There was no phoniness in the game with her and her girls. Their friendship was still as genuine as it was twenty years ago because they were all true blue.

Fatima added, "And when you wear your welcome out over here with *this* bitch, you can come stay with me. You know I'm all by myself since I kicked Wise out. My daughter's always at my parents' house. Sometimes I be kinda' scared up in there by myself."

Fatima looked down and studied her fingernails. She was quiet for a few seconds, and then she said, "I ain't gon' front, I kinda' miss that stupid ass nigga crackin' jokes all the time. And bumpin' his loud ass music in the crib."

Portia and Laila understood. They knew she loved her husband. But they all agreed that Wise needed to be taught a lesson so it was too soon to take him back. Portia knew that Wise was feeling it already though because Jay told her he spoke to him about it. He said he missed the hell out of Tima, and when he got her back he wasn't fucking up again. But only time would tell.

About an hour later, Fatima announced that she was going home, and Laila said she was going to bed so Portia could get back to her editing. Portia invited Fatima to stay the night but she refused. She said she had to learn how to live alone because she hadn't done so in a long time. She was tired of being so damn needy.

Laila walked Fatima out, and locked the door after she left. When she got upstairs to her bedroom and got in bed, she said her prayers and whispered hello to her baby in heaven. Then she laid there in silence for a while thinking about the house Cas got her. She and Macy did need to be getting settled wherever they were going to be soon before school started back. And Laila really wanted to relocate to New Jersey, but she had to sell the house she had in Brooklyn first.

She had contacted Khalil the past week, because she couldn't sell the house without him. They had a "joint tenancy" form of ownership. They were both equal owners on the deed, and neither of them could make a move without the other. That was why Laila was forced to reach out to him. She wasn't about to just walk away from her house. Real estate was just too valuable, and she wasn't leaving anything with her name on it in Khalil's unstable hands.

Since Laila called him the previous week, Khalil had called her twice begging her to come home. He kept on demanding that she stop acting up. Like she was the one with the problem. And for some reason he kept on talking about them having another baby. But Laila hadn't fed into it.

She had absolutely no use for his crack-filled sperm.

The last conversation she and Khalil had, they had agreed to put the house on the market. He told Laila to sell it and give him only a third of the proceeds since she had Macy with her. Laila had just put it on the real estate market two days ago.

She thought about it. Maybe she could take the house in Jersey from Cas now, and pay him back when her house in Brooklyn sold. She was asking $775,000 for it. It was a recently renovated two-family brownstone on Jefferson Avenue in Bed-Stuy, and the real-estate market had gone up drastically. After the house sold, she would just pay Cas back his money.

Laila picked up her cell phone and called Cas to apologize for seeming so ungrateful. After she told him she was sorry, she asked him if his offer was still on the table. He told her it was if she wanted it. Laila agreed to go and see the property with him the following day.

Laila noticed that Cas was keeping his answers real short and simple so she figured he was within earshot of Kira. She told him to call her back with a time and place, and they hung up. Laila laid there feeling a little guilty because a part of her hoped Kira had overheard their conversation.

Laila didn't know it but she had gotten her wish. A few blocks away at Cas' house, Kira had noticed that he left the room after his phone rang so she knew he didn't want her to hear what he was saying. She nonchalantly followed Cas into the kitchen and pretended she wanted a glass of orange juice, and she caught the last of his conversation. He agreed to do something "tomorrow" with whoever he was talking to.

Kira didn't comment but her woman's intuition told her that Cas had been on the phone with another woman. Kira knew that Portia's friend Laila had been staying with Jay and Portia for a while now but she hadn't spoke against it yet because she didn't have any proof that Cas was messing with her. But now Kira's suspicions rose like wild fire. Cas was fucking around on her. She knew it. And probably with that bitch Laila. Maybe it was time to confront her.

$$$

That night before Laila fell asleep she got a phone call from Khalil. It was the third that week. The first time he had called her and promised he was going to get it together, and begged her to reconsider coming home. The second time he called, he demanded that she give him a son. That's when Laila knew he'd lost his mind. He had to be crazy for thinking that one.

This time he started up again. He kept on talking about he wanted to try for a boy. Laila knew that was just a way for him to try and keep them together. He was only trying to make her think he was gonna get his shit together. She knew what his game plan was already and she wasn't buying it.

Ten minutes into their conversation, Laila got sick and tired of Khalil badgering her. She couldn't believe his stupid ass had the audacity to keep asking her to have another baby by him. Laila wouldn't even entertain the thought. She didn't want to deal with diapers ever again. And not to mention his serious drug addiction. Laila didn't want the headache. No way.

She didn't tell Khalil about the new house she had because she didn't want him all up in her business. She didn't want to be mean, so she politely cut their conversation short and bid him goodnight.

Laila was disappointed in Khalil but she felt sorry for him. She knew he was hurting. He had recently lost a child just like her, and he'd lost his family too. But she lost him also. It wasn't her fault. Laila couldn't help him because that damn crack had him by the balls. Khalil had to go to God on that one. He was the only one that could bring him through. Only God.

Chapter Twenty

The following week went by smoothly for everyone. Laila had seen the house Cas bought her, and she loved it. She was excited and ready to move in. She just had to decorate first, and Portia and Fatima were supposed to help her. Cas had offered to furnish the whole house but she turned the offer down. He had done enough. Casino was an angel but she wasn't broke. She made good money, and she wanted to maintain a fraction of her independence.

After all of that, Cas still insisted that she take twenty thousand dollars to get the basics. He refused to take no for an answer. Laila smiled when she thought about the way they had christened her new house. They'd had sex right on the living room floor. And then on the counter in her new state-of-the-art kitchen. And last but not least, in the master bedroom. Laila hadn't meant to give in so easily. But truthfully it was she who had initiated the first sexual encounter.

The house had just been so much more beautiful and bigger than she had imagined, she felt compelled to thank Cas. And she had done so on her knees. That was the first time she had done oral on Cas but she couldn't think of a more appropriate occasion than him purchasing her a 1.2 million dollar home.

Laila smiled mischievously to herself. She had made Cas' knees buckle. He deserved it. Especially after he presented her with that deed and told her to sign on the dotted line. Just as he said, the house was in her name with no strings attached. He told her she could have an attorney look things over if that would make her feel more comfortable.

After Laila signed, she thanked Cas and told him she would repay him after her house sold. He told her that wasn't necessary. Even more impressive, he'd given her some good advice. Casino told Laila that the brownstone she owned in Bed-Stuy would be worth well over a million dollars in a couple of years, so she should try to hold on to it until it appreciated. Laila explained to Cas that she didn't own it by herself so she just wanted to get rid of it.

Cas told her to buy Khalil out so his name would come off of everything, and keep the house. Laila told him that wasn't a bad idea but she couldn't afford to.

Cas had an idea, but he proceeded to ask the appropriate questions before he made his offer. Above all, Casino was a shrewd business man. He asked her how much equity she had in the house, and she told him they'd bought it nine years ago for $375,000, which was about half of what it was currently worth. She and Khalil had refinanced once four years ago, but they had only pulled out eighty grand for their later failed business venture. In that case they should have had at least a couple hundred grand in equity. Laila said Khalil wasn't dependable, but she paid her mortgage on time faithfully every month.

After hearing all of this, Cas had the necessary elements for his decision. He told Laila he would lend her the money to buy Khalil out, and then she could refinance once she was the sole owner of the property and pay him back.

During the next half hour Cas schooled Laila about building wealth, and how she had to acquire and maintain real estate in order to do so. Cas' motto was "money talks, bullshit walks". He told her to always remember that. He told Laila she had to make the right decisions, and then she would be able to pass her wealth on down. That way Macy would already be set when she grew up.

After Cas had enlightened her and offered his assistance, Laila was sold on the idea of buying Khalil out and keeping her house. She would just rent out the apartments and use the rental income to pay her mortgage.

Casino told Laila that his mother's office, or any other realty company could assist her with the tenant screening process and help her pick good candidates to rent to. That way she'd have to worry less about someone tearing up her house. She could even make arrangements to receive her rent in the mail.

After Cas dropped all that knowledge on Laila she felt an almost animalistic attraction to him. She thrived on his confidence, and his sense of wealth was invigorating. He was right, she definitely needed to buy Khalil out. She only hoped he went for it.

Casino suggested that she offer him two hundred thousand and see what he said, but he told Laila he was willing to lend her up to a quarter of a million. He was pretty sure that dude would take the bait because he had a weakness. But with the shit he was hooked on, having that much money at one time could kill him if he wasn't careful.

$$$

A few nights later, Cas and Jay were in the studio with Kira. She was remixing a hot single for her new album, and she and Cas had been bickering all night. Cas was really getting sick of Kira and her slick ass mouth. She kept on throwing pop shots at him, insinuating that he was fucking Laila.

Kira knew that Laila was staying with Jay and Portia, and she wasn't very happy about it. She was kind of tight at Portia, but pissed off at Jay because that bastard was her brother. Kira was supposed to be rapping but she was so mad she was in the booth cursing Jay and Cas out on the microphone.

"Cas, you fuckin' lyin' piece of shit! And Jay, you just as foul. You gon' invite Cas' *bitch* to lay up at your house. What type of shit is that? Ya'll mothafuckas in cahoots, huh?

Yo, stop try'na play me! Word up. Then when I spazz the fuck out, you niggas gon' be talkin' shit."

Jay and Cas tried their best to ignore Kira but she got louder and louder. Then she got real extra and came out the booth yelling in Cas' face. Cas told her to shut the fuck up and gave her a look that said he meant it.

Kira knew how far to go but she tested Cas nonetheless. She got all up in his face and mushed him upside his head. Casino didn't play that putting your hands on him shit so he snapped for a minute. He grabbed Kira by the neck and slammed her against the wall, and he warned her not to touch him ever again.

Kira started screaming and crying, pretending that she was more injured than she really was. That was the first time Cas had ever laid hands on her. Her feelings were hurt but she kept her tough skin on. She hissed, "I hate you, you fuckin' bastard. If you ever put your hands on me again, I'll put you on yo' fuckin' back, nigga!"

After Kira threatened him, Cas bit his lip in anger. He almost slapped the shit out of her for saying that. Boy, she was really provoking him to fuck her up. He took a deep breath and caught himself. He wasn't into hitting women but she was a stupid bitch sometimes.

Cas remained calm but he pointed at Kira and kept his tone firm. "Yo, I'ma tell you one time. Don't ever threaten me again." After that he just walked out.

Kira went after him. She wasn't letting him off that easy. She wasn't finished. Fuck that. She tugged at Cas' arm and demanded his attention.

Jay just shook his head. He knew his sister. She wanted more drama. Kira loved shit like that. Not wanting to get involved in their business, Jay just stayed out of it.

After Cas and Kira finished arguing outside the studio, he hopped in his Maserati and drove off, and she jumped in her Porsche and zoomed off in the other direction. Kira didn't know where Cas was going, but she was going over Jay's house to confront that bitch Laila. She had to find out if that bitch was fucking her husband. Kira stepped on it and headed for the parkway.

She got to the house in about twenty minutes. When she pulled up, she just hopped out of her car and didn't even bother to shut it off. Kira walked up to the front door and rang the bell, and banged on the door impatiently. Her nephew Jayquan came to the door and let her in. Seeing him changed her disposition somewhat. He was such a handsome little devil. And he was getting so tall.

Jayquan grinned and said brightly, "Hey, what up Auntie Kira?"

"What up, nephew? Look at you, gettin' all big. And your voice is gettin' all deep and shit. Let me find out my lil' nephew's becoming a man." Kira laughed and hugged him, and planted a big kiss on his cheek.

Jayquan blushed and told her to quit.

Kira put her hand on her hip and looked at him like he was crazy. "Boy, I can kiss you anytime I want to. I changed your stinky little pampers, so you *always* gon' be my baby."

Jayquan made a face. "Man, please. I ain't no baby. You were only like my age when I was born. You ain't even that much older than me."

Kira laughed. "You crazy, I was fourteen."

"And I'm almost twelve. Big difference."

Kira just rolled her eyes and laughed. She couldn't win with that dude. He was too sharp. She followed Lil' Jay inside the house and asked, "Is Laila here?"

"Yeah, she's in the there." Jayquan pointed to the kitchen.

Kira said, "Oh yeah? And where's Portia?"

"In there too", Lil' Jay answered.

"Thanks, boo", Kira said, and headed for the kitchen.

Jayquan followed her.

When she got in the kitchen, Kira saw Laila, Jazmin, and Macy. Then Portia's head popped up. She had on hot pink oven mitts, and was taking fresh baked chocolate chip cookies out of the oven. When she saw Kira she smiled and said hello. Kira smiled and greeted everyone, including Macy and Laila. They all spoke back. Jazmin ran over and hugged her, and she offered her some "shocolate tookies".

Kira laughed. "Hi, princess!" Her little niece was so adorable, and she talked so cute. She bent down and picked Jazz up, and she kissed her and pinched her cheeks.

After playing with Jazz for a minute, Kira remembered the reason she came. She put the baby down and got on to the business she was there to address.

Unsmiling, she walked right up to Laila. "Laila, can I talk to you?"

Laila played it cool, but she had a feeling she already knew what this was about. Oh boy, drama. She knew things were going too good between her and Cas to be true. She should've known something bad was going to happen. Laila hoped Kira didn't know about her new house. She wanted to suggest they go have their discussion elsewhere but that would make her look guilty. She didn't want the kids to hear any of this, but she was forced to stay there and say, "Talk to me about what?"

Kira turned up the attitude. "About my husband, that's what."

Uh oh, that was Portia's cue to round up the kids. "Macy and Lil'Jay, come with me. I wanna show ya'll something." Portia could tell by Kira's tone that there were about to be some things said that young ears didn't need to hear. She picked up Jazz and shooed them out of the kitchen.

Macy and Jayquan hesitated like they knew there was about to be a showdown they didn't want to miss. Portia called them again, so they reluctantly followed her. Macy kept on looking back.

Laila waited until the kids were gone to respond. She got on point in case that bitch tried to swing. "Well? What about your husband, Kira?"

Kira got right to the point. "Are you fuckin' him?"

"*Excuse me?*"

Kira placed her hand on her hip. "Ain't no trick question, babygirl. It's either yes or no."

Laila didn't like the tone Kira was using, but she wanted to keep it womanly. It was Cas' place to tell his wife about them, not hers. So Laila lied. "No. What would make you think that?"

Kira was fed up with Laila's little innocent act. She didn't believe that bitch. Not one bit. She should've known she wasn't going to tell her the truth. Kira took a deep breath. "Answer this question. Why are you here, Laila? Don't you have your *own* house to go to?"

Laila had to bite her tongue because she almost told her, "*Yes I do. Two houses, bitch. And one of them was a gift from your husband.*" But Laila was a lady. Instead she just said, "Yes, I do have my own house. But I'm staying with my girlfriend for a while, and I don't think the reason why is any of your business."

Kira fired right back. "Well, that might be true but I think you've overstayed your welcome. It's time for you to leave now. Don't you think?"

Laila laughed it off. She had to in order to keep from spazzing on that bitch. Was she serious? "Wow. You seem so concerned with where I'm staying. I'm wondering, do you own this house or something? Because last time I checked I was welcome by the *real* owners, Jay and Portia, to stay as long as I wanted to." Laila feigned confusion. "Unless something *changed*, and you paying bills up in here or something."

Kira smirked. This bitch had a slick mouth. Maybe she should just punch her in it. "Don't be cute, Laila. And by the way, home wrecking doesn't become you. I just want you gone so you can stay away from my damn husband. Don't you have your own one of those too? Go *home* to *your* husband at *your* house."

Laila forced a tight smile. "This seems a little personal, Kira. I wouldn't be a threat to you, now would I?"

"Oh, never that", Kira assured her.

Laila challenged, "So what's this about? You ain't never seen me up in your husband's face, or nothin'. So where is this coming from?"

After that, Kira lost her temper. "Bitch, just stay the fuck away from my husband!"

Laila was boiling but she still played it cool. "That'll be Miss Bitch to you, *little girl*. And you're throwing the word "husband" around pretty loosely today. *My husband, my husband, my husband*. Okay, we're all happy you're married. It just didn't seem that way a few weeks ago when you were all up in Young Vee's face at Wise' party."

Now Kira was fuming. That bitch had some nerve. "What the fuck are you watchin' me for?"

Laila laughed. "Darling, I wasn't watching you. Everyone in the whole damn club saw you playing yourself. You didn't care about your *husband* then. So who you try'na fool?"

Kira knew Laila was right but she wasn't about to let her disrespect her like that. Not in her damn brother's house. For lack of the proper words to express her anger, Kira reached over and slapped the hell out of Laila.

Laila couldn't believe that bitch hit her. No disrespect to Portia and Jay's house but there was no way she was letting that go. She jumped up and punched Kira in the face, and they started scrapping.

Kira had the height advantage of about nine inches, but Laila was older and wiser. She had been involved in more street fights and shit than Kira. Laila knew how to fight dirty. She rammed Kira into the refrigerator, and grabbed her hair and used her foot to trip her. When she got her down on the floor, Laila sat on top of her and laid her knuckle game down on her.

Kira bit Laila on the arm, and managed to roll them over and get on top. She wrapped her fist in Laila's hair and yanked it as hard as she could, and banged her head on the kitchen floor.

Laila screamed, "Get off my hair, bitch!" She mustered up all the strength she could, and flipped Kira back over. She had one hand around Kira's neck, and the other she used to punch her in the face repeatedly. Kira clawed at Laila's eyes and punched back.

Both ladies were throwing some serious blows. Their shirts were ripped open, Kira's tity was exposed, both their faces were scratched and bleeding, and they were pulling each other's hair out by the clump. Shit was really real.

Portia overheard the commotion and hurried downstairs to see what was going on. She had left with the kids so they wouldn't overhear Kira and Laila discussing their adult business, and now they were fighting like they were children. But the battle going on in the kitchen was vicious. Portia knew Laila was more mature, so Kira had to have thrown the first blow.

Portia did everything she could to break it up, but she needed some help because Kira wouldn't stop. And Laila wouldn't back down either. Those two were fighting like hell. She was glad when Jayquan and Macy came running in and gave her a hand. Lil' Jay was growing, and he was getting strong. Thank God he was able to subdue his crazy aunt because she wouldn't stop wilding. Portia was grateful because she didn't want Kira trying to say that she and Laila jumped her. Lord, she wished Jay was there.

After they broke up the fight, Portia and Macy had Laila on one side of the room, and Jayquan was holding Kira on the other. Jazz was in the middle crying and screaming at the top of her lungs. She was hysterical, but Kira still kept yelling, "Get off me, Jayquan! I'ma fuck that bitch up!"

Laila was still heated but she was calmer than Kira. "Come on, little girl. So I can bust that ass again."

Jay had sat at the studio for a few minutes after Cas and Kira left, and then he'd decided to go on home. He had pulled up and saw his sister's car carelessly parked and still running in front of the house, so he got out and quickened his step. He hoped Kira hadn't come over with any bullshit.

No sooner than Jay had put his key in the lock and opened the door did he hear Kira yelling, *"Get off me, Jayquan! Yo, that's my word! I'ma fuck you up, bitch!"* Jay hurried towards the noise. It sounded like it was coming from the kitchen.

Jay heard Laila say, *"I ain't scared. Let that bitch go."* He hurried, hoping to prevent a fight he could hear was in the making.

When he got to the kitchen he saw that he was too late. He had walked in on what was obviously a post-boxing match. Jay was shocked as hell. Laila and Kira were in opposite corners like they were De La Hoya and Mayweather in the middle of the twelfth round. They both looked like they had put it on each other pretty bad. They were scratched up, both of their hair was all over the place, their shirts were ripped and their bras were exposed. Damn, Kira's breast was showing. That was a damn shame. Jay just shook his head.

Jayquan spotted Jay first and called out, "Hey, Pop!" When Jazmin saw Jay, she stopped crying and ran over and grabbed his leg.

Portia looked over and saw Jay, and she thanked her lucky stars. Now he could restore some order to the house. His little sister was straight bugging.

Before Portia could say a word, Kira started in on Jay. "Jay, I'm glad you're here. You better tell this bitch to get the fuck out right now! I'm your fuckin' sister, and I want her gone! Tonight!"

Jay looked at Kira and told her to calm down. He didn't like dealing with irrational women, whether they were family or not. She was his sister but he wasn't a bad host. He had welcomed Laila into his home, and he wasn't about to kick her and her child out in the street because Kira was tripping. She might as well calm down.

There was silence in the room for a second as everyone waited for Jay to respond. Portia had a few words for Kira for talking about her friend that way, but she thought it best to let Jay handle that one. That was his immature ass sister.

Jay took so long to say something, Kira got pissed and spat, "Jay, I *said* I want this bitch gone. Tell her to get the fuck out! Now!"

Jay didn't like being pushed. Kira was getting out of line. Laila was a guest in his home. He said, "Kira, stop yelling. Calm yourself down. You want me to drive you home?" He put it as nicely as he could, but she still got offended.

Kira yelled, "What, mothafucka? You try'na kick me out for this bitch? Your *sister*? Your own flesh and blood? Nigga, you ain't shit! Fuck you, Jay!"

Jay just sighed and shook his head. His sister had a filthy mouth. He couldn't stand that. It was time for Kira to leave. She wasn't a kid anymore so her tantrums did little to move Jay these days. He politely asked her out of his house. "Go home, Kira. Please. Just go home. You need to change your shirt."

"Jay, fuck you! You ain't *shit*. Wait 'til I tell Mommy, nigga."

Jay remained calm. "Grow up, Kira. Why don't you grow the fuck up?"

Kira just clenched her fists, and looked around the room for something to channel her anger on. She zoomed in on Laila and stared at her hatefully. Jayquan had let his guards down when Jay came in so she broke loose and ran up on Laila swinging again. They both exchanged a few good blows before Jay picked Kira up and carried her out in the hallway.

Kira wouldn't quit giving him a hard time so he took her outside and closed the door behind them. Jay looked at her seriously and pointed at her. She knew he was getting fed up with her. He told her he was going back inside his house, which he didn't appreciate her disrespecting the way she did. He told her to grow up and stop blaming people for her shit, and start treating Cas like a man and showing him some fucking respect. Jay told Kira to have a good night, and he went back inside and locked the door. He loved his sister but she got on his nerves. He would call and check on her a little later.

When Jay got back inside he asked Laila if she was okay, and he apologized on his sister's behalf. Laila said she was fine, and she apologized to him and Portia for fighting in their house. She really hated that this had to have happened. Especially in front of the kids. What type of impression did that leave on them? And she sure didn't want Macy to think it was okay to fight over a man. Especially someone else's.

Laila told Jay and Portia that Kira had hit her first, so she'd been forced to defend herself. She thanked them for letting her stay there, and said she was very sorry for any conflicts she caused by being there. She was glad she would be leaving soon. Maybe she should just go on and move in her house before she finished decorating. She'd already had the utilities turned on in her name.

Jay and Portia both told Laila that she had nothing to apologize about. They told her she was welcome anytime, and they apologized to her for Kira attacking her in their home.

Jayquan and Macy just stared on quietly, still thinking about the fight they had witnessed. Macy asked her mother if she was alright, and so did Lil' Jay. Laila told them not to worry because she was just fine.

Just then, they all heard the sound of glass shattering. A few seconds later they heard tires screeching away. Jay knew Kira's dumb ass had thrown something and broken a window. He didn't sweat it though. His sister really needed to grow up.

$$$

The next day, Portia was at home working on her novel when she got a call from the hospital. They told her that her mother had been admitted! Portia ran to her room and got dressed in a hurry, and tried not to panic. Jazmin was on her bed asleep, and she woke up to see Portia stepping into her Louis Vuitton sneakers.

Jazmin sat up and rubbed her eyes. She asked sleepily, "Mommy, where you goin'?"

Portia told her she was going to the store, and would bring her back some ice cream if she was a good girl. Thank God Laila was still there. Portia was glad she hadn't moved out yet. She ran down the hall and knocked on her bedroom door and asked her to keep an eye on Jazz and Jayquan while she went to see about Patricia.

Laila was concerned and wanted to go with her, but she knew someone had to stay with the children. Jay was at the studio. She told Portia to run along quickly and not worry because her mother would be okay, and to make sure she called her.

Portia thanked her, and she made her way outside. She stopped short and decided to take a car with more speed. She ran back and grabbed the keys to Jay's Ferrari, and she hightailed it to New York. Portia's heart felt like it was literally deflating. She prayed the whole way there.

She made it to the City in nineteen minutes flat, and three minutes later she pulled up in the hospital parking lot. She had called Jay along the way to let him know where she was going but she got his voicemail. She left him a message telling him about the emergency.

Portia ran up to the information desk in the emergency room and asked where Patricia Lane was. The heavyset, nappy auburn wig wearing, Caribbean woman behind the desk impatiently sucked her teeth and rolled her eyes. She checked the patient roster and gave her directions to the ward where Pat was.

Patricia was in the intensive care unit, which frightened Portia even more. When she got to her room a doctor was standing over her. Portia stood there for a second, frozen with fear. She said another prayer and turned the knob.

A nurse called out to her, "Hey, you can't go in there."

Portia ignored her and stepped inside the room. The doctor turned around and greeted her. Portia said hello to him, and she stared at her mother. Patricia's appearance really frightened her. She looked real tired, and her eyes were deep and sunken. Portia had just seen her two days before, so she was shocked by how much she looked like she had aged.

Portia bent down and kissed Pat on her forehead. "Hey, Mommy. How you feelin'?"

Patricia squeezed Portia's hand and nodded a little to let her know she was okay, even though it was obvious that she wasn't. She managed a little smile. She was glad Portia was there.

Portia stared down at her mother and felt guilty about not being there for her more. She wished Pat had taken her up on her offer to stay with her. Portia made a promise to herself to never leave her side again when she got out of there. She was moving her mother to Jersey with her, and that was that. She stroked Pat's hair and wondered why God had let cancer attack her. It was draining her spirit and health at an alarming rate. But Portia knew she had to keep the faith.

She stepped outside to speak with the doctor for a minute. Dr. Kaiser informed her that Pat's condition had relapsed and the cancer was spreading quickly. It was too far gone to stop now. The hysterectomy she had undergone hadn't solved the problem.

Portia asked him what was next, and he told her that he was sorry to tell her but Patricia's days were numbered. Portia cut him off. She wasn't trying to hear that. She demanded a second opinion, and she went back inside with her mama. That doctor didn't know what the hell he was talking about. If anything happened to her mother she was getting an attorney and suing him for malpractice.

Portia sat by Patricia's side and held her hand. "Don't worry, Patty Cake. You're gonna be fine."

Portia saw a flicker of doubt in Pat's eyes, and that broke her heart. She picked up the Bible from the side of her bed. "Patricia Lane, you *are* gonna be fine. There's power in prayer, Ma. That's what *you* taught me. You just have to believe. You gotta have faith, Mommy. The size of a mustard seed. That's all you need."

Patricia nodded in agreement. She stared at her daughter through weak and sickly eyes. She was so proud of her. After her husband died, Portia was all she had. And she put everything she had into raising her. It had been a rocky road at some points, especially when Portia was dancing in those nightclubs for a living, but the Godliness she had installed in her prevailed. She had done a fine job. Her daughter was a lady.

Pat smiled and squeezed Portia's hand. She had no regrets. God had been good to her. She was leaving the house to Portia and Jazmin, and she made sure she had a good life insurance policy, of which Portia was the beneficiary. That way she wouldn't be troubled with her expenses.

Patricia pulled Portia closer to her. "I love you, and I'm proud of you, baby. Keep on writing, and take care of Jazmin good like I took care of you. Raise her with God, Portia."

Pat smiled. "You know, I can see you havin' another baby

soon. Real soon. Just watch what I tell you." She laughed feebly and placed Portia's hand against her face.

Portia was glad to hear her mother speak but she didn't sound well. And the way she was talking sounded so final. "Ma, please don't talk like that. You ain't goin' *no* where." She bent down and kissed her mother on the cheek.

When Portia kissed her, Pat whispered in her ear, "I'm tired, baby. Mama's so tired."

All of a sudden the wavy lines on the monitor above Pat's bed went flat and the machine made that long beeping sound that Portia had only seen on T.V. The sound that meant someone died. Portia couldn't believe it. Her eyes widened. "Oh my God!"

She quickly pressed the emergency button on the side of Pat's hospital bed to alert the nurses, and she ran to the door and yelled, "Hurry! Please come quick! My mother! Come do something! Hurry up! Oh God, please!"

A group of nurses and doctors hurried in and pushed Portia out of the way. There were about six of them, and they appeared to be checking Pat's vital signs. A resident named Carol immediately started pumping Pat's chest, but the doctor stopped her. "DNR", he said firmly.

The resident looked upset but she reluctantly backed off and left Pat alone. She looked over at Portia sadly for a second.

Portia looked around at the doctors and nurses like they were crazy. "Do something! Please! Why are ya'll just standin' there?"

The doctor looked at Portia and said, "I'm sorry ma'am, but she's gone."

Portia was in denial. She grabbed him by the collar. "What you *mean* "gone"? Do somethin' to bring her back! That's my mother!"

"I understand that you're upset, but please calm down." He pried Portia's hands off his shirt. "Ma'am, I'm sorry but she was a DNR."

Portia shook her head in disbelief. "What the fuck is a DNR?"

"DNR means "Do Not Resuscitate". It was her request. It's here in her chart." He proceeded to show Portia some papers from Patricia's medical chart, but she couldn't see straight.

She looked over at her mother's lifeless body on that hospital bed and was overcome with grief. She had to be dreaming. There was no way her mother could have just slipped away from her that quickly. That couldn't be real life.

Portia looked around at all the green scrub wearing nurses in disbelief. She couldn't really focus so their faces and bodies looked distorted. She made her way over to Patricia's bedside and stared down at her. Words couldn't explain her pain at that point. Portia laid her head on her mother's chest and held onto her for dear life.

After several minutes, the nurses tried to pull her off. They had to take Pat away. It wasn't personal. That was their job. When Portia saw that they were trying to separate her from Patricia, she completely lost it.

"No! No, no, no! I can't live without my mama. I need my mama! Please God, no! Don't let this be happening to me. No, no. Oh God, please no." Portia's soul deflated like someone had literally let the air out of her. At that moment in time she had no will to exist. Her mother was gone. Gone forever. She had never known pain like that existed. She'd have sooner put a bullet in her head and taken her own life then live through what she was feeling at that point.

Portia sank to the floor and just laid there crying, feeling like an abandoned child. And she wasn't being dramatic. Her legs had actually given out on her.

The nurses looked down at the poor weeping woman and pitied her. That was the part of their job they really hated.

Seeing how people reacted when they lost a loved one. They tried to subdue Portia and get her up off the floor.

Portia resisted their efforts. She just wanted to lay there and cry herself to death. She wanted to go with Patty Cake. She couldn't stay there without her. What would she do? Pat had taught her everything.

The pain in Portia's chest overwhelmed and consumed every ounce of her. She continuously cried. *"Mommy! Mommy! Please don't go. Please come back. I need you! Please, Patty Cake. Come back!"*

Meanwhile, Pat's doctor had ordered one of the nurses to give Portia a sedative. Portia was so out of it she didn't even see her coming with the needle. She stuck Portia right in the hip, and seconds later she was out. Whatever was in that needle was some powerful stuff. After Portia fell asleep, a few of the staff picked her up and put her on a stretcher and took her to another room on the other side of the hospital.

One of the nurses who had taken her off noticed her cell phone clipped on her jeans pocket. She took it off and checked the last few outgoing calls, and she saw a number tagged with the word "Hubby". Assuming that it was Portia's husband, she called the number.

Jay had just left the studio, and was driving along the West Side Highway when he got a call from Portia's phone. He knew it was her because he had a special ring tone for her. He answered and spoke in his Blue Tooth. "Yo, what up, P?"

Thankful that someone answered, the nurse introduced herself and explained why she was calling. "Hello, this is Nurse Pratchette, calling from Long Island College Hospital."

When Jay heard that, he knew something was wrong. He had been driving with his seat leaned back so he sat up and prepared himself for the news. He was almost afraid to ask what happened. "Yes?"

The nurse didn't know Portia's name so she asked, "Sir, do

you know the daughter of a Patricia Lane?"

"Yes, that's my wife. Portia. What's wrong?" Jay was on edge and his heart rate had increased substantially.

"Well sir, I'm very sorry to inform you that your wife's mother just passed away, and your wife was so hysterical that we had to administer a sedative."

When Jay heard that news he was crushed. That was real fucked up. He was so mad he hit the steering wheel hard as hell three times with the palm of his hand. *Bam, bam, bam!* Damn, his mother-in-law was dead. Jay was deeply saddened, and his heart grew heavier and heavier. He really loved Patricia. She was a good woman.

And poor Portia. Dear God, he knew she was taking it hard. "Is my wife okay?"

"Yes, sir. She's heavily sedated but she's okay. She's still asleep. I called you because I don't think it's wise to let her leave the hospital without an escort, considering the shape she was in before she fell asleep."

"Thanks. I'm on my way right now", Jay informed her. He had to go see about his Kit Kat. He got the number of the room Portia was in from the nurse, and he hurried to the hospital as quickly as he could.

Jay made it to the hospital in eleven minutes flat. He parked his Bentley and hurried inside. When he got upstairs where Portia was, he peeked in on her before he announced his arrival. She was just coming around. She opened her eyes slowly and looked around, obviously trying to figure out where she was.

Jay stared at his wife and his heart went out to her. Her eyes were puffy and swollen from crying so much, and her hair was a mess. He could tell from the look on her face that she just remembered what happened because her expression was suddenly sorrow filled. Jay stepped inside and let her know he was there for her.

When Portia saw Jay she didn't say a word. She couldn't.

She just reached out to him like an afraid child reaching for their father.

Jay rushed over to her bedside. "Hey, Kit Kat. How you feelin'?" He hugged her tight, and then he smoothed her hair back and planted a gentle kiss on her forehead.

Portia was groggy but she tried to sit up. "Baby, tell me I was just dreamin'. Mommy's okay, right?" She stared at Jay with a hopeful look in her eyes.

Jay could barely force himself to say the words. "No, Portia. She's gone."

Portia was quiet for a second. She was trying to let go of the pain but it was no use. She just started crying hysterically again, attempting to tell Jay what happened in between sobs. *"Jay, they let her die... They let Mommy die. They said she... was a DNR... They wouldn't... resuscitate... My mommy's gone, Jay. She's gone... Baby, I feel like I'ma die. Oh God, my mama's gone..."*

Jay just held Portia and caressed her, and let her cry on his shoulder. His woman was hurting so he had to be her rock. He could feel the wetness of her tears on his tee-shirt. Jay's eyes had water in them too. Patricia was a good woman. She was the best mother-in-law a dude could ask for. She was really understanding and easy to talk to. He had really loved her. Jay prayed that she would rest in peace.

After a few minutes, Portia calmed down a little. The pain hadn't subsided but she felt a little stronger, by the grace of God. She hugged Jay tightly. He also gave her strength. He was her black knight. He always came to her rescue.

Jay picked Portia up and cradled her in his arms like a baby. He loved her so much. He wanted to shelter her from all her pain but there was nothing he could do this time. He couldn't fix this, and it hurt. He just rocked her in his arms and whispered, "Don't cry, Kit Kat. It's gon' be ayight. Don't cry, baby."

Chapter Twenty One

Portia was out back by the pool, laying on a chaise lounge reminiscing. A month had passed since Patricia's death, and she was still in a fog. She just couldn't seem to get it together. A part of her was gone, and she felt hollow.

When the time had come for Portia to bury her mother last month, she had taken no shorts in planning her funeral. She had been in a daze throughout the entire ordeal but no expenses were spared. There were thousands of dollars worth of lovely floral arrangements, and Pat's casket was grand. It was made of the finest mahogany wood, lined in ivory satin, and trimmed in 24 karat gold. Portia had sent her mother home with class and style like the queen she was.

Her mother's sister Grace, who was an ordained minister, had delivered the eulogy. Portia knew that wasn't easy so her heart went out to her aunt. Jay, Laila, and Fatima had held Portia up and consoled her throughout the service, and Jazmin had cried uncontrollably from seeing Portia behaving so hysterically.

When she finally managed to get it together and go up and view her mother's body, Portia kissed Pat's face over and over and held on to her for dear life. They literally had to pry her from the coffin. She wasn't a bit of good.

After the service, Pat's casket was carried on a chariot pulled by two proud black stallions to the cemetery. Her gravesite was right next to Portia's father, Dwight's. Portia couldn't believe that both of her parents were dead and gone. The thought was sad and eerie.

After Patricia died, Portia had put in a special order for a beautiful, marble, custom designed, double heart shaped headstone. The headstone was wide enough to sit across both Dwight and Patricia's graves. Portia had a color photo

of her parents, smiling and in love, placed on the front. The
inscription was surrounded by flying doves. It read:

Rest In Peace
Mother   and   **Father**
Patricia Lane   **Dwight Lane**
Sunrise
May 27, 1951   **July 6, 1951**
Sunset
October 11, 2007   **March 12, 1996**

Together With God for Eternity
One Love

When it came time for the burial, Portia wanted to throw
herself in the ground with her mother. She really didn't want
to live her life without her. At the time she didn't think she
could've if she tried.

Now a whole month had passed, and she sat reminiscing
about the good times. Patricia Lane was a hell of a lady.
Portia thought about the old spiritual song, "Sometimes I
Feel Like a Motherless Child", by gospel legend Mahalia
Jackson. She couldn't believe she was now motherless. Her
eyes watered up at the thought.

Just then, her cell phone rang. It was Laila, calling to confirm
their meeting at her new house to finish decorating. It was
good to hear from her. Portia appreciated Laila's friendship.
She had pushed back her moving plans to accommodate her,
and stuck by her side since she was grieving and needed her
support. Laila was a true friend indeed. Fatima was too.
They had been all Portia had expected them to be. They were
both gems.

Portia was glad Laila had called. She needed something to
take her mind off things. She knew Laila was anxious to get
in her new place, which was lovely by the way, so she assured

her that she would be there. Laila told her that Fatima was
going to stop by and pick her up so they could ride over there
together.

After they hung up, Portia headed inside and went up to
her bedroom and took out her weed stash from her underwear
drawer. While she waited on Fatima, she poured a few buds
from the marijuana filled pill bottle and twisted up a nice
el in a honey flavored Dutch Master. She decided to wait
a little while to spark it. They could all puff when her and
Tima got over Laila's crib. She needed to ease her mind.

$$$

Wise drove along the parkway, speeding at over ninety
miles per hour in his Lamborghini Gallardo. He was just
returning from a fishing trip he'd gone on with a young
Italian acquaintance of his from the music business named
Telly. Telly was always talking about his boat and inviting
Wise to fish with him, so Wise had finally taken him up on
his offer.

Telly hadn't been lying about his boat. It was pretty big,
and it was nice as hell. Wise was ready to splurge on a good
boat for himself now, because fishing had become a hobby
of his. He had a lot of things on his mind, and he found the
sport to be relaxing. He was feeling himself because he had
caught two striped bass, and four bluefish. They were in the
trunk of his quarter million dollar sports car, tied up in a
plastic bag. He was going to stop by his mother's house and
have her filet and cook them for him.

Neyo's old CD was playing on the stereo. That was one of
Wise' favorites at one point, so he still bumped it sometimes.
He got tired of it so he shut it off, and flipped through the
radio stations until he found something else. He was "so
sick of love songs" his damn self. He didn't need to hear
Neyo keep saying it over and over. When he passed through

106.7 Lite FM, Wise heard a pop song he liked. It was by
this British white boy named James Blunt. Wise and he had
been introduced at a pre-Grammy mixer, and he seemed
cool. Wise sang along.
*"You're beautiful, you're beautiful, you're beautiful, it's true. I
saw your face, in a crowded place, and I don't know what to do
- 'cause I'll never be with you."*

That song made Wise think of Fatima. It was possible that
he would never be with her again. She made it clear that she
wasn't playing with him this time. He had been out of the
house for over a month now. Even the new drop top Bentley
he bought her hadn't softened her up.

He was tired of staying in a hotel. He had been renting a
penthouse suite by the week, dragging his feet on purchasing
something in hopes that Fatima would come to her senses.
Wise owned a few houses but they were all occupied with
tenants. He didn't want to move anyway. He just wanted
to go home.

Fatima didn't leave him after Melanie sued him but this
baby thing had really put a wedge between them two. They
had gone to court, and the judge had ordered a paternity test
in honor of Wise' request. The mother of the child was suing
him for back child support so he had a right to establish
paternity. Wise' defense was that he didn't know about the
child.

He didn't believe it was his, and that was the truth. He
did have sex with the girl before but he'd definitely used a
rubber. And that had been a minute ago. He really didn't
even remember that bitch. It was crazy how something from
so long ago could come back and haunt him like that. Wise
was learning time after time that messing with a bunch of
broads was just a damn headache.

Wise prayed that everything worked out in his favor. He
was scheduled to get the paternity results back soon. God
willing, Fatima would be pleased that he'd been telling the

truth about that kid not being his and take him back. It was time for them to be a family again.

$$$

Over the past few weeks, Laila and Cas had gotten quite close since she moved into the new home he'd purchased for her. When Cas found out about the fight Laila had with Kira, he had apologized to Laila with another lump sum of cash to pay off her car, so that she would have one less bill to worry about. The icing on the cake was that he upgraded Laila from her '04 Lexus GS to a brand new '07 Lexus LS 460. That was the big boy. That one had an eight speed automatic transmission, and not to mention an automatic parking system, so it parked itself. Laila was ecstatic over her new car. And it was already paid for. And so was her car insurance for a whole year. Cas was such a sweetheart.

Early that Tuesday morning, they drove the car into the City together to handle some real estate business associated with Laila's other property. Cas had kept his word and fronted her the money to buy Khalil out, so now she owned the brownstone in Brooklyn one hundred percent. They just had to go downtown to the municipal building and record her new deed, and then it was official.

After they were done, Cas went with Laila to her house so she could pick up her mail. Laila didn't think she had anything to worry about now that she was the sole owner, so she invited Cas inside. She wanted to show him what the contractors she hired were going to do. She got out to go unlock the house door while Cas parked the car down the street.

Laila's two-family house was a three story brownstone originally set up with a duplex and an upstairs apartment. As per Casino's advice she was putting in another entrance so she would have three apartments instead of only two, and more rental income. Laila was really starting to love Cas. He had really helped her out a lot. Especially by helping her buy Khalil's half of the house from him.

Speaking of Khalil, to Laila's disbelief when she opened the door that mothafucka was inside the house. She'd had the locks changed the week before, so he had obviously broken in. Laila knew she hadn't given him permission to be there.

She asked him what the hell he was doing there, and he had the nerve to say he was waiting for her to come home so they could be a family again. Khalil was talking stupid. Trying to act like everything was still the same and nothing had happened between them. He said she wouldn't give him her new address so he had no choice but to wait around for her.

Laila irritably told him to leave before she called the police, and they got into a big argument. She told him she had bought his part of the house from him, and he accepted the money. So now he was supposed to move on. He had no right being there. He was trespassing, and she was fed up.

She didn't pity Khalil. He wasn't some broke vagrant. She had just given him a check for two hundred twenty five thousand dollars. His ass could afford to move on. He was just hanging around trying to make her take him back. That was pathetic.

Casino had parked his car, and he came in a minute after Laila. He heard a man's voice so he stood back and waited in the other room, trying to mind his business. He hadn't known that dude was going to be there. If he had, he probably would've stayed outside. He felt it best to stay out of Laila's marital affairs.

Khalil got more and more fed up with Laila running her mouth. He grabbed her by the back of her neck and told her to shut the fuck up. She was getting out of control.

Casino didn't want to get into it with Laila's husband but when he heard the physical commotion arising he intercepted.

He walked in there and calmly but firmly addressed Khalil. "Yo, take your hands off of her."

Khalil looked at that nigga like he was crazy. Who the fuck was he supposed to be? That was his wife. "Yo, you better mind ya' business. This is between me and my wife."

Cas was glad he had his gun on him but he didn't want to have to use it. He just said, "You're right. I ain't got nothin' to do with it, but I don't like the way you're handling her. So I'ma say it nicely this time. Please take your hands off of her."

The men's dispositions were like night and day. Cas was calm and confident, and Khalil appeared shaky and full of doubt.

Khalil wondered who this nigga was Laila was fucking with. He was bold. Real bold. Khalil suddenly recognized him. That was Portia's husband, Jay's partner. Laila had obviously been laying up in New Jersey with him. That fucking bitch.

Khalil was a little intimidated because he knew that nigga had a lot of money but he had to show him that Laila belonged to him. And he had to show Laila that she couldn't disrespect him and get away with it. Not as long as he was her husband. With this theory in mind, Khalil drew back his arm and backhand slapped Laila across her mouth.

Laila fell against the wall and grabbed her face. No the fuck he didn't! She couldn't believe Khalil hit her like that. She reached in her purse for her pepper spray. She was going to blind that nigga. What the fuck was he trying to prove?

Khalil squared up at Cas. "Like I *said*, that's *my* mothafuckin' wife. And I'll discipline her as I please."

Cas bit his lip in anger. He couldn't help but smile and shake his head. "You shouldn't have did that, man."

Anyone who knew Cas would've told Khalil that he had made the wrong decision. He didn't know about Killah' Cas' infamous smile that signified a nigga going down.

Casino started to lift his hoodie and reach in his waist for his hammer but he changed his mind. Khalil was just a chump. Cas decided to give him an old-fashioned ass whipping. He stepped in and quickly three-pieced Khalil with his fists. Khalil just dropped. He was out.

Laila just stood there watching with her mace in her hand. There was no need for it now. Not since Cas had stood up for her.

Cas bent down and smacked Khalil awake. He told him to get back up. Khalil stood up on wobbly legs and swayed side to side. He used to be pretty nice with his hands but all the drinking and getting high he had done the last few days, along with that blow Cas had given him to his chin, had thrown off his equilibrium. Khalil should've just given up but he made a spectacle of himself. He was convinced that he could still fight so he threw up his hands.

Cas saw that he was no match for him so he didn't even bother giving it his all. He wasn't wasting his energy on some drunken crackhead. Cas was an experienced boxer. He fought in the Golden Gloves tournament years ago, and he knew where to hit a man to end a fight quickly.

Cas pounced Khalil out again with two hits. His left and right fists connected with Khalil's chin and jaw, and he just dropped. He was out like somebody shot him with a tranquilizer. Cas reached down to hit that nigga again but Laila grabbed his arm and begged him to stop before he killed him.

At her request, Cas didn't hit him anymore. He didn't have to anyway. Khalil was out cold. Casino turned around and asked Laila if she was okay.

Laila nodded, and just looked at him. She looked down at Khalil on the floor, back at Cas, and then down at Khalil again. She didn't know what to say. She stared at Khalil's chest to make sure he was still breathing. All she could hear in her head was Smokey from Ice Cube's movie "Friday" saying *"You got knocked the fuck out!"*

Sensing her worry, Casino bent down and slapped Khalil a few times to wake him up. He didn't mean to hurt him. He had been forced to knock him out. He had to teach him a lesson after he'd put his hands on Laila.

When Khalil opened his eyes, Cas pointed his finger at him like he was a child and warned him for his own good. "Yo, get your stuff and get out, man. And don't come back here again. I'm only tellin' you one time. When we come back tomorrow, you better be gone. You won't be told this twice." After that, Cas told Laila to come on. It was time for them to go.

Laila followed Casino without hesitation but she looked back at Khalil and felt sorry for him. She didn't love him anymore but she hated to see him that way. She'd just witnessed her husband get beat up by her lover, and the whole experience had been weird for her. That was like some television shit.

Cas opened the passenger door of the car for Laila in a protective gesture, and he walked around to the driver's side and got in. Laila glanced back at the house door to see if Khalil was coming after them. He wasn't.

Cas looked over and saw Laila looking out the window at her house. She was probably trying to see if that dude was coming after her. Cas started up the car and slowly drove off.

Inside the house, Khalil sat there on the floor for a minute and rewound what had just gone down. He had just gotten his ass beat and watched his wife leave with another man. The last few drops of pride and dignity he possessed had completely evaporated.

He really had to get his shit together. He was weak. He knew it now. He believed everyone. He really had a problem. Khalil knew he needed help but he'd much rather continue getting high. It was just easier. He thought about the piece of rock he had in his jacket pocket, and he got up and went to search for it frantically. He needed an escape.

Khalil found what he was looking for and he got ready to take a blast. As he put the pipe to his lips tears ran down his face. Every ounce of manhood he had once possessed was out the window now. He had sacrificed it all. He felt like he could literally feel his balls shrinking by the second.

In reality, he couldn't even fault Laila for moving on. He had pushed her away and into the arms of another man. He hadn't even been there for her when their baby daughter was murdered. And he had gotten himself hooked on drugs. What a loser she must've thought he was. And she was right too.

Khalil hit the pipe and took the easy way away from his problems. He sucked on that glass dick like he was trying to make it cum. As the crack smoke filled his lungs and clouded his brain, his heart rate quickened like he had just taken a shot of pure adrenaline. Now he felt powerful and mighty. That was the part he loved about getting high.

$$$

Every time they were in the midst of trying to get money and take care of business, there was always some bullshit brewing when it came to Hop. Jay and Cas had recently been informed by a couple of their cohorts in the dirty south that Hop had robbed this rapper named Trey-Black from ATL for his chain, and they wanted it back.

Hop was said to have been seen disrespectfully sporting the chain in public, and boasting about the way he'd obtained it. Jay and Cas were forced to play the part of mediators. They called Hop in for a sit down and "suggested" that he give the chain back because those boys were their alliances. They asked him again why he kept trying to start unnecessary beef with everybody in the industry when he should be focused on trying to make something happen in the studio. He hadn't produced a solid hit yet.

After Jay and Cas shot down Hop's rebuttal, he agreed to return the chain. He smiled at them like everything was okay but there was malice in his heart. He felt like him giving that chain back made him look like a sucker. And now he felt that Jay and Cas were soft.

Hop didn't understand that they were just trying to keep the peace and get money. They were successful millionaires who just didn't want to be bothered with petty and unnecessary static, but Hop took it personal just like he took everything else. He was the epitome of what Jay-Z meant when he said, *"sensitive thugs, you all need hugs."*

Hop decided that it was time to get some get-back. Those dudes kept on playing him and treating him like he was a sucker. He was gonna be the last one laughing. Them niggas would see.

Hop knew Jay was throwing a party for his wife in a few weeks. His wife Portia wrote books and shit, and she was coming out with something new. That would be the perfect time for dudes to strike. Hop thought about it and he decided that the benefit outweighed the risk.

A few days later, Hop contacted The Scumbag Brothas and tipped them off on the time and place the party was being held. They came to terms on a split, and they all agreed to keep in touch until the shit went down.

$$$

The next few weeks were busy for Portia. She was preparing for the arrival of her new shipment of books. Portia couldn't wait to see them. The book had a great cover, and she had dedicated it to her mother.

Her book shipment was due from the printer in about eight more business days. She and Fatima had agreed to print ten thousand copies initially. God willing, they'd be on the next print run soon. There was a pretty decent demand for the book because Fatima had been promoting shamelessly, so Portia anticipated a good sales volume out the gate. That was how they usually did. Tima handled most of the marketing and stuff, and Portia did the writing.

Portia was excited. She looked forward to all of the business that came along with the release of a new novel. All of the book signings, advertising, giveaways, on-line chats, interviews, etc. She and Fatima were taking Sinclair Lane Publishing and going big this time. They had advertised in all types of magazines, including Essence, Don Diva, VIBE, Vibe Vixen, XXL, and The Source.

Jay and Wise had cushioned the company's budget so they could afford billboards and radio commercials, and Portia had even hired a publicist this time around. And courtesy of Jay's wallet, this time her book release party was going to be huge. Portia was getting nervous because the date was approaching so fast.

$$$

A few days later, Jay sat in his office and made phone calls to make sure plans were moving along smoothly for the ultra fabulous book release party he was throwing Portia that weekend. This new novel's release would be the turning point in her career, and he wanted to make sure everyone knew that.

Portia had proven to Jay that the urban book market was lucrative. After she showed him the figures of her first two books' sales he had been forced to take his hat off and respect her new hustle. That's why he didn't complain when she spent so much time writing. He was supportive of her career. It was good that she had her own thing going. He liked that Portia was still business minded.

Jay thought about back when he'd first met her, when

she was dancing in that strip club. He had known then that
Portia was a hustler. The fact that they shared the same type
of mentality made them compatible.

For Portia's upcoming big night, Jay had hired a professional
party planner who worked with Portia's new publicist,
Rebecca, and her agent, Penelope, to form an A-list guest list
that consisted of a mélange of bigwigs from the music, film,
and publishing industries.

$$$

When the night finally came, everything went along as
planned. Portia was so happy she was floating. She smiled
all night long, and she looked beautiful.

Towards the end of the evening, Jay stood up and
commanded everyone's attention. He made a toast to Portia,
and all the sexless nights they had while she stayed up until
dawn writing her book. Everyone laughed, especially when
Jay said that now that she finished the book, she could make
it up to him.

That night Kira had stayed home because she wasn't feeling
well, and Cas and Laila flirted openly. Jay didn't even have
anything to say about it because he knew Kira was doing
her. She had lied and told Cas she was sick. Her behind
was feeling fine. She was out with that nigga Young Vee. Jay
wasn't stupid. He had called her to make sure she was okay,
and he'd heard a dude's voice in the background. When he
asked her who that was she just giggled and shit. Kira played
a whole lot of games. Cas was Jay's main man, and it seemed
like Laila made him happy.

As usual, Wise was trying to holler at a chick that night.
But this time the chick was his wife. But Fatima wouldn't
give him the time of day so Wise felt low. He knew she
was hurting but he had at least hoped she would've spoken
to him. Fatima's behavior towards him threw off his whole

night. Wise found himself watching her from afar during the entire event. He purchased two copies of Portia's book that night, and he went up and asked her to sign them for him. Fatima was sitting right beside her but she wouldn't even make eye contact with him.

Unbeknownst to anyone, The Scumbag Brothas were in the vicinity that evening blending in amongst the well dressed attendees. They were professionals. They knew how to look the part.

After the party was over, Portia rode back home with Laila and Fatima. Jay stuck with his boys, Cas and Wise. Hop tagged along with them too. They made a few stops in the City and hung out until about four AM.

On their way home, they traveled down the West Side Highway because there was no traffic that time of the morning. Something told Cas to check the rearview mirror of his Rolls Royce Phantom. There was a van that he kept on seeing a few cars behind them, and it seemed to be everywhere they went.

Casino made a few turns to make sure he wasn't bugging. After a few blocks, he realized that he was right. The suspicious looking van was still behind them. Cas knew he wasn't crazy. They had company, and his instinct told him something was up.

Casino got on point and kept his eyes on that vehicle but he kept on talking to his homies like nothing was wrong. They were in the middle of a conversation about Wise missing Fatima, and wanting to do right by her.

Cas looked over at Jay and Wise and smiled. "Ya'll don't react or look back, but there's a van following us. You niggas better get ya' hammers ready, 'cause for some reason I think it's a hit."

Jay nor Wise took what Casino said lightly because he was smiling. They both knew Cas always smiled when he sensed beef brewing. They were all from the streets. They weren't naïve enough to doubt niggas. They knew that being millionaires automatically made them targets for thirsty dudes with something to prove. Wise got his mind off of Fatima and got in battle mode. They all took out their heat and got ready.

Hop was quiet but he was a little nervous. He hadn't planned on Cas noticing the van behind them. He hoped everything went down smooth. Hop took out his gun and pretended he was an ally, when he was in fact the person responsible for the van following them in the first place.

Between Jay, Cas, Wise, and Hop, they had a total of six guns in their vehicle. At Cas' suggestion, they pulled over and acted like they were having car trouble. Cas shut off the engine and faked like they had a flat tire.

When the men in the van following them saw the Phantom pull over with a flat, they immediately sensed victory. The shit was about to go down. The Scumbag Brothas weren't shook because they were outnumbered by the vics. They had gone up against and taken down larger crews than that. Their theory was simple. Whoever didn't give it up got it. And they got it in the worse way. When they saw the car pull over and the driver hop out and look at the front tire, they knew that jux would be even easier than they thought. The setup was just too sweet.

The Scumbag Brothas pulled up a few feet behind their would-be victims. Powerful shut off the lights and the engine, and he and Mike Machete both adjusted their hammers and got out. Black baseball caps pulled down over their eyes, they approached the Rolls Royce in front of them.

Cas knelt down on one knee like he was checking the tire but he watched the two suspicious looking thugs from the corner of his eye. Jay, Wise, and Hop hopped out of the car. Each of them was armed with already cocked handguns of different calibers but only two of them planned to cover Cas.

Cas stood up just as the dudes walked up, and his henchmen appeared right at his side. They were all ready for combat. They weren't about to give dudes a chance to walk up on them and murk them. They had families to get home to. Fuck that.

There was a brief stare down between the two crews. The Scumbag Brothas paused because they saw that those Street Life cats weren't going to be easily had. It was in their eyes. Before Powerful or Mike Machete could even utter a word, Cas, Wise, and Jay opened fire and aired it out.

The Scumbag Brothas pulled out and fired back fearlessly. They were no strangers to combat. They stayed prepared for a gun battle. The men on both sides scattered for cover as bullets flew in every direction, whizzing by their heads like tiny missiles.

The Scumbag Brothas hadn't contemplated those dudes spraying on them like that. They were running out of ammunition quick so it was time for them to reload. They had to get back to their vehicle. They used their last few rounds to back their way out.

Jay ducked and paused to reload, not realizing that he was in the line of Powerful's fire. A hot slug pierced his face and tore through his flesh. The impact knocked Jay backwards slightly but he caught himself and didn't fall. He ate that bullet and came back up blasting. For the one he caught, he threw four back. *Boom, boom, boom, boom!*

Jay saw two of his bullets strike the taller of the grimy pair as they ran the other way. He had hit the one who shot him. Those bitch ass niggas were trying to flee. They jumped in their van and sped off.

Cas saw Jay get hit so he kept dumping at those shiesty assed dudes. He prayed his partner was okay. Determined to kill them niggas, he and Wise chased the van as they drove off. Hop ran over to see about Jay.

Cas and Wise emptied their pistols on that van. They

knew those mothafuckas had to be hit up pretty bad. They sure hoped so. After all that gunfire they wondered how they were still breathing.

After the van screeched off, sirens could be heard in the distance. Cas and Wise wanted to jump in the car and chase them but they thought the better of it now that the police were in the vicinity. And they had to get Jay to the emergency room. They hurried over to see about him.

Satisfied that Jay was still breathing but worried sick nonetheless, they hurried and got him in the car and sped off in the other direction. Thank God he was conscious, but he had to see a doctor. Fast.

Chapter Twenty Two

On the way to the hospital, Wise was silent as he pushed the pedal all the way down to the metal. He was worried sick but he wouldn't panic. He couldn't. Driving upset at that speed could kill them all. Wise kept glancing back at Jay to make sure he was alright. He was praying for his bro. Jay's face was swollen big as a watermelon, and he was bleeding profusely onto a towel he had pressed on his jaw.

Hop sat in the passenger seat quiet as a church mouse. Just like the rest of them, he knew that this was no laughing matter. Jay got hit in the face. Hop's cell phone kept ringing the same hip-hop ring tone but he wouldn't answer. Had he been smarter, he would've just shut it off. Whoever it was wouldn't lay off so he finally picked up.

Wise could overhear the caller on Hop's phone, and they were pretty upset. In fact, they were yelling through the phone. Wise played it cool and listened close. He could hear some dude saying, *"You was s'posed to set that shit up right, but your sloppy ass work got Powerful hit up. I told him let's not fuck wit' no new, inexperienced niggas! Nigga, I just want you to know that if my brother don't make it, you finished! That's word on my life, nigga! You finished!"*

Hop had a good response for that but he simply said, "Ayight man", and hung up. He kept quiet but that nigga Mike Machete had really pissed him off talking to him like he was some type of bitch. He was lucky Hop couldn't pop off at the time because he'd have let that Philly nigga know where the fuck he was. They were in New York. That was his town.

Wise squinted at Hop through the corner of his eye. That nigga was a snake. His bitch ass had set them up! He had glanced over at Hop during the shootout and saw that he

wasn't firing, and now he knew why. At the time he thought
Hop had got scared and just bitched up but now he knew
the truth. That nigga wasn't afraid to shoot. He had no
intentions on helping them. And Jay messed around and got
shot behind his bullshit.

The more Wise thought about it, he became enraged.
The fury he felt was so strong he could taste revenge. He was
tempted to grab his hammer and put a bullet in Hop's filthy,
lowlife, traitor skull right then and there. Wise only resisted
the urge because getting Jay to the emergency room was his
priority. Hop would get dealt with later. That was for sure.

Casino sat in the back with Jay, who was laid across the
backseat. Cas kept his head elevated so he wouldn't choke on
the blood that gurgled dangerously from his mouth.

He held Jay's hand and told him, "Just hold on, ayight
son. Just hold on. We gon' be at the hospital in a minute.
You gon' be ayight, man. You hear me? You gon' be ayight."
Cas was praying to God as he spoke.

Jay wanted to answer Cas but he couldn't talk. And he
couldn't feel his face either. He prayed silently. He sure
hoped God was going to give him this one. He squeezed
Cas' hand to let him know he was holding on.

Cas took that hand squeeze as a good sign. A sign that
meant Jay would make it. He couldn't imagine life without
his closest comrade. They were brothers from other mothers.
Straight up. Jay had to be alright. He just had too.

$$$

A short time later, Portia got a phone call from Cas. It
was five o'clock in the morning. She hadn't been long gone
to sleep but she got up out of the bed. From the way Cas
sounded, she had a feeling it was something serious.

Portia told him to tell her what was wrong. He told her
that Jay had been shot, and she almost had a heart attack.

"What?! Oh God! No! Jay got shot *where*? Oh God, is he okay? Cas, where is he?"

Cas told Portia that Jay was alive but he honestly didn't know much about his condition yet. Portia found out what hospital he was in, and told Cas she was on her way.

After she hung up she stood there for a moment. The feeling in the pit of her stomach was indescribable. She felt weak and afraid to move. How could it be that Jay got shot? She had just seen him a few hours ago at her book release party. God, she hoped he was okay.

The kids had been asleep but they overheard Portia yelling so they hurried in to see what was wrong. When they saw her crying they both just stood there frozen, like they knew it was real bad.

Jayquan and Jazmin looked terrified. Jayquan was old enough to understand. And poor little Jazz had seen so much grieving and mourning lately at all the funerals they had attended that year, she now associated crying with people dying and never coming back. First Humble, then Pebbles, and then her grandmother, Patricia. All of their deaths had occurred one behind another. That was a lot of sadness for a little girl her age to endure. Portia prayed that her daddy wouldn't be next.

Portia's heart went out to her kids. They were just babies. She walked over and hugged them tightly, and they both started crying in her arms.

Jayquan just belted out, "I'm scared, man! I'm scared Pop is gonna die, Portia."

Portia was scared too but she held them close to her and rocked them back and forth. She had to stay positive. "Don't worry, baby. Your daddy's gonna be fine. He's gonna be alright. Just have faith. Jay's gon' be fine. Pray, baby. You gotta pray."

Portia told Lil' Jay to hurry and get dressed so they could get to the hospital. She quickly threw on a pair of jeans and sneakers and got Jazz dressed, and in two minutes they were en route to see about Jay. Along the way Portia prayed her heart out.

She fought to keep her eyes on the road. It was if heartache had blinded her. She asked God to keep her and the children safe. As she sped along the highway she couldn't help but wonder what they had done to deserve so much bad luck in the course of a year. It had just been one devastating blow after another.

$$\$\$\$$$

When Portia and the kids got to the hospital they were greeted with the blessed news that Jay was in stable condition. When Portia heard that she broke down and cried. But this time she shed tears of joy because it felt like she regained her ability to be. By the grace of God her husband had made it.

She learned from Jay's doctor that he had been shot in the face. Luckily, the bullet had made a clean exit through the other side. It shattered his jaw bone to pieces but he was lucky. Jay just had to stay in the hospital for a little while until the doctor decided to release him.

The following week, Portia spent most of her time right by his bedside. The funny thing was that Jay was laid up in the hospital with wires and stitches all throughout his face, but he still wanted to have sex.

At first Portia protested because she thought it was too soon but Jay assured her that there wasn't anything wrong with his dick. That being said, during the course of his hospital stay Portia spent a lot of time bent over the bathroom sink while he hit it from the back. That was the most convenient way for them to make love under the circumstances. The bathroom was small but they didn't want to risk getting caught. Jay had a private room but the nurses were in and out all day.

Jay was having a pretty speedy recovery, so he was able to

go home after a few more days. He was so grateful to God. His jaw was still wired shut so he couldn't talk but it was all good. While he was in the hospital, he and Portia had developed a system of knocks. Jay knocked one time for "no", and two times for "yes". Three knocks meant he was in pain.

When he came home, Portia catered to his every need. She spent the greater part of her day by his side while he delegated his responsibilities to her. She had gotten him a clipboard to write on, and all day long he ferociously scribbled down things that needed to be taken care of.

Whatever Portia could do herself, she did, and the rest she got on the phone and called Casino about. Cas was usually up on what Jay had to do before Portia told him. He always told her to tell Jay not to worry. And he stopped by every chance he got. Wise did too. The three of them had always had each other's backs, and nothing had changed now. Those boys really loved each other. Portia guessed that was the reason they had been so successful.

Poor Jay couldn't eat solid food yet. He could only sip through a straw so Cas, Wise, Kira, his mother, and everyone else kept on bringing him cases of protein drinks. Jay had every flavor of Ensure and Nutriment from chocolate to peanut butter. The drinks tasted okay but they gave him a terrible case of gas. At first Portia complained about his farting until he scribbled on his notepad, *"You know I can't eat. I ain't got nothin' on my stomach but air, Ma. I can't help it."*

Portia just wrinkled her nose and laughed. She loved his stinking butt regardless.

Despite Jay's efforts to make up for his missed meals by sipping high calorie shakes, he had lost a lot of weight. He had also lost some muscle tone when he was laid up in the hospital. Now that he was feeling better he developed a daily workout routine which he did twice a day.

Portia kept telling him to take it easy but he was ready to get back on top of his "A" game. Jay knew Portia was right though. His jaw wasn't healed yet. His doctor told him it had been shattered pretty bad, and it would probably never heal to its original condition. He said Jay's bite would probably be different, and there was some nerve damage so there might be some involuntary twitching in his facial muscles. But even knowing all of that, Jay was still glad to be alive.

Hop had visited him a few times in the hospital, and once since he'd been home. Jay had detected nothing but pure phoniness off of him. That dude just didn't seem sincere.

Jay told Portia about Hop setting them up to get robbed, and he made her promise not to blow it up. He just wanted to heal, and then he was going to take care of it. Cas and Wise were eager to smoke Hop but after a debate with Jay, verbal on their part and written on his, they agreed to handle it the way he chose.

They had heard through the grapevine that one of The Scumbag Brothas was dead. Cas told Jay that this news had been confirmed. It was the one named Powerful. They immediately put a price on the other brother, Mike Machete's head. They pledged a hundred grand to the first person to take him out and bring them proof, and fifty thousand to whoever pointed out his whereabouts. The idea of that nigga still walking the streets didn't sit well with any of them.

$$$

Kira was feeling down about her and Cas drifting apart. She knew she had played her part in their splitting up, especially by fucking around with Young Vee. But now that the shoe was on the other foot and it was Cas fooling around, she just couldn't deal with it. It was really killing her. She wasn't even that interested in Vee anymore. Now that she knew there was another woman in Cas' life she really wanted to hold on to him. That bitch wasn't getting her husband.

In a last desperate attempt to save her marriage, Kira awaited Cas sexily clad in black Charnos lingerie and stilettos that night. They each had their own master bathrooms, and she made sure his was candlelit and smelling of a masculine fragrant sandalwood medley she had placed in the potpourri burner. She also turned on the surround sound in the bathroom and put on an R. Kelley's greatest slow jams CD.

When Cas came in the door, Kira took his hand and led him to the hot tub she had run for him. Cas wasn't in a romantic mood when he came in but he just played along with her. He'd had a long day so he didn't protest to the bath, but he wondered where all of this came from. He and Kira had been on the outs for months and now all of a sudden she was trying to seduce him. What the hell was she up to?

Cas undressed and got in his bath. The spa water felt good so he decided to soak for a little while. He was a busy man so he didn't get to enjoy his hot tub much. He just wanted to be alone but Kira came in and laid down on the side of the tub. She dipped ripe strawberries in chocolate and fed them to him. After the second one, Cas told her he didn't want anymore.

When Cas got out of the hot tub, Kira slowly towel dried him and rubbed lotion all over his body. Her touch aroused him. They had problems but Cas was still a man. And she did look sexy in that black corset. She smelled good too.

When Kira was done moisturizing Cas' body she sank to her knees in front of him. She took his big hard penis in her hands and stroked it gently. She'd almost forgotten how beautiful it was. Kira placed it in her mouth and went to work. She knew Cas loved getting some good head. Someone was sucking his dick so it might as well be her. She was his wife.

In a sense, Kira knew that her theory was sort of stupid

but she figured that if they had sex he would remember how much he loved her. Cas hadn't touched her in a while but he didn't resist her advances. He had his head leaned back and his eyes were closed. To Kira's delight, it looked like he was savoring the moment.

After a minute, Casino told her to stand up and bend over. Kira obeyed, and he slid inside of her and began to stroke. She started moaning like it felt good. Cas beat it for about twenty more humps and he felt himself about to cum. He groaned, and pulled out and shot off all over Kira's ass. Afterwards Cas felt terrible because he'd thought about Laila the whole time. He wiped his dick off with his washcloth and excused himself, and he went and got ready for bed.

Kira watched Cas walk away, and she felt even worse than she'd felt before they fucked. There was so much distance between them during their intercourse. It was like Cas wasn't even there. Kira felt like she was just a piece of meat.

Later on, she laid in bed crying silently with her back turned to him. Cas was laying next to her snoring lightly. She knew his body was there with her but his heart was on the other side of town. Kira knew she had to let it go. There was too much damage between the two of them. It was over.

The following morning, she woke Cas up and told him she wanted a divorce. Cas didn't respond at first. He wished she would've at least given him a chance to brush his teeth and wash his face before she said that.

He thought about it quietly for a minute. When he finally spoke he simply said, "Ayight, I'll leave. You can have the house."

Kira was shocked. Damn, he didn't even protest. She had prayed deep down inside that when she told him, he would tell her he loved her and beg her not to leave him. But it seemed like he was relieved. Boy, the truth really hurt. Kira just walked out of the room. She didn't want Cas to see the tears forming in her eyes.

$$$

As soon as Jay got the wires taken out of his jaw, he was ready to get at Hop for setting them up. Jay called him up that Tuesday and told him to meet him at his house. He had cleverly thought up a scenario that was television-like enough for Hop's dumb ass to believe.

When Hop came over, Jay fixed each of them a straight shot of Jack Daniels and told him to join him out on the veranda. When they got outside, he told Hop to have a seat. Jay told him that the reason he had arranged a private meeting between the two of them was top-secret. He told him not to breath a word of what he was about to tell him to another soul.

Jay's face was still healing so he spoke a little slower these days. "Hop, while I was layin' up healing, I came to some conclusions. I decided that I want out of the game. I just wanna chill now, and raise my kids. I done took a bullet in the face, man. That's my cue to exit the stage. But I need a good, reliable man to turn the coke operation over to. Somebody with some heart."

Jay looked at Hop sincerely. "Son, I think *you'd* be a good candidate. I believe you got what it takes, but do you think you could handle all that responsibility?"

Hop's greedy ass had already gone for the bait. He knew them niggas was still hustling. He'd asked them if they were before but they wouldn't admit it. Hop pictured himself a drug kingpin, smoking a Cuban cigar and wearing a straw Tommy Bahama hat. He liked that vision a whole lot. Hop nodded at Jay earnestly. "Yeah, son. I can handle it. Definitely."

Seeing that Hop was interested, Jay continued. "Okay, that's good money. We gon' fly out this weekend, and I'ma introduce you to the connect."

Hop nodded enthusiastically. He thought about all the

perks that came along with meeting the connect, including use of his body disposal warehouse. Bodies were bound to start piling up now that he was taking over. He had plans to make niggas get down or lay down.

It was that type of reckless thinking that would ultimately destroy Hop. He was what you would call "overly and unnecessarily gangsta". That dude was just too extra.

When the weekend finally came, Jay, Wise, Cas, and Hop boarded Manuel's private jet en route to Cartagena, Colombia. As far as Hop was concerned, he was going on a top secret mission to claim his throne. He was in a good mood the whole plane ride because he knew that when he returned he would be the king. He was excited at the prospect of supplying the whole industry with cocaine. That was a big money business and he just couldn't wait.

When they landed in Cartagena, the breeze was warm and welcoming. There was something calming about the air. And the beaches were beautiful. It seemed like a place the men could really enjoy once business was taken care of.

Just as he promised, Manuel came to meet them at the landing strip. When they got off the plane he pulled up in a white Rolls Royce stretch limousine. The driver got out and opened the door for him, and Manuel stepped out of the car with extended arms.

"Bienvenido! Welcome, my friends", he bellowed. Manuel heartily greeted each of them with a firm handshake and a fatherly slap on the back. He asked them how their trip was, and then he told them to get in the limo so he could show them to their quarters.

Inside the car, Manuel smiled and let them know of the joys their trip would bring. He promised them the time of their lives. He knew there was a rat amongst them and he already knew who it was, but he was a classy gentleman. The type of host that treated all of his guests well. He was a very

powerful and well polished man, who oftentimes had smiled
and treated people like family, while having intentions to kill
them all along. Manuel was a descendant of the Colombian
Cartel, and he would administer a death sentence without
batting an eye. Whenever it was necessary.

Jay, Cas, and Wise dug the fact that Manuel treated Hop
like he treated them. He was already aware of their plans
to leave Hop in Colombia, and he didn't give the shit away.
That was how real gangstas did it. They showed you the time
of your life, and then popped you.

In the limo, Manuel offered them adult beverages and
refreshments. They all declined and told him that the staff
on his private jet had treated them well. They'd had their
choice of top shelf liquor, and Manuel had an onboard chef
named Basco who specialized in cuisines from nine different
countries. The dude could really cook his ass off.

A few minutes later, they arrived at Manuel's house. It
was located on acres of his own private beach, and it was
absolutely exquisite. His property straight up looked like
something out of a movie. Jay, Cas, and Wise all had grand
estates but they had to give that man his props. When it
came to residences, he definitely had it.

When they finally got to their quarters, which were
rooms the size of double presidential suites, they all decided
to unwind for a little while. Jay, Cas, Wise, and Manuel
had all previously agreed that Hop would be the evening's
honoree on their first night there. It was like a private joke
that everyone was in on except for him.

When Hop found out that night at dinner, he was thrilled.
A toast was made in his honor, and then he was wined,
dined, and treated like a king. Hop ate up every ounce of it
too, knowing that the star treatment came along with taking
over. He played the part well with a Cuban cigar Manuel
had given him in the side of his mouth like the gangsters in

the movies.

After dinner, Jay stood up and announced that it was time for the induction. He told Hop to stand up, and he reached over and placed an iced out Street Life Entertainment medallion around his neck. Jay patted Hop on his back affectionately and told him he finally got up. Now he was officially a made man. Jay congratulated him, and the others stood in line to do so as well. Manual handed out cigars in celebration. Cas elbowed Wise because his silly ass kept on laughing.

Hop was so proud. His adrenaline level soared. He was finally made. Them niggas finally respected him. He smiled like a champion and gave pounds and hugs to his cohorts when they lined up to wish him well.

Manuel snapped his fingers, and his servants bought out the bubbly. Cristal bottles were popped, and out came five beautiful Colombian women who had been pre-instructed to make Hop feel like royalty. The ladies took him away to the Jacuzzi with plans to fulfill his every fantasy.

Hop had enough weed, liquor, and pussy for days. He partied well into the wee hours of the morning until he was like a sexed out, drunken zombie. The fellows made sure he had a chance to shine in his final hour.

The following morning at ten o'clock, Manuel's servants served them a hearty breakfast. After they all ate, Manuel took them to the east wing of his house and showed them his fine collection of weaponry. He had over two hundred guns in his possession. Every kind and caliber you could think of. Manuel invited them all along to target practice with him. He offered the use of his weapons so they could participate as well. The men accepted Manuel's invitation without hesitation. Each of them was given extra rounds of the proper ammunition for the weapon they chose.

As Manuel walked them across his sprawling estate to his firing range, he pointed out where everything was. Amongst other things on his land, he had an Olympic sized swimming pool, a real racecar track, and a full golf course.

When they finally arrived at the range, Manuel told them he enjoyed friendly competition. He said that the man with the best aim would be rewarded well. Jay, Cas, and Wise all had their turn, and then it was Hop's go.

Hop was anxious to prove that he was a no-nonsense gunner. He felt the need to impress Manuel with his aim because he was taking over now, and he wanted to assure him that he would bust his gun and not miss if need be. Hop looked around at everybody confidently, and he stepped up to the plate and took aim. He fired three shots, and got real close to the bull's eye twice. Hop was so engrossed in trying to astound them with the perfect shot that he didn't notice the other men step to the side out of Jay's way.

They all knew that Hop's murder was a long time in the making, and it was time for him to go. That nigga was a snake. He had set them up. Jay had been shot in the attempted robbery so Jay would do the honor of clapping him.

Jay had waited a long time for this day. When he thought about the fact that he could've been eighty-sixed out of his kids' lives forever all because of Hop, he was filled with rage. Jay bit his lip in anger. The desire to kill Hop engulfed him. He pointed his .44 caliber Desert Eagle at his dome piece and mercilessly squeezed.

Hop didn't even see it coming. The bullet spun from the chamber and made a permanent part in his freshly brushed waves. Part of his skull flew off, and tiny red dots of blood splattered on Cas and Wise' white tees. They quickly removed their shirts before the blood soaked through to their wife beaters.

Jay apologized to them for being messy, and Manuel called for a cleanup crew on his walkie-talkie. About two minutes later, two men showed up in a black pickup truck. After a few words in Spanish with Manuel, they quickly proceeded to scrape Hop's body and brains up off the ground and into a big, black, heavy-duty plastic bag.

The cleanup men left as quickly as they had come. Manuel looked over at Jay, Cas, and Wise and smiled. The deed was done. The rat was dead and soon stinking, so now they could resume their vacation.

Manuel knew without question that the three men standing before him were not the imitation kind. They had proven themselves to him already, and they had all made a lot of money in the process. It had been his pleasure to help them dispose of that snake in their camp.

Manuel called another manservant and had him collect their weapons, and then he insisted that his friends join him in visiting Hop's final resting place. He pointed to some nearby golf cars and instructed them to each hop in one. All driving separate golf cars, they followed Manuel to see what he was referring to.

When they all stopped a few minutes later, Jay, Cas, and Wise couldn't believe where they were. Manuel had a private zoo. A real fucking zoo. He had everything from monkeys and elephants, to lions, tigers, and bears. There were beautiful exotic birds, all kinds of tamed creatures, and ferocious beasts.

The Colombian cleanup men in the black pickup truck had been instructed to wait until they arrived. When they got there, Manuel yelled out some type of command in Spanish. A moment later, Hop's corpse was dragged into a huge cage and emptied from the plastic bag onto the ground.

The men from the pickup truck hurried away from the corpse as fast as they could and quickly relocked the cage. Just then, two lions came out of a cave inside the cage. Both men wiped sweat from their brows with the back of their hands. They had missed an encounter with the lions by seconds, and it was obvious that they were relieved.

Hop's body was put in the lions' den about an hour before feeding time so they were real hungry. They circled Hop's remains slowly and growled, both baring atrocious dagger-like fangs.

Now Jay, Cas, and Wise understood what Manuel had meant. That caged lions' den would be Hop's final resting place. They were all hardcore, gun-toting men who had all looked death in the eye a time or two in their lives, but when they witnessed the massive and menacing lions' vicious fangs tear into Hop's torso and effortlessly rip him apart they all winced. It was like he was made of nothing. Their stomachs turned, and they watched in silence as the lions mangled and devoured what was left of Hop's carcass. He was lucky he was already dead.

After they killed the rat, Jay, Cas, and Wise stayed in Cartagena for a few more days.

The remainder of their vacation was filled with sun and fun. They rode jet skis, parasailed, and did every other fun thing they could do in the water. It was a well needed getaway for all of them.

That Tuesday evening, they flew back home to the States. It was time to get back to business as usual. There was a lot to do.

When they got home, Jay made up a story to tell Hop's baby mother, Nisha. They told her that Hop had gotten drunk and thought he was superman, and he tried to rob this big time dude in Colombia, and had been gunned down by his body guards in the process.

Nisha had no reason to doubt what they told her because she knew how her man got down. Hop stayed robbing niggas. That was how he was living. She was just grateful that Jay and Casino gave her a hefty good faith check on behalf of the record company for her and her child, because Hop hadn't left them anything. She decided to take the money and move down south to Virginia where her mother was.

Chapter Twenty Three

About two weeks later, Jay woke up late one morning and stretched. He yawned and looked around the room. Portia had been redecorating, and the new curtains were really nice. Jay got out of bed and put on his slippers, and he headed for the bathroom. He washed his face and brushed his teeth, and then he went downstairs to get a glass of orange juice.

Jay was feeling pretty good physically. He had to admit that. The only evidence of him getting shot was two faint scars on his cheeks. He had grown out his beard so you couldn't even see them. He was basically the same old Jay. Luckily he hadn't developed the muscle twitch in his face that the doctor had warned him about. At least not yet. He'd been working out, eating right, and he was physically fit.

But spiritually and emotionally Jay was in a slump. Something was eating at his soul, and deep down inside he knew what it was. He was a man of God with a good heart and he knew right from wrong. He was feeling a bit remorseful about the lives he had taken. He had done a lot of dirt the past year.

Jay wouldn't call everything he'd ever done in his lifetime justifiable in God's eyes but it certainly wasn't senseless. He had gotten revenge on every person that crossed him or brought harm to his loved ones. But it just wasn't enough.

Before he had gone to Colombia, Jay had promised himself that once he took care of Hop that was it. He really had to get his life in order. He didn't need anymore bad karma. There was something going on inside of him, and he couldn't explain it. He guessed he just had to talk it over with God.

Jay didn't play with God. He knew better. He knew God made all things possible for him, and a lot of the stuff he did he should've just left up to Him to handle. The more Jay thought about it, resorting to violence hadn't really made him feel that much better. In some cases he just did what he had to do because that was the code of the streets, and it was expected of him.

After he got shot, he knew it was time to get right. He had just been straight wilding lately. Jay knew deep in his heart that getting shot was a sign from God. That was a warning for him to slow down. He had to leave that life alone. God had given him another chance. He had no business living like that anymore. He was entirely too blessed.

Jay was a praying man, and at that instant he prayed for God to melt the malice in his heart and change him. He just felt like he needed something.

Portia had gone out early that morning, and the kids were in school so Jay was home all alone. He decided to get dressed and break out for a little while. He was thinking too much in the crib. And he had to go to the city for a meeting with his attorney about some new contracts a little later anyway.

While Jay was getting dressed he got a call from his aunt. Yaz had been calling to check on his condition every couple of days since he'd been shot. Jay assured her that he was feeling okay. He could finally eat solid food again so he agreed to have lunch with her. Aunt Yaz was good people, and she was also a renowned sculptress.

About two hours later, she and Jay were sitting in a restaurant in Soho. Halfway through lunch, two of Yaz' artist friends joined them. They were both white. Yaz cheerfully introduced them to Jay. There was a lady named Tilly, who specialized in ice and wood sculpting, and a dude named Josh, whose thing was canvas art. They seemed cool.

After they ate, they took a walk to a nearby Soho gallery where pieces of their work were on display. Jay being the fine art connoisseur he was, he was glad to tag along with them.

Jay knew art, and he was nothing short of impressed with their work. He stood back and studied one of Josh's paintings. That particular one was called "The Ascent", and it was intriguing. It was a painting of a woman whose soul was en route to heaven. She had pastel rainbow colored wings, and her features were so lifelike.

Looking at the painting gave Jay an idea. He wanted to do something nice for someone, and he thought about Laila. Jay pulled Josh to the side and discussed his wishes to have him paint a friend's deceased child as an angel. Jay explained to him that Laila had just moved into a new home so he wanted something large and framed so she could hang it up over her fireplace. He said he needed it done as soon as possible, and asked Josh how much he would charge.

Josh and Jay settled on ten thousand dollars cash, and Josh told him he needed a photo of the little girl. Jay promised to send it to his email address pronto, and they shook hands and sealed the deal.

When Jay got home that evening, he told Portia what he had planned and asked her if she had a photo of Pebbles. That way he wouldn't have to ask Laila for one and spoil the surprise. Lucky for him, Portia had a bunch of cute photos of Pebbles.

Portia took three of the cutest pictures from her photo album and scanned them, and she emailed them to Josh for Jay. Looking at Pebbles' pictures really made her misty eyed. She was such a beautiful child. That was just so fucked up what had happened to her.

Portia shut down her computer and flipped through more pictures. She laughed out loud at a photo of Pebbles in a dance contest she had won at a block party when she was little. She looked so cute. Portia couldn't help but wonder why God had let her go like that. She hadn't gotten a chance to live her life yet. She was only a baby. It was just so unfair.

Jay saw Portia staring at the photos so he walked up

behind her and placed his arms around her waist. He asked softly in her ear, "You ayight, Kit Kat?"

Portia nodded, and turned around and hugged him. His getting Pebbles painted as an angel for Laila was the absolute sweetest thing he could have done. Jay was just a thoughtful guy. Portia placed a soft kiss on his sexy lips. She loved that man so much.

About two weeks later, the painting was finished. Jay paid Josh in cash, just as he had requested. Jay understood that he wanted that bread to be tax-free so he didn't mind at all. And Josh had done an excellent job. The mahogany frame was nice too.

Before he had the painting crated up and delivered to Laila, Jay stood back and admired it. Pebbles looked so lifelike. God bless her little heart. She was so beautiful he had literally gasped when he first laid eyes on it. His heart truly went out to Laila for her loss. He couldn't imagine one of his kids dying before him. And the heinous way Pebbles was killed. That was just horrible. Jay prayed she was resting in peace.

Jay called Portia and told her to let Laila know to be expecting a package the following day. He was sending it to her overnight express.

The following evening, Laila had just taken a shower after her workout and was getting dressed when her doorbell rang. She knew Macy was downstairs and could answer the door so she didn't bother rushing down to see who it was.

Laila stepped into a pair of comfortable pink fleece lounging pants and she heard Macy yell upstairs, *"Ma! It's a delivery for you!"* Laila figured that must've been what Portia was talking about yesterday. She had told her to be expecting something. Laila couldn't wait to see what it was. She slipped on the matching shirt to her pants, and hurried downstairs.

Whatever the delivery was, it was huge. Laila signed

for the giant package, and the delivery guy asked her if she needed assistance with it. Macy started tearing the paper off before she could answer.

"Oh my God", she screamed. "Ma, look! It's Pebbles!"

Laila hurried over to see what Macy was talking about. She helped tear the rest of the paper off so that the whole thing was exposed. When Laila laid eyes on the painting she covered her mouth and gasped.

"Oh my God", she whispered. It was Pebbles. And she was an angel. It was the most beautiful piece of art Laila had ever seen in her life.

Macy said, "Ma, look how pretty she looks. Oh my God, this looks just like her. I wonder who painted this."

The delivery guy could see that it was an emotional time for them but he was off the clock in a few more minutes. He politely reminded Laila that he was standing there. "Uh, excuse me, lady. Do ya' need some help gettin' this thing up?"

Laila said, "Oh yeah, I'm sorry. I do need help." She wiped her eyes. She was so awed by the painting she was teary-eyed, but she did need help mounting it.

The guy went to the door and summoned his partner Larry, and the two of them anchored the painting high up on the wall above the fireplace. It was framed in fine mahogany wood, and it looked amazing.

When they were done, Laila thanked them and offered them a tip of twenty bucks each. Both of the men refused adamantly. They told her that the guy who'd hired them had already tipped them pretty well.

Laila smiled. That big tipper had to be Jay. She bid the gentlemen goodnight and locked the door behind them.

Laila turned around and looked up at the larger than life image of her baby as an angel with lovely pink and white wings. Pebbles was smiling and flying in a blue sky by the golden gates of heaven. That was just the way Laila had often pictured her, up there with God. And with her grandparents. Laila couldn't take her eyes off of her. She was glued. Pebbles looked so serene and so lifelike.

Macy asked Laila if she was okay. Laila nodded, and told her she was fine. She told Macy to go on and finish her homework.

Thirty minutes later, Laila was still standing there staring at Pebbles when her doorbell rang. She peeked out the window and saw Portia's Benz, so she opened the door.

Laila grinned at her friend. "Hey, girl. What's up?"

Portia hugged Laila and asked how she was doing. Her eyes were red and swollen, so Portia could see that she had been crying. She hoped that painting hadn't been in bad taste. Jay hadn't intended to make her sad.

Laila hugged Portia back tightly. "Girl, I'm okay. Come on in."

As soon as Portia stepped in the house, she saw the huge painting of Pebbles proudly displayed on the wall. Portia gasped. It was her first time seeing it, and it was truly breathtaking. She couldn't even speak for a second. She just looked at Laila, who nodded and smiled.

Portia smiled, and nodded back at her. There was no need for them to say anything. That picture told a thousand words. That was indeed the portrait of an angel.

Laila said, "Thank you, Portia. Thank you."

Portia told her that Jay was responsible, but she would surely thank him for her. Laila immediately got on her cell phone and called Jay to thank him personally.

Jay told Laila it was nothing. She didn't have to thank him. He just thought it would be nice. At her request, he told her he would stop by and check it out on his way home.

Jay was with Cas at the time, so when he hung up he asked him if he wanted to ride with him over Laila's crib to check out the painting. Cas agreed, and a few minutes later they headed that way.

Cas didn't bother to tell Jay that he'd had plans to go see about Laila later on that evening anyway. He guessed that now he could save himself a trip.

When they got there, Portia and Laila were sipping on what they called raspberry "Laila-ritas". Jay and Cas were both amazed by the painting as well. They agreed that it was beautiful.

Cas looked at Laila. She was smiling, and he was glad she seemed happier. He looked around at the house, which she had furnished elaborately. She definitely had good taste. Laila was a fine woman, and he was fond of her.

Cas hadn't told her that he and Kira were getting a divorce yet. He didn't want it to seem like he was trading in one woman for another. That wasn't the way he operated. That was tacky, and Cas was a gentleman who liked to do things with class.

Cas, Jay, and Portia stayed and chilled with Laila for a while, and then they decided to call it a night. It was getting late. Portia and Jay said goodbye and left out first to allow Cas and Laila the opportunity to say goodnight to one another. Cas came outside a few moments later, and they all drove off together.

Laila and Cas had tightly embraced each other at the door before he left, and Macy stood at the top of the stairs watching them. Laila locked the door after everybody left, and she looked at the painting of her baby once more. That pain in her chest just wouldn't go away. It was the pain of loss, and sometimes it got stronger.

It hit Laila again and she was deeply saddened. She didn't know why God had let that happen to her baby. She couldn't front, she was real angry at God about that. She wanted to believe in His will but right about then it was hard.

Laila was a strong woman but she was weary. Her faith wasn't as strong as it normally was but she knew she had to praise God through the good and the bad. She sank down to her knees crying, and she began to pray. She thanked God for sparing her sanity and keeping her whole throughout her ordeal because an enormous chunk had been taken out of her. A part of her had died with Pebbles, and that wound would surely never heal.

Laila also thanked God for giving her the strength to be there for her other baby, Macy. Macy was the reason Laila had been forced to pull it together and keep on living. But during the process she hadn't really had time to grieve. The long cries she often had at night were all she had.

Macy peeked downstairs and saw her mother crying again. She knew Laila had to let it out but she hurried down there to console her. Macy gave her a comforting and much needed hug. She knew it wasn't easy. She missed her little sister also. She still cried for Pebbles too. It was really heartbreaking.

Laila and Macy stayed up late that night engaged in a real heart to heart. Laila knew her daughter was intelligent so she wanted to inform her of what was going on. They were a family so she had a right to know. She finally told Macy that she had filed for a divorce from Khalil. Macy was pretty adult about it. She told Laila she understood because her father needed some time to get himself together. She had seen him at her sister's funeral and he hadn't looked well.

Macy then switched the topic to Casino. She told Laila he seemed like a good guy, and she could tell that she liked him a whole lot. Macy said she liked Cas too, and was glad he made Laila happy, but she should be careful because Jayquan told her that Cas was leaving his Aunt Kira. Macy said that she believed in love, but she just didn't want Cas to hurt Laila like that.

Once again, Laila's daughter had put things into perspective for her. She valued Macy's opinion. Laila thanked her, and then she suggested they bake some Tollhouse cookies and watch a movie. It was Friday night, so both of them could sleep late the following morning.

Chapter Twenty Four

That Saturday it was nice outside so Fatima had the top down on the new Bentley Continental GTC Wise had bought her. She drove home from the hair salon bumping "Irreplaceable" by Beyonce on the stereo. She was dedicating that song to Wise. Fatima sung along.

"To the left, to the left. Everything you own in a box to the left... You must not know 'bout me, you must not know 'bout me. I can have another you in a minute. Matter of fact, he'll be here in a minute. Baby, you must not know 'bout me, you must not know 'bout me... Don't you ever for a second get to thinking, you're irreplaceable. To the left, to the left... ooh..."

Fatima was jamming so hard she didn't even notice the red light change. The cars behind her beeped their horns impatiently. Fatima laughed and hit the gas, and she continued her journey on home to her empty house. It was the weekend so Falynn was at her parents' house as usual. Fatima was all alone.

Suddenly she didn't feel like going home. She really hated to admit it but she missed Wise. He was an asshole but his presence just seemed to liven up the house. Fatima had been toying with the idea of taking him back but she knew it was too soon. She was still hurting too bad about that paternity suit. What if that was his baby? He shouldn't have cheated on her in the first place. Then it wouldn't have been a possibility. His ass was always cheating.

Fatima felt like she needed some emotional support. She needed to be around her girls. She decided to stop by Portia's house to see what was up with her.

$$$

Laila was riding along the New Jersey turnpike on her way home from shopping. She got off at her exit and paid the toll, and she headed on. Along the way she'd been listening to Wendy Williams' radio show on WBLS, and they were talking about these "Strip for My Man" classes that women could sign up for.

Laila had been feeling a whole lot sexier lately, and it was all due to Casino. He made her feel like a natural woman. She wanted to repay him with a little treat. She wanted to do an exotic dance for him.

Laila punched the number for information on the "Strip for My Man" classes in her cell phone. She started to call but she hesitated. The more she thought about it, she realized that she could ask Portia to teach her a few moves. At one point and time her girl Portia was queen of the night. She used to be an exotic dancer.

Laila made a detour on her way home. She needed to holler at her homegirl. She knew how to be sensual but she needed some moves, and she knew Portia could teach her. Laila knew Cas and his friends went to strip clubs sometimes, so he was obviously into that. She wanted to give him a lap dance he would never forget.

To Laila's delight, when she got to Portia's house Fatima was there also. Laila hugged both of them and told them why she had come over. Portia and Fatima both cracked up, but Portia agreed to show Laila a few moves.

Fatima had been celibate since she'd kicked Wise out, and she had ended her semi-lesbian affair with Raven after Wise caught them by the pool. She didn't have anyone in her life to strip for right about then. She participated in Portia's booty shaking school just for fun. And who knew, her new tricks might come in handy one day.

Portia told her two best friends that while they were on that subject, she had a valuable gem for them. After she said that they both looked interested in what she had to say.

Portia told them that first they had to swear they'd keep it to themselves. Laila and Tima giggled but they promised her that they were sworn to secrecy forever.

Portia looked around carefully to make sure no one else was listening before she continued. Even though they were the only ones there. She stared at Laila and Fatima with a serious look on her face and asked them, "Do you bitches know the way to a man's heart?"

In unison they both blurted out, "Yeah! Through his stomach!"

Portia laughed and shook her head. "Nah, that's the old school way. I'ma tell ya'll 'bout the new way." She gave her speech a dramatic pause. Her girls were so on edge it was hard not to bust out laughing.

After about ten seconds of them demanding that she tell them, Portia let it out. "Ladies, the new way to a man's heart is through your booty! If you wanna keep your man, you gotta learn how to make your booty clap! I'm living proof. How ya'll think I kept Jay all these years? 'Cause I make it clap, bitches!" Portia dropped it like it was hot right quick. She made her booty touch the floor and then stood back up.

Laila and Fatima laughed. Portia was so stupid. They both made faces but neither one of them could dispute what she said. She and Jay had been strong pretty long.

Fatima said, "So tell us how, P. Teach us."

Both she and Laila wore serious expressions like they were really in a classroom yearning knowledge. They listened intently, waiting to hear what Portia had to say like she was a Harvard professor about to lecture.

Portia had to laugh. Those two were so stupid. She told her dizzy girlfriends, "Ya'll first lesson is free, but next time these mo'fuckas gon' cost you bitches $39.99."

They both laughed, and Laila threw a pillow off the sofa at her. Portia ducked and laughed. She picked up the stereo

remote control and switched it on, and she demanded that
they get down to business.

The next hour was spent teaching Laila and Fatima the
art of seduction and dirty dancing. Portia had no mercy on
them. She coached them hard and relentlessly. Her goal
was to shape them into the best booty clappers ever. She
shouted out orders and instructions like she was a military
drill sergeant.

"Come on, ladies. Move it! You heard what the record
said. Shake ya' money maker like somebody try'na pay ya'!
That's right, shake that shit! Laila, loosen up. Damn girl,
move! All that ass you got, please. Come on, shake that shit!
Loosen up your hips. It's all in the hips, Lay. That's right,
Tima. Get it, girl. Drop it like it's hot! Ow! Oh shoot, Laila
got it now. Do that shit, girl! That's what's up!"

Portia was so proud of them. She told her homegirls that
they had both gotten an "A-plus" in her bootleg dance class.
They were both "Certified Bootylicious Divas" now. They
had mastered the booty clap, and that would hereby be their
secret weapon from that day forth.

Fatima twisted up and they puffed a blunt in celebration.
She and Laila felt real sexy with their newfound talent. It
was like they had developed super powers.

$$$

The following week, Portia had a routine physical exam
scheduled with her doctor. During her visit, she learned that
she was almost three months pregnant. Her mother had told
her that on her death bed, and she had been right! Portia
couldn't believe it. She was going to have another baby.

The old proverb "The Lord giveth, and he taketh away"
came to Portia's mind. God had taken away Patty Cake but
he had blessed her with a baby. If it was a girl she was going
to name her Patricia, after her mother. Or Patrice. That was

a pretty name also.

When Portia first found out she was sort of scared but the more she thought about it, it was perfect timing. She could really use something new and beautiful in her life right about then. She couldn't wait to tell Jay. She knew he would be so excited. Portia couldn't believe he messed around and got her knocked up while he was in the hospital, with his horny self. She believed Jazmin and Jayquan would be happy also.

Portia couldn't believe she was pregnant. Wasn't that something? She placed her hands on her belly and whispered a prayer for her unborn child that would be born into such a harsh and cold world. Her protective motherly instinct had kicked in immediately. Especially when she thought about the way she had been forced to bring Jazmin into this world. She'd been born premature, from the rape and abuse Portia had suffered at the hands of Wayne-o, when he and those dudes had forced their way in the house.

At the thought of Wayne-o, Portia spit on the street to her left. She still hated that dude, even after his death. She shook it off and put her mind back on God and her baby. God willing, this pregnancy would be stress and event-free.

That night when Jay got home, Portia blessed him with the good news about the baby. He was so thrilled he got down on one knee and hugged her around the waist, and repeatedly kissed her belly.

Portia grinned from ear to ear and rubbed his head affectionately. She was glad he was happy. She asked Jay if he wanted a girl or a boy this time.

Jay stood up and tilted Portia's chin up towards him and gently kissed her lips, and then he kissed her on the forehead. He told her he didn't care what it was as long as it was healthy. He already had a fine young man for a son, and a princess for a little girl. An addition to the family would be well welcomed no matter what sex it was.

Portia climbed in bed, and a few minutes later Jay slid

A Dollar Outa Fifteen Cent Part II

in behind her. He wrapped his arms around her, and she instantly felt safe. She loved him. They had a beautiful family. Portia's only regret about this pregnancy was that her mother wouldn't be there to help her this time. Lord knows if it wasn't for Pat, she didn't know what she would've done with Jazmin when they first came home from the hospital. Jazz was so tiny Portia had been almost afraid to hold her. But by the grace of God, and with Patricia's much welcomed guidance, she'd winded up being a good mother.

Portia hadn't told her girlfriends yet but she was so tired. She would call and tell them the following day. She was sure Laila and Tima would both be delighted. Becoming a new auntie was more fun than becoming a new mommy in a way because aunties got to go home when mommies had to stay up all night with a screaming kid.

Portia thought about all the sleepless nights and diaper changing, and she laughed to herself. She couldn't believe she and Jay would be going through it all again.

Jay laid on the other side of the bed holding his dear wife, who had given him the best news he could've asked for that night. He was gonna be a daddy again. Jay kissed Portia on the earlobe and whispered in her ear, "I love you, Kit Kat."

He rubbed her belly gently. "Thank you, beloved. Thanks so much."

After that, Jay whispered a word of thanks to God. That baby had given him a new perspective on life already. This was just what he needed. His prayers had been answered.

Jay mused over the way his priorities had shifted lately. He hadn't been acting like a family man at all. He hated to admit it but he'd been ripping and running so much he'd been slipping. Portia and the kids were very understanding about it but he knew his presence was missed.

Jay decided to make some adjustments. He needed to be more like a Cosby dad. He had to get deeper involved in his children's lives. All three of them, God willing.

$$$

The next morning Wise was on a phone call with his attorney. He was smiling because he had just received some good news. "Okay, that's what's up. Thanks, man. You have a good day too."

Wise ended his conversation and hung up the phone feeling glad as hell. His lawyer had just called to inform him that the paternity suit against him had been dismissed from court because the DNA test revealed that Wise was 99.999% not the father of the little boy in question.

That news was music to Wise' ears. He immediately called Fatima and told her the good news. She had told him to prove to her that it wasn't his kid, and now he had the proof she needed. Wise figured that now she would finally come around.

When Fatima answered her phone and found out why he had called, she was happy on the inside but she played him indifferently. She acted like she didn't care one way or the other. In a monotone and bored voice she told Wise that he was lucky he wouldn't have to pay all that back child support, and she just hung up the phone.

Fatima hanging up on him really pissed Wise off so he called her right back. He swallowed his pride once again and told her he wanted to come home. Fatima just told him she didn't think that was such a good idea. She said that his apology, and the paternity test results were both too little and too late. Fatima told Wise that their marriage was over, and she hung up on him again.

Wise was so tight he grinded his back teeth. Damn, the baby wasn't his. What the fuck else did she want from him? If Fatima wanted to play like that, then fuck it. He guessed it was really over. He wasn't going to keep making himself look stupid, fucking chasing after her and begging her to take him back. That was it. He was giving up.

After Fatima hung up on Wise, she got really misty eyed. She loved that bastard. She really did. She just couldn't stand the way he took her for granted. And she was just getting used to being alone. That was something she'd really had to learn how to do because from the time she'd left her parents' house, she had been in relationships with different men.

The past few months of living single had taught her a lot. Sometimes a person had to cut everybody off to learn themselves. She had learned that loving God was just as good of a substitute, and even better. He was the only man she really needed in her life.

And this discovery had made Fatima cling more to her daughter. She had to teach Falynn that she didn't need a man for anything either. Not even for emotional support. A man was nice to have if they treated you right, but you didn't need one to make you whole. Only God's love and mercy could do that.

Fatima hadn't quite axed out the possibility of taking Wise back yet but she knew they needed space. She was waiting for a sign from God. He would let her know when the time was right.

Fatima had taken her mother's advice and prayed on it so she refused to worry about it anymore. She had given it to the Man upstairs. Now she and Wise' marriage was in the hands of God.

$$$

While Fatima and Wise had drifted apart, Laila and Cas had taken their affair to a whole new level. Laila hadn't admitted it to her girlfriends yet, but they were having unprotected sex. It had just sort of happened one night, when Cas had stopped by to see about her. She had given him an intimate lap dance, and then they had gotten in the hot tub and fooled around.

In the hot tub, she had just sort of slipped and fell on his dick. And they didn't stop until both of them climaxed under water. But Laila did recall Cas pulling out before he came.

Laila was a nurse, and she was certainly no naïve teenager so she knew the risk they had taken. Before Cas had left her house, she had gotten up the nerve to ask him to go with her to get tested for HIV. Casino didn't get offended, and she liked that. He told her that it was no problem, and they could go the following day if she had time.

Cas told her he'd been tested last about a year ago during a routine physical, and he wasn't out there like that. Laila believed him. He seemed to be a selective guy. It was Kira that she couldn't vouch for. The only pussy she could speak for was her own.

The following day when Laila got off work, she called Cas and asked him if he was ready to make that move. He told her that he had gone and got tested earlier that day, and would provide her with a copy of his results.

Laila told him she had a copy of her last HIV test results from about two months ago. Her occupation as a Registered Nurse required her to get tested quarterly. She told Cas that she hadn't been sexually involved with anyone over the past year except him. And they had been using condoms until the night before.

Cas told Laila he would bring a copy of his results over later on. She told him that was cool, and she would show him hers as well. They agreed to see each other later on, and hung up.

Later that night Cas and Laila exchanged written proof that they were each safe, and then they engaged in acrobatic sex. As quietly as possible of course, because Macy was in her bedroom sleeping.

At about three AM, Laila walked Cas to the front door

and kissed him goodnight. She was glowing with sexual satisfaction. It was true what they said. Sex was good for you. Her body was just tingling. She felt invigorated like she'd spent a weekend at the spa.

Before Laila went to bed, she sent Portia and Fatima a text message that read, *"Good dick is like a pillow. It helps you sleep good at night, and it doesn't mind if you slobber all over it."* When her homegirls got that they wouldn't need to ask her how her night had gone. Casino had some good ass dick, and that was her testimony.

That night Cas also told her that it was over between him and Kira. He said he was moving out. That was the only reason Laila had unprotected sex with him again. She was a responsible adult so she knew she had to get on some form of birth control because she had a feeling they were going to continue carrying on that way. To Laila that meant there was some type of bond between them but she didn't want to get knocked up. She needed to get back on the pill.

Laila knew she was speeding but she was really fond of Casino. She loved him with all her heart. His company and friendship had proved to be cathartic in her chaotic world.

Chapter Twenty Five

A few mornings later, Laila was on the telephone with Khalil arguing. He had called her and started a fight about the same old thing. He didn't want to give her a divorce. He kept on asserting that he had himself together, so she and Macy should come home immediately. Laila could tell he'd been drinking. He was bugging, talking about he wasn't selling her his part of the house anymore.

She and Cas had gone back and checked, so she knew he had finally moved out of the house. She assumed that he had gone on about his business. She wished he would quit talking that "come home" shit. They no longer had a home together. Laila grew impatient with Khalil and just told him the truth. He had signed the Real Property Transfer forms and cashed his check, so it was too late. It was already a done deal.

After Laila had handed Khalil that check, she no longer felt responsible for him. He had close to three hundred thousand dollars at one time. That was more than enough for him to get a new start. He needed to straighten up and get a place so he could play an active role in Macy's life. He was some kind of father.

Khalil said he would give her back the money, but Laila told him it wasn't that simple. He was really starting to get on her nerves. She was on the verge of hanging up the phone on him. She told him she had to go because she was busy.

Khalil got really pissed at Laila's brush-off. He guessed she was rushing him off the phone to get back to her new life with that nigga. Was he laying beside her in bed now? It finally sunk in, and he realized that Laila wasn't coming back to him. He was feeling real salty.

Khalil was full of spite. He said, "Yo, fuck you, Laila.

You's a dumb bitch! And you know what? You stupid for stayin' in New Jersey with Portia. That bitch ain't your fuckin' friend."

He must've been crazy talking to her like that. Laila didn't bother telling him that she didn't stay with Portia anymore because she had her own house now. That was none of his damn business. She barked on Khalil's disrespectful ass. "Fuck *you*, nigga! With a sick dick! You bitch ass, punk mothafucka! Fuck you too! And don't worry about my friends. Matter of fact, Portia's more than a friend. That's my *sister*. And she was there for me and your kids when *you* weren't."

When Laila screamed on him like that, Khalil just hung up the phone on her. He was pissed. That bitch ran her mouth too much. Laila had gotten out of control. Khalil knew deep down inside that her words had stung him so badly because they were true. But who the fuck was she to judge him? She was a married woman sleeping with another man.

The more Khalil thought about it, he was sick of Laila with her "I'm holier than thou, I'm such an angel" bullshit. She acted like she was perfect. Like she was sitting on the right-hand side of God or something. Homegirl was on some brand new shit. That bitch had a swollen head.

Khalil turned his liquor bottle up again and took a healthy swig of Bacardi Dark. The more he thought about it, he had to bring that bitch Laila back down to size. She was really trying to style on him. He knew just the reality check she needed. Fuck her. She had him up there begging her to take him back like he was some little bitch. Khalil worked on his bottle and got drunker and drunker. He didn't give a fuck.

A few minutes later, he called Laila back and gave her some very unwelcome news. As soon as she picked up the phone he blurted out, "Bitch, fuck you! I don't give a fuck 'bout you neither. That's why I should've made that whore Portia *have* my baby instead of gettin' rid of it. Try'na hide shit to keep *you* from gettin' hurt."

Laila just knew her ears had deceived her. Lord, she must've been hearing things. "What did you just say?"

Khalil plunged the knife in deeper. "You heard what I said! You stayin' over there at Portia house like she your friend. If that bitch is such a friend to you, then why did she get pregnant by me? *Huh*? Don't be fuckin' stupid, Laila. You need to bring your dumb, naïve ass home."

Laila wished he was standing in front of her so she could slap the shit out of him. "Mothafucka, you better stop lying on my friend!"

"Oh, I ain't lying. Trust me."

Laila said, "What the fuck you mean, nigga? What the fuck you try'na say?"

Khalil yelled into the phone, "I ain't *try'na* say shit! You *heard* what I said! I fucked your girl and got her pregnant! And I *should've* made her keep it. That could've been the son that you don't wanna give me now. You know what, Laila? You a stupid bitch. You *made* me tell you that shit! You fuckin' made me!"

On the other end of the line, Laila was so aghast she could hardly stand. She prayed to God that Khalil was lying. Those drugs had to have made him lose his mind. Portia couldn't have done that. Or could she have? Laila was completely stunned. She dropped the telephone and stood there with her mouth open.

She had to ask Portia about this shit. Right away. And face to face too. She had to see Portia's reaction with her own two eyes. Laila grabbed her car keys and ran out of the house. She hopped in her car and sped off blindly. Before she knew it she was on the highway headed for Portia's house.

Laila's mind was racing. She didn't know what to do. If it was true, she was just gonna go off and punch Portia in her fucking face for violating her like that. Laila remembered that Portia was pregnant now, so she couldn't even fight her. She had just informed her two days ago that she was expecting another baby.

Laila tried to shake it off and stop thinking the worse. She didn't think Portia would do that to her. She just wanted to see what her initial reaction would be when she asked her. She just had to ask her.

When Laila turned down Portia's road, she sped down that long winding driveway faster than she ever had before. She hit the brakes and screeched to a halt in front of the house, and she jumped out and banged on the front door.

Portia just happened to be downstairs when she heard the loud knocking. She ran to the front door and looked out of the peephole. When she saw it was Laila, she swung the palatial oak door open. Portia could tell something was wrong because Laila looked upset. "Hey, Lay. What's the matter?"

Laila shook her head. "Nothin', I'm good." She faked a smile and tried to play it off.

Laila wasn't fooling Portia with that fake smile. She wondered what was wrong with her. The last time they had spoken they were picking out baby names for Portia's bun in the oven. What was this about? "Come on in", she told her friend.

Laila shook her head again. "Nah, I can't stay. But girl, let me tell you. The strangest thing happened. I just got off the phone with Khalil, and he was talkin' some crazy shit. You know what he had the nerve to say, girl? Check this out, P."

Laila kept her eyes locked on Portia's with her next words. "He said he should've made you keep his baby when you got pregnant by him. P, what's *that* about?"

When Laila said that, Portia swallowed hard. She hadn't been prepared for that one. Wow, that was the last thing she had expected Laila to say. She was glad the kids were in school so they hadn't overheard that. Portia was totally shocked. That incident had been a total mistake, and it happened so long ago. How could Khalil bring that up?

Portia realized that Laila was waiting for an explanation so she quickly snapped out of it. She played it off like she was totally offended. "What?! What the hell are you talkin' 'bout, Laila? Is Khalil crazy? Why the fuck would he *say* some shit like that? Hell no, that ain't true!"

Laila just backed up and shook her head sadly. Tears welled up in her eyes. Portia was breaking her heart. She couldn't believe it. Laila knew Portia like a book. They had been best friends for twenty years. She was lying.

Laila covered her mouth in disappointed amazement. "Oh my God! It's true. It's true! Portia, how *could* you?"

Laila was stunned. She couldn't believe Portia had done her dirty like that. She had to get away from her before she spazzed the fuck out. That bitch was lucky she was pregnant. Laila just ran and jumped in her car. She ignored Portia calling after her, and sped off so fast she burned rubber.

As Laila drove off, she was filled with disbelief. She kept on seeing the look on Portia's face when she asked her. She had denied it vehemently but her initial reaction was definitely guilty.

Laila thought back a few years and remembered when Portia was pregnant that time, and she'd tried to talk her into keeping the baby. Portia had kept on saying, *"I have my reasons. Trust me, I have my reasons"*, but she would never say what her reasons were.

Something hadn't really seemed right to Laila back then about the way she'd been so adamant about getting an abortion. Especially since they'd both always said they would never do that. After all of this dawned on Laila, she knew that those horrible accusations Khalil had made about her homegirl were more than likely true.

Laila was so deep in thought that she didn't look to her left at the stop sign, before she crossed it. She slowed down and looked right, and she just accelerated. Laila then remembered to glance to her left but it was a little too late. An eighteen wheeler was approaching at full speed.

Laila panicked and gunned it, but she only managed to get half of her car out of the way. The big truck slammed into the rear side of her Lexus and caused her to spin around in the two-lane highway two times before slamming into a ditch and flipping over. When Laila's car crashed upside down, it exploded and burst into a fiery inferno.

Onlookers and fellow motorists quickly pulled over to the side of the road and ran to try and assist the driver of the Lexus that had just crashed so terribly. People called for assistance on their cell phones as they watched the car burn in horror.

Inside the car, Laila was strapped upside down in her seatbelt. The airbag had deployed, and the impact had knocked her out temporarily. She came to and realized that her car was on fire. Dear God, she had to get out of there! Laila realized that she didn't have any feeling in her arms and legs. She couldn't move. The only thing that seemed to be working was her brain. Laila panicked.

God was on her side. She was really blessed because there just happened to be a fire engine coming along, on its way returning from a bogus call. When the firemen saw the burning car, they pulled over and immediately sprang into action.

They successfully extinguished the flames, and managed to rescue Laila from the car. By the time the firemen freed her from the wreckage, the police and paramedics had arrived. She was placed on a stretcher and hooked up to oxygen, and they immediately rushed her to the hospital.

$$$

Back at Portia's house, she felt just terrible. Khalil was really a lowdown son of a bitch for bringing up that incident after all this time. That shit happened more than six years ago, and he knew it wasn't even consensual on her part.

Boy, that nigga really played his self. Portia had denied it, and would do so until the day she died, but she knew Laila didn't believe her. Especially from the way she had stormed off and sped away in her car. She hadn't even bothered to hear Portia out.

$$$

At the hospital, a nurse had gone through Laila's belongings and found her insurance card. For her "In Case of Emergency" contact numbers, she had Portia Lane-Mitchell, and Fatima Sinclair-Page listed. The nurse tried Portia's number first, but it went straight to voicemail. She tried Fatima's next.

Fatima picked up on the third ring. When the nurse informed her that Laila had been in a bad car accident, and was in the trauma unit of Jacobs Memorial Hospital, Fatima almost dropped the phone. Oh God, why Laila? She was worried and afraid, but she sprang into action.

Fatima asked the woman for the hospital address, and she thanked her. As soon as she hung up, she called Portia and told her what happened. They agreed to meet each other at the hospital because it was only about five minutes away.

The friends were scared to death. They both prayed hard for Laila as they shuffled their ways to the hospital as fast as they could. Fatima and Portia each thought about the night Simone had killed herself. They had rushed to the hospital the same way but Laila had been there with them mourning Simone's loss as well. Portia and Fatima prayed they wouldn't have to bury another sister. Neither of them would be able to bear it.

As Portia rode along, guilty pains racked her abdomen. That couldn't possibly be good for her baby. It was always something. Portia felt bad because she knew deep in her heart that the accident was her fault. Laila had to have been upset and not thinking straight.

Laila was usually a careful driver, so if she had an accident, she couldn't have had her mind on the road. And it was all because of that bullshit Khalil's dumb ass had told her. If Laila died, Portia would never be able to forgive herself.

It was crazy how something that happened so long ago, and had been swept under a rug could resurface and just mess everything up. Portia thought that getting raped by Wayne-o while she was pregnant with Jazmin had been her punishment for getting pregnant by Khalil. She thought she and God were even, but they obviously weren't. He couldn't take Laila away from her.

Portia thought about that old saying, "What goes around comes around". That was really true. The bullshit you do comes back around again and again. Her heart was heavy with guilt. She had so much on her mind, she didn't even think to call Jay and Cas to let them know about Laila's car accident.

Fatima was thinking more on her toes. She called Casino from her car and let him know what happened. She told him what hospital Laila was in, and he said he was on his way immediately.

When Cas heard about Laila's accident he was worried sick. He called Jay and told him what happened, and they both hurried to the hospital.

Portia and Fatima pulled up in the hospital parking lot at almost the same time. Fatima beat Portia there by about fifteen seconds. They both parked and ran to the emergency room entrance.

Inside the E.R. the ladies quickly approached the information desk and asked where Laila Atkins was. After they got a location they hurried to where she was, praying the whole time. Both of the girlfriends' hearts were racing, and their hands were sweating profusely.

$$$

When Fatima had called Cas, he was at the house with Kira. He had just come by to check on his son. His little man had just started kindergarten that year, but he was home because he wasn't feeling well.

Kira was standing right next to Cas when he got the call, and she heard a woman's voice. The bitch on the phone sounded upset, so Kira studied his reaction. He seemed genuinely concerned. That was obviously a woman he really cared about. Kira knew they were going through a divorce, but it still hurt to know he was messing around.

After Cas hung up the phone, he just mumbled something to Kira about seeing her later. He kissed his son and told him he loved him, and he got ready to leave. Kira grabbed his arm and demanded to know who that was on the phone, and where he was going.

Cas wouldn't answer her. He pushed her out of the way, and told her to get out of his face because it wasn't the time. That's when Kira knew it was really over. The other woman had won. Kira couldn't front, it hurt because she still loved him.

When Casino got to the hospital, he headed up to the trauma ward where Laila was. When he got up there he saw Portia and Fatima in the hallway.

Portia and Fatima were glad to see Cas. They told him the doctors said they couldn't go in Laila's room yet because she was in surgery. Cas looked like he was worried sick. Portia and Fatima thanked him for coming. They could tell that he was genuinely concerned. They knew Cas had mad love for Laila. They asked him to help pray for her.

Casino was a God-fearing man above all. He knew Laila's fate was in God's hands. He told them he'd been praying ever since he found out. Cas couldn't imagine life without

Laila. She was so special to him. They hadn't made it official yet but he wanted a life with her. He'd just needed some time to get out of the situation he was in. And so did she. Cas felt it in his heart with Laila. He knew she was the one. God had to bring her through.

A few minutes later, Jay arrived. The minute Portia laid eyes on him she hurried into his arms. He made her feel safer and more secure. Jay had always had that power.

Jay hugged Portia and massaged her back. His poor baby had been through so much. She had just gone through her mother's death, him getting shot in the face, Laila's little girl's death, and Humble's murder. It had been a rough ass year. And now this. Jay hoped and prayed Laila would be okay. The news about her accident was just terrible.

Portia held onto Jay and cried in his chest. Crying was her only release because she couldn't tell anybody that the accident was her fault. She felt horrible. Her best friend was in the hospital clinging to her life, and it was all her fault.

Fatima watched Jay comforting Portia so lovingly, and it really made her miss Wise. She could sure use his comfort right about then. She wished he was there.

Fatima's prayer was answered a few minutes later. Wise got off the elevator and came walking up. Fatima thought she saw a ghost but it was really him.

Jay had called Wise in the car and told him about the accident, so he had come to see about Laila. And he also wanted to be there for Fatima. She was still his wife, and he loved the shit out of her. Even if she wouldn't take him back.

When Fatima saw Wise she just started crying. His presence brought back a lot of feelings and emotions, and right about then she just felt weak and helpless. She needed his strength.

Wise didn't say anything at first. He just walked over and put his arms around Fatima and held her. Then he whispered in her ear, "Don't cry. I love you, Ma. Everything gon' be ayight."

At that instant, Fatima forgave him. She wanted him back. She needed him. His embrace had melted the ice in her heart. She didn't want to be alone anymore.

Just then, the doctor came out with an update on Laila's condition. He told them she was alive but she was in a deep coma. He said they had performed surgery because she had broken her neck in the accident, and there was spinal damage. He informed them that Laila's chances were slim, and even if she came out of the coma, she would probably suffer some type of paralysis and possibly never walk again.

After hearing that news, everyone grew more somber. They were all so quiet you could have heard a pin drop. Each of them was deep in thought. This thing was really serious. Laila had to make it. She had to pull through. They all loved her and wished her well. And she was a mother. Her child needed her. Laila couldn't leave yet. There was no way.

Chapter Twenty Six

Unbeknownst to Cas, Jay, and Wise, there was an enemy lurking in the midst. The last of the Scumbag Brothas, Mike Machete, had been tailing them for the past week. He'd been careful to disguise himself differently each time he followed one of them, and he also made sure he was driving a different inconspicuous looking vehicle.

Mike Machete had played it smart this time because he knew those Street Life niggas' prudence had been the reason his brother was killed. He and Powerful had waited until those dudes were drunk and tired before they attacked, but things hadn't gone as smoothly as they had anticipated.

Mike Machete was angry, and out to avenge his brother's death. Those Street Life cats had to pay for what they did to Powerful, and he was ready to settle the score. He had also heard about the one hundred thousand dollar bounty Jay and them niggas had on his head. Those two factors played the biggest parts in the war he was determined to declare on them.

Mike Machete reached over and lifted the corner of the towel laying in the passenger seat next to him, and peeked underneath at his artillery. At the sight of the small arsenal of fully loaded weapons, he felt reassured. There was no doubt in his mind that he was riding away the victor that day.

Mike Machete thought about his brother's untimely death, and his blood began to boil. He literally saw red. He was ready to body something. He wanted to finish those dudes off immediately, but he knew he couldn't just go up in the hospital blasting. Mike Machete was smarter than that. He waited patiently out in the parking lot for the opportunity to attack.

$$$

After hearing the bad news about Laila, Casino felt like he needed some air. He told Portia and Fatima he'd be back in a minute, and he headed outside. Jay and Wise went with him because they could both sense that he was in a fog. They knew how Cas felt about Laila, so they could understand.

Portia and Fatima understood how Cas felt too, so they let the men go. It was no secret that men and women handled their pain differently. Fatima and Portia took a seat in the waiting area until they were allowed to go in and see Laila. They prayed for their dear friend while they waited.

When the fellows got outside, Casino told his mans what he was feeling. He admitted that he was scared for Laila. He said he would rather it had been him getting hurt instead of her because she had already been through too much. Especially when she'd lost her daughter. And now this had to happen.

Jay and Wise told Cas to keep the faith and Laila would be okay, God willing. They felt Cas' pain. It showed all in his face. Their hearts went out to him.

$$$

Sitting in his car in the hospital parking lot, Mike Machete saw the three men in the world he wanted dead the most appear. It was those Street Life mothafuckas. He was so delighted he chuckled out loud. They had just come out of the hospital and were standing out front talking, lined up like sitting ducks. Killing them would be a lot easier than he thought.

Mike Machete reached underneath his seat and pulled out his black tech-nine. She was his favorite. He kissed her barrel for good luck, and he slowly rolled down his tinted driver's side window. He shined the infrared beam on Jay's jaw, he pointed at Cas' neck, and then at Wise' temple. He didn't know who to take out first. It was a tough decision to make, but he took great pleasure in the fact that he had a clean shot of all three of them mothafuckas.

But he wanted them to see his face when he killed them. Those niggas needed to know where the heat was coming from. That was the only thing that kept him from pulling the trigger right then. He could have easily finished them all from the car, but Mike Machete was a real killer. He had a lot of heart.

He had earned his moniker "Mike Machete" when he cut off a dude's head back in '91. He was infamous in seven states for cutting off niggas' limbs if they crossed him or got in his way. His heart was ice cold, and he wasn't playing with a full deck. Mike Machete never handled shit like a coward. He was no bitch. He put an extra gun in his waist and got out of the car, and he proceeded to set it on them Street Life niggas.

A parking lot security guard, this white dude named Harper, had been watching Mike Machete for some time. He wanted to make sure he wasn't going to get out and leave his vehicle sitting in the "no parking" zone he was in. When Harper saw Mike get out of the car, he rushed over and stopped him.

"Uh, sir? Excuse me, buddy. I'm sorry, but you're not allowed to park here. This is a "no parking" zone, so I'm afraid you're gonna have to move... "

Mike Machete didn't want any problems. He wasn't in the mood for talking either, so he silenced the guard the only way he knew how. He fired on him twice. *Boom, boom!* He gave him one to the torso, and one to the head to finish him off. Mike Machete didn't like to leave any witnesses, so that parking lot security guard never even had a chance to pray.

Another guard, a young brother named Andrews, sat just a few cars away. He had just arrived seconds before, and he witnessed his coworker's cold-blooded murder with his own two eyes. Andrews was in shock, and afraid to make a move. He quickly ducked and radioed the police for backup. He wished he was sitting in a more inconspicuous looking vehicle than a white hospital security patrol car.

Andrews was scared to drive off, and too shook to even think about getting out and doing his job. He was just a flashlight security dude trying to earn a paycheck. He didn't even have a gun. What was even more fucked up was the fact that he was off that day. He had only come in to earn some overtime to help pay for his girl's engagement ring. Boy, his timing couldn't have been worse.

Andrews just sat there crouched down in his vehicle praying that the coast was clear. A few seconds later, he raised his head slowly to peek out the window and see what was going on. He hoped that psycho dude had left the scene already. He knew he wasn't going to try and stop him from fleeing. Not as long as he had that gun.

As soon as Andrews looked up, he found himself staring down the barrel of Mike Machete's ratchet. Andrews prayed that he would notice that he was a brother like him and spare his life, but it was no use. He was shown no mercy. Mike Machete heartlessly blew his head to smithereens. Afterwards he continued creeping towards his prey, crouching down alongside parked cars along the way.

Jay, Cas, and Wise had heard the shots so they knew something was up. Luckily, they were all armed. Wise had started to leave his hammer in the car, and now he was glad he hadn't.

They listened to see what direction the gunfire was coming from. Wise suddenly noticed a red dot on Cas' chest. It was an infrared beam! He instinctively shoved his homie out of the way. "Get down, son! Yo, it's a hit! Oh shit!"

As soon as Wise said that, bullets started flying their way. They all got low and quickly scrambled for cover. Not on no sucker shit, but they had to protect their dome pieces. They knew they weren't bulletproof.

When the comrades were all safely covered behind parked cars, they peeked out carefully with their heat drawn. They all saw that the shooter was none other than Mike Machete, the remaining Scumbag Brotha. A nigga they had ironically put a hit out on. They had a nice price on his head.

Jay, Cas, and Wise stayed low. They were each crouched down on one knee. They fired a few rounds just to hold Mike Machete back. Their plan was to make him run out of ammo. They knew what they were doing. That mothafucka had to stop and reload soon, the way he was wasting bullets. Jay, Wise, and Cas held their fire and waited, each eager for the opportunity to take the winning shot.

They had projected the truth. Mike Machete had been firing so recklessly he ran out of bullets on both guns. He fished in his pocket for a fresh clip for his tech-nine. He knew he wasn't covered, and the seconds he took to reload could cost him his life, but he didn't give a fuck. He had faith in his bullet proof vest.

When Mike Machete paused to reload, Jay, Cas, and Wise blasted on his ass. They fired simultaneously and barraged him with bullets. None of them wanted to take a chance on him getting back up, so they Swiss cheesed him up something proper.

The slugs ripping into his body made Mike Machete dance involuntarily like he was a puppet, and then he fell back on the cold concrete. He laid there still. Them niggas had hit him up pretty bad, but they didn't know his vest had absorbed the bulk of the shots. He'd been hit in the legs a couple of times, but he was still alive.

He just laid there and played dead. He wanted to bring them boys out of hiding. He still had to finish them off. And he would too, as long as he had breath left in his body. Fuck that, them niggas had killed his brother so they were going to die.

Jay, Cas, and Wise saw Mike Machete fall to the ground, and they were all satisfied. They had taken that crazy mothafucka down. What a relief.

That nigga was laid out on the ground and it looked like he was dead, but Wise wanted to finish him off with a headshot just to make sure. He knew it had to be done quickly because they could already hear sirens in the distance.

Wise hurried over and stood over Mike Machete's body and aimed at his skull. Cas and Jay followed closely behind to cover him.

Wise didn't know, but he had moved a little too fast. When he looked down he was surprised as hell. That nigga was still alive! Mike Machete winked at him and raised his gun.

Wise and Mike Machete fired at the exact same time, and they both struck their targets. Wise' bullet hit Mike Machete in the forehead right above his left eye, and Mike Machete's slug pierced Wise' neck.

Jay and Cas stared on horrified as their man dropped right in front of them. Oh shit, that mothafucka shot Wise! That nigga had to die!

When Jay and Cas looked at the damage Wise had done to that lemon already, it was clear that their vengeance would have been in vain. It would've been a waste of bullets because Mike Machete was already dead. Wise had literally pushed his wig back. His left eye was hanging out, and his skull was exposed.

Wise knelt down on one knee clutching his throat. He was gasping for air and spitting up blood. He pleaded with his mans through his eyes. He needed a doctor fast. Jay and Cas quickly put away their hammers, and Cas stuffed Wise' gun in his pocket. He and Jay carefully picked up their bro and hurried inside the hospital.

"Just hold on, son! You gon' be ayight", Jay told Wise

assuredly. "Just hold on. The doctors are right here."

Wise nodded his head to let Jay know he was good, but the truth was he was really scared to death. His heart was racing.

In the hospital Jay and Casino demanded that someone get a doctor immediately, and they carefully laid Wise on a stretcher that was sitting next to the triage door. Cas squeezed his young bro's hand. "Be easy, man. You gon' be ayight. Just breathe, son. Hold on."

Wise was listening to Cas, but his voice sounded far away. He felt like he was drifting. Everything looked foggy and distorted, and it was getting dark. He tried hard to focus. Finally, he could see a light through the cloudiness. It was in the distance but he was relieved. It was so inviting, Wise was drawn to it. He slowly started towards it, wanting to seek refuge in its warmth.

As he was going, he could've sworn he heard his little girl's voice. She kept on saying, *"Daddy, don't go. Daddy, don't go."* Then Fatima was calling him. He knew they needed him. Wise turned back around and followed the voices instead of going to the light.

Just then, some doctors and nurses came running, and they whisked him away to an operating room. Jay and Cas ran alongside them, but they weren't allowed inside. They waited in the hallway and prayed hard that Wise would pull through.

Portia and Fatima had been upstairs sitting in the hallway by Laila's room waiting for the doctor to allow them to see her. They overheard two nurses talking about a shootout that had just happened in the hospital parking lot. One of them said it didn't look like the guy who was shot in the neck was going to make it. Then she said he was on the third floor being operated on.

When Portia and Fatima heard that, their hearts stopped at around the same time. They both had a feeling that their

husbands were involved. They hurried down to the third
floor to see what was going on.

Portia and Fatima were best friends who had never once
wished the other any harm, but they both prayed selfishly
that it wasn't their husband who got shot.

As soon as they got off the elevator, they saw Jay and Cas
standing down the corridor. Seeing Jay was a tremendous
relief for Portia.

Fatima didn't see Wise so her stomach flipped, and she was
overcome with dread. Her knees weakened, and it felt like
her legs gave out on her. Wise was the only one of the three
musketeers missing, so he had to be the one that got shot.
Fatima was terrified. She broke down at the thought.

Jay and Cas saw Portia and Fatima coming down the
hallway, so they went and met them halfway. Fatima was
crying hysterically like she already knew. It was difficult for
them, but they had to tell her the truth. They told her that
Wise got shot, and then comforted her and told her to be
strong and have faith that he would pull through.

Through her sobs, Fatima managed to ask, "Wh-what
happened to him?" She wanted some answers. Why was
Wise the only one shot? What the hell had gone on?

Cas briefly ran down the facts for Fatima and told her
how they'd been fired upon. He felt terrible about the whole
situation. Jay felt bad too. That was some fucked up shit
that happened. They hoped their man pulled through.

It wasn't the time, but Jay knew they had to get rid of
those guns. He pulled Portia to the side and told her he
needed her to get rid of them for him before the police got
up there. On the low, he collected Cas and Wise' hammers
from Cas, and he pulled Portia into the men's bathroom on
their left. Inside, he locked the door and wiped the weapons
free of prints, and he stuffed them all in Portia's leather Gucci
hobo bag.

Jay knew it was probably only a matter of minutes before

the pigs would be there to question them. He had looked down out the window and seen a bunch of cop cars already.

Jay and Portia went back out to comfort Fatima. The minutes they all waited to see about Wise' condition seemed longer than eternity. Finally, a white middle-aged doctor with horn-rimmed glasses on stepped out of the O.R. to update them.

Fatima, Jay, Cas, and Portia all held their breath and prayed for good news. The doctor informed them that every possible method of treatment had been used to save Wise, but he had succumbed to his injuries. He was gone.

When Fatima heard that, she literally had a fit. She doubled over and hollered out in pain. *"NO! No, no, please God, no!"* Fatima fell down on her knees and cried. She couldn't believe her husband was dead. Only minutes after they got back together. And at a time when she needed him most. That was heartache to an undefined power. Lord, it couldn't be. How could she make it without him? And what would Falynn do? Fatima was crying so hard she could barely breathe.

Portia got down on her knees with her best friend and cried with her. She held Fatima in her arms and rocked her. Her heart went out to her. Why did this have to happen to Wise? What the hell had happened out there in that parking lot? And so fast? It seemed like everything just happened in a split second. And right when Laila was holding on to her life from the accident she had been in. Who would've thought things could get worse.

Jay and Cas were stunned. The pain they were experiencing at that moment was unexplainable. Both of them had huge lumps in their throats and watery eyes. They knew they had to be strong for the women, but at the time they were wrapped up in their own grief.

Cas and Jay were crushed, but also enraged. Somebody was gonna pay. They had just lost a brother. They couldn't help but shed tears for that man. He was their brother from another mother, and they felt responsible for his death. They both felt like they let him get killed, and that would stick with them for the rest of their lives. Wise was a good dude, and life without him would never be the same. He was a fallen soldier.

Just then, the elevator opened and two detectives stepped off. They spotted them and started down the corridor. Jay had predicted right. They were there to question them.

The detectives walked up to Jay and Cas and flashed their badges. They introduced themselves, and got right to the point. One of them said, "We'd like to talk to you guys about the bodies."

Jay and Cas both played it cool. "What bodies?", they asked in unison.

The detectives looked at one another and shook their heads. They could see they had two wise guys there. The taller cop sarcastically said, "Why, those three bodies in the parking lot. One unidentified African American gentleman, and two on-duty hospital parking lot security guards. And now we hear that your friend is dead too."

Jay and Cas were hurting over Wise' death, but they gave the pigs no response and kept their expressions blank.

The shorter cop said, "Come on, fellas. I think you two know what we're talkin' about. We just need you to tell us what went on out there, and then you're free to go."

Jay and Cas glanced at one another. They both knew that was bullshit. They knew better. The cops weren't going to let them go if they started talking. Those pigs were going to do whatever they were going to do regardless, so they both stuck to their stories. They acted like they didn't know anything. Neither of them was willing to cooperate with police.

The detectives saw that they weren't getting anywhere, so they patted Jay and Cas down to see if they had weapons. Dissatisfied that they didn't find anything, they were even more determined to get something on those assholes. As a result of that parking lot shootout, they now had a total of four dead bodies. The detectives knew a serious gun battle had taken place because there were shell casings out there from more than four different handguns. They had to get to the bottom of those homicides.

Portia was still comforting Fatima, but she was on point. She knew those were detectives over there talking to Jay and Cas. She had to get those guns as far away from them as possible. She didn't really know what had gone down, but she knew Jay told her to hide those guns for a reason. Portia whispered to Fatima to come with her, and was glad homegirl didn't ask any questions. Fatima saw the look of urgency in Portia's eyes, so she pulled it together as best she could, and walked off with her towards the elevator.

One of the detectives was pretty smart. Speaking loud enough so that Portia and Fatima could hear, he said, "Now let me guess. These ladies are breakin' out 'cause they're holding the guns for you."

Portia and Fatima just kept walking and didn't respond. Fatima was grief-stricken, and could barely even think at that point, so the last thing she wanted to do was talk to some damn police. And Portia knew what she had in her bag could put her husband and Cas away for a very long time. Or possibly worse. Her heart was racing but she played it cool.

Fatima played it cool too. She wanted answers about Wise' murder, but she wanted them on her terms. She didn't want to deal with the cops. Not yet. First she had to find out what happened from Jay and Cas. She couldn't speak to the police without speaking to them first. But she would save her questions for a later time, when there were no cops present. She didn't want to get them in trouble.

Jay didn't say anything to incriminate himself, but he prayed the cops wouldn't give Portia a hard time. He really regretted dumping those hot guns in her bag now. Why had he put her in harm's way like that? What the hell was wrong with him? She was pregnant with his child, for God's sake. He just hoped she would be cool and keep her mouth shut. Those pigs were just talking. They didn't have any proof.

Jay had schooled Portia a thousand times on the rights she had when dealing with police, so he hoped she'd been listening. The more he thought about it, his doubts diminished. He knew how Portia was built. She was a standup chick. She wouldn't fold.

The detectives had already spoken with some of the hospital staff downstairs, so they knew Jay and Cas had carried Wise into the hospital. That was why they weren't buying their story. The cops believed they knew what happened, and they also believed they had everything to do with it.

The taller cop smirked at Jay and Cas, and he went over and approached the women. In a not-so-friendly tone, he said, "Look ladies, just hand over the guns. Because if we find them in your possession, we're gonna pin the murder charges on *you*. There are *dead bodies* out there in that parking lot. And I know these guys gave you the murder weapons to hide for them. Don't get caught holdin' the smoking guns for some knuckleheads. These fellas wouldn't throw their lives away for *you* that way. Trust me." He studied Portia and Fatima's faces carefully to see how much effect his words had on them.

Portia knew he was bluffing, but she was still nervous. She tried to swallow but the lump in her throat wouldn't go away. She couldn't let the cops see her sweat. This was a test, and she had to follow the code of the streets. There was no way she was handing those guns over to the police. Her heart was racing, but she looked the officer in his eyes and told him that his insinuations were ridiculous.

The detective wouldn't give up, so Portia asked him to please quit harassing them so they could be on their way.

She'd been thoroughly schooled by Jay on police contact, so she knew her rights. They couldn't search them without their consent.

Fatima was quiet, but her expression didn't change. She kept a stone face so the cop couldn't read her. She had grown up in the 'hood too, and the rule was "no fraternizing with police". And if Wise was there, she knew he would've told her to keep quiet too.

The detective saw that the girls weren't going to cooperate, so he decided to go with another plan. He let Portia and Fatima go, and watched them get on the elevator. He didn't take his eyes off Portia's pocketbook. He just had a feeling in his gut, and his gut never lied.

As soon as the ladies were out of his sight, he radioed downstairs to some uniformed officers and gave them a full description of them. He told the blue and whites he believed the girls were holding the murder weapons, and ordered them to detain them. The detective smiled to himself at the thought of those girls thinking they made it home scot-free, and then being approached by the three female officers down in the lobby and getting searched. If he was right about them having those guns, they would be making some arrests in a matter of minutes. He smiled wickedly at Jay and Cas, and rubbed his hands together in anticipation.

Jay prayed that Portia and Fatima wouldn't leave the hospital yet. They had no way of knowing the police were waiting for them downstairs, but he hoped they used common sense. He wished he could've warned Portia, but those dickhead cops were pressing him and Cas hard. *"Think smart, Ma. Please don't go outside"*, Jay thought.

He would never forgive himself if something happened to Portia. He was so burdened with guilt, tears almost welled up in his eyes at the thought. Damn, he loved her. Jay knew the law. If they caught Portia with the guns, she would be arrested too. Even if he stepped up and said the guns were all his.

Jay tried to keep the faith, but he knew there was an extremely thin line between him and his wife's freedom, and a life in prison. Cas would be finished too. If they caught Portia with those guns, they could all kiss their black asses goodbye for long indeterminate lengths of time.

Every time it seemed like shit couldn't get worse, it just did. Laila was in a coma, Wise was dead, and now they could be locked up for a long time if Portia got caught. And then who would be left to look after the kids? Jay hoped God was riding with them on this one.

To be continued...

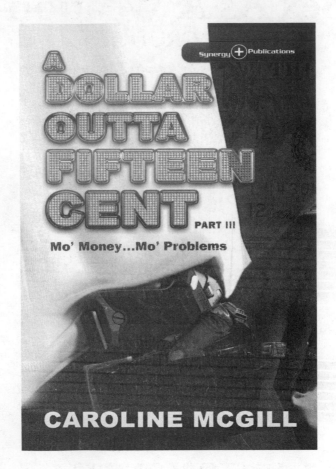

Ladies & Gentlemen
For your reading pleasure,
Synergy Publications is proud to present
A complimentary sneak preview of ...

Sex As A Weapon
THE GRUDGE

An Exclusive By Caroline McGill

IN STORES NOW!

Chapter One

Hen-Rock came back from taking a piss in the bathroom just in time to see video hopeful number sixteen grinning, as she was obviously confident that she'd be chosen for the shoot.

Eager to burst her bubble, Hen-Rock exclaimed loudly, "Nah, not her. Hell no! Bring the next girl out here!" Hen-Rock waved his hand and dismissed the 5'7" caramel bombshell from the video audition.

The girl, whose name was Nadia, looked at Beef and Broc to see if they were going to stand up for her. She hadn't come in there on any bullshit so she didn't deserve to be treated like that. When no one said anything on her behalf, Nadia decided she wasn't leaving before she let that rude bastard who'd just shut her down know how she felt.

She turned to Broc and asked about Hen-Rock indirectly. "Hey, what's ya' man's problem? Why is he so mad? He seems to have a lot of personal issues. He ain't on the damn *Down Low*, is he?" She gave Hen-Rock a look of death and rolled her eyes at him.

Hen-Rock retorted, "Trick, ain't nothin' sweet about me. And I ain't mad, I'm just short of patience. We're lookin' for a dime, and you're only a five. So kick rocks, bitch."

"Fuck you, asshole", she yelled at him.

Hen-Rock knew he'd gotten to her because he heard her voice crack like she was about to cry. He laughed and waved his hand at her like she was wasting his time. She gave him the middle finger, and then rolled her eyes and walked out.

After the bad assed, thick brown skinned sister in the orange string bikini cursed Hen-Rock out and left, Beef and Broc looked at one another and shook their heads

Broc and Beef, collectively the Hip Hop duo Beef & Broccoli, looked at their manager Hen-Rock with disbelief.

Broc exclaimed, "Unbelievable! That bitch was flawless. This dude got a problem with every black woman that comes through. Am I the only mothafucka that's starting to see a pattern here? Hen-Rock, what up son? You color struck or some shit?"

Beef co-signed, "Word up, Hen. What's good with that? Why you running all these pretty, big assed and big tity chicks up outta here like that? Don't be so hard on the sistahs."

Victor Reyes, the absolute "who's who" of video directors, looked at Hen-Rock and sighed impatiently. "Look man, did you forget that this record is about women with big asses. We must have black women in the shoot also. They epitomize big asses. That girl looked great in a swimsuit, and this is for a beach scene. Get real, Hen-Rock. What ever hang-ups you got, get rid of 'em, because we're gonna finish casting today. All we got so far is a bunch of flat assed white and Asian girls, and I'm not dragging this thing out any longer. It's not as if we have a bunch of dogs to choose from. These women are stunning. I fuckin' love black women. What the hell's your problem?"

"I ain't got no problem, man. I just hate black bitches", was the calm reply Hen-Rock offered. Henry Jacobs AKA Hen-Rock, 31 year old manager of multi-platinum Hip Hop recording artists Beef & Broccoli, was just being honest that day. He hated black women more than anything on the face of the earth. In his opinion, there wasn't a lower form of life. That's exactly why he had wifed his young Vietnamese beauty, Sai. His Cajun Asian and he had been married going on three years now. He didn't exactly have Russell Simmons' type of bread yet, but Kimora didn't have shit on his baby. Sai was only twenty one years old, and he was certain he was the first and only man to tap that. He knew because he'd paid to have her transported from Vietnam. Their marriage was prearranged. Hen-Rock had been determined to find a virgin, and he bought the best his money could buy.

Not that he had to pay for pussy, because Hen-Rock was a devilishly handsome man with a boyish charm the ladies found irresistible. He was 5'11", with a slim athletic build, walnut complexioned with dark eyebrows and bedroom eyes, clean cut and well groomed. Hen-Rock was just particular about a woman's race, and to him black was wack. Not even good enough to suck his penis, a lowly black bitch couldn't do anything for him but clean his house.

Beef asked what everyone was thinking. "Why Hen? Why you hate black bitches?"

Everyone, including Beef and Broc's bodyguards, Mittens and Nifty, looked at Hen-Rock and waited for his reply. Hen-Rock became really agitated with all of them. He wasn't about to answer their questions. "Fuck this shit, man. I'm out." He stood up and bounced without another word.

Beef, Broc, Nifty, Mittens, and Victor Reyes all looked at one another and shook their heads. "That dude is seven thirty", Broc mumbled as he rolled his trademark trees in a honey flavored Dutch Master. He and Beef knew Hen-Rock preferred non-African American women but they didn't know it was that serious.

Victor was anxious to wrap it up, so they got back to their casting. Beef and Broc were getting impatient as well. As usual, Nifty and Mittens had plans to pick out a couple of get-rights from the video rejects. It was sad to say, but even after some of the women didn't make the cut, they hung around with stars in their eyes hoping for another chance. That second chance usually involved them getting down on their knees and auditioning with their mouths.

Hen-Rock left the building to get his Aston Martin from the parking lot. After he got in his car, Hen-Rock instinctively reached under his seat to make sure his gun was in place before he sped off. Growing up in the East New York section of Brooklyn had educated him quite well in street protocol. Part of the uniform was a hammer to protect yourself if anything jumped off.

Hen-Rock decided to head on home. He figured he could get a nap because he knew his wife was probably out shopping somewhere. Lately it seemed like she lived to spend his money. Sai was becoming Americanized at an alarming pace. The other day he'd had to resort to violence because she had gotten an attitude when he told her he wanted some head. He'd come home feeling tense from a long day and needed a release, and Sai was dressed in a little red Valentino dress and getting ready to go clubbing with her little crew, which Hen-Rock disliked immensely. They were all C-List class coke snorting whores below age twenty-five, looking for the next cock of success to ride to industry wife status. Sai was anxious to go out with her slut-buddies Tulane and Olivia to party all night, so she told him she didn't have time to give him a blow job.

That was the first time she'd defied Hen-Rock that way so he backhanded her across the mouth, and when she fell on the floor, he kicked her in her ass. Afterwards, he'd walked away and left her there on the floor, and Sai whimpered and crawled after him like a bruised, affection starved puppy. Strangely, Hen-Rock's abuse made her want to do it. She grabbed at his ankles and begged him to let her suck his dick. After ten minutes of groveling, he allowed her the opportunity to pleasure him. And she licked everything too, including his toes, elbows, and asshole. That night Hen-Rock discovered that Sai was a pain freak. That worked for him too. He could seriously get with that. Being able to smack the shit out of a bitch for fun was an instant hard-on.

After Hen-Rock got to his crib, located in an upscale section of Long Island, he took off his Timbs at the door because he didn't allow shoes on his plush white carpet. Not even his own. He slid on his slippers and poured himself a glass of Hennessy, and he settled down in front of the 64 inch flat screen in the movie room of his home. Hen-Rock looked around, and was overcome with a smug satisfaction. He had such high aspirations that it wasn't quite the crib of his dreams yet, but he definitely had bragging rights. The spacious 3 story, 5 bedroom, 3 bathroom, and 4 car garage home sitting on 1.5 acres of land, which included a small private lake and a huge outdoor swimming pool, was a big accomplishment for him. He didn't come from money. He never knew his Pops, and his Moms was a dope fiend. The only silver spoon he was born with in his mouth was the one his mama used to cook her dope on so she could shoot up.

Thinking of how his moms had let that heroin shit destroy her caused him to shake his head. She was weak. "Good riddance", Hen-Rock said aloud. He poured himself another glass of Henny and thought about his exit on Vic and Beef & Broccoli earlier. He knew it was immature of him because that was business, but his personal feelings towards black women had superseded his professionalism. "*Why can't I let this shit go?*", he thought. Hen-Rock stared into his glass of cognac as if the answer to his question lay in the bottom. That was how he got his nickname, Hen-Rock. Not only was his first name Henry, but Hennessey had been the drink of his choice since he was a young man. His best friend Mel had given him the moniker "Hen-Rock" ten years ago.

The baggage Hen-Rock was referring to letting go was the contempt he held for his deceased mother, and every other black woman in the world. His mother had never nurtured him and loved and provided for him the way a mother should do her only child. They'd never bonded and she hadn't once in his life done anything good for him. So as far as Hen-Rock was concerned, black women were all no-good bitches with no morals, respect for themselves, or decency. He had come to these generalizations all because that was the only type of black woman he had ever been exposed to. Ever since he could make his own decisions, he'd never allowed himself to get tangled up with a dirty black bitch.

Hen-Rock reminisced about his childhood. To say he had grown up hard would have been an understatement. He remembered back when he was like four, his mother had beaten him with an extension cord when he had mistakenly knocked over her fix. That was almost thirty years ago but he could remember it like it was yesterday.

Anxious to get off "E", Octavia ran inside her apartment and kicked the door shut with her foot. She had contemplated sniffing the bag on her way home because she was so dope sick, but Octavia knew she was a shooter. She would've had to sniff three bags of P-funk to get the rush a needle gave her. She ran straight to the kitchen table and grabbed a book of matches and her favorite spoon, which she used to melt her dope on to fill her needle. Before putting the match to the bottom of the spoon, she realized she didn't have anything to tie around her arm. Rolling up her sleeve and searching for a good vein along the way, Octavia ran to the bedroom to find something. The entire time she'd been inside she'd failed to acknowledge her son, little Henry, whom she'd left alone inside her apartment for thirty-six minutes while she shamelessly turned a trick for her morning bag of heroin.

Little Henry was so used to being neglected and left alone, he didn't even cry. He was so weak from hunger, he couldn't have cried if he wanted to. After his mother ran in the room he wandered over to the table and stood on his tiptoes and reached up and grabbed the spoon, hoping it would lead to something to eat. Its contents overturned, and Octavia came back just in time to see her fix falling to the floor. She ran and tried to catch it but she didn't make it in time. The heroin quickly disappeared into the dingy gray carpet.

"No! Oh shit! You little stupid, ugly, ignorant, black, cocked eyed muthafucka! Look what the fuck you did." She grabbed her son and pointed her hypodermic needle dangerously close to his eye. "You ever touch my shit again I'll kill you, you little piece of shit! You hear me? I'll fuckin' kill you! I'll stick this

needle in your fuckin' eye!"

Octavia shook Henry hard and shoved him across the room. "Oh God! What I'm a do?" She sank to her knees desperately holding her needle and began to cry like she'd lost her will to live.

All of a sudden she jumped up and ran over to the living room electric socket and unplugged an extension cord, and she angrily charged at her little son. Henry didn't understand that she was so irate because she was dope sick.

"I'm a show your little ass how to sit down and stay the fuck outta my business. You fucked with my shit? Huh, you little asshole? I can't stand your little ugly ass!" Octavia yelled and whipped her poor defenseless child with the speed of a tornado. Little hungry, feeble Henry threw up his arms and tried to grab the cord. He had bloody welts all over his tiny body.

Hen-Rock snapped back to his present setting. "Damn", he said aloud. That memory was too vivid. That was just one of many occasions. Hen-Rock poured himself a refresher and leaned back in his recliner. Beef & Broccoli's last video for their number one hit, "Leave 'Em Where They Stand", was playing on MTV. Hen-Rock was reminded of his affluent status as their manager and couldn't help but smile at how well he had done for himself. To hell with his mother and black women. He was living the good life now. His artists had two multi-platinum albums under their belt, and were still doing serious numbers on the last joint.

Hen-Rock stared at his boys on the video and felt as proud as a father watching his only sons that made it. Beef and Broc were stars. Whatever "it" was, they had it. Their chemistry was bananas. What was even hotter about them was the fact that they were nothing alike. They were equally handsome dudes, but Beef was a 5'9", broad shouldered, dark brown skinned dude with super spinning waves and a goatee, and Broc was a 5'8" slimmer light skinned cat with "good hair", braids, and freckles that the ladies adored. And their rap styles were just as different as they looked. Their chemistry plus Hen-Rock's capitalization ability equaled chi-ching! Neither Hen-Rock, nor Beef, nor Broc was on that pretty boy shit, but chicks found all of them sexy as hell and they had access to pussy by the pound.

Seeing Beef and Broc's video made Hen-Rock think of Beef's question. *"Why? Why you hate black bitches?"* Hen-Rock knew deep down inside it wasn't entirely because of the beatings and abuse from his mother. He hated to think about the real reason. His no-good bitch of a mother had let the unthinkable happen to him. Hen-Rock closed his eyes and tried to block the memory out. He didn't want to relive it again. He had relived it so many times in his nightmares.

Octavia was fiending a little more than usual that day. Desperate for get-high money, she waltzed into the corner store to proposition the fat Puerto Rican store owner for a blow job. The store owner, Pablo Lopez, was better known as "Pork n Beans", which the neighborhood kids had nicknamed him for being severely overweight.

Pork n Beans immediately rejected Octavia's offer. "Hell no! Tavia, you're worn out. I wouldn't touch that mouth or that pussy with a ten foot pole. Don't ever ask me that again. Get outta here!" Irritated, Pork n Beans waved his chubby hand at her and turned his back.

Determined to score, Octavia insisted, "Come on Pork n Beans, I'll do anything. Anything, baby. I just need my medicine. I'm sick. Help me out, Pork n Beans. Fuck wit' me, come on. Daddy, please. I need to get off "E", baby. Help me out wit' a lil' fuel."

Pork n Beans remembered that Octavia had a kid. He was into kids. Preferably little boys. It wasn't unheard of for him to give some of the local little boys free candy and things from his store in exchange for their cooperation in letting him touch them. He liked to rub their little penises. He had never dared to go further than that out of fear that one of them might tell their parents. But Octavia was just a dope fiend with a kid she didn't give a rat's ass about. It was the perfect opportunity for him to delve into his sick fantasy of giving it to a little boy. He so desperately wanted to lunge his small sausage penis into the firm rear end of a boy. He agreed to give Octavia money for two bundles of dope, if he could play with her son.

Dope sick at the time, Octavia thought about the twenty bags of heroin that would be in her possession if she said yes. She agreed, and Pork n Beans followed her to her apartment and gave her the money. She led him to her son's room door, and left the apartment to go cop her fix. Pork n Beans pushed open the door and licked his thick greasy lips when he saw little Henry sleeping on a dingy looking mattress on the floor. The too small pajama pants he was wearing aroused Pork n Beans imagination. He longed to see his little penis. He went over and gently removed sleeping Henry's pajama bottoms and admired his maleness. He stroked his small shaft until it became erect. Pork n Beans bent down and planted a kiss on it.

Henry woke up in time to see the fat man from the corner store touching his penis. Frightened, he tried to jump up and run. But Pork n Beans was a large man. He held Henry down with one arm and turned him over and placed him across his knee. He licked his pudgy finger and stuck it in poor little Henry's bottom.

Henry screamed and fought as hard as he could to get away. Pork n Beans stuck his finger in deeper, and with a satisfied glaze in his eyes he began to finger the four year old across his knee. Little Henry would soon find out that he was only priming him for penetration of the real deal.

Hen-Rock wiped the tear that was starting to form in his right eye. No need to cry about it. It happened and he survived it. It just hurt like hell to know his mama sold him to a pedophile for dope money. She was a no-good black bitch with no heart. That's why he hated black women. He had a huge grudge against them all. But Hen-Rock couldn't ever tell anyone that story. Ever. That's why he'd walked out when Beef questioned him.

All of a sudden Hen-Rock heard his mother's voice in his head. That happened to him sometimes. Octavia would taunt and antagonize him mentally. Hen-Rock braced himself because he wasn't in the mood for the bullshit.

Octavia said, "Boy, man up and stop crying. All that shit happened in the past, so get over it! Just move on."

"Man, fuck you. Get out of my head and go back to hell."

"You the one livin' in hell, as long as you let that Pork n Beans shit cripple you."

Hen-Rock fired back, "Oh, you mean like you let that fuckin' dope cripple you?"

Octavia chuckled eerily. "Well, that is true, and I ain't too proud of that. But the apple don't fall far from the tree. You turnin' into a fuckin' drunk. You're using that Hennessy as a crutch."

"Well, I damn sure couldn't lean on you. Not even once in my whole life."

"Man, there you go bitchin' again. You're my son, not my daughter. Quit complaining like a little girl. So I wasn't the perfect mother. Move on! When life deals you lemons, you know what you do? You make lemonade, mothafucka!" Octavia laughed again and her voice faded out.

Hen-Rock bit his lip in anger. He collected himself and poured himself another shot of troubles, and then he shook his head to make sure she was gone. He couldn't fuckin' stand that bitch. As much as he hated to admit it, Octavia was right about one thing. Sometimes he drank too heavy.

Hen-Rock resented his mother so much it frustrated him. He was tense and needed to release. Where the hell was his wife when he needed her? She was supposed to be submissive, and at his beck and call. That's how it used to be. The last few months Sai had been tripping. Hen-Rock dialed her cell phone to tell her to bring her ass home.

<u>Chapter Two</u>

Sai was luxuriating at Crème De La Crème, an upscale day spa in Soho, enjoying an eight hundred dollar full body massage when her cell phone rang. Annoyed that someone was disturbing her "me-time", Sai frowned at the phone. It was her husband calling. What the fuck did he want? Sai hesitantly answered. "Hello?"

Hen-Rock didn't waste time on small talk. "Yo, where you at? How much of my fuckin' money did you spend today? Am I broke yet, Sai?"

"Don't be silly. We are far from broke, Hen-Rock", Sai told her husband in her thick Vietnamese accent.

"Well, lately you've been shopping like you try'na break me. Get yo' ass home, Sai. Now."

"But I'm in the middle of massage", Sai whined.

"Well, ain't that a bitch. I need a massage from my wife, and she out gettin' a massage from another mothafucka. And I'm pickin' up the tab. I don't believe this shit. You gon' make me take away your plastic. I'm a put you on punishment from them credit cards if you don't get your ass home."

Hearing him threaten to take away her Titanium Am Ex and her Black Card, Sai realized that Hen-Rock meant business that day. She usually held him off with sweet talk when he called with his demands, but this day she took heed. She didn't want to mess up her free ride. "Okay, Daddy. I'm coming now. I have a car outside." Sai motioned to her masseuse to stop.

The young Polish woman didn't respond so Sai sat up and yelled, "Pay me some fucking attention, you idiot! Leave me! Go get my clothes now. Quickly!" She snapped her fingers and the girl ran to obey. As usual, Sai carried on like an Asian diva, tossing about orders like she was Donna Trump.

Sai stood up naked when the girl returned with her things. She stepped into her La Perla underwear and then buttoned her Yves St Laurent mini coatdress, and stepped into her thigh high Zanotti boots. Afterwards, Sai grabbed her Birken bag, tossed her glossy black hair and sashayed out of there like she was on the runway. That was how she always did it because she knew she was a knockout. A shapely, caramel skinned, slanted eyed bombshell of 5'6", she had the beauty and confidence of a supermodel, and enough attitude to give the most ghetto chick a run for her money.

When Sai got outside to her limo she saw her driver, Habib, snoozing behind the wheel. She banged on the driver's side window and startled him. *Bang bang bang!* "Wake up you asshole, and stop sleeping on the job! Get out and open the fucking door for me!"

Alarmed, Habib jumped, and then he hurriedly got out and opened the back door for her. "I am very sorry madam", he said in his Indian accent. "I am taking final exams at the university I attend this week, and I was up very late last night studying."

"I don't give a fuck about your finals. You sleep on the job again, and that will be your *final* fucking paycheck." Sai pressed a button and closed the partition before he could respond. She knew she was being a bitch lately, but she didn't give a fuck. Nobody ever gave a fuck about her. Now she had a husband with money and she was living her dream. In her short life of twenty one years she had seen and done so much, it had been a long time coming.

On the ride home, Sai thought back three years ago to before she married Hen-Rock. At eighteen, she was young, but no where near as inexperienced as the demure virgin he thought she was. Sai had a very dark past. In her native homeland of Vietnam, she had been a child prostitute since she was twelve years old. Six whole years prior to meeting Hen-Rock, she had sucked and fucked British and American tourists in the capital city of Saigon to keep her empty belly full and clothes on her back. She owed being in America to a friend of hers back home. She recollected the conversation with him that had spawned her American dreams.

Late one night Sai had met with her friend and self proclaimed bodyguard, Nyuan, to smoke a joint. He asked her a question she would never forget for the rest of her life.

"You wanna go to America?"

"Fuck yes! I want to go live my dreams."

"I know a man who looking for young virgin girls to marry rich American men. They want young pretty Asian wife to cook and clean for them."

Sai sucked her teeth at the thought of cleaning for a man. "I'm no virgin anyway."

"Don't be stupid! You young, you pretty. Act like one. Then you get to America and be yourself again. By then you got a green card."

Sai smiled and agreed to let Nyuan introduce her to Hui, the man in charge. He saw her and was pleased that she looked young enough to be a virgin. Not even three months passed before Hui told her he had prearranged her marriage to a rich man in her dream land. She had no idea how much money she was sold for, but she was excited at the possibility of escaping Vietnam for America.

Sai's only fear was that her new husband would be able to tell that she wasn't really a virgin. She had voiced her fears to her older sister and mentor, Mao, who was the one who taught her how to whore after their mother died. They prostituted themselves as a means of survival. Their mother was a hooker too, so that's all they knew. She had died of an opium overdose five years before. Sai asked Mao, "What if he can tell I'm no virgin? He will reject me and send me back here to Vietnam. Then my American dreams will be shattered."

Mao laughed at her. "My silly sister, there is no need to worry. If you think and act like virgin, then you will be virgin.

Continue to do the exercises I taught you. They will keep your vagina so tight he will never know a thing. Men very easy to fool. You must make him believe you are innocent, submissive little girl. Big dumb man have big dumb ego. Continue to stroke this, and you are in charge."

To this day Sai faithfully practiced the Kegal exercises Mao had taught her. Sai was grateful to Hen-Rock for giving her a better life, but it was hard for her to love any man because of the way so many of them had used her for their sexual pleasures and sick bondage fetishes as a young girl, barely leaving her with enough money for a light meal. But those days were over now. She had Hen-Rock wrapped around her little finger. Her submissive act had worked. She had him, so now she could be herself.

When the limo finally turned into the long winding driveway, Sai let out a sigh. Hen-Rock was home early. It was going to be a long day.

Hen-Rock looked at the monitor connected to the surveillance camera pointed at the driveway and saw a black limo coming in. He couldn't believe that bitch. She was on some real Hollywood shit lately. His bills had quadrupled in the last half year because of her spending unnecessary money. Sai had done a 360 degree turn on him. What had become of her innocence? It was those no good whores she called friends rubbing off on her. He should've kept her locked in the house instead of flirting her around on his arm in the industry life. Then she wouldn't have gotten to know her way around or met any friends.

On another one of the six surveillance monitors, he watched Sai's driver get out and open the door for her. She stepped out like she was the First Lady and adjusted her dress and shook her hair. She walked towards the house and snapped her fingers, and the limo driver reached into the car and retrieved about eight Saks 5th Avenue and Bergdorf Goodman shopping bags and followed her to the front door.

Hen-Rock headed downstairs to greet her. Sai tipped the driver a fifty, and then she looked up at Hen-Rock and spoke before he could. "Hi sweetie. How you doin'? Home early today, no?"

Hen-Rock ignored her and asked, "What you do, buy the whole fuckin' store? This is what you do all day, shop?"

Sai rolled her eyes. She hated when Hen-Rock came with that cheap shit. "No sweetie. Today is special day." She watched as her driver got back in his car and drove off.

"What's so special about today? It ain't Christmas."

"Today is my holiday. Sai Day. Yippee!" She left her bags and ran over to Hen-Rock and jumped into his arms and planted a huge kiss on his lips. "I love you sweetie! You are the best husband in the world."

Despite himself, Hen-Rock couldn't help but smile. Sai had mad game. He picked his sexy slender wife up and threw her over his shoulder and spanked her bottom. "Fuck is you walkin' on my carpet in these boots for? You need your ass spanked, girl."

Sai giggled and said, "Ooh, you know I like it like that so much! Spank my ass, you mot-a-fucka. And you take that big, black dick and knock my boots off!"

Hen-Rock laughed at Sai. She sounded so funny cursing and talking dirty with her accent. Now he was turned on and ready to hit that. With her still across his shoulder, he slid his hand up her dress and pulled off her panties. When he saw they were red, he was pleased.

Sai squealed. "Put me down, Daddy. I want suck you big cock."

"Say please", Hen-Rock commanded.

"Please? Please can I suck your dick, Daddy? I need so bad."

Hen-Rock grew a big hard-on hearing her beg like that, so he flipped her upside down so that her face was near his crotch and her legs over his shoulders. Sai wrapped her legs around his neck and unfastened his jeans and freed his penis. She hungrily took him in her mouth like a starving animal.

The intense head she was giving him was overpowering him. Hen-Rock felt his knees weakening. He buried his face in Sai's furry patch and ran his tongue along her slit. Hen-Rock fingered her, and her pussy was so wet he slipped a finger in her ass with no problem. Sai was going crazy on his jump-off as he sucked her pussy. The vertical "6-9" was too overwhelming for Hen-Rock. He put Sai down and stepped out of his pants and boxers. She unbuttoned her coatdress and stood in front of him wearing a sexy red La Perla bra and lacy garter. Her panties lay on the floor at his feet. Sai rubbed her pussy and sucked on her finger seductively, and then she sank to her knees and finished handling her business.

After she took both his balls in her mouth, Hen-Rock decided to lie down and enjoy the royal treatment. His snow white carpet was so plush he sank down into it like a mattress.

Hen-Rock was always so busy running around trying to make money he hardly got a chance to enjoy his home. That's was what life was all about. He folded his arms behind his head and stared up at the exquisite Austrian crystal chandelier hanging from his cathedral ceiling. The whole inside of his home was done in white, including most of the furniture. He had grown up in such a dark, dreary apartment with such nasty carpet, he wanted to live in a bright and cozy environment. Hen-Rock's eyes rolled back in his head as Sai swallowed him. Feeling the walls of her throat around him was too much. She was really milking him.

"Aargh, aahhh. I'm 'bout to bust." He wrapped his hand in her hair and grabbed the back of her head.

Sai smiled up at her husband like a champion and took every drop of him into her digestive system. She looked down at his curled toes and knew she had him.

Hen-Rock tried to catch his breath. Damn, he had taught Sai well. Her head game was bananas. When he first got her, she couldn't suck a dick worth a damn. Now she was a pro. He'd molded her right into the freak he wanted. All the bomb sex he desired, he had at home now. This had made him slow down a lot. He was never really into that groupie shit. Now Sai was even taking it in the ass, so that was all she wrote.

There was too much shit out there to be fucking around with mad hoes. That's why he'd got married in the first place. Hen-Rock was the type of man that took care of himself. Before he got married he used to get tested for AIDS twice a year, even though he generally used condoms. He knew Sai was safe because he was the first man to tap that. She'd only been with him and him alone.

Hen-Rock didn't bother to have her tested for anything because she came with papers guaranteeing that she was a disease-free virgin. And he had paid twenty thousand in cash for Sai. He had seen her picture and fell for her immediately. Little did he know, he got more than he bargained for. Sai had only let him think he taught her how to please him. She had been rocking grown men's worlds since she was a kid.

Coming Soon from Synergy Publications...

A Dollar Outta Fifteen Cent IV:
Money Makes the World Go 'Round
An Exclusive by Caroline McGill

Guns & Roses
A Street Story of Sin, Sex, and Survival
Another Exclusive by Caroline McGill

Sex As a Weapon 2:
Steaming Hot Coffee
Another Exclusive by Caroline McGill

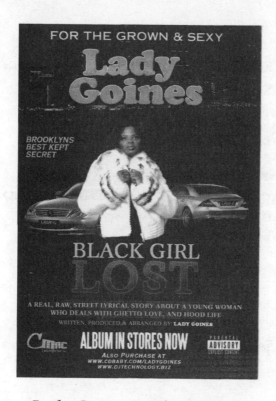

Order Form

Synergy Publications
P.O. Box 210-987 Brooklyn, NY 11221
www.SynergyPublications.com

_____ A Dollar Outta Fifteen Cent $14.95

_____ A Dollar Outta Fifteen Cent II: Money Talks… Bullsh*t Walks $14.95

_____ A Dollar Outta Fifteen Cent III: Mo' Money…Mo' Problems $14.95

_____ A Dollar Outta Fifteen Cent IV: $14.95
Money Makes the World Go 'Round   *(Available Fall 2009)*

_____ Sex As a Weapon $14.95

_____ Sex As a Weapon 2: Steaming Hot Coffee   *(Available 2010)* $14.95

_____ Guns & Roses   *(Available 2010)* $14.95

Shipping and Handling (plus $1 for each additional book) $ 4.00

TOTAL   (for one book) $18.95

_____ TOTAL NUMBER OF BOOKS ORDERED

Name (please print) :_____
　　　　　　　　　　　　First　　　　　　　　　　　　　Last

Reg. # (Applies if Incarcerated): _____

Address: _____

_____

City: _____ State: _____ Zip Code: _____

Email: _____

*25% Discount for Orders Being Shipped Directly to Prisons
Prison Discount: ($11.21+ $4.00 s & h = **$15.21**)
**Special Discounts for Book Clubs with 4 or more members
***Discount for Bulk Orders - please call for info (718) 930-8818
WE ACCEPT MONEY ORDERS ONLY for all mail orders
Credit Cards can be used for orders made online
Allow 2 -3 weeks for delivery
Purchase online at **www.SynergyPublications.com**